WORST CASE SCENARIO...

"That was the scene five minutes ago at a downtown Seattle location. Wolf Amundson left the press conference and his location is currently unknown. So far, government sources have remained silent on any response to Amundson's accusations. In related news, a family of four was killed when a crowd at a local shopping mall took matters into their own hands when a patron was accused of being Gifted. In the ensuing chase and melee, John Stubbs and his wife, Lorraine, and their two infant sons were trampled. Authorities are calling it another example of innocents paying the price for Gifted presence."

Xavier turned the T.V. down and slowly turreted back to the table. "It is the purges come again."

His head hung low, Jack nodded. He covered his face with his hands.

"Purges?" Vallon asked, curious about what could make Xavier look so ill.

The two men looked at each other and finally Xavier nodded. "It is part of our history all Cartos would choose to forget, and it is not spoken of in polite society. I therefore apologize." Glancing back at the muted television, he sighed. "You see, eons ago, Cartos began a war. During the struggle, they did something so horrific that suddenly the unGifted were aware of the Change. They rose up against the Cartos and the world ended. Cities were brought down to dust. The earth was reduced to ash by volcanoes. Cartos were slaughtered and scattered to all corners of the earth, including their part-bred children. Those few that survived either hid in secret enclaves or intermarried, once more diluting the blood. It split our people and left us with less than nothing. It took many generations to come together again."

As he spoke, Vallon's vision spread a grey pall across the room and she tasted bile.

Wavering, she held onto the counter, her heart pounding, her lungs unable to catch a breath as swirling ash filled the room and the others voices became the sound of the wind. That was when she understood.

Her world was ending, too.

BOOKS BY THE AUTHOR

***The Cartographer Universe* series:**
The Warden of Power

The Cartographer's Daughter

Afterburn
Aftershock
Aftermath
Afterimage

Terra Incognita
Terra Infirma
Terra Nueva

Also by the Author
Mutable Things
Emberstone
Ice Dragon
The Crystal Courtesan

Written as Karen L. McKee
Ashes and Light
Shades of Moonlight
Judas Kiss
Second Spring
A Different Nightmusic
Shadow Play

Afterimage

Karen L. Abrahamson

For Marcelle,
who put up with me through the whole series.

The world today is sick to its thin blood for lack of elemental things, for fire before the hands, for water welling from the earth, for air, for the dear earth itself underfoot.
Henry Beston, The Outermost House (1928)

CHAPTER 1 —BREATH AND COPPER BLOOD

The end of September, Interstate 5, North of Anacortes, Washington

The pain drilled into Vallon Drake's chest and the night-bound world of the streaking white line outside the fast-moving vehicle reduced to the leather back seat, Fi Murdoch's supporting arms around her, and the simple act of breathing. Breathe in, in a painful gasp, and she would stay alive, but the pain hazed even the Porsche Cayenne's dashboard lights that lit the world green. Breathe out, and for a moment, relief flooded in and the powerful engine of the vehicle purred up through her body as Xavier de Varga expertly guided it through the night. If she could hold her breath forever. If she could just breathe differently, shift her body, but something cold and hard and jagged in her side stabbed her each time she moved and sent fresh blood flowing warm and sticky down her side.

If she could just stop breathing.

But that was impossible, and even now she struggled to get enough of the copper-tainted air.

I'm going to die. Did she deserve it? The pain was a constant reminder of everything that had happened. Her escape from Jason only two days ago, leaving him with the crumbling remains of her horrible attempt to resurrect his wife. How she'd tried to save the kidnapped children and how she'd lost them—not all, but most, including Keira—trapped and lost in the explosion that had done this to her. She'd trusted in herself and failed, and she was going to die as a result.

Just breathe.

The SUV dipped and swayed as it sped down the highway, taillights of other vehicles painting bright red slashes on the darkness. Fi's whispers drilled into her, begging Vallon to stay with them. Maybe she didn't deserve to. All her life, she had sworn to use her power to protect life. To preserve it.

Except this time she hadn't.

Two mewling puddles of melting life, white research coats around them.

She'd actually killed someone using her Gift. Her judgment was wrong. Just like she couldn't trust her father's or Landon's judgment, she couldn't trust her own. Yes, she'd been trying to protect Keira, but that didn't make it right. She jerked back from the memory and the thing—metal shard, probably—in her side stabbed her from within, in a well-deserved payback.

Fi must have heard her moan. Her arms tightened around Vallon and seemed to trap her here on the too-slick leather seats with the pain. Xavier, too. His dark gaze reflected back at her from the rearview mirror. He was a good man. Would things have ended up differently if she'd actually waited for him to go into the warehouse with her?

Strange, after she'd left him and had forced him to wait for her return, that it was his will that held her here. His will that would not allow her to let the pain cut the rest of the way through her chest. That would not just let her stop breathing. Those dark eyes held her and the pain eased a little.

Just breathe.

Love could do that, she supposed. But she'd dragged him into trouble, first with her people in the American Geological Survey, then with Homeland Security, and now with his own secret Cartos Council.

There was no question: Vallon Drake was not good for Xavier de Varga. Actually, it seemed that she wasn't much good for too many people. The people closest to her were always the ones who paid.

Just breathe. Blood bubbled in her chest and sent her into a paroxysm of coughing.

Since her father left her as a child, she had always been a loner. Perhaps that was how things were meant to be. Instead, she'd dragged people into her trouble, and now too many innocent Gifted were going to die at the hands of Wolf Amundson.

Not much you can do about that, now, pigeon. She could hear Landon Snow's voice. Landon, her mentor, who had turned out to be a traitor, too, just as her father Francis Drake had turned on her. It suggested she was fatally flawed and deserved the pain, the way blood ran down her side, the way it was so hard to breathe.

§

The white lines on I-5 led on into the darkness and nothingness, much like Xavier de Varga's life. White lines for the straight and narrow path he had lived for so long as an agent for the Cartos Council. Darkness for what his life would become if anything happened to Vallon. Trees—cedar, pine, and fall-yellowed poplar—caught in the headlights and pressed in from either side. The copper scent of Vallon's blood made it hard to breathe. Or maybe it was the twisted feeling that strangled in his chest. It wasn't a new feeling. Failure had always brought it. Failure all these years to satisfy his father. Failure, now, to protect the woman he loved.

He drew in a breath, held it, and released it slowly. Always before, he had held himself still and breathed through the sick feeling. But this time, the woman he loved lay dying in the back of his car and all he could do was drive.

Drive, and pray to Mother Pangea, and wonder whether this was what came of breaking an oath to the Council. Would he be left with less than nothing?

His hands gripped the leather steering wheel harder, guiding the powerful Porsche around the highway traffic as fast as he dared, but not fast enough. In the rearview mirror, Fi Murdoch cradled Vallon against her. Fi's face was ashen and tears streaked her cheeks as she stroked Vallon's face. Vallon, well, if Fi was pale, then Vallon was the color of ashes from the injuries she had sustained trying to rescue the Gifted children from the warehouse-turned-research-facility north of Seattle. The wound in her arm bled, but she could recover from that; the wound in her chest, though, that was another matter. She'd been caught in the explosion that killed most of the children, and some projectile had buried itself in her flesh too deep for anyone but a skilled surgeon to fix—or a healer. Her lovely eyes were huge and dark and luminous with pain as she struggled to breathe. The sound was a horrific burble over the humming of the Cayenne's wheels. The coppery scent overwhelmed the vehicle's new-car smell.

"Hold on, *Bela*. Hold on." His voice grated in his throat and sounded rough and desperate from all the smoke he had inhaled, bringing her out of the inferno.

In the mirror Fi squeezed her friend and stroked her hair. "You can't leave me like this. We just found each other, Vallon. We just fixed things between us. You promised you'd be there for me. You hear?"

Sentiments he echoed, though there were no spoken promises between them. Though Vallon had said they would stay together, already she had left him and the result was her injury. It left him as anxious as he had been as a small boy, trying to gain his father's approval. His long life wandering the world on missions for the Cartos Council had been such an attempt—until he had found this woman. His *Bela Menina*—his beautiful girl, like a part of his life he had never realized was missing. He could not lose her now. She was all that mattered. All his work for the Cartos Council was a futile endeavor to keep watch and mete out consequences to the young Cartos progeny left to wander the world with little to no guidance except Council edicts of what was forbidden. The role of a spy and—what was the term?—a hatchet man. Or a hang man, more like, for the consequences were severe.

And then he had found Vallon.

He caught her eye in the rearview mirror. "Stay with us, love. We will be at the border soon. There is a rest stop ahead and we must clean ourselves and the car. We must plan on there being photos or drawings of at least Vallon and possibly myself at the border, given our friend, the detective, seems to have teamed with your Amundson."

Vallon shook her head and grimaced. Her ghostly face was grim. "Not *my* Amundson. Not any Gifted's." Her voice was a hoarse whisper, stabbed by a cough that sprayed blood down her front.

The Gifted—those upstart Americans with the Cartos talent to rewrite the landscape using only their minds and vellum and pen—had mostly been employees of the American Geological Survey, an ultra secret department of Homeland Security charged with the protection of America from possible terrorists with similar talents. But the Gifted were not the whole story. Unbeknownst to the Gifted, but theorized by some to exist, were Others with the Gift. The Cartos, a far older bloodline, with greater talent. Xavier was one, and the first to confirm their existence when he went against the Council's orders and revealed himself to Vallon. And became a hunted man.

"Well, Amundson is our first problem. He will have the borders closed to us. Normally I would simply transmute across, but that is beyond me at this time." Loss of blood—courtesy of Landon Snow—had left him too weak, and Vallon was injured, and Fi could not do it alone.

The sign for the last rest stop before the Canadian border came up and he took the exit into the parking lot. Orange-colored streetlights turned the night amber, and late September insects formed clouds around the glowing globes of light that lit up the low concrete building that housed washrooms and travel brochures.

Praise the Creator, the parking area lay empty. He leapt out and went around to the rear passenger door. Fi fought to get Vallon fully upright as Xavier reached in and gathered Vallon in his arms, then eased her out of the door. For a woman who was a force of nature in everything she did, she felt too small, too light in his arms, even though she was five feet nine. He placed a kiss on her forehead.

"We will get you bandaged up a little better before we try for the border." He prayed to the Creator that it was possible.

Cradling her against him, he strode to the washroom building, Fi limping behind him. Inside, he locked the bathroom door, then seated Vallon on the double-sink counter beside the long row of stalls. She sagged there, the fluorescent lights painting frightening darkness in the hollows of her eyes. Her white t-shirt and jeans were crimson-black with precious blood from her wounds. Fi had tried to keep pressure on them, but moving her had sent a bloom of new red down Vallon's side. She swayed at the edge of the counter.

"*Dondo*! I am a fool!" Xavier caught her gently and eased her back against the fly-spotted wall.

Much more bleeding like this and she was not going to make it. That much was clear. She needed a physician quickly, but his only medical assistance lay across the border in Canada. Getting there was the problem. So risk taking her to an American doctor who would likely turn them in to Homeland Security, or risk the border and Vallon bleeding out in the interim? A breathless sense of impending doom filled his chest.

He explained the risks to the two women.

"Get her to a doctor," Fi said from where she leaned heavily against the wall.

Vallon shook her head, eyes closed. "The border. We have to cross. If we stop—we'll all be caught. You—have to get to safety." Her throat worked and she opened her eyes. "You two—are too important. Fi—I'm so sorry. I shouldn't have used you. Xavier—how could I have found you only now?" She lifted a blood-stained hand for him, but it collapsed in her lap before he could catch it.

"Stop it!" Fi came off of the wall like a she-bear defending her young. "You stop it, Vallon Drake. Just stop it now! You are not going to die, because we won't let you; so you just quit acting like you are! You hear?"

He could not have said it better himself. The ferocity was surprising, coming from the meek, pixy of a woman. She tossed the Cayenne's medical kit on the counter and opened the top, then turned a furious face on Xavier. "I don't know how to do all this stuff. You do."

This time he had the harsh light to see what he worked on. When he pulled up Vallon's bloodied shirt, blood burbled from the ragged wound in her side. Inside it, like a reef in a sea of blood, poked the angry end of some kind of shrapnel. He didn't dare pull it free for fear of hurting her worse. Instead, he padded the wound as best he could and then started tightening bandages around her torso.

Vallon's skin practically matched the grey wall.

"*Bela*, I am so sorry. It must be done."

She sucked in a breath and nodded, but no matter Vallon Drake's will to live, how long could her body continue to lose such amounts of blood? She was covered in it. They all were. Not exactly the way he wanted to face the border. For himself, he could pull on his coat to cover the blood; the women, however, could not.

"We need to get you two clothes."

Fi shook her head. "We don't have time. A doctor first and then clothes. Or we wash them out here as best we can."

Xavier nodded, and Fi pulled off her shirt. No time for modesty. Water ran red in the metal sink as she rinsed it. Vallon was too badly injured to care, and her shirt too blood-covered to ever come clean. She started to slide down the counter, so Xavier pulled her into his arms.

"We need to go," he said.

Vallon was too still, too cool in his arms, and the copper-penny scent of blood masked even the miasma of bathroom. Her own scent of ashes of roses had vanished. He had to get her medical help.

If Homeland Security didn't find them first.

§

Blood. Blood on his hands. Copper-scented blood caked in his manicured cuticles, on his shirt, and soaked into his moccasin soles.

Landon Snow, ex-researcher for what had once been the American Geological Survey, stood next to the operating table in the white room that doubled as his lab in his secret retreat in the Nevada desert. On the table lay the body that was once Gregor Gleason, Chief of the AGS, in a pool of congealing blood. The chrome and white-painted surgery room where he had previously held Xavier de Varga prisoner gleamed around him. At least that venture had been moderately successful.

Sorrow and the fatigue of long labor slumped his shoulders over the messy remains of Gregor's open chest cavity. Whatever the man had been through to reach Landon, the wounds he'd borne had devastated too many critical organs for Landon's relatively meager surgical skills to heal. Gleason had required a whole team of thoracic surgeons, and even then, his chances of survival would have been slim. For him to be dependent upon only Landon had basically sealed his fate.

And so Landon had failed him as he seemed to fail in so many things these days. Even the calm of his meditations seemed to elude him.

He held up his bloodied, gloved hands, wiggled his fingers, and felt his gorge rise. Why, he wasn't quite sure. These hands had been as bloody with Xavier's blood, and that had been the result of his efforts, not trying to save the man.

Torture, a part of him whispered. *You tortured a man and inserted a tracking device as if he were an animal. All because you had to be able to track Xavier and Vallon to the Others*—those Gifted who, he'd always theorized, fell on the upper side of the bell curve. Gifted whose blood was rarified beyond any Gifted agent in the AGS.

Gleason's drying blood slicked between his fingers. Gleason had been a good man—not a particularly Gifted agent, certainly not in Vallon's league—but he'd been committed to his country and to keeping it safe. He'd been a moral man. A man strong with ethics, who truly cared.

And he was dead because of Amundson.

"I'm sorry, old friend. I truly did everything I could." It was the truth. When Gleason had driven into Landon's hideaway, the police hard on his heels, Landon had run out to Gleason's vehicle only to find the ex-head of the American Geological Survey collapsed over his steering wheel, seated in a pool of his own blood. Somehow, with only Landon's assistance, Gleason had walked into Landon's research facility, his breath a burbling, gurgling wheeze. He'd collapsed unconscious on the surgery table, leaving Landon to administer anesthetic and attempt emergency surgery. The police must have been wholly stumped when their prey simply disappeared in the middle of the desert, but Landon's hidey hole was like that—a bit of territory left off the maps—and so it eluded the unGifted's senses. They would likely chalk it up to the proximity of Area 51, but that was no concern of his.

When he'd cut open Gleason's chest, he'd wanted to immediately sew it up again. Whatever type of ammunition had hit Gleason had ricocheted around inside him, torn up his lungs, and yet somehow missed his heart and arteries. To try and find enough flesh to mend was an impossibility, yet he had tried—until Gleason's mighty heart stuttered to a stop. How the man had driven all this way into the Nevada desert, and then walked inside, was a testament to the strength and fortitude that had been Gregor Gleason.

Lost now. As were the connections Gleason had to the politicians who might stop what was coming at the hands of Wolf Amundson.

Landon sighed and sought a needle and thread on the tray of surgical instruments. Swiftly he sewed up the chest cavity and stood there shaking. From the body rose a faint scent of Gleason's Old Spice aftershave through the stink of charnel house. He bowed his head.

"Creator, take this man from the dust he will return to and transform him into the gold he always was." He stepped back from the table and filled a basin with water, then gently began to wash his old friend.

CHAPTER 2 —NIGHT MISTS AND ANGRY SPARKS

Coils of smoke and bursts of sparks lifted from the burning warehouse-cum-research facility and filled the Pacific Northwest night sky above Anacortes, Washington. The sparks looked like hornets battling an angry smoke serpent, and he, Francis Drake, was the serpent. Damn Vallon Drake and her friends. Damn his daughter for betraying him. No true daughter would walk away when her father needed her most. Not and take with her the resources she had—Fiona and the strange, dark man who radiated more power than any Gifted. Damnation and damnation and hell take all three of them!

They'd left him with the exhausted, huddled remains of AGS Gifted in the cold wind on the muddy, salt-rimed shores of Fidalgo Bay. They'd left him to once more convince the remaining Gifted that following him, into the battle to come, was worth the risk. They could do this: they could defeat Amundson and his plans.

The blazing remains of the warehouse Homeland Security had used as a holding and research facility had become a pyre for the Gifted students they had kidnapped from the American Geological Survey Academy. Most had died in the massive explosion caused by the National Guard artillery fire, and beneath the screeching of scorched and toppling metal came the sound of sobbing from his people.

His sheep, more like. At least they looked it at the moment, cowed and milling together in their grief.

A whining missile wound through the air toward them, but fell far short and exploded in the forest around the warehouse. The ground shook and the few surviving children that Vallon *had* rescued whimpered in the sheltering presence of their mothers and fathers. Almost an entire generation of Gifted children lost. A steep price to pay, but still worth it if his plan succeeded. A gust of wind brought acrid wood smoke and sparks around them before the wind twisted direction again. The trees had caught fire, and flame leapt from tree top to tree top.

His people's eyes glittered red from the flames. Yes, a herd of sheep. They refused to see the power they held. Gregor Gleason had indoctrinated them well into the belief their power was only to preserve life.

"People," he yelled over the sound of gunfire from beyond the burning research facility. Some Gifted were still among the trees, fighting to escape the National Guard assault and setting quicksand under the feet of the advancing soldiers. Those he stood with awaited their loved ones and, he prayed, would stand and fight with him. "I grieve with you for our children, but more Gifted children can be born. Your freedom, once lost, you will not get back, and we are facing not just loss of freedom, but extermination! The American public does not love us. Our government has made sure they are afraid. And so they should be, because the days of hiding our power are over for the Gifted. Open your eyes! Behold the blaze of power we possess!" He shifted his gaze to Gifted sight, and the entire landscape changed. Yes, the warehouse still burned, but it dimmed before the blaze of burning tapers that were his people's Gifted presences. Each of them was linked to the power of the earth.

"See our glory? We are the next step in the evolution of the human race, and we will take our place as leaders. What we do tonight, our children's children will sing of as the beginning of a dynasty that controls not only America, but the world!"

It was like the night went still around them. Then some—too many—of the tapers shivered. He shifted to his normal sight as the Gifted stirred. The true sheep amongst his people—mostly those whose children still lived—shook their heads.

"We're not killers or warriors," one man said. A young girl clung to his side, a woman beside him. Other heads nodded agreement. "We're agents of the United States. We don't fight our government."

"Well, circumstances will make you a warrior, or you and that child of yours will die. Look at the sky, man." He waved up at the circling lights of the media helicopters and aircraft. "Think! Even if the only images from tonight that get out are of the burning warehouse, do you think the American government can just let you walk away? It might have been Amundson who exposed our existence and said we were a danger, but after the battle tonight—hell, even if we did nothing except try to free your children—the government will have to side with him that we are too dangerous to exist as free men and women. The public will demand it. It means we—our kind—are the enemy."

There were murmured protests.

Francis stabbed his finger at the sky. "That is the media. That has sealed our fate as evil in the public's eyes unless we're the ones that write the history books. The only way to do that is to be victorious!"

"No!" A man stepped forward to face Francis. Jake Murphy, the agent Francis's team of agents had rescued with his family from an AGS take-down team in the Olympic National Forest. Francis had been there, but Murphy had been far less than grateful because his wife had died in the process.

Now he stood, hands clenched into fists, his dark face even darker under layers of sweat and soot. He had been one of the few of the team on the far side of the warehouse who had made it back here to his children, who—lucky for Murphy—he had pulled from the AGS Academy for a special family vacation before Amundson's men got there.

"I can't speak for everyone here, Francis, but I didn't sign on to attack our own people. All my career, I've tried to keep things calm and together for everyone. I'm not about to change that now. I was hanging around to see what we could do to put things right, but if you lead an attack against the National Guard, count me out. Me and my kids—we're going to head some place safe."

Swallowing back an acidic response to this betrayal, Francis stepped up to Murphy and clasped the man's hands.

"Good luck to you, then, but where will you go? There's no place safe in America. Not for Gifted. And your face and those of your family are known to the AGS. They'll be known to every law enforcement person in America. Your vehicle's also known. They'll be looking for you." He let his voice carry. Let the others hear what he had to say.

Murphy glanced back at his children, two adolescent girls huddled together. "I'll—we'll—head for the border then. Canada will be safer until things cool down."

"Are you so sure? News of the Gifted will undoubtedly go farther than our borders. Gifted could very well be hunted across the world. Don't do this, Jake. Don't endanger your family any further. We're only going to be safe as long as we stick together. We have power then. Enough to keep ourselves safe."

Which was true, if this rabble would quit debating and *do* something. It was like the deaths of their children had stolen their brains. He should just let them go and be captured or worse, but he needed the additional trained minds and the power they brought. If he could just get them thinking again.

"Together we can take a stand. Together we can show that we are more than just a band of homegrown militants staking out territory. Together we can remain safe. After this, we can return to the old AGS Academy and together exert ourselves over Redmond and Seattle and then all of Washington and the Pacific Northwest. After all, who can stand against Gifted power?"

He looked around at the fire-glazed eyes. Most were exhausted. Most despaired and all grieved for what they had lost—homes, friends, and family.

"Friends, they have taken everything from us. Our homes are beyond us now. Our friends turned against us and our children are dead at the hands of men who will stop at nothing to imprison or kill us. You might be prepared to run and hide from these men, but I say let us make them pay for what they've done. Let them pay for the loss of your homes. Let them pay for the loss of your loved ones. Let them feel the loss as we do. We have the power to do it—not with weapons like guns, but with the power of our minds, and none can stand against us. Let us take from them and leave them like the fools they are—unable to remember the power they once had." He let his voice fall away from a sonorous speech.

"No." Murphy broke the ensuing silence. "No one will win in a war. They might not remember, but I know that I've lost my wife. I'm not going to chance losing anything more. I should have taken off when they got Vallon out of here fifteen minutes ago, not stood here listening to you."

Francis' hands curled into fists, because that was his true failure. He should have forced Vallon to use her talents against their adversaries. Instead, she'd gone for the children in the warehouse, and the grey streaks in her aura before she'd left with Fiona said she'd almost certainly gotten herself killed. Stupid, futile heroics, but it was so like his daughter. Destroy herself to help others. That was a fine quality, but the waste of her power hurt the chances of his success.

Murphy turned away and Drake swallowed back the twisted need to grab his shoulder and drag him back, to slam his fist into his face until he changed his mind.

Instead he turned back to the other Gifted. Backs had straightened and the red light of the fire seemed to come from within. Anger and revenge were powerful substitutes for grief. Good. His speech had worked. At least for most of them.

"He will go and he and his children will die," Francis said. "Here is what *we* will do."

§

The four rotors of the Sikorsky S-92 helicopter pounded the air so loudly that it was difficult to hold conversation even with the ear protectors and radios on. Ex-Detective Jason Bryson peered out the portal, down into the darkness of Puget Sound and the dotted lights of the San Juan Islands, and let the rotor vibration run through him. Ahead lay the string of lights of Whidbey Island, and further north, like an outpost in the darkness of the water, the brighter cluster of Anacortes. But just to the east of the town of Anacortes, the darkness was illuminated by the red beacon of the burning research facility.

He glanced over to Amundson, who sat, facing forward, across from him. Amundson was a tall man and fit, with broad, muscled shoulders and a Teutonic look, with heavy brow, ice-blue eyes, and short, white-blond hair that made him look almost formidable in what must be a thousand dollar suit. Beside him sat Page, his right hand man, a huge hulk of a man with a bald-shaved head and the smarts to make him a lethal weapon as Seattle Station's Assistant Chief. The two of them had accepted Jason's help in exchange for free access to Vallon Drake if and when she was captured again.

Because the bitch had already betrayed him once.

Jason was the only unGifted who could sense the changes the Gifted caused. That made him valuable to Amundson and Page. Between the three of them, they'd established a secret research station in their Seattle headquarters—until the Gifted took the station out. Jason, Amundson, Page, and three other agents had barely gotten out as the Gifted Change wiped the building and all it contained off the map.

Amundson, thankfully, had enough common sense to believe Jason's report of events, and so when Jason had sensed Change at the Anacortes research facility, they'd headed out. The other three agents had been sent to see if they could renovate the old AGS facility to become a new Homeland Security headquarters.

Amundson motioned toward the flame and gave a thumbs-up. The fire would hit the Gifted where it hurt, especially if they hadn't gotten the students out. The past week had been one of destruction upon destruction. The Homeland Security Offices in Seattle, various of the retrieval teams gone to pick up former AGS agents, and now the research facility. The loss of the research facility, though, took it to a different level, given that children were involved. That would hopefully sap the Gifted morale, just as his loss of Cheryl had sapped his. Of course, there was a chance they *had* got the young people out, too. On the maps and building schematics Jason had monitored, he had noted Change happening, so at least one Gifted *had* gotten inside the installation and attempted to get the children out. Given what he knew of them, he had a pretty good idea who it had been.

Vallon Drake always seemed to be at the heart of every Gifted action. She had been in the Murdoch affair. She had been in New Madrid. Then he and Vallon had left New Madrid intent on returning to Seattle to free the children Amundson had taken into custody—protective custody, the head of Seattle's Homeland Security Station had claimed, though they both knew it was a lie. So Jason and Vallon had journeyed across the country, and the whole time Jason had felt breathless with the single most important question he had to ask her—until he'd drugged her and taken her prisoner.

He'd held her in the rear of the log cabin while he lounged in the main room, nursing his beer as he reclined on the worn blue couch in front of the stone fireplace that yawned empty as his life. He'd ignoring the angry cries from the back bedroom of the cabin and the plaintive meows from the cat carry case in the hall. His sock-covered feet rested on the round, tufted ottoman covered with Cheryl's piebald crochet squares. Even in the sunlight through the streaked windows that flanked the front door, the brightly colored squares had been faded with dust and wear. Outside, the wind sighed in the cedars and spruce. Inside, the sweet scent of dust and old mouse droppings only reminded him of all he had lost. His job as a Seattle PD detective. His friends, such as they had been. Cheryl.

Most of all Cheryl.

He'd swallowed back the old pain with a gulp of Rainier beer from a can that sported the outline of the mountain the cabin stood on and studied the photo in his lap. The woman laughed out at him in that way that had always made him laugh. She was entirely different from the bitch he'd captured. Wavy, auburn hair grazed the tops of Cheryl's shoulders. She wore a t-shirt and jeans with a man's plaid shirt over top as a jacket. Her green-brown eyes crackled with life and she had a light smudge of dirt on her perfect nose. Not for the first time, he ran the pad of his thumb over the glass covering the image.

That was what he had done to Cheryl long ago, when she came running into the cabin to tell him that she had finished planting a small garden around the cabin's porch. She had been so excited. He had stroked her smooth flesh and he'd kissed her as she dragged him outside to marvel at the results of her work and they had hugged in the light breeze off the lake that sighed in the forest around them.

"The garden's gone, too, Cheryl. I couldn't save it, either." He closed his eyes at the memory. Failure upon failure. The garden long lost to weeds and cold weather, just as the cabin itself was slumping into gradual decay. And all his efforts to force Vallon to use her considerable powers to bring back Cheryl had only resulted in the most horrible of trickery so that he'd had to relive Cheryl's loss again—this time as the woman he loved collapsed into sand.

Her face melting, she had looked up at him with Cheryl's loving eyes until they, too, melted into dust and nothing.

His hands clenched into fists and he closed his eyes, but Cheryl's terrified gaze peered back at him from the darkness that vibrated and thumped with the helicopter's rotors.

He would make Vallon pay for that—after he forced her to do what he'd asked. That was what his life had become: no more loving Cheryl, just a heart that beat for revenge. Just let him catch Vallon and her lover. She could watch Xavier de Varga die an agonizing death, just as he had watched Cheryl die—or she could help him. Those were her only options.

But first catch her. Amundson would see to that, and the place to find her was here, at the remains of the research facility at Anacortes.

The helicopter swung in low along the Whidbey Island ridge and then swooped down toward the burning building beneath the media copters and planes circling like vultures. They might see the flames, but their cameras would never record the changes the Gifted caused. South of the warehouse, a barricade of National Guard vehicles blocked the only road from the highway into what had once been the research facility.

The facility itself was consumed in flames that had already collapsed the upper floor so that the flames licked up the side of a twisted metal bowl as they consumed everything. Around the warehouse stood a forest that his Changed maps indicated hadn't always stood there. He craned around to peer out of the window toward the darkness of Fidalgo Bay. A glint of fire on metal and something moving.

There were people there. Gifted. He'd lay money on it. He pointed out the window for Amundson to see, but the view of the waterline was lost as the chopper sank toward the paved road behind the array of National Guard vehicles, drawn up on muddy soil that faced the burning warehouse.

Amundson shook his head, so he hadn't seen what Jason had.

The rotors still spun as Jason and Amundson leapt from the aircraft onto the sodden soil, Page behind them. Page pulled what looked like a camera from his pocket and swung around as if filming. A uniformed man strode toward them and saluted.

"Colonel Bryce Dawson, I presume," Amundson said over the roar of the helicopter engine. He stuck out his hand. "Wolf Amundson, Seattle Station Chief, Homeland Security. What's our situation?"

As usual, no introduction of either Page or Jason.

Dawson nodded and barely glanced in their direction. He was a typical career soldier, with the buzz cut hair, rigid posture, and squinting eyes of someone who had spent too many hours at attention and too many hours squinting through gun sites into the sun.

"We've got them on the run in the forest west of the research facility. We've been pounding the forest to stop them from organizing, and my men are after them to mop up as we speak."

The concussive explosion of one of the missiles going off made speech impossible for a moment, but Jason moved up beside Amundson. When the noise died back, Jason shook his head.

"I think you may have missed something. On our way in, I noticed a group gathering by the water, that way." He pointed, then reached out his hand. "Jason Bryson, Seattle PD."

The cool look from Amundson said he might have erred in giving this information.

"Mr. Bryson is an advisor to Homeland Security," Amundson allowed.

"We've no intelligence of targets massing in that direction," Dawson said.

"Well, maybe you'd better get intelligence aloft. Spotter planes. Hell, if you don't believe me, radio the media circling. I'm sure *they've* spotted them."

Dawson's face darkened but he nodded. "It's a little tough to get air support over from Spokane. Come with me."

He strode off toward a truck, Jason, Amundson, and Page in tow, but a haze in the air and a tingle across his skin made all the hair on Jason's flesh stand on end. Reddish haloes coalesced around the incandescent floodlights set up around the military array. Mist seemed to roll across the trampled earth and under the wheels of the Hummers, Bradleys, and M1 tanks, lined up facing the warehouse. It was no ocean mist he'd ever seen—as if the floodlights, the earth, and the vehicles all gave off the mist themselves.

Jason grabbed Dawson's arm. "Do you see that?" He pointed at mist that rolled toward them.

Dawson ripped away. "See what? I see you stopping us from getting to maps that will allow you to show me this hypothetical massing of targets."

Jason ignored the sarcasm. "The mist? Do you see the mist there?"

He pointed at a bank of mist, growing around the vehicles and the soldiers near them.

Dawson was looking at him like he was crazy. Jason spun around to Amundson and Page. "Do you see mist there?"

At least they understood why he might ask such a strange question. Both men shook their heads. Page pulled out the camera device again.

"A little something Loadstone research has been working on. This is the prototype," he said as he put it up to his eye. "Shit! There is something."

Jason swung back to Dawson. "You have to get those vehicles and men outta there."

"What the hell is this?" Dawson demanded.

"Just do as I say if you want to save those men's lives!"

Too late. A shout, and one of the Hummers sank up to the axles; the man beside it sank up to his knees. The ground beneath Jason's feet softened. Page still filmed. Another shout and a Bradley shifted and sank— quickly this time, up over the wheels. The earth seemed to slurp at the vehicle's sides. Beside it, the lone M1 tank slowly tilted onto its side.

Mist filled the air and the too-well-remembered horror feeling of being stretched came over Jason.

"We have to get outta here," he yelled. He yelled for Dawson to get his men moving. Already one man was up to his waist and sinking fast. A dozen others were up to their knees. The damned Gifted weren't killing these men outright, they were toying with them and burying them bit by bit in quicksand, and he'd be one of them. They were trying to instill horror in the unGifted population.

He grabbed Amundson's arm and Page's and turned them back to the chopper, interrupting the filming. The mist clouded around the helicopter and seemed to thin the rotors. Could the damn thing even lift off?

He shoved the two men back to the chopper, leapt in. "Get this can in the air!" he shouted.

The engine whined on and the rotors slowly, too slowly, began to spin and pick up speed, but the mist seemed to stream off of them as they spun. Jason grabbed the camera from Page and started filming.

Flames from the warehouse placed a red glare over the surreal scene. The first Hummer was almost gone, the man only a head above ground that quickly disappeared. The M1 tank pointed uselessly skyward, the Bradleys with their chain guns had sunk up to their bellies. But worst were the men. Mist streamed off of Dawson as he shouted orders, his essence stripped away by the Change. The same happened to the soldiers in a sickening display of Gifted power.

People needed to see this. They needed to know.

He kept filming as the chopper suddenly lurched and began to lift. They were going to make it. They were.

Whup, whup, whup and the helicopter lifted free of the mist.

"Keep circling," Jason ordered, without bothering to check with Amundson. Jason pressed the camera against the window and kept filming. Beneath them the line of vehicles sank and those left behind began to dissipate, streaming away like flags in the wind. Dawson was a thin reed in the wind off the ocean and then was gone. His jeep suddenly bloomed like a puffball exploding and disappeared in a cloud that was swiftly tugged away by the wind. Dust spattered the helicopter windscreen as they circled the scene, and he had the sickening thought that it was part Dawson out there.

And then it was over. The National Guard vehicles—what remained of them—stood like weird sculptures, their weapons odd lumps of metal pointed harmlessly in other directions. Nothing moved between them—at least, nothing human.

Then the chopper turned away and Jason caught a glimpse again of the darkness of the waters of Fidalgo Bay, and right near its edge the glimmer of lights. Headlights, heading away from the bay and the vicinity of the fire.

Jason stopped filming and looked back at Amundson and Page. The big Assistant Chief was pressed into his seat, shocked disbelief in his eyes. Amundson was pale, but his eyes carried a look of satisfaction.

"They're getting away," Jason said and pointed out the window.

Amundson shrugged. "We have police roadblocks. That should catch some of them at least. Did you get it?" He nodded at the camera Jason held.

"If it's possible to film Change, then I did."

Amundson closed his eyes and leaned back against the bulkhead. "Good. That gives us ammunition to go to the people with."

"What do you mean?"

Amundson's cold blue eyes opened again. "I mean that we can expect the Gifted to go to the media to try to sway public opinion with their sad little tale of how I tried to take their innocent children and how they were only trying to rescue them." He leaned forward and confiscated the camera. "If this came through, it will be the perfect response to show the American people what we're dealing with. No way in hell any red-blooded American is going to let monsters like these live in their midst. We've got them, Jason. There's nothing they can do except run and try to hide."

Jason looked at the triumphant way Amundson held up the prototype camera and had the weirdest sensation that this was all a well-orchestrated play. But that couldn't be. Amundson wouldn't purposely end the lives of all those researchers, the children, and the National Guard just to get proof on film of what the Gifted could do. But then again, he *had* coerced Gifted into spying on the AGS for him. Who knew what he would do?

He had to have film of the experiments in the main Homeland Security research facility.

A facility that didn't exist anymore. And he'd come here with a prototype camera that supposedly could film Change.

Jason's heart beat a little faster. Amundson had understood exactly what would happen if he took the Gifted children. He'd planned it all out and thought the loss of the children, the researchers, and the National

Guardsmen was worth it to ignite a nation. Jason looked out the window at the flames of the warehouse and the sparks spiraling up against the night sky and a shiver ran through him.

Those were the sparks that were going to do it.

CHAPTER 3 —LIFEBLOOD

Vallon lay on a giant slab of stone, another slab above her pressing down, down, down on her chest so each breath took every bit of her strength. Wolf Amundson hung over her with a white wolf smile. Jason was there, too. Once her friend and lover, now someone she didn't understand, with a dangerous talent for recognizing Change when no other unGifted could. Her father, Francis Drake, screamed at her of betrayal. The young girl, Keira, dead now, looked at her with accusation.

[I'm sorry I let you die.]

But the slim girl with the cardamom scent just peered down accusingly.

Did she, Vallon, deserve to die for her part in the deaths of the children and her part in the downfall of the AGS and for the devastation that would come? Gild the Lily, her father's plan to place the Gifted in control, was nothing compared to what was happening. This, though, this was war that would leave no safe place in America for her kind.

She needed to warn the Gifted, but it was so hard to find the strength with this stone pressed on her chest.

A small cat was crying.

Maggie?

Her eyelids flickered open onto darkness except for a slight glow of reflected green dashboard lights off the vehicle's roof liner. The frightened cat cry came from the space behind her, as did the overripe scent of cat piss, so Maggie was here, tucked into a cage in the back of the Porsche because neither Vallon nor Xavier could be sure they would ever get back to the boathouse where the car had been stashed. Gifted anise and mint and cedar of Lebanon-scented presence pressed in on her and she coughed. Coughed again, and coppery liquid flooded her mouth.

Blood, her mind supplied. Hers.

She lay, half supine, her legs stretched into the foot space, her previously white t-shirt now stained dark. Beside her in the back seat sat Fi, her BFF all the way back to high school.

"Damnation. There is a police car following."

Xavier's voice. The weight on her chest eased just a little. So she hadn't imagined the cedar scent. Xavier was still here, with her.

"Where?" The effort to form the word set off another bout of coughing.

"Vallon? You're awake?" Fi's face swam into view, the concern in her gaze enough to tell Vallon just how grave her injuries were.

She nodded and tried to smile.

Fi grabbed her in an anise and mint-scented hug that unfortunately undid all the good Xavier's presence had done. More coughing sent blood streaming out of her mouth. Fi grabbed a cloth and cleaned her off.

"You stay still. Don't try to talk, okay? We're going to a doctor. You'll be okay."

But she wasn't going to be okay. She wasn't okay *now.* She managed to grab one of Fi's fluttering hands. "Where. Are. We?" she tried again.

"I don't know. Somewhere around Lynden, according to Xavier. We're trying to find a doctor because Xavier doesn't think we'll pass the border inspection." Her blonde hair fell around her pixyish face.

But if Amundson's men caught them, they were done for.

"The border." She squeezed Fi's hand. It was their only hope.

Fi shook her head. "Xavier says that with all the blood and you so injured, we just can't chance it."

Red and blue light strobed over the ceiling panel and Xavier swore from the front seat. The Cayenne leapt forward, its engine roaring.

Fi jerked upright. "What's going on? What's happening?"

"Your Homeland Security has somehow tracked this vehicle. The police are now pursuing." The Cayenne's wheels whined over the pavement as the vehicle's acceleration pressed on Vallon's chest. She tried to push herself upright, but failed until Fi helped lift her.

She slumped against the door. Sticky warmth ran down her side again, but at least she could breathe. At least a little.

Darkness filled the world beyond the vehicle, with the occasional pinprick of light that must be farmhouses. In front, the blue-tinged headlights highlighted a two-lane highway and the centerline that seemed to pull them along into comforting darkness. Behind them came oscillating red-blue and the high whine of a siren. There was no way they could just outrun them. The police would have already called it in. More police cars would be converging, and Homeland Security would be on their way.

She closed her eyes and found the strength. "The border."

More coughing and blood filled her mouth. She was going to be sick, but somehow she swallowed it back and her head fell back against the seat. Just breathe. Just breathe and let her heart stop racing. The air was so frigid she'd never get warm again. Not a good sign. Neither was the blood-copper taste of her mouth. But she had to tell them—remind them. Her fingers found Fi's and dragged her down.

From the front seat came what sounded like a curse in a foreign language and the Cayenne swerved violently. Tires squealing, they came around a corner, throwing Fi across Vallon's lap.

"My apologies. It seems other vehicles have joined the chase."

The rear window of the Cayenne suddenly exploded and cold night air rushed in. Maggie screamed in terror and kept on screaming.

Fi pulled Vallon down again. "They're shooting at us!"

"Fi." Vallon squeezed her friend's hand. On her back again, her breath gurgled like deep water, but she had to do this.

"Just stay down," Fi said and went to lift her head to peer over the back seat.

"Fi. Listen." It came out in a barely distinguishable gasp.

Fi's eyes were a worried luminous grey in the darkness, her short hair a bed-head mess around her face. "What is it? What can I do? How can I help?"

Breathing was so damn hard. Vallon swallowed and inhaled, fought off the coughing. "The border." Barely a whisper.

"I know you want us to cross it, but Xavier says we can't get through. They'll be waiting for us. Now you just lay back and concentrate on living, okay?"

She tried to ease Vallon back, but no way was Vallon letting this go.

"No. You have to." A cough gushed warm and rich into her throat and silenced her voice. She couldn't breathe. Choked on thick gobs of the coppery stuff. She scrabbled for a hold to haul herself up, but Fi's hands held her down—too easily. She gave up and rolled on her side and vomited a rush of blood onto the floor. The metal in her side stabbed the clenching muscles so she started to cry. Bile and copper filled the air. But she could breathe.

For the moment.

She heaved herself back with Fi's help and gasped in air. "Change it. Change the border."

She collapsed back on the seat. Please let Fi understand. It had been done before, when she was a new agent on her first assignment, her training partner had accidentally shifted the Canadian border in the Red River Valley. Or she'd thought it was an accident—at first. When she'd found out the truth, it had changed her whole relationship with the AGS; but it had proved it could be done. An imaginary line could be Changed.

Fi peered down at her a moment. Then suddenly she was yelling at Xavier over the back of the front seat. There was a rapid discussion and then Fi was back. "Have you still got the pen and vellum, Vallon? Xavier said you had them?"

Moving her hand to her pocket seemed beyond her at the moment. She managed a nod and Fi stuck her fingers into Vallon's bloody jeans pocket and tugged out a black Mont Blanc pen and a tattered bit of still unstained vellum.

Then she was gone, throwing herself into the front seat to slouch beside Xavier. Vallon closed her eyes and concentrated on breathing. If it worked, it could save them, but it was all about the timing. Fi didn't have the skill to do it—not as untrained as she was. But Xavier could do it in a heartbeat—just not while he was driving.

A sickening darkness and cold roared through the shattered rear window and tore away her vision and what little warmth she had.

She closed her eyes and prayed that even if she didn't make it, Fi and Xavier would.

§

"How is she?" the dark man asked as Fi slumped down into the front passenger seat. The green dashboard lights placed an unhealthy glow on his haggard features. Xavier de Varga might be powerful, but at the moment he looked like someone stretched to the ends of his strength.

"Not good." Her teeth chattered together. "She can barely breathe for the blood." She chanced lifting her head to peer into the rear seat and tried to stop her legs from vibrating. *Live, Vallon. You have to live.* Thankfully, the cavalcade of pursuers had fallen back enough bullets might not be a threat. For the moment. Turning back to Xavier, she smoothed the worn vellum on her uninjured thigh. The other one had been wounded in the confrontation at the warehouse, but she'd almost forgotten it because Vallon was so much worse off.

"You are injured as well." Xavier's already hard jaw went rigid and muscle corded his neck. If anything, he looked more dangerous than he usually did. "Then we must do this together. I will not let her die."

There were already sketches on the small scrap of paper: a hallway, what looked like a series of rooms connected by entries, and another that looked like a set of stairs.

"There's not much free space," she said.

"There must be enough, no?"

She found a bit of unmarked space and opened the fountain pen. The golden nib was stained green in the dash light. "So what do I do?"

"Draw for me." He placed a heavy hand on her forearm and a surge of his Gift jolted through her, but then changed to a pulse of warming power that matched her heartbeat. Flashes of anger. Deep desperation. Determination so strong it almost swept her away. An image of lines, crisscrossing like streets and roads.

"A map," she said, recognizing it.

The dashboard lights placed a sick pallor on his nod. She looked over her shoulder. Vallon still slumped by the door. It was impossible to tell if she was breathing.

"It is the map you must draw if we are to save her." He glanced down at her. "Yes. She still lives."

The small bare spot on the vellum would force her to write very small and neat. With the bumps in the road she wasn't sure she could do it.

Xavier's power continued to pulse as she set the pen to the paper. Ink blotted out of the pen nib. She lifted it up, then sketched quickly, all of the old AGS Academy training coming back. At the bottom of the drawing, the lines were father apart, as farm fields separated them. She was running out of space. A flare of streetlights southward through the window caught her eye.

"Lynden," Xavier said. "Keep going."

On the northern half of the drawing, there was a maze of tightly wound streets that pressed up to an imaginary line that separated north from south, city from farm land. The border, she realized. The northern area of America was less populated, while the southern edge of Canada held most of that country's people. Here was proof.

"Now what?" she asked.

"I need both hands to drive. You must hold the connection."

She wasn't sure she could do it, but slid her hand up over his arm, never breaking the connection between them. She'd messed up so many times before and she couldn't afford to this time. The vellum slipped on her thigh and she grabbed it with her pen hand. When she looked at the road ahead, a sickening double exposure filled her vision. The image in her head vibrated over the current reality. It had been like this in school, too, when she'd been in training.

The road ran straight, but then signs said it turned sharply left toward the border. At the turn ahead, a cadre of red and blue police lights strobed through the darkness.

"Roadblock. There's no way we can get through that."

"Hold on." Xavier said and cranked the wheel. The Cayenne careened north off the road and came down hard into a farmer's fence. Barbwire fencing shrieked and then they bounced and were through and into a stubble field. The Cayenne's wheels dug in, but the vehicle churned forward. The phalanx of police cars followed behind them, but the lower-slung vehicles got caught on the fence.

Fi crowed triumph.

"We are not yet through. Get ready."

She clutched the vellum to her thigh and clung to his arm. The Cayenne slewed through the muddy ground and threw her against the door. Xavier aimed kitty-corner across the field, but already the lights at the roadblock were breaking up as the police raced northward to cut them off.

The Cayenne hit the next fence with the sound of shattering headlights. One of theirs went dark. Then the Cayenne ploughed through and they climbed the slight bank. Tires once more hummed on pavement. But the colored lights were coming fast behind them.

"Quickly, now! Draw a line behind where we are. Draw a building across the road. Imagine it is a customs checkpoint."

His power still flowed, but she had to close her eyes against the sickening double vision and hold the vellum with the heel of her drawing hand at the same time as she drew. There was the new line. She slashed ink across the farm land. There was the border-crossing building. She sketched a square box on the new borderline where it crossed the road, and imagined it as gleaming metal building with five traffic lanes for crossings.

"Now!"

A surge of power shot through her and flooded her with heat. Her flesh melted and became one with the earth. Or seemed to.

But then she was back in herself. Cold, ozone-tinged air poured in the rear window and the Cayenne's lone headlight streamed ahead as they entered a well-lit shopping area, filled with the late hour's empty parking lots. The scents of anise and mint and cedar of Lebanon mingled and were overwritten with ozone—the scent of her and Xavier's use of power.

She dropped the vellum and was up on her knees to peer behind them. Red and blue lights placed stains across the darkness behind them and silhouetted the low-slung, border buildings. Buildings she had created.

There was nothing all those police cars could do because she and Xavier and Vallon were in Canada now.

"Woohoo!"

She pumped a fist and thumped back in the seat and felt Xavier's regard, heavy and sensual like dark moist places and hands caressing skin. She swallowed and looked up at him, a surge of heat running deep and low in her body.

"We're free," she said, her voice suddenly husky. "We did it."

A jerked nod of his fine head as he skillfully drove.

Should she touch him? Would he touch her back? It would feel so good. She liked his profile and the way his powerful hands gripped the wheel. She could understand why Vallon was attracted to this man. She reached out to stroke the back of his hand and he jerked away.

"No, Fi. That is afterburn you feel. You must deal with it, yes? As I have done." He glanced over his shoulder at the rear seat. "How is Vallon?"

Vallon. Of course! What was the matter with her? It was like her brain was as scrambled as the unGifted's memories would be at the Change.

She scrambled over the seat back, careful of her wounded leg. Vallon had tumbled off the seat, probably in their crazy race across the fields. She lay face down and unmoving in her bloody vomit.

"Oh God. Oh, God!" Fi scrambled to help her. Vallon didn't even groan as Fi struggled to get her back onto the seat.

The contact sent the afterburn flaring. That had to mean Vallon was still alive. Didn't it?

"Please be alive. Please be alive." She placed an ear against Vallon's chest. A painfully slow *thump, thump* greeted her.

"Thank God." She pulled Vallon onto her lap and held her upright so she gave a gurgling sigh. "She's alive, but I don't know for how much longer."

The Cayenne picked up speed. "I have a healer who can provide what she needs, if we can get there before Homeland Security can scramble the local police."

The vehicle careened through a typical suburban area of fast food restaurants, big box stores, and chain hotels, topped by tight rows of houses on the hillsides above. Then they were suddenly on a highway, traveling over a hill. The first hint of dawn showed the faint pink of mountain peaks, closer than they'd ever been in Seattle. The suburban landscape shifted to farmlands. She kept checking over her shoulder, but they were alone on the road except for long-haul truckers. South, against the blushing sky, stood the silhouetted volcanic might of Mount Baker.

Then the Cayenne turned off the highway; through a small, darkened village; and onto a side road, flanked with huge poplar trees. The air through the shattered rear window smelled of water and growing things and rich mud.

The Cayenne bumped onto an unpaved road, or maybe it was a driveway. From the rear of the Porsche came a querulous mew.

"Maggie!" She craned around and almost dropped Vallon. "Maggie, are you all right, girl?"

Another less than tolerant meow.

"A good thing Vallon thought to put her in the vehicle, or she would be beyond us now," Xavier said as they bumped along.

"She sounds hungry."

Xavier nodded, but said nothing. Fi hung an arm over the back of the seat, and felt for the pet carry cage. A cat nose nudged her through the bars. "Hey little kitty-girl. Just hold on. We'll get you fed, but we have to take care of your mistress first."

She brought her arm back and hugged Vallon close. "You have to live. Maggie needs you, and so do I. I'm so sorry I was mad at you. I'm sorry I couldn't explain better why I wouldn't cycle the power for you. I just don't want you turning like my mother, Vallon. You're so much better than her."

Vallon didn't move. It was hard to tell whether her chest rose and fell.

She would not lose her best friend! Fi squeezed her eyes shut and willed her power into Vallon, but Vallon's usually brilliant, Gifted presence was faded grey and streaked with darkness. She held Vallon tighter. She wasn't someone powerful like Xavier, but maybe she could give her strength to Vallon to save her.

Fi inhaled to steady herself and then reached out to her friend, imagining enveloping Vallon with her aura. Another deep, calming breath, and she flowed out of herself and into Vallon.

Ashes of roses was Vallon's scent. Her heart thumped slowly, desperate to keep going, but the blood so necessary to life was fading, depleted. Veins and arteries collapsed and her lungs labored against the pressure of the blood pooled within them. She was drowning in lifeblood at the same time as the rest of her body starved for it.

No and no and no and no! She would not let Vallon die. Not when they'd only found each other a few months ago. They were BFFs. BFFs didn't let each other die.

Like Vallon had shown her, Fi -reached- for the earth and the power that ran in its ley lines. She hauled rose-scented power up. Ran it through her body and poured it into Vallon—roses for ashes of roses. Vallon's body lay in her arms, cool as a glass of water on a hot day and just as clear. Almost as if her flesh faded and Fi could look inside Vallon's body. The tattered lungs. The laboring muscle of the heart. The bones and tissue, shattered by the piece of metal in Vallon's chest, all like a ghostly red-tinged vision. Her arteries and veins were like gossamer threads, growing fainter. Blood. She needed blood. But there was no way to do a blood transfusion. The power had to help her. That was all Fi had.

Vallon jerked in her arms and her back arched violently. Then her eyes flew open in dark brown shock and she ripped loose of Fi's arms.

"Wha…?" The word was truncated by coughing gouts of blood. Fi tried to hold her, but Vallon fought her off, bent over, and vomited more blood onto the floor.

"What is happening back there?" Xavier yelled.

"I don't know. I don't know. I fed power into her. I was trying to help her."

What should she do? She held Vallon's head. She helped her sit upright. Wiped her face with the edge of her t-shirt. Vallon had her eyes closed, her head straining back on the headrest as her chest strained for breath. But she was awake. That had to be better. But her heart raced, her chest rose and fell too rapidly as she strained.

"You have to be calm, Vallon. Be calm, so your heart isn't pushing your blood so fast."

More blood streamed down Vallon's side in a silent, dark flow. Blood rouged her lips. She didn't have enough blood in her to do this. She'd be drained dry. The back seat of the Cayenne was soaked in the coppery red of Vallon's life force, and all Fi could do was hold her.

God, she was useless. Less than useless. Her best friend was dying and she couldn't do anything to help. In fact, she'd made it worse.

Tears ran down her face and she scrubbed them away, not caring that she was getting Vallon's blood over her.

Then the Cayenne's engine shut off and the night was suddenly still except for Xavier's rough movements as he tore off his seat belt, scrambled out, and came around the car. Each of Vallon's gurgled breaths was a knife stuck in Fi's heart. The back car door pulled open and Xavier leaned in on the other side of Vallon.

"*Bela*. We are here. There is a doctor. It will hurt when I lift you up, but stay with me, yes?" He placed a kiss on her forehead and then gently lifted her up into his arms, leaving Fi with only Maggie's terrified squall.

Fi fought the carry case over the seat back and then stumbled out of the car and almost fell when her injured leg gave. She stood in utter darkness. Where were Xavier and Vallon?

Then her eyes adjusted. Darkness, yes, but there were lighter patches. Walls with windows. The sweet scent of old hay and older manure. A barn, probably. She inhaled deeply and Maggie mewed.

"It's okay, girl. We aren't any place to be afraid of, or else Xavier wouldn't have brought us here. At least he wouldn't have brought Vallon here." She limped around the Cayenne, its engine softly ticking in the cool air, and found an open doorway, filled with faint grey dawn. She stepped out into light wind, the scent of mud, and the sound of a river running.

CHAPTER 4 — WATER COLORS IN RAIN

Landon Snow leaned back in his office chair, trying to quell the sick feeling in his stomach, and considered the completed news feed on his computer screen. The headlines—frozen at the moment the news story completed—read *"Monsters Massacre National Guard."*

He looked up at the pristine white walls, at the alchemical tomes he had on his bookshelves, and at the azoth drawing that had always—until now—inspired him to seek balance. The triangle with the face of the practicing alchemist in the center, the star and triangle surrounding the face, the procedures he must do to transform the *prima materia*—the First Matter—into the final, perfected stone. Usually these calmed his mind and allowed him to begin his meditations. The body of the alchemist symbolized the four elements, and the whole of the azoth was a meditative representation of the journey the alchemist must take to shift his own poor 'first material' into the perfection that would allow reunion with the Creator.

But this time it was just an archaic picture, not even its artistic merits worth considering.

"What in the Creator's name were you thinking, Francis?" He drew in a deep breath and his chair squeaked as he placed his feet flat on the ground.

The air of his secret installation still tasted of blood. Or maybe it had gotten into his nostrils and skin and he hadn't yet been successful in scrubbing it out. He'd washed his hands. He'd soaped and lathered them many times since cleaning up after Gleason. It had not been pretty. First washing the body, then wrestling the big man onto a gurney and rattling down the hall to the freezer for storage until he got around to digging a grave. Then there had been the arduous job of cleaning up the surgery.

So much blood. Good, Gifted blood spilled from a good man, a colleague and friend. Gregor had fought to get here. He'd made the long journey by car from Washington, but the Las Vegas news had shown the pursuit as Gleason fought to make it to safety in Landon's hidey hole. The news clip had shown the roadblock and escape, Gleason's car shuddering under the gunfire, and yet with superhuman strength Gleason had kept going. The news feed's overhead shots had shown the battered car speeding through the desert, the police and Homeland Security in pursuit, and then the sudden disappearance of Gleason's vehicle as he entered the little fold in reality that was Landon's hidey hole. This place, that had been left out of the edges of maps and that even GPS hadn't marked yet. In ancient times they would have called it Terra Incognita. Here Abide Monsters, and Landon was the monster.

He was safe here, because the unGifted couldn't sense this location and could drive right through it, never sensing its existence. But now there were Homeland Security and police nosing around outside the narrow wedge of land that held his sweet facility. It was going to make leaving this place a tad more difficult. The cameras he had set up at the edges of his safety zone showed agents setting up some kind of equipment. Motion detection, most likely. He was pretty sure he could deal with that—when he decided to go.

But damnation, what was Francis doing? The man was a wild card and always had been—in that, Francis Drake had rubbed off on Vallon. Years ago, Francis had tried to convince the then-Chief of the AGS of a project he had code-named *Gild the Lily*. It had been an audacious plan to use the Gift to build power in America and to connect with other Gifted across the world so that Gifted would assume control. Francis had even taken the first few steps to make contact. The Chief had turned down the plan, and not too many years later, Francis had disappeared during the event that had traumatized Vallon more than any other. Landon knew. He'd been there. Had driven her home from public school because once more Francis Drake was too busy for the child who idolized him. But when they got home that fateful day, the house was gone and Francis Drake with it. The low-slung rancher off Seattle's Broadway had been replaced by a two-story blue heritage house.

Years later, after Gleason assumed the mantle of AGS Chief, Landon had received a cryptic message that could only have come from Francis, asking if *Gild the Lily* might still be of interest, given Francis had left 'tools' behind. Landon had answered in the negative, but the contact had been made and Landon had always been one to keep his options open. So he'd supplied Francis with information on Vallon, the true lily to be gilded, and somehow it had all led here.

He stabbed the computer *play* button again and the news feed once more played on the screen. An aerial view of what looked like a burning warehouse, the announcer's voice talking about a Homeland Security research facility under attack by the very people the Seattle Chief of Station Wolf Amundson had denounced as terrorists dangerous to the nation. So far, no comment had come from Homeland Security Director Ray Fitzsimmons.

Then the scene on the screen shifted. It showed a line of National Guard vehicles, pulled up under floodlights, and a helicopter with rotors slowly turning just at the edge of the lit area. Soldiers smoothly operated the guns on the tops of the vehicles, shooting at something or someone in the forested darkness around the burning building. Then something happened. A haziness seemed to flood part of the screen. Vehicles and guardsmen suddenly sank into the soil. Then the filming cut off and suddenly whoever held the camera was lifting off in the helicopter. Below them the scene became blurrier. The soldiers became wavy lines and then the whole scene *ran*, like watercolor paints in rain. The men, the equipment, twisted and faded, leaving a clearing filled with twisted, tilted metal like strange sculptures under floodlights.

The camera's aerial view then shifted to a brief shot of a shoreline and dark water and a dimly viewed group of people scattering to vehicles and the lines of taillights speeding away.

The scene froze as the commentator came back on screen.

"This video was released by Homeland Security a short time ago. Media outlets across the Pacific Northwest also received a video communiqué from the leader of these terrorists. We've been asked by authorities not to show it, but we can say that the video tries to convince us that Gifted children were being held and experimented on in that facility. They go on to say that they take this aggression as an act of war. Homeland Security Director Ray Fitzsimmons has been unavailable on this topic as well. In Washington, Congresswoman Gillian Black has demanded accountability for the government secrecy surrounding these Gifted."

The screen cut to the fifty-something-year-old congresswoman in a blood-red business suit, her graying dark hair cut in a bob. "The existence of these—these creatures—should have been shared with the American people. How else are good folk of these American states to protect themselves? I demand the resignation of the Director of Homeland Security and answers from the White House and the Homeland Security Council."

The newsfeed cut back to the announcer. "Locally, Governor Robinson is demanding the full weight of the law be brought against these monsters for killing these good men and women of the National Guard. And in other news…"

Landon stabbed his finger at the feed again. The news froze on the screen. Damnation and damnation. Did Drake really understand what he was doing? This could incite a race war that could spread worldwide and that would be very hard for the Gifted to win. The witch purges of the Middle Ages came to mind, because the unGifted had no more means to tell if a person was Gifted than the Middle Ages magistrates had when they'd thrown a person weighted with stones into a pond. Either way, the accused witch drowned.

He shivered and pulled the collar of his cardigan up around his neck. For some reason, the air conditioning ran colder today. The astounding fact that Amundson had somehow *filmed* Change, when it had never been possible before, told Landon that the rules of engagement were changing, too. If Amundson could do that, maybe Amundson *did* have a way of identifying Gifted. The thought was terrifying.

He shifted the computer cursor again and clicked. Another feed came up on-screen, showing a view of North America, the eastern seaboard under mid-morning sun, the band of division between night and day sweeping across the mountains toward the Pacific Ocean. Global Positioning System (GPS).

He stabbed the key again and the screen shifted and flowed northwestward, gradually zooming in over the Pacific Northwest, then further north. A single red bead pulsed on and off like a heartbeat, and his breath caught in his chest as the landscape solidified with the red bead coming to rest north of the longest unguarded border in the world.

The tracking device he'd placed was working.

If Xavier de Varga had been at Anacortes, he had lived through the events. Now he was on the move and leading Landon to the people he had to find just as *Gild the Lily* had planned: the Others.

CHAPTER 5 —SWEET, LIKE OLD DEATH

The sound of rushing water flowed around Fi as she stood in the semi-darkness of early morning. Wind rustled the yellowed leaves of the tall poplars that encircled the yard and ran along the driveway of the low house. The air was moist and heavy and northward, clouds clung to the mountains that were lit by early sunlight. Southeastward, the pre-dawn sun limned Mount Baker.

But where was Xavier? A light came on over a side door of the low-slung farmhouse hunkered across the yard. It illuminated the black-clad man and the woman he carried. A dying Vallon. Fi limped after them, carrying a strangely silent Maggie, as the door pulled open to reveal a slim, blond man with a tatty red-plaid bathrobe pulled tight around him. He rubbed sleep from his eyes as Fi came up to them.

"De Varga? Bloody hell! You shouldn't be here—not if you don't want to be turned in. You know my loyalties rest with the Council." He spoke with a fading British accent.

Xavier ignored him and pushed inside. Fi trailed after, the pain in her leg pulsing viciously now that the adrenaline was fading. As she brushed by the blond man, she caught a whiff of cut grass and apples, and her afterburn flared. She froze and -reached-.

Gifted. This man was Gifted, but not like she was. No, this guy was GIFTED, just like Xavier.

"Holy shit," she said, turning to him, and looked up, way up, into entirely-too-blue eyes. "Oh my."

He wore a pajama top that exposed just a little too much rock-hard chest. Not as tall as Xavier, but just tall enough when she wasn't very tall herself, with a nice tangle of blond hair falling down to his shoulders. A flush ran through her so she figured it would be a perfectly good idea to cultivate this man up close and personal.

She stepped up to him. "Hi. I'm Fi." A winning smile.

The guy backed up a step, then turned an uncertain face to Xavier and followed after him into an old-fashioned kitchen, with yellow-tiled counters and scarred maple cupboards, but the newest stainless steel appliances. Xavier had shoved a stack of livestock magazines and papers off a butcher block table in the middle of the room and laid Vallon on it. Her blood dripped on the cream linoleum floor.

"What the hell's going on, de Varga?"

"What do you think is going on? I brought you a patient. Three patients, actually." Xavier seemed to actually grow to fill the room, the darkness of him filling corners and reflecting the light. He stroked a hand gently over Vallon's head. "She's gravely injured. I need you to save her. Fiona and I have also have injuries."

The blond man's gaze flickered over them and down to Vallon. "Shit. You were there, weren't you? You were part of the madness going on down south. The television and radio are full of it."He shook his head. "The Council will have my head if I help anyone not Cartos."

"Well then, look at her and you will see you do not have to worry about your pretty blond head being placed on a platter. Now heal her. She does not have much time left. She has been bleeding out for the past hour and a half."

Blondie's gaze widened as he studied Vallon. "But how? Who?" He glanced at Fi and she felt the weight of his power. "She's not."

"Well *she* is, and it is a long story for another time. Now move. If she dies, I will personally drown you in the Fraser River. Understand?"

It was as if the blond man suddenly came to life. He walked to the door and flicked a switch, and stronger lights came on in the kitchen. He stepped up to Vallon, gently unwrapped her wounds, and his gaze widened. Then he placed one hand on her forehead and another lightly on her abdomen. He closed his eyes.

"What's he doing? Don't we need to find a doctor?" Fi asked.

"He is better than a doctor, Fiona," Xavier said, stroking Vallon's cheek. He glanced up and must have seen her confusion. "He is a healer, Fi. A precious few still exist among my people. Jack has been here as support to my ventures in your country."

But…. "Healer?" The room filled with the ozone reek of power use. It radiated off of Jack until it was as if he and Vallon existed in a bubble of power in the center of the room. Jack's hands slid over Vallon and touched the dagger of twisted metal in her side. It glittered for a moment, then wisped away.

Xavier glanced up at Jack. The blond man's eyes were closed and his breathing had slowed to match Vallon's.

"Long ago, certain amongst my people were blessed by the Creator and mother Pangea with the gift to heal without the assistance of the surgery and drugs Western civilization uses now."

It sounded like so much woo-woo, and yet Jack had just done something to the wound. "Do you mean faith healing?"

Xavier looked thoughtful. "In some ways. He must hold himself pure for the power of Our Mother."

"Pure?" She rounded to look at Blondie. "You mean he's a virgin?" Because that would indeed be a tragedy for such a good-looking man. His most-attractive scent of cut grass and apples seemed stuck up her nose for all time.

Xavier burst out laughing, the sound rumbling warmly around the room. She realized she'd never heard him laugh before, but it was a good laugh and full of life. He caught her and pulled her into a one-armed hug—swiftly released—as beyond him early sunlight through the kitchen window warmed the worn wood of the cupboards.

"Thank you, Fiona. I have not had a laugh like that for too many days." He shook his head. "No, Jack is no virgin, but he keeps his power pure by not using it for more mundane tasks like making maps."

A soft groan sounded and Fi spun around, her leg almost giving out until Xavier steadied her. Vallon lay on the table, still pale as a west coast fog, but her eyes shifted under their lids and one hand rose up, reaching. Xavier rushed to catch it in his injured hand and brought it to his lips as he knelt beside her. Fi caught her other one.

Jack, however, sagged against the table. When he opened his eyes, they showed a fiery afterburn as they came to rest on Fi. He smiled and a surge of heat roared through her.

"It's done," he said. "As best as I know how. She will still need rest for many days, but she is no longer at death's door."

He might have spoken to Xavier, but his deep blue gaze never left Fi's face. His intensity seemed to pull her in.

"I do not think she would have lived if not for your healing attempts, Xavier," he said.

Xavier looked up from where he knelt beside Vallon's head. He lightly kissed her cheek. "I did not do anything except bandage the wound. I was focused on driving to get her to a doctor."

"Well someone helped her. I tasted the anise and mint in her blood. Someone was there before me."

The two men's gazes turned to Fi, too hot, too intense, and she stumbled back to the counter for support as an answering heat climbed her neck.

"Fiona?" Xavier asked softly, his gaze gone black. "What did you do?"

So this was what a bird felt like when cornered by Maggie. She swallowed. "I—I only meant to help. She—she was empty and almost gone. I—could feel it. I just tried to give her more blood, except then she was drowning in it. I'm sorry."

In two steps Xavier was around the table and grabbed her hands. His eyes did his glittery Cartos thing and she felt like he was looking right into her. Then he dropped her hands and stepped back. "That is—most unexpected. Thank you, Fiona. Thank you for what you did."

Not in trouble.

"You," Jack said, shaking his head in obvious disbelief. "It cannot be, but it is." But then he swept into a gallant bow like some knight right out of one of those old costume movies. "Welcome to my home, little sister."

But the heat in his gaze was anything *but* that of a man speaking to a sibling.

§

Stretched thin and bled dry, that was how she felt, and yet not. The landscape she stood on lay grey and empty and spread into the distance as far as she could see in all directions. Here and there, the husk of a long dead tree stuck broken branches and trunk up through the desolation. Above, thick clouds muffled the horizon where there might be a hint of mountains.

Where? Was this a dream? The entry to whatever hell existed, or was she already dead and confined to purgatory?

She started forward, her feet crunching in the deep ash underfoot and sending up small whirlwinds of the stuff. The wind smelled musty and sweet, like old death. Nothing was alive around her.

No sound of water, though she was sure she had smelled it once, not too long ago. There had been a sound like a river and she had run toward it, the thirst in her throat like a creature clawing at her neck, and she was going crazy with the pain.

But there was nothing here. Nothing but death and endings, and by the look of it, it spread across everything. The place she deserved to be for what she had done in the warehouse. Two people melting into formless puddles, the children dying.

A soft cry disturbed the wind's sigh and she turned. By one of the dead trees, something floundered in the ash and she ran toward it. A child!

No. Not a child. It was Keira, who had led her to rescue the other students. Fourteen-year-old Keira whom she had tried to rescue from the warehouse, but who had died in the final explosion. But this Keira was alive, or at least as alive as either of them was in this place. The girl's slender body was trapped in the ash up to her waist and she was sinking fast. Her hair tangled around her heart-shaped face and spread out on the wind.

"Keira! I'm coming." She ran, had to save her, had to save herself, but the ash caught at her feet and clung to her legs.

Keira looked up. "Help me! Help!"

"I'm coming!"

"Vallon! Please!"

But the wind held her back and slowed her down. So hard to move her legs and arms.

"Keira, I'm coming. Just hold on!"

But it was as if weights held her down. She was failing again—Keira, everyone. Herself. She fought the weights, waded through the landscape as someone called her name.

"Vallon!"

Her eyes flashed open and superimposed on the grey lands hung Xavier's face on one side of her. On the other side stood Fi and a fair-haired stranger. But the grey lands were still there, faded, perhaps, like a movie played in sunshine, but present as a nascent future. Was that what it was? A vision? But Keira was there, and Keira was dead.

She couldn't quite find the answer. Unless this was the transition into death, but that didn't make sense, because who was this stranger, and why, judging by the cupboards and the sink she saw beyond Xavier, was she lying on a kitchen table?

She struggled to sit up, but Xavier stopped her, his cedar of Lebanon scent tarnished with the scent of smoke and ash.

"It is okay, *Bela*. You are safe and well. My friend Jack, here, has healed you—apparently with the help of Fi."

The double vision made her stomach queasy and she closed her eyes. *Healed her?* But Xavier's voice sounded normal. Himself. Concerned. His hand on hers was warm and so were his lips as he brought her cold fingers to them.

Alive, then. Her breath hitched in her chest, but a knife no longer sawed at her with each breath. Alive was a good thing, but the grey lands seemed to lie like a transparent membrane over this room, and that wasn't normal.

She managed a small smile up at him as she fought back the fear. At least she could breathe. At least the pain was gone. A wave of exhaustion rolled over her and her eyes closed again.

The grey lands waited.

CHAPTER 6 — CHOICES

Ray Fitzsimmons stood in the cool morning air of Boeing Field and inhaled the scents of jet fuel and the Puget Sound salt flats as he watched the helicopter come in for a landing. The sky was still the pale blue that preceded the full impact of a rising sun. He was a big man, but hunched and hooked-nosed, so that most people who were not his friends described him as a vulture. He didn't care for the description, but he didn't mind, either. When you were head of Homeland Security and eternally having to show your face picking through the debris of America's worst disasters, it was easy for such a moniker to stick.

But this time he was trying to avert such a disaster—at least he thought he was. And deal with an employee who seemed to have taken the bit in his teeth. It would not keep certain powerful men happy, but it was the right thing to do, even if it would ruin the strategies of far more important men than Wolf Amundson would ever be. Already in transit to Seattle to deal with Amundson, he had received and viewed the Gifted video setting out their grievances and could imagine how he would have felt if it had been his Evangeline in the Academy. He knew what loss was like—had been there every step of the way as his beloved Evangeline was stolen from him by leukemia when she had filled his life for only five years. It had destroyed his marriage and part of his soul in the process.

He ground his teeth as the concussive *whup-whup-whup* of the helicopter overwhelmed the rush of the traffic on nearby I-5 as the copter settled onto the helipad and disgorged three men. One, Amundson, he knew well by his spike-short blond hair and broad shoulders and investment-banker suit. The second, Page, was the big, contracted employee Amundson had dubbed his second in command. The last man he recalled from briefings—the detective, Bryson. All three men's suits were slightly askew, their hair not quite so perfect, and Amundson had the slightly shaken look of people who had just run for their lives, which, by the television coverage Ray had seen, was exactly what they had done.

He crossed his arms and let them come to him.

Amundson initially looked nonplussed at seeing Fitzsimmons waiting, but then his expression smoothed. Bryson and Page just followed doggedly along, though Amundson said something to them. His words were masked by the helicopter's engine on cool-down.

"Ray. How good of you to come. I hope you haven't been waiting too long," Amundson said.

Jesus, the man was cool. He made it sound like he had asked Ray to attend to him, when he'd no more known his boss was coming to ride herd on him than he had known that Fitzsimmons had backed Francis Drake's actions in New Madrid.

"Cut the bull," Ray rumbled. "You've created a disaster and now we need to fix it." He lifted his chin at the limousine idling at the edge of the helipad. "Get in. We've got things to discuss."

The blond man's shoulders hunched slightly and the muscles in his neck corded. Not happy, this one. Then he shrugged. "Fine. But you'll listen to us, too. You don't know what's going on."

Fitzsimmons barely held himself in check. As if this wet-behind-the-ears station chief was going to lecture him on which way was up. The damned man didn't have half the information he thought he did. He didn't dignify Amundson with an answer and simply led them to the car and slid inside. Amundson slid in across from him, leaving Page and the detective standing in the morning sunshine beside the car.

Ray made a show of studying the detective through the tint-blackened window. "Perhaps we can start with something small—like why Detective Bryson is involved in Homeland Security business? I don't believe I've approved any requests for clearance."

Amundson stiffened, his blue eyes turned to ice, but the temperature in the car seemed to increase a couple of degrees. Amundson, who had always played his cards so well, wasn't hiding his reactions as well as he used to. Interesting.

"There was no time, and Bryson has skills our agency needed."

"And those would be?" Ray kept his voice soft and watched Amundson swallow. The man knew the danger he was in for not keeping his boss informed—and well he should worry.

"He can recognize when Change is happening and can remember what existed before." Amundson fell into the clipped report of a soldier—only directly answering the question. But the facts he revealed were interesting.

Ray turned his regard on the detective. "How long have you known he had this talent?"

Amundson shrugged. "He came to me before New Madrid with a story I would have thought was crazy except he knows Vallon Drake. So I had our researchers perform a little experiment. Turns out he can do what he says." He shrugged again. "It seemed like a good idea to keep him close in case the Gifted attacked. He saved my life. I think that gives him security clearance."

"Not good enough. We have rules, procedures, in this organization, not the least of which is keeping your superior informed."

"That would be the same organization that allowed the Gifted to grow and prosper and develop their powers?" Amundson crossed his arms over his chest and sat back, relaxed, as if he knew the flack Ray was taking from the powers that be.

"That would be the organization that is supported by a number of very powerful people in Washington whom you have now royally pissed off. And that was before you released a video that is going to rock the foundations of this nation and the world."

Amundson went still.

"So just where did the technology come from, Wolf? We both know the Changes aren't normally filmable." Ray used Amundson's first name as a clear sign of warning. "How long have you been hiding that little breakthrough, and just when did you intend to tell me about it? At the same time you were going to tell me about the detective? And while we're on the topic of communication, I also didn't see the approval requests to release said video to the media. Care to enlighten me about where it was lost?"

Amundson leaned forward so suddenly Ray fell back against his seat. "You listen to me, old man. You need me. I didn't do this alone. Francis Drake turned the Gifted into a terrorist organization and I had no choice but to respond. I released the video because it had to be done.

People had to be warned. Now you need me, because the American people are going to demand that something be done and they know that I'm the heart of that response."

The snarl on Wolf's face showed his true rabid nature. Always he'd kept a smooth, unruffled exterior before. He'd wanted control of the AGS and its Gifted agents so badly it had been a pleasure to manipulate him with that carrot, but....

"You got control and then realized just how little control you really had, and that terrified you, because that's what you're all about, isn't it?" said Fitzsimmons. "Control of everything? HS was the perfect place to build your little empire, but even though the Gifted worked *for* us, the power of the Gifted eclipsed everything you thought you were and you couldn't have that. *You* couldn't have that because *you* don't trust and so *you* took their children and brought us to this."

Understanding the man's motivation had always been the path to controlling him, and at the moment, control was all Ray could hope to regain. The figurative horse was literally out of the barn, and there were only so many ways he could hope to stop a bloodbath and anarchy from sweeping the nation.

"You will come with me to Washington, where we will hold a press conference and you will apologize and announce that your previous pronouncements were premature and that there are no Gifted and there is no danger. The film coverage was not due to any Gifted power, but due to an experimental weapon developed by the Pentagon that unfortunately deployed when the National Guard column was sent out in error. Not everyone will believe it, but without you fueling it, the crisis will blow over."

Amundson shook his head. "No way. Do you really think the American public is that gullible? It will ruin me."

As if that mattered. Here was another sign that the brash young station chief had lost his mojo and perhaps his mind.

"You're already ruined, son. With what you've done, your security breaches, there's no future for you at all, but I'm prepared to let you have a chance at life. Do this and you can sink back into obscurity amidst the rank and file. But you'll be alive and have a job."

The ice in Amundson's gaze seemed to chill the limousine compartment. "Do you ever really think about what you're doing, *Ray?*"

The question, and the use of his first name, was so unlike Amundson it sent a tremor running down Ray's back to settle uncomfortably in the pit of his stomach.

"You sit here and tell me my life is pretty much over, when all I see is an old man past his prime, scrambling to hold onto power. They're out for you, aren't they? Congresswoman Black is already leaving messages for me on my cell phone." He patted his pocket. "Did you ever think that maybe you're the one going to be blamed and shamed and then left to obscurity? Or maybe, in your case, it'll be infamy as the friend of the Gifted who gave them the chance to seek power over America." Amundson's icy gaze only grew colder. "Those monsters have to be stopped and contained. Their presence anywhere on the globe is a danger to mankind. Now you can either work with me or I'll go through you. You understand?"

Ray breathed in slowly. He'd foreseen it might come to this, but he'd hoped it would be otherwise. Amundson was a man of his convictions, he'd give him that. But the corporate plans for the Gifted could not be allowed to go so far off the rails. If he could stop Amundson, then there was a good chance that Francis Drake would calm down and focus on the projects that corporations were asking for. Yes, they might change the face of the nation, but it was a change for the better, surely. At least, it would be better for one Ray Fitzsimmons, and it would not result in the death toll that Amundson was promising.

His hand slid in his jacket and he pulled out his Sig, silencer already fitted. "It's over, Wolf. I can't have you running loose like some rabid animal."

Amundson launched himself. Ray got off a shot, but the faster, younger man knocked the gun aside as he flattened Ray back in his seat. A fist plowed into face. His head filled with the crunch of shattering cartilage and pain, and blood spilled out of his nose. Realizing just how wrong he'd been about the situation, he brought the gun up again, but Amundson knocked it aside, then twisted it from his grip and sank back on the seat facing him, gun cradled in his lap. Someone was pounding on the vehicle roof.

Amundson's face twisted into a mocking smile. "Just so we've got this straight, I want you to know that when I do my next press conference, it will not be to renounce my previous announcement. I *will* be remaining in my position as Seattle Station Chief and head of the AGS. Have you got that? I will also be assuming responsibility nationally for dealing with this crisis. Congresswoman Black will see to that, *Ray*, because you're just a tad irrelevant right now. Understand?"

To buy time, Ray fumbled a tissue at his bloody nose. Useless to stop the blood. Amundson looked at him like the wolf he was named for. He raised the gun, and oh, Christ, he really was going to do this.

The silencer spat twice and a huge, invisible hand slammed him back into his seat. Horrendous pain and heat rocketed through his chest. He couldn't move. Couldn't breathe, just looked down to see the crimson blooming on his chest.

Amundson casually pocketed the gun and slid past Ray to open the door. A gust of wind blew in dust that clotted on the blood, clotted in his nose, and it was so hard to breathe. He choked and raised his hand for help from the two other men standing there.

Ducking his head, Amundson slid out the door and stepped up to the big man, Page. The other man had turned away in an obvious case of willful blindness.

"Give him a minute to finish dying," Amundson said, with a pat on the big man's arm. "Then I want you to take care of the car."

CHAPTER 7 —THE END OF ALL THINGS

The air smelled heavenly of bacon and maple, and Vallon stirred under the warm covers and smiled. Morning, it was morning and time to get up. Fi must be cooking, and that was both a pleasure and a surprise, because Vallon hadn't really trusted her in her kitchen to this point.

She rolled onto her side and a stab of pain brought her out of that lovely, half-asleep state and her eyes opened wide.

Queen-sized bed. Dent in the pillow beside her, and the white-and-yellow checkerboard duvet showed signs of recent occupancy. A pale yellow wall held a variety of small, black-and-white nature photos of fern and mushroom and the curl of Madrona bark. Nice. Calming—except she clearly wasn't in her own bedroom and she hadn't a clue where the heck she was. And she was naked under the covers! She tugged them up to her chin.

Beyond the foot of the bed, another pale yellow wall had plaid yellow curtains—closed—above a sturdy-looking brown dresser. Sunlight backlit the curtains and cast a golden light over the room. Not any place she knew, but it was morning and she was alive and—and she had almost died.

She eased onto her back and her breath caught at the pain. A grey pall seeped into her vision from the edges. Grey stubs of trees, poking out of grey, parched earth. The taste of ash filled her mouth and Kiera's face suddenly filled her head.

She froze as everything came flooding back. New Madrid. Jason's betrayal. Finding Xavier, and the mad race to save the children. And her abject failure.

Forearm over her eyes, she fought back tears and the replay of the frantic attempt to save them and the helplessness at the explosion that killed Kiera and most of the others. If she'd only been faster. Worked smarter.

If she hadn't killed those people with her power.

She'd always believed that the power she held was for good and for life. At least that was what she had always used it for. Never had she killed anyone—at least not that she knew of. Not until now, and it left her feeling ugly and permanently unclean. Sure, she might have done a few things right—Seattle and New Madrid, for example—but her judgment, her actions, were faulty too often.

Rubbing at her arms, she struggled to sit up, and a little cry escaped her at the pain. She deserved the pain. Hell, she deserved to be dead for what she had done. *The scream that swiftly became a strangled mewling as the female researcher's legs melted under her and her body became a toxic spill.*

Her stomach rebelled as the door on the other side of the room pushed open. She swallowed her self-loathing as Fi entered, along with the sound of voices and a television's low drone. Trailing Fi came a chubby black-and-white cat that immediately leapt up onto the bed and began to purr and meow as she rubbed against Vallon's arm. Vallon tugged the covers up modestly to cover her nakedness.

"Maggie, you little minx. Let me guess: you want me out of bed and a fresh bowl of food immediately."

A chirrup of agreement and a head butt with a little dry, pink nose, and Maggie leapt down off the bed and scooted out the door as if to show the way.

"So much for cat loyalty," Vallon sighed, turning away from the view of the upright tail and furry white cat bloomers.

"She's been checking on you all morning and wouldn't leave your side all night—according to Xavier. I fed her."

Fi leaned against the door frame. She wore a pair of too-large jeans and a man's shirt that was many sizes too big and rolled up at the sleeves. Her blonde hair was still slicked-back from a shower, but she looked downright pleased with herself—sort of a cat-that-ate-the-cream satisfied. She held what looked like an old-fashioned telescope, playing with the extensions.

She turned back to the hall. "She's awake," she called, and then crossed the room to the bed to throw her arms around Vallon. She caught herself just in time and gave a gentle squeeze and a kiss on the cheek. "My God, you had us worried."

As if on cue, Xavier appeared in the doorway, a blond man who looked vaguely familiar behind him.

Across the room in one stride, Xavier sank down beside her and gently pulled her into him. He kissed her hair. "I prayed to mother Pangea and Creator that they would give you back to us."

The gentleness of his touch was almost more than she could bear. She didn't deserve it. She didn't deserve people like this around her at all.

His lips ran down to hers and his incense and cedar of Lebanon scent filled up her senses. Against her wishes, she relaxed against him. Love and safety enfolded her and she didn't deserve it. She'd lost the children. She should have stayed and stopped her father. She should have somehow stopped Amundson before he spread his hatred any further and got more people killed.

When Xavier pulled back it was almost a relief.

His black gaze was tender and he chucked her under the chin. "It has been too long, *Bela Menina*. We shall make the time to cherish each other properly. But right now, I would like to introduce you to our host and your healer."

Vallon frowned and pulled the covers up further, because the grey pall seemed to cover the other man's face, even as Fi slid in close beside him. He smiled down at her.

"It's something simple, isn't it? Jim?" she said, blinking against the grey. "You introduced us before, didn't you?"

It felt as if the man was not quite there, or perhaps it was her who was removed somehow. She shook her head, trying to dislodge the pall. It didn't work. Even Fi's face was faded and drained of color, regardless of her happy smile.

"Jack Henry, meet Vallon Drake."

Jack half-bowed, just as Xavier had when she had first met him. So he came from somewhere else, as well.

"A true pleasure. I am glad to have been of service." His accent said British, with something southern European thrown in for good measure. Odd, given his name and his almost hippy-long hair.

"Service?"

"He healed you, Vallon. Remember?" Xavier's concerned gaze said she should, and what had previously been slight lines of worry now seemed etched permanently on his face.

But the memory just wasn't there. She swallowed back her ill-ease. "Of course I remember."

Xavier eyed her as if he saw through her lie. And why she lied to him, she couldn't say. Perhaps it was the grey that lurked over everything— even across Fi and Jack, standing so close their flaming auras mingled. She needed to understand what was happening. She didn't want to worry him anymore than she had.

Fi showed a possessiveness toward Jack that Vallon hadn't seen before. She looked back to Xavier and raised a brow. Was something going on there? He gave the barest of nods. Well Lordy, Lordy, little Fi had found herself a man.

"They both helped to heal you. In the Porsche, somehow Fi kept you alive long enough to get here. Then Jack healed you. They dealt with the afterburn together after Jack healed Fi's leg."

Fi colored prettily, but Jack pulled her into his side. "There are surprises under the sun even now, that one so young and only Gifted could do what she did and without any training."

Surprises were an understatement. Healer? Fi? There'd never been any hint of that talent amongst the Gifted, and Fi? Really? But she looked like she'd grown up years since the wreck of house Vallon's father had occupied in Anacortes. That had been—last night? Vallon had basically discounted Fi as being under the influence of Francis Drake. Up until she and Fi had met at that house, the childhood trauma Fi had experienced had left her, well, childlike.

But not now. Now Fi looked and acted like a woman who had realized her own competence as she pulled away from Jack and crossed her arms. For the moment, at least, because Fi seemed to always revert back to a child-like state or pouting and tears.

"I had *some* training," Fi said."I did go to the academy for a few years. And Vallon showed me lots of things, didn't you?"

It was true. Both times Vallon had had to deal with predators attacking America, Fi had been there. Vallon had had to enlist her help because there hadn't been anyone else to turn to.

"Fi's a quick study," she allowed and saw the pleasure bloom across Fi's cheeks.

Jack and Xavier exchanged glances and then Jack nodded. "There is that. Of course."

"Let me guess. Your people don't think much of the AGS training program."

Another exchange between the two men so that Vallon suspected they were conversing in some way.

"All right. Let me try it this way. You don't think much of the AGS *or* the Gifted. Is that closer to the mark?" She crossed her arms over her chest and winced. "Even though the two Gifted in the room dealt with Seattle and New Madrid."

Xavier inhaled. "Yes. Yes, you did, and the Council will need to hear about it. You are far more than they give you credit for."

Typical. Amundson thought the Gifted were too bad to exist, and Xavier's people thought they were too little to care about. So much for being in the middle of the bell curve. Didn't exactly lengthen the Gifteds' life expectancy.

"So we have breakfast made. Do you feel strong enough to join us in the kitchen, or do we bring the breakfast to you here?" Jack asked.

"Definitely the kitchen!" She pasted a bright smile on her face. "Just let me get dressed."

She shushed them out of the room after being brought a t-shirt and robe and tried to blink back the vision of ashes. Her clothes had been ruined and Xavier had yet to make it to a store to replace them. When they were gone and the door was closed, she gingerly shoved the covers off and slid her legs over the edge of the bed.

Sitting upright, her head swam a little and the gray haze thickened. The taste of ash coated her tongue and she really didn't think she could eat a thing, but she'd try. She held onto the edge of the bed, fighting the panic. It was just because she'd been injured. It had to be. The taste of ash seemed to wash through her and leave her feeling half dead. Was that what it was? The result of almost dying, so she walked with a foot in this world and one in the next?

Stupid idea. She didn't believe in 'next worlds.'

Focusing on the clothes, she pulled the t-shirt over her head. It was emblazoned with a hockey team logo and just raising her arms left her sweating and pale. The robe, which smelled of cut grass and apples, was plaid flannel and thankfully easier to get into. She slipped her arms in and tugged it over her shoulders.

A soft knock came at the door. "May I come in?" Xavier asked.

"Always."

He helped her to stand and then his arms came around her, his broad hand on the small of her back as he pulled her in to kiss her forehead.

"I held you all night, praying you would wake and be well. But something has happened. I see it in your eyes." He looked down at her and gently shifted a lock of blond hair that showed signs of someone washing it. "Tell me."

She shook her head and looked down at where their bodies connected. How could he act this way after what she'd done? Was he just hiding his real feelings? "It's nothing. I think I'm just tired. Could—could you help me to the washroom? I want to brush my teeth." Because her mouth tasted of copper and she was sure her breath stank.

His knuckle raised her chin and he studied her eyes. "I respect your privacy, *Bela*. But I am here for you. Always. You can tell me anything. We will work it through together."

But he took her to a small, yellow bathroom in the hall—didn't Jack know how to paint any other color? and waited as she relieved herself, did her teeth, and studied herself in the mirror. Her eyes held deep shadows that looked deeper in the pallor of her skin. Her hair was a tangle and she really needed a shower, but a wash-cloth scrub was all she had strength and time for.

When she stepped out of the bathroom, Xavier was still there to offer her support. Leaning in, his heady incense and cedar scent filled her senses and sent the grey fading. Perhaps that was all it would take—more time with this man. She lifted her face to him and his lips covered hers and she answered the hard-soft need of him with her own. A pleasant fizz of afterburn blazed between them like man-made lighting.

Xavier pulled back and his lips curved wickedly. "That tells me you heal better than any words. Perhaps it will not be too long until we can have dessert instead of breakfast."

A quick grin and she shuffled after him down a narrow, landscape-photo-lined hallway toward a sun-filled kitchen. Clearly, someone liked the outdoors, for the house was cool and, though the robe covered her almost-nakedness down to mid calf, the air chilled her ankles.

The kitchen, though, was a sunny place, warmed by sunshine and an unexpected small fireplace that crackled merrily in a stone hearth. On the yellow counter lay an idle electric waffle iron, and a large, batter-coated bowl filled the porcelain sink under one of the large windows. On a corner of the tiled counter under the scarred maple cupboards, a small television droned on a twenty-four hour U.S. news channel. Over the gleaming stove, an old-fashioned cast-iron baker's shelf displayed antique plates, while in the center of the room, the butcher-block table had been set for four.

She stopped and looked to the ceiling—faux beams across painted gyprock—and swallowed, remembering. She had lain on that table, but now the wood surface was scrubbed to glistening blonde and laid with placemats with bright, fall maple leaves on them, and heavy cream-colored stoneware plates and silverware. A steaming platter of waffles sat in the middle of the table along with a pitcher of what could only be maple syrup and a carafe of coffee. Jack and Fi had already started and Maggie munched crunchies in the corner.

"We didn't know how long you'd be," Jack said and gave them a sly look. "I understand it has been some time since you two have had a chance to relax together."

Xavier helped her into a chair and then sat across from her, watching. To test her appetite? To make sure she was truly on the mend? Or…?

She silently accepted the large waffle Xavier slid onto her plate and buttered it and then poured the warmed maple syrup over top. She studied the melting butter for a moment and then dug in, though in truth the grey pall left her less than hungry.

Even here in the warm kitchen with the friendly conversation of Fi and Jack and Xavier and the drone of the television, the grey waxed and waned like an incoming tide. She'd chewed the cardboard-tasting piece of waffle in her mouth until it was no more than mush and forced herself to swallow and smile.

"Wonderful! Who's the cook?" Even though she could barely taste the maple through the ash.

Jack raised his hand and she congratulated him, but Xavier was watching her too closely. He'd know something was wrong if she didn't do something and soon. She cut another piece of waffle.

"So what are the plans, because I've been thinking." She looked from person to person as she took the bite. More ash. More chewing. Great. She forced a smile and shook her head. "I figure we need to get back across the border and deal with things. Between my father and Amundson, they're just going to make things worse if they're not dealt with." She nodded at the T.V. "What's been happening?"

Xavier looked at Fi and Jack, who seemed to have smiles permanently pasted on their faces. "Perhaps we should leave such discussions until after the meal."

That couldn't mean anything good. The waffle-cum-ash-flavored-cardboard caught in her throat. She set down her knife and fork. "And perhaps you should stop trying to coddle me. Or is it that you don't trust me? I might have been injured, but I'm here. I know I screwed up big time, but I'm a trained agent and a big girl. Now tell me."

Xavier stopped eating and set his fork down. So did everyone else. She waited.

Finally, Xavier nodded. "I thought to give you time to heal. The process can leave one disoriented."

In other words, like there *was* something the matter with her. "Like I said. I'm a big girl."

"You need to rest or you're liable to delay your recovery," Jack said with a shake of his blond head. Unlike the dangerousness Xavier evoked, he looked like an escapee of the flower child '70s, with his hair loose over his collar and wearing a cotton tunic over faded, torn jeans.

"Would you just tell me!"

"There've been lynchings in a few states and riots in Los Angeles and Washington," Jack said. "Politicians are calling for the head of the president for sanctioning such operations and for keeping the existence of Gifted a secret. Of course, nighttime radio is ablaze with conspiracy theorists saying they've known for years that aliens lived side by side with humans and were planning a takeover of the planet. The unfortunate thing is that some of those conspiracy theorists have spilled over into mainstream news like FOX and CNN. There's been speculation that the president will have to replace the head of Homeland Security with this Amundson." Jack cast an apologetic glance in Xavier's direction. "Sorry. She has a right to know and she'll learn it sooner or later."

"I would prefer it be later after what she has been through. It has only been three days since she was injured."

"Three days!" The grey seemed to thicken in the room. "I've been here three days? Oh, my God, there's no telling how much damage Amundson's done."

She struggled to stand, but her legs failed her. Xavier caught her hand and sent a surge of calming power into her. Then he sighed. "That is a danger and we have been watching, but the bigger challenge is potential for this reaction to spread internationally. BBC reports demonstrations in London demanding to know if such Gifted exist there. There have been reports of quiet roundups of minority ethnic groups in some parts of North Africa. Most of Europe has kept the lid on, but for how long we don't know. There is no news out of China because all the news feeds and the internet have been shut down. The Japanese and Taiwanese are on high alert and so are the Koreans. There's no news out of the former U.S.S.R. At least that is what Jack's sources tell us."

Which had to be through Xavier's Council. The two pieces of waffle curdled in her stomach. "So fast."

"It is only the beginning." Xavier pushed his plate away and caught her hand protectively.

"Then it makes it even more important that we act. I have to get back across the border and stop my father. If the Gifted don't react to Amundson, there'll be nothing for him to feed the news on. It can put the fire out before it begins."

"No. That is too dangerous. You barely survived the last time. Your father uses you as fodder for his ventures. Please, *Bela*. Do not do something so foolish."

"So? What? You're my handler now? My boss? There are a whole lot of people down there who are going to die if we just leave this. This is something I have to do, Xavier. You have no say in it."

It was like she'd slapped him. He released her hand and clutched the edge of the table in visible self-restraint. "Vallon, this is not a decision you should make quickly. Not when you are still recovering."

The grey pall pulsed over everything, momentarily blinding her to Xavier and the others. Kiera was screaming as she sank into the ash.

"No!" she yelled and lunged forward, slamming up against the table. Dishes rattled, something fell and shattered, and she fought when someone grabbed her and held her back from Kiera. "No! Damn you, no!"

She fought with her fists, but Xavier caught them, his scent of incense and cedar of Lebanon acrid up her nose.

"Let me go. I have to help her."

When he did, she crumpled to the kitchen floor, but Xavier went with her and pulled her into him.

"Vallon." His hand cupped her head, held her face toward him. "Tell me what happens. What do you see? Who is it you try to help?"

Blinking, she pulled back from him. Could barely see him through the grey and the ash that blew across the landscape. *Trust him when he was trying to stop her from doing what needed to be done?*

"It's Kiera, Xavier. She's trapped in that place." She could just make out his features, the question on his face.

"Place, *Bela?*" As if he doubted her sanity. Perhaps she should as well.

She shoved him away and fought to get her legs under her. Then she was up and swaying with her back to the counter. Xavier, flanked by Fi and Jack, faced her, but they were ghosts in the ghastly landscape. Clearly, they did not understand.

She squeezed her eyes shut again. "I'm not crazy. I'm not. But I'm seeing something. A landscape." She told them what she saw. Then she looked at each of their faces. She had to make them understand.

The television burbled and rumbled behind them on the counter, showing scenes of the fire she knew too well. The warehouse. She pointed, as the image switched to a smiling Wolf Amundson on a stage speaking into a microphone. Jason Bryson and a big man she recognized as one of Amundson's agents stood slightly behind him. Wolf Amundson's blond hair gleamed and, if anything, he looked pleased, instead of like a man who had just lost a cadre of men.

Jack leapt to turn the volume up.

"Thank you for agreeing to attend this news conference, because you have placed yourself at risk to do so." Amundson raised his hands to quell any possible questions. "You see, the government wishes to remove me from my position. They wish to silence me about our situation." The room around him erupted in voices and he held up his hands again, smooth, confident, his expression one of apparent sorrow at his predicament. He shook his head. "But the reasons behind the decision are what trouble me. They did not threaten to cast me out, they threatened to kill me unless I recanted the truth of the Gifted existence. But that I cannot do after the tragedy of Anacortes." Another theatrical shake of the head. "It seems our leaders do not want us to be able to protect ourselves. First they wanted our guns and now there is this. But I say to you, as long as I am a free man, I will fight these creatures alongside any man, woman, or child who wishes to hold onto their freedom."

The sound of sirens came through the television.

"And now I am afraid I must leave or be arrested. You may wish to question those who come for me about who they work for and who they are truly protecting."

He and Jason and the other man stepped down from the stage and disappeared into the crowd of reporters, just as armed, plain clothed men burst onto the stage. The reporters seemed to close in around Amundson. Then the scene was replaced by a newscaster.

"That was the scene five minutes ago at a downtown Seattle location. Wolf Amundson left the press conference and his location is currently unknown. So far, government sources have remained silent on any response to Amundson's accusations. In related news, a family of four was killed when a crowd at a local shopping mall took matters into their own hands when a patron was accused of being Gifted. In the ensuing chase and melee, John Stubbs and his wife, Lorraine, and their two infant sons were trampled. Authorities are calling it another example of innocents paying the price for Gifted presence."

Xavier turned the T.V. down and slowly turreted back to the table. "It is the purges come again."

His head hung low, Jack nodded. He covered his face with his hands.

"Purges?" Vallon asked.

The two men looked at each other and finally Xavier nodded. "It is part of our history all Cartos would choose to forget, and it is not spoken of in polite society. I therefore apologize." Glancing back at the muted television, he sighed. "You see, eons ago, Cartos began a war. During the struggle, they did something so horrific that suddenly the unGifted were aware of the Change. They rose up against the Cartos and the world ended. Cities were brought down to dust. The earth was reduced to ash by volcanoes. Cartos were slaughtered and scattered to all corners of the earth, including their part-bred children. Those few that survived either hid in secret enclaves or intermarried, once more diluting the blood. It split our people and left us with less than nothing. It took many generations to come together again."

As he spoke, the grey pall spread across the room and Vallon tasted bile.

Wavering, she held onto the counter, her heart pounding, her lungs unable to catch a breath as swirling ash filled the room and the others voices became the sound of the wind. That was when she understood.

Her world was ending, too.

CHAPTER 8 — ASH AND GREY WIND

When Vallon started to topple, Xavier's heart clenched. The kitchen was strangely silent after the drone of the television. Jack and Fi stood frozen and the rich waffles and maple syrup and bacon curdled in his stomach. Vallon's face had gone strange and the usual light in her brown eyes had faded to grey.

He caught her before she hit the floor, picked her up so her head rested on his shoulder.

"No. No. I understand now." Her knuckles jabbed his chest. "Put me down." Stronger. "I'm fine."

She looked anything *but* fine. He just wanted to hold her, tell her all would be right, but her gaze rebuffed him. He placed her in her chair.

She looked ill: full lips drawn thin, her head skeletal.

He rounded on Jack. "You said she was healed?"

"She is. At least of anything physical. She should just be a little tender—and tired."

But it was more than fatigue with Vallon. He ran his palm over her cheek. Her great golden presence no longer had the blackened streaks of imminent death that she'd had during the horrendous run for the border. But something had tarnished her golden flame. He went to his knees beside her and cupped her face.

"Vallon. What is happening? Tell me."

Her brown gaze twitched over his face, and then came to rest on his hands. "Your hand. It's healed."

Avoiding his question, then. And it reminded him too much of his father and his childhood. He nodded at Jack. "He took care of me this morning and showed Fi how it is done. *Bela, please.* Tell me what ails you?"

Because there had to be something he could do. So much in the greater world was now beyond his control. He had to focus on Vallon and keeping her safe and well. That was all that mattered, because once before he had failed someone he loved. And right now, the woman he loved was grinding the heels of her hands into her eyes. When she stopped and squinted her eyes open again, she visibly sighed and leaned back in her chair.

Then she gave him a wan smile that eased the tightness around his heart. "I don't think this is anything Jack or Fi could heal. You see, right now, as I look at you, an ash-laden wind fills this room and the world beyond. This room has faded, is fading, almost as if it never existed, and all I see is desolation."

Xavier frowned and ran his hands down her arms. She was frozen, even in the flannel housecoat. He scooped her up and headed down the hall for the bedroom. Get her under the covers and warm, because something was clearly going on.

"I'm not seeing things, Xavier," she said trying to stop him. "I'm not. And I'm not sick—well, maybe a little. But that's not what's going on here. After what you said—what you described of the purges—I think—I think I'm seeing the future." She shivered in his arms. "It's not good."

§

Blue fluorescent lights lit the pedestrian tunnel through the basement of the hotel, and the bare concrete walls reflected Amundson's and Jason's hurried footfall. Page's longer stride fell in syncopated rhythm as he gave terse orders into his cell phone. Old urine and spilled wine filled the dead air.

The plainclothed men who'd broken up the press conference couldn't be far behind, and it wasn't likely that they'd hesitate to shoot after the bloodbath he'd left at the heliport, the HS left headless, at least for the moment. The limo driver, unfortunate collateral damage. The question was how the plainclothed men had found him so quickly.

"Boss!" Page's voice echoed down the tunnel. "I've got a car coming for us. They'll meet us in the alley behind the hotel. We just have to get our asses from this door to theirs."

"Good man." He patted Page's shoulder and hurried on, the detective unusually silent beside him. "Don't tell me you've still got a problem with my actions."

Bryson's dark eyes met his. "I just didn't think you had it in you. Should have known better, given Anacortes."

Anacortes and all the 'innocent' deaths, as the media called them. They were a necessary call to action. If people didn't like it, too bad. "So now you know."

Let the man have his thoughts and his doubts. He didn't care anymore. The technology was coming, and soon he wouldn't need Detective Jason Bryson anymore except as another little science project. Hell, if they could figure out how Bryson did what he did, then no one would ever have to fear the Gifted again.

The end of the tunnel came up, a solid metal door with a not-so-solid lock that, by the urine stains on the walls by the door, had been used by the street people for a long while. Page elbowed his way past and shoved the heavy metal steel door open wide enough he could just peer out. The hushed whine of Seattle traffic came in on a gust of sea-salt air. Just let them get out of this place and home, back to what had previously been the AGS compound. He'd already sent men to secure the site. If HS wanted to take him down, there'd be a fire fight; but so far there'd been no word of any movement against the hilltop compound. Maybe, just maybe, Fitzsimmon's demise had had given whoever was driving that show a sober second thought.

A whiff of car exhaust and then Page nodded.

"Now!" he shoved open the door as a yellow cab rolled to a stop and the rear door swung open. Wolf leapt out the door, his head down, and dove for the rear seat. Bryson followed more slowly, but he held a service revolver ready and climbed in beside him. Page let the door slam shut and rolled a garbage bin in front of the door, then climbed in the front seat.

"Go!" he said, and the cabby went.

Well, perhaps not just a cabby. He was a big, broad-shouldered man, made from the same mold as Page: shaved head, strong jaw, and a silent authority that he wore like a robe. No chatty Seattle immigrant here.

The car roared down the alley, aiming for the street. Get into traffic and they'd be that much harder to stop. The car barely slowed as they hit the end of the alley and a man threw himself at the windshield.

Not plainclothed. Not an agent, but someone he knew: mid forties, clad in a blue windbreaker and jeans, with short black hair and golden skin. The driver slammed on the brakes and slewed the car sideways into moving traffic, but the crazy man on the hood of the car held on, blocking all view of the street.

"Amundson! Wolf Amundson!" The voice came through the window.

"What the fuck is this?" growled the driver.

"Hell if I know," Page yelled. 'Stop the car, I'll pull the fucker off."

"No! Just get him inside." Amundson broke his stunned silence; he recognized the man plastered across the window. "That's Sukh Sandhu. Dr. Sukh Sandhu. I thought he was dead."

The car screeched to a halt and Sandhu went sliding half way up and over the roof of the car before Page grabbed him, and stuffed him in the back of the car. Then the taxi roared away toward the highway.

"Sandhu? What the hell were you thinking, man? You could have been killed." Wolf grabbed the man by the scruff of the neck and righted him, somehow finding space between himself and Bryson. "I thought you were dead with the others at Seattle Station."

The researcher's head bobbed on his thin neck. "Seattle Station. Is that what it was called? I couldn't remember. To be honest, I thought I was dead, too. I wondered about it when I suddenly found myself walking around Seattle and I didn't know what to do, where I worked, nothing. Then I saw you on the news and I remembered that I worked for you. I was in the lounge in the hotel bar when your last news conference came on and I tried to catch you. So here I am."

He gave the ridiculous little head-waggle of his culture and closed his eyes. "I am going to hurt like hell tomorrow."

"You're lucky as hell I didn't just drive over you," the driver growled as they took the ramp onto I-5 North headed for the 520 that would take them out to Redmond.

Wolf looked from Bryson, who was studiously ignoring the scientist—that was right, Sandhu had overseen the experiments on Bryson—and back to Sandhu.

"You chose the right time to find me. I've got work for you."

Sandhu nodded and fumbled a sheaf of papers from a pocket inside his windbreaker.

"Sir, it's fortunate I found you, because I had planned to speak with you the day HS headquarters was destroyed." Sandhu held out the sheaf of wrinkled papers. "These are the results of some side research I was doing. We'd been looking at drugs and bloodletting as a means to control the Gifted power. I decided to look for other options, as well. I had just written this report for you when everything happened. This is the only copy in existence."

Wolf scanned the title. *The Role of Ley Lines as a Source of Gifted Power.* Interesting.

"Sir, I think I know how to stop them."

Interesting indeed.

CHAPTER 9 —THE LAVENDER OF HERET

Vallon looked so fragile nestled amid the pillows he had placed around her on the bed. Even with the sun through the windows, the warm yellow walls only placed a sallow pall across her skin, almost as if what she said were true. A vision. A vision of the death of the world, but that made no sense. A Cartos could not cause such damage because of the edicts that governed them. And though bombs and environmental degradation had proven the unGifted capable of immense stupidity, surely disaster was not in their immediate future. Leastways it was difficult to believe, in the fall warmth of the sunshine lighting the bright, checkerboard bedspread.

"I know it makes no sense at all," Vallon said.

Xavier fought the need to cradle her in his arms. She would not accept it. She'd pushed him away when he settled her on the bed and had complained when he tucked the covers around her. So he stood here, uselessly, beside her bed. He had felt like this once before and had disliked the sensation then, as well. On the other side of her bed, Jack waited and Fi fidgeted anxiously.

Vallon shoved the covers down farther and pulled the red plaid robe around her neck as if the room, the house, the world was a cold dark place, but she still had to prove she did not need him. Her brown eyes had gone so dark all the iris had disappeared.

"But this vision suggests that something bad is going to happen," she continued. "It looks like the earth is dead or dying as far as I can see. And no, it's not a desert. Deserts have lots of life in them. This was ash and crying winds and death. I know. I can still taste it."

She had been through so much, had her mind fractured under the strain? Jack's gaze held judgment, and Fi? Well, Fiona seemed to fight back tears and would not meet Vallon's gaze.

"Would you stop looking like someone died? I am *not* crazy," Vallon flared at them. "I had those dreams of the kids from the Academy, and that turned out to be true."

Xavier sat on the edge of the bed, caught her hand. "Those were foretelling dreams, *Bela*, not a walking daytime vision," he said softly. "It is known that people sometimes learn things through their dreams."

She pulled her hand free. "Damn it, Xavier, I'm not some fragile flower. Consider this like a waking nightmare, because I'm damn well seeing it, and right now the ash is blowing so hard I can barely see you." She clenched her eyes closed as if something pained her, and if anything, her skin grayed further. "Think about it. If things are so bad that your Pangea will be affected, wouldn't she want someone to do something about it? Like ask for help?"

"But why you, Vallon?" He shifted beside her. The flow of her Cartos power seemed normal; her scent of ashes of roses almost overwhelming. "Why not some Cartos of the Council?"

"Gee. Maybe because I'm in the middle of things, not hiding away on the other side of the world? I've been using the power a lot lately. Maybe that got your mother goddess's attention. I mean, how the hell do I know? She's not my mother goddess. But there could be some connection created by my power use."

He caught her hand again. "There are many Cartos who use power, *Bela*."

She yanked free and glared. "Don't call me '*Bela*'. My *name* is Vallon. And I don't give a damn if you believe me. When we make love to deal with the afterburn, there's a moment when we connect to everything. Well, I had something like that when I dealt with the Seattle volcano and when I dealt with New Madrid. I reached so far and spread so thin I really couldn't tell where I ended and the earth began. Maybe that's why I'm seeing this. Or maybe it's the fact I'd be frigging dead if it wasn't for Fi and Jack's meddling."

She pulled the robe around her and pushed to the far side of the bed and stood defiantly, even though she swayed. Her small feline began to thread around her ankles and almost looked like she could push her mistress over.

"The bottom line is this: I will not just sit here and do nothing. Something is happening that threatens the world. I'm going to take care of it." She glowered as if daring him to contradict her.

She was the most stubborn woman he had ever known, but she had always worked for the greater good. In every instance, she took matters into her own hands, no matter what wiser heads said. In all his years of watching her, he had seen that. And even pale and barely recovered, she was adamant about this, so something had her truly afraid.

She squinted and wiped her eyes as if she stood in a harsh wind. Was her mind truly gone, or was she actually experiencing something?

Her bright gold aura filled the room, overlapped in places by Jack's presence. Fi's lesser light was like a shadow in the incandescence. But there *were* differences in Vallon's aura, small eddies in the golden vortex that he had missed until he looked closely. They spoke of emotional reactions to something very real.

He -reached- for her and saw her start at his gentle intrusion.

[What?]

[Show me what you see.]

Nothing happened for a moment, except that cold radiated into him. Then layers of gossamer curtains parted to reveal a scene rippling as if seen through the deep water of another's perceptions. *Barrens that fled into hazy distance, a taste of ash so acrid it burned away the taste of maple and of Vallon's kisses. He -reached- into the earth, but found nothing but stone darkness as a desolate wind scoured his face.* He winced and pulled back and found his hand shielding his eyes.

Vallon looked up at him, her expression pleading.

A weight settled into his chest and it was hard to breathe.

Only stone and darkness. What did that mean? Simply that he could not sense the earth through Vallon's vision? Or that something more had happened? For him not to feel the flow of Pangea's blood through the ley lines spoke of death far greater than he could comprehend, and the weight on his chest was so great he had to fumble for the edge of the bed.

He sat down hard and looked up at Jack's disbelieving face. "She speaks the truth."

Jack's expression hardened. "You know what that means?"

Xavier sighed. This went against everything he had tried to do. "It seems you get your wish, old friend. Didn't you wish to do this, right from the start?"

His lips in a hard line, Jack gave a curt nod. "I will let them know." He left the room.

"Let who know what?" Vallon demanded from behind him.

He turned to her and caught her hand. "*Bela*—Vallon—please sit down. You are weak and your little cat is likely enough to make you fall."

She resisted just as always, and it reminded him of another woman who always tried to appear so strong—until it killed her.

"I believe you. I do. But you must conserve your strength for what is to come."

Slowly she allowed herself to be coaxed back on the bed. Maggie meowed in disdain and then turned tail out the door.

"So is this the men in white coats you're calling?" she asked.

He sighed. "I fear it is far worse, but I will protect you or die trying."

"Protect me?"

He pulled her into his side, pulled the covers around her to keep her warm, for the vision was a cold, dead place, indeed. He would not wish to dwell in it as she did, just as he did not wish to take her to the Cartos Council. What would they do when they saw her? What would it mean to her? He pulled her back against him and rubbed her cold arms. "I have asked Jack to contact the Council. To tell them that I will turn myself in, because they must hear what you are saying. The Council is very conservative, Vallon." Her name tasted cold and remote on his tongue and left his chest hollow, even though he held her in his arms. "They are all about remaining hidden and retaining the status quo, but if what you see is the future, then they must take action to stop it. Our mother is more than the source of our power, she is life itself for this planet. Nothing must harm her. You must show the Council what you see, just as you showed me."

He could not bring himself to tell her of the risk to both of them. After his latest betrayal, the Council's first response might be to kill both of them.

"I planned to go back to Seattle myself. I—I don't need their help."

But he stroked her hair and kissed her forehead. Her hands trembled and shivers wracked her. "Aah, Vallon, please. In your condition, you will do no one any good."

She sighed and it was as if she gave up the fight—at least for this moment—and for this moment alone, he had accomplished something, protected her.

"All right," she said, weariness radiating off of her. "We'll go to them together, and I'll tell them what I know. Then we can come home and I'll do what I have to do. So you'll make the travel arrangements? When will we go?"

The sound of too familiar voices came from the hallway and Xavier stiffened.

"Xavier?" Her brown eyes looked up at him.

Fi went to the doorway and then stepped back as Jack came back into the room, followed by the two people Xavier least wanted to see. Both were naked. Carlos, his elder brother, was broad of chest and as hawk nosed as Xavier, with sun-darkened skin and lines around the eyes. Leticia, his wife and the Council's interrogator, was as pale as the moon with her night-dark cascade of hair around her naked shoulders. Her haughty gaze swept the room, touched on Xavier with ice, and came to rest on Vallon with clear distaste.

Xavier loosed Vallon and stood to face them.

"I see the contagion spreads," Leticia said and stepped further into the room. Fi averted her gaze from the naked man and woman and stepped up to Jack's side—a move that did not escape the ever vigilant Leticia. She turned to Jack. "I had always thought better of you. You would involve yourself with such as this." She raked Vallon and Fi with a glance.

"Beloved, I am sure that Jack would not call upon us unless there was some dire need," Carlos said.

She considered for a moment and then inhaled. "I suppose. He has always been—responsible."

A pointed look in Xavier's direction made it clear he had not.

"We must go before the Council," Xavier said, placing his body between Leticia's anger and Vallon. "There are things happening that require their action."

One dark brow arched in a look that could shrivel most men. "Well that, for once, is the truth. The Council must pass judgment on you and—this." She nodded at Vallon as if she were an inanimate object.

"Then praise the Creator that you are not the Council and that cooler heads sit on that illustrious body. We need your assistance to take us before the Council."

Vallon stirred beside him and her hand found his. "Xavier…? Is this a good idea?"

"A moment, please." He turned to Carlos. "I request safe passage for Vallon from you, a Council member. She has done nothing but try to maintain Pangea according to the edicts and the secret of our existence. If there are to be repercussions, they fall to me and me alone."

"Xavier, no." She struggled up to face Leticia. "Your Pangea is in mortal danger, but unless you guarantee safe passage to both of us, we'll stay here and do what we can ourselves. You and your Council can go to hell."

Ferocious. Beautiful. Angry. Vulnerable. He remembered another woman, long ago. His mother, when she was young and he was no more than a child. Cold rippled through him.

"*Bela*—Vallon—no." She did not need another enemy, and certainly did not need to face Leticia's malice. Not when the Cartos Council would already be inclined against her.

"Why should we involve them, Xavier?" Vallon rounded on him. "Why, if they are just going to hurt you?"

"So sweet, the defense of so weak a creature for her better. Is this why you keep her around, Xavier? For her small delusions of grandeur? Or perhaps because she views you as a god?"

He curled his fists as she looked up at Carlos. "When did you cease such defense of me, husband?" Her contempt was barely veiled.

Perhaps it was when she cuckolded him for the fourth or fifth time, or when she showed herself a heartless bitch, but that had been so soon after their marriage that Xavier wondered if they had ever been happy. But it was so like Leticia to leap to conclusions regarding Xavier's relationship with Vallon and to let her old enmity for her husband's brother blind her to the woman before her.

Carlos stayed silent, but met Xavier's gaze and must have read the truth there. He nodded.

"Vallon," said Xavier, "We need the Council's aid to discover what has caused this thing and to prevent it. You are too weak, and they have great knowledge and records that go back almost to the great purge. They will know what this is and how to stop it." He looked up at Carlos. "You must help us and ensure no repercussions fall on Vallon."

"And Xavier." Vallon's voice was hard.

"I will do all I can, brother." But could it be enough? Carlos clasped Xavier's hand in an almost unfamiliar show of kinship. A long-lost surge of family warmth ran through his aura. When had the last time been? Xavier could not remember.

"Leticia, take her."

Her pale features twisted at the order, but she caught Vallon's free hand as Xavier gripped the other. *Please, let Vallon at least get through this unscathed. Let old secrets not harm her.* Then the world swirled and fell away around them. The lavender of the heret ley lines filled his nose, and North America swept behind them.

CHAPTER 10 — A POX UPON HER FAIRNESS

She should not have let Xavier bring her here, even though it was like entering a dream. The problem was that the grey pall gave a troubling double vision that was both dream and nightmare. She was never truly sure just what was truth anymore.

Except that she and Xavier were prisoners.

Vallon stood, blinking back the ashes, on the third floor balcony of the Villa de Polo, or so Xavier had named it, overlooking a narrow, winding black canal, with just as narrow a view of watery blue sky. With the refracted blue sky and balcony staring back up at her from the canal, it was difficult to remember which way was up. Venetian sunlight placed bright pixels on the constant ripple of the dark water and filled the air with a muddy humidity. The close-knit villas that grew straight up from the water provided little in the way of handholds she might use to escape from her prison and blocked out the wind and so the air hung dank and heavy, even though the room behind her was filled with refracted light. A faint scent of jasmine filled the air from a bush that, if she leaned far out from the marble balcony railing, she could just see escaping over a wall some ways southward. The sound of voices came from along the canal—the gondoliers calling, the laughter of roaming tourists, the sound of a guitar and singer—and yet the house behind her remained silent, the grey pall grew, and her chest clamped slowly shut in panic.

"You look like a horse fretting at its tether," Xavier said, padding barefoot up behind her.

He placed his hands on her shoulders, but they simply added to the weight on her chest. She should not have let him talk her into this. She would have found a way to stop what was happening in Seattle herself, but instead she was trapped here while disaster waited in Seattle.

"It will not be long. They need time to pull the Council members in from around the world. In the meantime, you should rest and enjoy your surroundings."

She turned under his hands. "How can I enjoy Venice, trapped in this room? How can I enjoy anything, knowing something is happening? Judging by Leticia's gloating, they've already passed judgment and we're just waiting for the execution. It's been two days, Xavier, and nothing has happened except we've wasted time in this room, and all the time the grey pall is there and, if anything, the news on CNN says things are getting worse back home. I'm worried about Fi and Jack and my cat, not to mention all the people south of the border. I mean, how long is this going to take? We haven't seen *anyone* except the people who bring us our meals, and they're silent as monks."

Xavier pulled her into him, but it didn't change the facts. This morning on CNN had come stories. Out of New Orleans had come the story that suddenly the meager levees protecting that city had disappeared overnight. It left the river flowing into the barely recovering city, even as hurricane season began. There was no way New Orleans would survive any type of tidal surge, let alone a full-fledged storm. Millions would die and a beautiful city would be destroyed. Refugees were flooding up through the Mississippi Valley. And the worst part of it was that the broader population seemed to remember the Change. Was it just that the Change was too massive and New Orleans' vulnerabilities too well known, or was it something else? Were unGifted somehow gaining the ability to recognize Change?

From somewhere in Oklahoma had come a story of three families on vacation in their R.V.s taken into custody on suspicion of being Gifted. A vigilante group had broken them out of the jail and burned the lot of them as witches. And the disturbances were spreading, not only across America, but into Canada. The world's longest unguarded border was now guarded, as neither country wanted Gifted crossing their borders.

Xavier's warm scent of incense and cedar of Lebanon gave her momentary release from the fear and the ash that swirled around her. His warm palm cupped her head. "My poor Vallon. She strains like a wild desert mare to be away and protect the world from itself. What she forgets is that sometimes it takes more than one person to win the good fight. They will come. They are just scattered at the moment."

He was forgetting that she had always done things herself. Yes, others might have come along for the ride, but each time it was after she'd already decided her own course of action. That was how she worked. Those successes were because of her.

And her failures. Keira and the children in Anacortes.

She cringed at the memory. "I feel stuck here, Xavier. A prisoner, no matter what assurances your brother gave you. We don't have time to wait. The grey pall is thickening. Sometimes I'm parched from its wind, and nothing I drink slakes my thirst. It's as if the pall is becoming the reality and this—this place, this world—is barely a dream I once had."

She pulled away and paced back into the room. It might not look like a prison, with its high, ornate, mural-covered ceilings and the overdone pale blue walls with the golden scrollwork and the artful murals and original paintings displayed around a four poster bed and sitting area, but it was. The golden duvet on the bed and gleaming ebony furniture were five-star-hotel lovely—but a guard stood outside the door, and the presence of so much water in the canals and the sodden soil that underpinned the sinking city made it more difficult to use the Gift and to -reach- out and feel things. The intent of the Council, apparently. It made the use of the Gift less likely.

They were trapped—she was trapped in a gilded cage that she had walked into willingly. She could not trust her judgment, nor Xavier's, apparently, when it came to the Cartos Council.

"I'm going to go crazy just standing around waiting," she said with a frustrated flip of her hair over her shoulders.

"Then perhaps we should not let this gift of time go to waste," Xavier said softly. "We have had so little of it together."

She turned back to him, and the heat in Xavier's gaze said what he had in mind as he caught her wrist and pulled her into him. A distraction. It was totally a distraction, but his touch sent heat surging through her as he leaned down and captured her lips with his.

Since Jack's healing of his hand, Xavier's recovery seemed to have increased in speed. His arms trapped her and he stepped into her, his mouth sliding away from hers to taste the shadows under her hair. A shiver of pleasure ran through her and she stood on tiptoe and placed her arms around his neck. Kissed him back, and the pleasure as his hands slipped from her back to trace the sides of her breasts was enough to set her skin humming. Not afterburn, just the pleasurable desire for this man.

She pulled back from the kiss and found him studying her. "You make a very good case for imprisonment," she said and tried to look stern. "We *should* take advantage of this gift of time." Which was true as far as it went. Far better this than fretting at reflections. She caught his hand and led him to the bed.

It was a sensual dance to undress each other and cherish each other amid the amber-colored pillows. Their moans and whispers filled the shimmering silence of the room until Xavier rose above her and she opened herself so he could take her. Their movements twined together in a slow ebb and flow of tides, of grasping his hard shoulders and buttocks and pulling him closer and deeper. If she could just hold this feeling of him, become one with the sensation of him inside her, surely the intensity would burn away the strange, grey pallor. The world would be new, then, refreshed and young.

"Take me there," she whispered, her fingernails digging into his back. "Make us one."

Because wrapped in Pangea's bliss, she could surely overcome anything.

A smooth movement of his shoulders pulled her legs higher as he drove deeper. Sensation tore her breath away. His gaze held her, forced her to look deep inside them, to fall upward into him, even as he found his way deep inside and the slick of sweat brought their electric flesh together, the friction igniting their auras. She reached for his hips to help him, to draw him in, her body pulsing, her breath caught in her chest, and he drove into her again and threw his head back and yelled and the room pulsed once and faded around them.

They hung in blue mist, the warm scent of sun-heated green grass all around them even though they could see nothing. He still pulsed within her and she tightened her limbs around him so they might never be parted.

"Pangea," he breathed into her hair and kissed her earlobe, his arms strong but tender.

His word blew through the mist and tore it away. The earth spread out before them and they hung above it. Night and day, chasing each other like a dog chasing a rabbit across the landscape. But something wasn't right. Something hauled them down toward North America, away from their bodies, away from the politics of the Cartos and the twisted veins of Venice's canals.

Down into the grey lands of the western desert. Down into the dry bones of Las Vegas. Something was there. Something that Pangea wanted her to see. A whiff of baby's breath could only mean Landon, but before she saw anything, they were whisked away northwestward toward Seattle and the redolent green of the landscape. Rain fell and the city woke under grey clouds. Rain fell and water cascaded through the streets, in the storm drains, and down into the earth, where the ley lines lay so close to the surface one actually burbled up to run through the cracks in her basement.

She -reached- for them because they were a comfort. Because they filled her up when she was feeling weak and scared and didn't know what to do.

She couldn't find them.

Even in Xavier's arms, cold stone pressed around her. Cold dead stone and darkness filled her and yet left her empty.

The ley lines had to be there. They were Pangea's lifeblood, the source of everything. She -reached- farther, stretching, and found the flow of power still ran under Mount Rainier and Olympia and along the border, but here, in Seattle and Fremont, there was only cold stone and nothing, the earth an empty pie crust, a salt pan that remained after all the water had dried. Trees reached roots down into nourishment that wasn't there. Stone crumbled. Tectonic plates rumbled. Her city and her house teetered above nothingness.

A single minor trembler and the entire area would collapse, or so it seemed.

She froze in Xavier's arms, because she had to understand this. How had it happened? Where did it come from, because this couldn't be natural? She turned her vision on the Gifted, but there were none to be seen—at least not in Seattle, nor Fremont, nor as far east as Redmond. The end of the ley lines meant the end of the Gift, but wouldn't it also mean the end of life?

She -reached- for Xavier. [Do you see it?]

But she couldn't feel him. Had lost him when she reached into the earth, had lost the sublime union in her scramble to understand. Where was he? Where were the Gifted?

She reached farther, and faint flickers upon the land spoke of Gifted scattering. Some, closer by, at least still lived, though their auras were diminished.

Just as Pangea was diminished, a pox upon her fair face.

She closed her eyes and opened them again and found herself empty and looking up at the ceiling, a sensual mural of a man and woman—the Creator and Pangea—coming together and the stars and earth who were their offspring, Xavier had explained to her. The Cartos belief. He stirred at her shoulder and ran a long hard palm down her side, then pulled her into him, and the way they clung together, she knew he had seen.

He knew, even as the grey pall closed in and stole her away into ash and barrens. Her vision realized, as dust coated her tongue.

It had begun in Seattle.

§

Landon sat in the blue jeep Xavier had purchased for them in Las Vegas on their long drive from New Madrid. The scent of heated leather filled the air, and copper anxiety filled his mouth from where he had chewed the inside of his cheek to bleeding. It seemed like months ago that he had stopped in Las Vegas with Xavier, but really it was less than two weeks. How could the world have changed so dramatically in such a short time?

Beyond the windscreen and the air-conditioned interior lay his green wedge of safety, a few hundred yards of verdant green and a babbling brook along with his hideaway research installation, all hidden in the midst of a desert in the midst of a country that was becoming increasingly inimical to him and his kind—not that he'd ever actually used power like the others, but he was Gifted insofar as he could sense the power in others. He wanted to do more.

He'd watched the news. He'd seen the reports, and they were only coming in more frequently as the idiot Francis Drake tried to take the battle to the nation. Well, not the nation *per se*, because so far, the government had remained uninvolved, although politicians of various stripes were establishing their positions. No, this was working its way up to an all-out war between the Gifted and the unGifted.

Not a good idea when the Gifted were so few. It was a good way to wipe out the Gifted and to so firmly embed their presence in the minds of the unGifted that any future sign of power would result in immediate and permanent solutions. The comforting cool of the air conditioner turned momentarily cold, but he'd sat here musing long enough. Xavier de Varga was on the move. He'd left the country somehow and was now—if the GPS tracker he'd implanted in Xavier could be believed—on the other side of the world, in Venice, no less.

That meant something, because Xavier de Varga was not the kind of man who would simply run away from what was happening in this country, not if Vallon were involved, and not if she were in danger. And if the country was in danger, Vallon would be trying to do something about it. That was who she was, and who she'd been since she was a child. His pigeon—always rescuing puppies, always solving mysteries, always in trouble.

So that meant he had the answer he'd sought for years. There were Others, the greater Gifted, and they were centered in Venice if Xavier had done the expected and reported in regarding what was happening in America. Landon patted the computer bag beside him. With the GPS readings, he could pinpoint them exactly. But first he had to venture out to the larger world.

He dropped the jeep into drive and eased forward. His perimeter cameras had allowed him to track where the military had placed their motion sensors after they'd tailed Gleason to the point where he disappeared into Landon's little hidey hole. The place existed only because the original surveyors of the country had left out this small wedge of landscape when they took their readings. So far it had been safe because the area around Area 51 and the military testing ground of Nellis Air Force Base were semisecret installations and not subject to the same satellite surveillance as other locations. How long that would continue was another matter entirely.

Unfortunately, whoever had arranged the monitoring had done a creditable job, given they had no idea of the perimeter of his hiding place. There was only one place it seemed they hadn't monitored, and even that was questionable. He eased the jeep forward up to the unseen edge of his domain. At least there were no guards in the area that he'd been able to detect.

Go or stay. One would mean he would never be the great man he hoped to be. The other meant he was prepared to take a chance for what he wanted.

He gripped the steering wheel. Raised his chin and tromped on the gas.

The jeep leapt forward through the invisible barrier that protected his safe haven from the austere Nevada desert. Dry all around him and flat for miles until one reached the mountains of California, but he drove the car farther north toward Area 51 to avoid the military sensors, and then turned back toward the highway that would lead to Las Vegas and the nearest airport.

The jeep jounced and slewed over sand and over rock. Low brush tore at the undercarriage and scratched the paint. Back where he knew the wedge of safety existed there was nothing but the shimmering haze of heat mirage and the scar of the road that ran through it.

Let this work. Let him avoid the military and Homeland Security and get where he needed to be. The alternative was unthinkable.

Dust rose from his car's tires in a giant fish tail that could not be avoided. He scanned the landscape for anyone approaching. No other dust trails showed. He was going to do this. Ahead, in the distance, was the long line of passing trucks, cars, and tour busses bringing the ubiquitous gambling tours to Vegas. Good luck to them. They'd be lighter when they headed home fleeced of cash.

He hit the highway and joined them southbound, opening the window to allow the dust that had seeped through the ventilation systems to clear in the diesel-and-sage-tanged air. The tires hummed, and he relaxed a little, easing his shoulders back into the seat, and drank a sip of cool bottled water. He was doing this. He was going to make it and they still had not discovered his hidey hole.

The mountains that rimmed Vegas were stark gray in the harsh sunlight, as if they disapproved of the decadence in their midst. The oasis of Las Vegas grew out of the grayness with the overwhelming glitz and tawdry glamour of the gold-chain-bedecked entertainer. And just like the entertainer, Las Vegas couldn't help herself. She had to wear the glamour of the biggest and brightest and yet everything she did was barely a copy of the real Venice and Paris and Egypt. For all its fountains and fervently irrigated green, Vegas was at best a wound on the tottering American economy, and the people who flocked here the carrion flies seeking the source of riches they'd all bought into with the American dream.

The airport flanked the strip of hotels, while the miles of development provided housing for the casino workers. He slid into a parking lot at the airport without incident and paid for parking, then pulled his one meager computer bag with a change of clothes over his shoulder. There wasn't much he could do about his stature, but he pulled a baseball cap over his shock of white hair and instead of wearing his usual suit, he wore jeans, a Bellagio t-shirt, and sunglasses like so many of the tourists who flooded around him.

He just had to hope there was no one watching.

The American Airlines ticket counter came up in front of him and he set his computer down.

"I'd like to a book a flight, please," he said to the petite Latina woman seated behind the counter. She wore the usual navy jacket over striped shirt with a red scarf tied at the neck. "To New York."

From New York he could get a flight direct to Venice, but he didn't ask for the forwarding flight. He didn't want that information so clearly available.

"Let me check on availability," the young woman said. She looked down at him and frowned. "Your identification, please?"

He fished out the forged documents he'd always held against just such a day. When he handed them over, the attendant's frown cleared. "Well, Mr. Horvath. We have a flight departing immediately at 2:30." She checked her watch. "If you run you could probably catch it. Our next flight isn't until six tonight."

He bought the ticket using a credit card in the Horvath name and ran.

CHAPTER 11 —THE WHITE GNOME'S POWER

The low bunker that had once been the headquarters of the American Geological Survey hunkered like a cowed beast on the hilltop of its treed Redmond Campus. Wolf Amundson strode the long central corridor of the building, liking the image, because while his enemies might say he had only entered the belly of the beast, he *knew* that he was the beast that had devoured the AGS from within. It was—*satisfying*.

The AGS's articulated dragonfly desk hung like a dragon skeleton above the abandoned map pit in the center of what had been the AGS control room. Once it had been the heart of AGS operations, supposedly directing efforts to maintain the American landscape. The electric stink of the chair's motors had faded from the air, and the hushed slosh of the liquid nanite map had finally gone dark and silent. It was like he could breathe here, finally, instead of feeling like he was running a race to just walk through the thick air of the room. The Gifted threat no longer filled the space.

But half-heard whispers still seemed to fill the air-conditioned air, and there was still a troubling sense of something happening just beyond his ken. And that was unacceptable. When this was all over, he'd have the infernal place bulldozed to the ground. But in the meantime, he'd make do with the pitiful office that he'd ripped from the grasp of ex-AGS Chief Gregor Gleason. He pushed into the cramped office in the corner of the map room and slapped Dr. Sukh Sandhu's report on the oversized desk. Then he settled himself in what had once been Gleason's custom-made chair to read just how Dr. Sandhu was going to help him vanquish his foes from America. It was just a matter of time.

Gregor Gleason.

Landon Snow.

Vallon Drake.

He flipped open the file.

The names of his enemies, and with this report he would deal with them. A soft knock came at the door.

"Come." He looked up.

Jason Bryson stepped inside looking haggard and, if anything, worse than before. Dark shadows rimmed his eyes, and his face and body had gone skeletal gaunt as if he had his own personal Wolf Amundson consuming him from the inside out. Possibly he did, because Bryson seemed to vibrate even when he was still, like now, standing behind the lone, hard-backed visitor's chair. His dark hair had gone greasy and hung in his eyes and over the tops of his ears, a far cry from the detective who'd come to him with a bargain only a week ago, let alone the man he'd met less than six months ago. That man had made an effort to impress with his looks. This man looked like he no longer cared—or cared too intensely about something else.

"What is it?" Amundson asked.

Jason's fingers whitened as he leaned on the back of the chair. He scanned the photos of Wolf glad-handing politicians hung on the wall behind him. The man's jaw worked and then firmed as if he'd made a decision. "This research you and Sandhu are doing—what is it going to mean for the Gifted?"

Wolf closed the file and straightened. "Mean? I suppose it means they won't have powers anymore. That they'll be just like you and me and we'll be able to round them up just like any criminal."

For the man Wolf had known, it took an inordinately long time for Jason to formulate a response. His gaze strayed back to the photos. "How long before the field covers the U.S.?"

"Covers the U.S.? Jason, what is this? I'm just reading Sandhu's report. We don't even know if this will impact the Gifted yet. It's only been a day since he got his equipment set up. It'll power up today."

"But in theory it should work, right? It worked on the prisoners. So the Gifted will be stripped of their power...." Jason's gaze had gone darker as if the brown of his eyes had been consumed by some void within him. Not good. Jason was his front line of defense until Sandhu's work proved viable. Jason Bryson was a man he had been forced to trust with his life.

"What's this all about, Jason?" He motioned at the chair. "Why don't you sit down and we'll discuss what's on your mind and take a read of this report together."

A slight hesitation and then Jason perched on the edge of the chair, his hands between his knees. He looked both like a supplicant and someone ready to leap for escape. What the hell was going on? Then Jason inhaled and met finally met Wolf's gaze.

"When I agreed to help you it was in exchange for time with Vallon."

Wolf nodded. "As soon as she is apprehended, you'll have your time."

Jason shook his head. "No one has seen her since she escaped from your men in Tacoma. There's been no sign at all, except for the incident with the Porsche making a run for the border. That's the kind of vehicle her lover would drive. She could be in Canada, and we're doing nothing to find her."

There was an unusual emotional tremor to Jason's voice. The man was falling apart for some reason that wasn't yet clear.

"Just relax. Everything is going well. Fitzsimmons might have wanted to cut off funding, but now that he's out of the picture, we can take advantage of friends in high places. Congresswoman Black has become one of our most fervent supporters and has been placing pressure in all the right places, including with the Canadians. With the money coming in again and corporate donors, there's been enough coming our way that Sandhu has his lab and technicians back and has been able to try out his theory." He tapped his forefinger on the report. "We can read about it here."

Again, Jason's dark gaze seemed to rest like a weight—this time on the report. Finally he nodded. "What does it say?"

"Let's find out." He flipped the first page open to the executive summary.

In Sandhu's initial research report into the source of Gifted power, he had pulled a great deal of information from AGS archives. Those files—once the purview of the white gnome—had discussed the source of the Gifted talents from the perspective of what the Gifted knew. It had been invaluable information from inside the enemy camp.

Along with the apparent link between the Gifted's strange power and their actual blood, had been information that when the Gifted worked

Change, they accessed a source of power in the earth's crust. At first Sandhu and his team had thought the power might be thermal heat rising from the earth's core. This had made sense, given the heat the Gifted reported when they used the power and the afterburn that the agents dealt with. But thermal energy didn't make sense, given it would be available everywhere on earth, and the AGS files clearly stated that certain areas of the United States were more attractive to the Gifted. The Pacific Northwest was specifically named and that was why AGS headquarters were here.

He looked up from reading aloud. "Interesting. Did you know any of this?"

Jason shook his head. "Not in so many words, but it makes sense with what I do know."

"Which is?"

A shrug of Jason's broad shoulders. "That they use what's in the earth somehow. It was how Vallon stopped the New Madrid quake. At least I think so. And Gleason and de Varga work with whatever it is, too."

"de Varga?"

Jason looked away, toward the door. "Drake's lover. I told you. The likely driver of the Porsche. Works for some place called *CartosNationele* out of Lisbon and Venice. He's done a lot of traveling in North Africa and Europe. For a while I thought he was a terrorist."

A little thrill of excitement ran up Wolf's spine and he made a note of the information. A link to foreign powers would only sell the danger. Something else to have Loadstone research. "So what you're saying is together these two could be trouble."

A smile sketched across Jason's features. "It's Vallon Drake. When has she not been trouble? The trouble is, we're not looking for *her*. The longer we wait, the more chance she'll be beyond our reach. We need to go after her, and the best person for that job is me."

The resolve on the man's face said that this was what he'd come to say: he wanted to leave and that would leave Wolf unprotected. Wolf chose to ignore it for the moment. He turned back to the report and continued reading.

Sandhu had theorized that there must be something else in the earth that the Gifted connected to, given the frequent reports of that connection, but it flew in the face of what was known of geology. No geologist had ever reported currents of power in the earth's crust. But there *was* the pseudo-science that spoke of ley lines as a product of torsion field spin, which the same pseudo-science proclaimed led to talents like faith healing, telepathy, telekinesis, and levitation, amongst others. Sandhu hypothesized that a portion of the Gifted's brains had an ability to impact the mass and makeup of the landscape through a direct physiologically-based ability to manipulate matter, similar to how physicists had found that the perceptions of the scientist could affect the outcome of experiments.

He hypothesized that if the Gifted were impacting matter through a connection to gravitational currents—the ley lines—then the disruption of the gravitational currents in the earth would disrupt their abilities.

Amundson scanned ahead through the report of Sandhu's experiment and a flood of warmth ran through him. He looked up at Jason. "We may have found our answer."

"What do you mean?" Jason looked confused and still, like he was waiting for something.

"I mean that Sandhu has been testing a theory. He's been busy with his team, placing the grid of ferromagnetic disruptors around Seattle. They are supposed to disrupt the ley lines—not to redirect them, but simply shatter them apart and disperse the torsion spin field. He placed a series of them around the AGS headquarters two days ago and it appears to be working, given tests with our *guests*. The larger grid installation around Seattle and Redmond is ready to go next."

All the stress of the past few months seemed to lift off of his chest. He could breathe fully again, when he hadn't even realized his chest was constricted—something else to blame on the Gifted. He smiled up at Jason. "So you want to go get Drake, is that it? You're afraid you're going to lose her?"

Jason nodded. He looked like he'd be up and gone in an instant, like a too-long tethered dog.

"Well then, go get her. It appears this place and the city are protected, and it will be interesting to see just how insubordinate she'll be when she has her powers stripped away."

Jason, already out of his chair and to the door, suddenly stopped and turned back to Wolf. "So let me get this straight. Sandhu has found a way to disrupt the Gifted power permanently."

Wolf nodded. "He's been working on a couple of areas of research. The body-blood connection and the connection to the earth. In experiments, when their power source has been disrupted, it has been successful in stopping them. If it works over the Seattle area, there's no reason it can't work across the U.S., or anywhere else, for that matter. I can't imagine that the rest of the world will want to leave themselves unprotected, either. Hell, we can make our fortune selling the technology."

The way Jason paled, something wasn't right. He should be jubilant. Had the man lost his mind? He *had* become more silent and more withdrawn. Thank God Sandhu had placed the disruptors around his new headquarters first as a hoped-for means of protection, because Jason didn't look like he could protect anybody at the moment.

"We're going to stop them, Jason. It's over and you can rest. The bastards have holed up in the old AGS Academy, thinking we won't notice, but what they don't know is that we've got people out placing disruptors around them. They've lost and they don't even know it yet. We'll be the heroes," he said softly. And Ray Fitzsimmons could roll over in his grave as Wolf Amundson rose like a phoenix to eclipse everything the ex HS chief had ever been.

"I see," Jason said. He nodded once and was gone out the door.

Strangely, he did not look happy.

§

The hallway through what had once been Vallon Drake's place of work was too long and too empty—not like the night six months ago when Jason had come seeking Vallon and been turned away almost right at the door. The placed no longer hummed with an unseen electric energy. In fact, at the moment, he felt like he had to swim through a vacuum. The air even smelled *vacant*—as if whatever had made this a place of the Gifted was gone. The hairs on his arms stood on end. *Maybe* it was just the urgency that had been building in his chest as each day passed since the events in Anacortes. Each day without sight of Vallon. Or maybe it was something more—the thing Amundson had been going on about. Maybe the disruptors around this place caused the sense of emptiness that was actually more like a feeling of coming apart at the seams.

Him included. Which meant he had to move fast.

The corridor echoed with the hiss of fluorescent lights. Ahead, the door to the left led to Sandhu's research facilities and the holding cells. Go in and destroy whatever it was Sandhu was building? Or disrupt the Gifted power? Strip Vallon of *her* power?

His stomach did an uneasy flip-flop. How the hell would he ever get Cheryl back if the woman with the power to bring her back was stripped of all power? He had to get to Vallon outside of Amundson's disrupted zone before that zone covered the earth.

He buzzed out of the locked main doors of the installation into the crowded parking lot. Amundson had pulled in a lot of staff from somewhere and they were obviously working in research, or else in security, which was housed in what had apparently once been two apartments at the back of the facility. Watery September sunshine filtered through the tall cedars that surrounded the bunker, and the wind through them was a constant hush as he climbed in the brown sedan he'd driven across country.

At the moment, getting to Vallon meant following the sightings of the Porsche Cayenne. It had crossed the border into Canada after a chase that still had the U.S. and Canadian border services scratching their heads. No one could remember how or where the car had crossed the border. He keyed on the ignition and the sedan roared to life. Yes, Vallon could be anywhere, but north of the border there had to be clues.

CHAPTER 12 —ROSE-SCENTED ANGER

The tall cedars beyond the lawns and empty circular driveway at the front of the abandoned AGS Academy were a green-gold in the westering sun through Francis Drake's office window. The light slashed across the floor and dark maple desk like a beacon and spot-lit Francis's chest. Once the room had been the headmaster's office, but the headmaster, along with the entire faculty, had been slaughtered when Wolf Amundson made his first overt move against the Gifted. The trouble was, no one knew or believed it, except the Gifted.

Thankfully the slaughter hadn't occurred here, in this office, and the room only smelled of stale coffee and old books. It was actually quite comfortable, with its bookshelf-covered walls and the old wooden desk and oversized chair. Not too different from the kind of place he had built himself in the ill-fated New Madrid installation. It would be that much more comfortable once he had sorted things out with Fitzsimmons.

Except the distant ringing of the phone he held to his ear must have drilled into his brain fifteen times now, and still Fitzsimmons hadn't answered on their private line. That wasn't like him. Since Drake had contacted the Director of Homeland Security ten years back and had made his quiet overture to make them both very rich men at the expense of a number of large multi-national corporations, Fitzsimmons had always been available at the end of this particular phone number. Fitzsimmons had brokered the deal between Drake and the corporations, with the Indian Ocean tsunami as proof of what the Gifted could do. But for the past two days, he hadn't answered.

Drake set down the phone and looked out the window. A few of the Gifted families that had stayed with him instead of running like scared hens out into the world, where Amundson would surely catch them, had a soccer game going on the playing fields he could just glimpse to the side of the school. Children dashed around their parents, apparently blithely unaware just how much was wrong with the world.

But he was going to make it right. Let him succeed and children like that would be the elite. They would stand shoulder to shoulder with the Others that his old friend Snow had always obsessed about. The Gifted as the rulers of the world, because no one could stand against them. So Fitzsimmons had damn well better get his act together if he didn't want to be *very* low on the totem pole of power after the battle was over.

He picked up the phone again and dialed a different number. It rang once, twice, then the line clicked open.

"Fitzsimmons," came an unfamiliar voice at the other end, too young, too smooth to have ever been Fitzsimmons

"Who the hell is this?"

The sound of shuffling papers and low voices. "Mr. Fitzsimmon's assistant."

What the hell? Fitzsimmons never handed control of his phones to anyone.

A soft knock came at Francis' office door and it opened to show one of the youngest of the AGS agents, tanned and red-haired Drew Libernaum. Libernaum had been one of the AGS New Madrid agents 'recruited' by Francis to fuel his grand scheme to hold America hostage. He been saved from the destruction Vallon had wrought in New Madrid and had made it back to Seattle only to barely avoid arrest. He was a pretty boy—a waste—who slid by mostly on his good looks, even though the incandescence of his Gifted aura suggested he had talent.

"You got a moment?" Libernaum asked.

Francis covered the phone with his hand. "I'm on the phone, if you're blind."

"I need to talk to you."

"I'm busy. Not now."

Libernaum seemed to hesitate and Drake refocused on the phone and swung his chair around, all his attention on the voice asking who was calling. The soft sound of the door closing came from behind him.

"This is a friend calling. Fitzsimmons would never ask me to identify myself on this line."

There was silence on the line a moment. "Then, *friend*, you should probably know that Mr. Fitzsimmons met with an accident. He didn't make it."

The chill of the voice nearly froze him, and Francis stabbed the cell phone off and tossed it on the desk. For a moment he couldn't breathe as all the ramifications sank in. His alliance was gone, and that meant resources through his corporate financiers were gone, too. The Gifted were on their own, and Amundson was out of control with no one to stop him. Hands shaking, he scooped up the special phone and flung it across the room. It clattered against a bookshelf and tumbled to the floor, too strong to break, too useless for him to care if it had.

§

In the Villa de Polo, the watery light of the canals reflected off the ceiling murals so that the images of Pangea and the Creator in the act of creation seemed to breathe and move. The muddy, warm breezes off the lagoon stirred across Xavier's skin and lifted the fine hairs around Vallon's face, but her scent of ashes of roses still filled his senses. He could still taste the salt-sweet of her skin and her secret, shadowed places.

He held Vallon to him on the cool sheets of the wide bed. It had taken hours for him to quiet her after what they had discovered at the end of their lovemaking. She had been almost inconsolable when they finally pulled back from the mists of ecstasy, and that was not like her at all. At first she had curled into a ball on the bed, then had stormed the door, demanding to be let out, then had raged around the room, avoiding his comfort until finally her strength gave out—she *was* still recovering from the depletion of her injuries—and she crumpled onto the floor in the corner.

He had gathered her up, then, and brought her back to the bed to lie with her. They were both only partially clothed. Vallon wearing his hastily pulled-on black shirt, her legs bare. He in his black jeans, his chest bare so he felt her light breath on his skin. He ran a palm over the smooth back of her head and pulled her into him again. "What will I do with you, my heart, my *Bela*?"

He spread his aura around her, forming a protective shield between her and the world, but it was not enough, for it was becoming clearer and clearer that he could not protect Vallon. She would forever keep leaving him behind and running into danger. She had proved it one more time when she ran into the warehouse to save the children. She had proved it just now by leaving him on the bed. Yes, he might do the same thing from time to time—it had been his career—but her unwillingness to let him help her... His chest tightened at the jumble of memories it evoked of a much younger Xavier being stopped from helping when his help might have saved his mother.

He placed a gentle kiss onto Vallon's sweat-stained hair. At least she was safe now. Until she faced the Council. He prayed she would understand what he had done and not view it as betrayal. The soft, reflected light of the canal filled the room as if they lay encased in a renaissance painting—until she stirred and freed herself of his embrace once more. Her troubled gaze found his.

"It's serious, isn't it?" At least her voice was steady again, the panic and grief passed through and gone, leaving only steel behind.

"Perhaps more serious than either of us know. The blemish on Pangea's flesh—it is an absence of anything living."

She stiffened, swallowed, and twin small lines formed between her brows as if she placed boundaries around her emotions. "Are they all dead, then? All the Gifted and partially Gifted of Seattle?"

Xavier shook his head. "Not dead yet, I think. They might still breathe and go about their business in the midst of that area, and trees might still grow, but for how long? In that darkness, bereft of Pangea's blood, can anything live for long?"

She closed her eyes and her face worked as she fought back emotion. "And it's not natural, is it?"

"I—think not. Certain rock formations and certain megalithic monuments like Stonehenge created vortexes in Pangea's ley lines, but I am not aware of any natural event obliterating Pangea's power flow. At least not within the memory of the very long-lived Gifted."

She sat up and swung her legs off the bed and hunched there, slim and vulnerable, her blond hair tumbling over her shoulders. "So that means that it's man-made. Amundson. He's the kind of idiot who would do something like this without thinking of the consequences. All he'd care about was stopping the Gifted from accessing the power. There'll be nothing living left on the earth if he blocks all the power."

"That is my assessment as well." He placed his arm around her shoulders, but she stood.

"That's what my vision is telling me, Xavier. That's what's going to happen."

A single sharp knock came at the room's door.

"It is time, de Varga. The Council waits."Leticia's gloating voice came through the ornate wood.

Knowing her, she had worked to turn them all against him and Vallon.

"A moment, please," he called and went to Vallon.

Stroking back her fine blonde hair, he tilted her face up toward him. Nightmare-fogged, exhausted eyes looked up at him. She opened her mouth to speak, but he masked her words with a kiss. Her lips became soft and yielding under his, though they hid the steel that was so much a part of his beloved. He dragged himself away. "The situation is grave, but together we will make them understand. Together, yes?" He leaned in, forehead to forehead. "Together we can do anything."

She nodded, but stepped out of his arms. "We need to get ready." She crossed the room for the small bathroom, leaving him to inhale the remnants of her ashes of roses. Gone again.

When she came out, he was already dressed in cream trousers and tunic provided by the Council. Vallon's hair was dark with damp and sleeked back in a simple, sultry ponytail. She changed from the towel she was wearing to a simple, sleeveless, cream-colored shift out of the closet of clothes provided in the room.

"Do I look okay?" She did a single turn for him. The dress clung to her in all the right places, and he felt old and haggard next to such beauty.

"Lovely. You are always lovely." And he caught her hand. "Together. Just remember, I am with you always."

She nodded, but new lines had formed around her eyes. Fatigue, pain, grief all mingled.

"Are you ready?"

She held up a bare foot, then strode across the room to pull on the docker boots she had demanded when they first arrived. Somehow, on Vallon, they went with the dress, hard and soft and incredibly sexy and strong, all at the same time.

"Ready," she said.

Blessed Pangea, let it be so.

Another single rap on the door and it opened on Leticia, perched on impossibly high Italian heels and dressed in the form-fitting black leather she preferred. Her gaze slid from Xavier to Vallon and her gaze hung on Vallon's boots. Leticia's full lips turned down toward her ample décolletage that escaped her form-fitting leather corset.

"So. If this is your ready, we go." She turned on her heel and led them, click-clacking, hips swaying, down the marble-floored hall. It was broad and filled with breezes from a central courtyard that sent the air whispering around them as if a gallery watched them. Perhaps they did. Unobtrusive security cameras filled small fissures in the carvings that framed a high, domed ceiling, covered in murals of the Creation. Painted in fading blues and greens and golds, on the seventh day the Creator shed five drops of blood onto the soil of Pangea, and those drops sprang to life as the first Cartos. On the courtyard side, potted palms rustled in sunshine and jasmine perfumed the air. On the other side of the hall, tables holding huge vases filled with cloyingly fragrant lilies flanked broad, closed doorways.

They followed the hallway around the sun-filled courtyard to the one door that mattered. Decorated with a broad disc of bronze set into dark wood, the sight of it quickened Xavier's pulse. He caught Vallon's hand in his as Leticia knocked once, and the sound boomed through the door. Vallon glanced up at him, but there was no worry in her gaze—only determination—as the Council Chamber opened before them into the high-ceilinged room he had once thought so grand.

Enemy territory. More clearly so given there was no hint of friendship on any face in the room. The room was broader than it was long, with nine chairs set in a curved arc across the floor. Behind them, a dark tapestry hung like a curtain, hiding the far wall. The marble floors were light and dark and carried an inset disc of bronze like the one on the council room door. The walls were as gilded and ornate as the rest of the house, and at one end of the room, the wall opened onto a sunlit balcony and life beyond. Life he might not see again.

The Council sat as they had the last time he was here, though this time their frowns made it clear that his long service to them meant nothing. When they looked at him, they saw only betrayal, a risk for their people. Neither were something the Council would take lightly, and penalties would be doubly hard given he'd betrayed their trust before. He could not let their anger color their dealings with Vallon, for she had done nothing except accept the possibility of their existence. He stood beside her in the center of the room.

Leticia bowed low to the Council. "The prisoners, Most Noble Elders." She stepped back, beside the now-closed door, leaving Xavier and Vallon to face them.

There were nine members of the Cartos Council, facing them in the nine heavy chairs, each chair carved to represent the part of the globe represented by the Cartos member—Italy carved to look like grape vines; Portugal to look like ship's sails; Spain with the curveting forms of Andalusian horses; Northern Europe with the look of medieval fortresses; North Africa with the image of pyramids; the Middle East with a map of the two great rivers; China with the great wall and writing strokes; India with its many grappling forms of the Hindu pantheon; and Southeast Asia with the faces of the temples of Angkor—and Lisbon, shaped like a ship, as the city that held more Cartos history than any other. There were no representatives from America or Australia, as they had no indigenous Cartos population, and the Cartos of Southern Africa were so few that they had no chair.

Blond Wark of northern Europe sat with his mouth down-turned. Lovely Voda of India, with the curtain of black hair, would not meet his gaze this time, though she had previously been his ally. Isabella Polo from Italia, in heels as high as Leticia's, simply looked out the window toward the canal, while Aziz from the Middle East adjusted the drape of his robes over his knees. The cherub mouth of Norvanahpum, the tiny woman from Southeast Asia, belied her deadly, unforgiving gaze, while business-suited Chan of China whispered to old Victor of Lisbon, who was the oldest person in the room but still had blond hair, though streaked with gray. On the far left side of the arc sat Carlos, his brother, filling what had always been their father's seat representing Portugal. Clothed, now, Carlos studiously avoided Xavier's gaze.

In the center sat Hector Gonzales in Spain's seat, the man who had once been his friend and who was currently the elected voice of the Council. He was also the youngest member of the Council by only a few months, being the same age as Carlos, and that left him vulnerable to the manipulations of the older Council members, not to mention Leticia. He was a slight man, with a rider's slim, upright build and the fading robustness of someone overwhelmed by the demands of his life so that he no longer got the exercise of his horses. Being the head of the Council was telling on him, then. Today, he wore a formal suit of Italian silk and his graying dark hair was slicked straight back, leaving his strong features severe and gaunt.

The Council's disapproving regard weighed on Xavier, but then skipped to settle on Vallon. He tensed and his fingers tightened on hers. *Shove her behind him. Better still, shove her out the door.* Too late now.

There was no mistaking the slow shock that filled the faces of the eldest in the room. One look at Vallon and they knew, just as he had known. It was written in the fall of her blonde hair, in the way her chin narrowed to a feminine point, and in the depth of her brown-green eyes. A small gasp escaped Voda.

Old Victor of Lisbon leapt to his feet. He was old, even for the long-lived Cartos—the eldest of them all—and held in greatest esteem for that fact. His graying-blond hair flocked back from a high, lined forehead and his thick brows jutted over piercing black eyes and a turned down mouth. He wore an old-fashioned tweed jacket in an old-fashioned cut, too-close to the body and worn around the cuffs, and baggy trousers shiny from too much wear, though rumor said his fortune had weathered the meltdown in Portugal's economic fortunes. Frugal, some named him. Stingy was a better description, and Victor had been stingy in many things.

"What is this?" Victor bristled and turned from Hector and back to Xavier and Vallon. "What trickery are you trying to pull? Who is this woman?"

Vallon glanced questions in Xavier's direction, but he just shook his head. "She is as you see her. My dalliance, as you have named her. Council members, may I introduce Vallon Drake of the American Geological Survey." He half bowed in her direction, but kept hold of her hand even when she tried to slip it loose.

"Xavier, what's going on here?" she asked softly.

"But—but it cannot be." Old Victor interrupted as he left his chair and strode to her. He looked her up and down. "She may be taller, but she is the image of my Lianna. This—this is a Gifted—not of the blood? How can she look like my Lianna? How can that be possible?"

Aah, Lianna, named for her forebear, who brought together the first Cartos school at Sagre. The creation of that school had reclaimed the Cartos powers and saved them from being forgotten.

The room went silent, all eyes upon Vallon. She, in turn, turned a stony gaze on Xavier. He held his tongue, for though Vallon needed answers, this was not the time. They needed to be a united front while these old men and women digested what they saw and filled in the blanks, just as Xavier had done long ago. If he tried to tell them what he surmised, they would not believe him. No, let them come to their own conclusions and let Vallon be innocent of all the possibilities.

Questions filled Vallon's gaze. She twisted her fingers loose and stared up at him, then faced the Council, her entire body rigid.

He tensed, for the Council might be elders, but they were able to wreak havoc should they so choose, and there was always Leticia, hovering like a dangerous harpy at the edge of the room. Who knew how many weapons the woman had secreted on her person?

Vallon's throat worked. Then she stepped forward and bowed. "I am honored to meet you, men and women of the Cartos Council." Her low voice seemed to reverberate through the marble-floored room and her ashes of roses scent seemed to flood the air. "I come as emissary from your far brethren, the Gifted of the United States of America, to bring a warning and to beg for your aid."

Trust his *Bela* to get to the point. The trouble was that the elders were not listening, and the air seemed to ripple with the many non-verbal conversations flying between the Council members.

But Victor still stood. His old gaze caught hers and then his eyes turned momentarily golden. "Who are you?" he asked when they'd returned to normal.

"As he said." Vallon motioned to Xavier. "My name is Vallon Drake. I'm an agent of the American Geological Survey. Or at least I was when the AGS existed. I don't think it does anymore. That's part of the emergency that has sent me to seek your aid."

Victor reached for her face, as if to pull off a mask, and Vallon fell back a step beside Xavier. He caught her hand and squeezed her suddenly cold fingers.

"Why do you do that?" she asked.

"You are the image of my daughter."

That stopped her, and her fingers went stiff. He squeezed them. *Hold tight, Vallon. You will understand soon enough.*

"How old are you?" Victor demanded.

"Twenty seven," she said, then hesitated. "Why does it matter? I've come to ask for your aid for all our people. I'm sure you've seen the news that exposed the existence of the Gifted. It has led to a battle and will likely lead to a war before this is over, and not just in America. Acts against suspected Gifted have already bled into Canada and Mexico."

Victor waved her words away as if they didn't matter. He swung back to the rest of the Council. "She is of an age. I've told no one, but Lianna was with child when she disappeared, though she thought I did not know. Like so many of our youth, she was a wild child, determined to live her life beyond the boundaries of our kind, and when I gave her an ultimatum that she return to our home or be disowned, she chose to leave. It is my shame, when all I wished to do was to care for her and my grandchild. Instead, she left in a storm and was not seen again." He turned back to Vallon and his withered hand came up again, as if to touch her face.

Vallon avoided his touch and turned to Xavier. "What the hell is he talking about, Xavier?"

"He believes you may be his lost granddaughter, *Bela*. I believe it is possible." Please let her accept the possibility for the moment. Let her let it go and focus on their mission.

But her eyes widened slightly. She pulled her hand loose and turned to Victor. "Impossible. My father is Francis Drake, a Gifted."

"He *claims* to be your father, *Bela*. That does not mean it is so." The wrong thing to say. He knew it from the way her spine stiffened and the way her silence echoed like water in the catacombs beneath the sinking city. Through the open windows came the sounds of boat motors and voices drifting from off the Grand Canal. Vallon's ashes of roses scent swirled around her.

Her face had gone pale as she turned back to Victor and then twisted back to him. "Are you saying that you've known this all along? That I might be something other than Gifted? That my father might not be Francis Drake?"

The skin around her lips had whitened. Brands of color had found her cheeks. Then she slapped him so hard it sent him back a step.

"How dare you! How dare you not tell me and then bring me here!"

"*Bela*... Vallon..." But what could he say? That he had thought her honest shock would prove her innocence to the Council? His cheek stung with the tattoo of her palm and he knew that he had failed her again—failed to protect her, just as he had failed to protect so many things. The weight of it came crashing down.

Vallon whirled back to Victor. "I don't know if I'm your granddaughter, and frankly I don't give a damn. I didn't come here for a family reunion. I came here to warn you. A war has started between the

Gifted and unGifted and something has happened. Something has stopped the flow of power under Seattle, and the land is dying. Your Pangea is dying—will die unless we stop such blockages from being used across the world. Whatever the unGifted are doing, if they increase it, it could get more serious very fast."

Hector Gonzales stood, his suit whispering at his movement, his dark, graying hair falling around his handsome Latin features. All their old friendship had drained from his expression, as he left the arc of chairs and came up to them.

"What game is this, de Varga? You knew the uproar she would cause," Hector said in Spanish. "Did you plan to turn this Council into a circus?"

Xavier's body was heavy with fatigue and the weight of Vallon's anger. It was hard to think. Hard to respond, when all his life he had been trained to respond. Hector smelled of tidal pools and leather. Enough scent it spoke of the man's anger. Emotions—too many of them—roiled through the air and he was almost a child again, charting a course through the eternal miasma of his parents' stormy marriage.

He sighed. "The truth?" he answered in Spanish. "I would have hidden her forever—even from herself—but circumstances demanded she be revealed. What sane person would wish to associate with this Council of rigid ideas and medieval practices? I do not. Not anymore. But Vallon speaks the truth about the danger looming in America. If you look, you will see. She would take on the entire battle herself, and she could not succeed like that. So I brought her here to seek your help—and to protect her."

Vallon's scowl said she understood some of what he said. Not a good thing.

"*Bela*, truly, I am sorry. I did not wish to harm you—or to keep secrets from you—but I knew what would await you on this side of the ocean amongst our people. I knew how they would see you. Your shock at their reaction had to be real, for them to believe."

Her jaw was set. Her fists were clenched at her sides. "And just what is it that you wanted them to believe, Xavier? Because I have exactly zero idea what the hell is going on, except apparently I'm not who I thought I was, and the man I thought loved me has betrayed me by keeping the truth from me."

Say it? Put into words the fears of this Council and chance exposing others who had trusted him?

Hector rocked impatiently on the balls of his feet. The other Council members leaned forward like vultures, feeding on the drama, but Leticia had stepped away from her place at the wall and her eyes had gone golden with power. She was prepared to intervene, should he or Vallon try anything, and she was prepared to use her gifts to do it, while the Council might dither. He had to keep Vallon calm, for Leticia was never to be trifled with and Vallon had not the other woman's breadth of training in the art of murder.

"Whether I betrayed you is a matter for another time. You must show Hector what you have seen. The vision. He must understand why we have come."

She seemed to swallow her anger. "You're Hector?"

Before he could nod, she grabbed his arm.

Leticia leapt to intervene. Xavier caught her around her narrow waist. The flash of steel was so fast he barely warded off the stiletto knife she plunged toward his neck.

He knocked her striking arm aside and then caught her wrist. She was muscle and sinew and old rage that writhed like a snake in his hold. The rest of the Council was on their feet. Old Victor had fallen back. Hector stood frozen, his dark gaze gold-tinged and distant.

Then Vallon released him and he staggered back. Xavier shoved Leticia at Carlos. "Restrain your wife."

Leticia snarled and leapt for him again, but Carlos, praise the Creator, caught her arm.

Vallon trained a fury-darkened glare at Xavier as Hector's expression cleared. His gaze skipped from Vallon to Xavier.

"Carlos." His voice was imperious. "Get them out of here, but return immediately. We must discuss what we have heard and what I have seen."

CHAPTER 13 — BLACK FEATHERS, ROSE SCENT

Gold tinged the cottonwood trees along the river as Fi and Jack followed the dike that guarded the rich farmland from the murky Fraser River. Right now, in the fall, the water ran dark and sluggish, its currents swirling over unseen rocks, much like her situation. Vallon and Xavier were gone, scooped up and taken in some strange fashion that left only their empty clothes in a heap on the floor and the scent of ozone and ether on the air.

She'd freaked when it happened. Had screamed until Jack caught her in a bear hug grip and forced her to look at him. "They are okay. Truly. They have only gone traveling to somewhere else. It is a talent some of my people have."

She had looked up into Jack's blue eyes and had finally believed. "Why doesn't anyone tell me anything? I *hate* being treated like a child."

Then Jack had tipped her chin up to him and looked her in the eyes. "Then I vow that I will not treat you so. You are Fiona Murdoch: a woman with the healer's power. That is a great gift and nothing a child would have."

"Really?"

A nod of his blond head. "Truly. There were never many with the healing talent, and now that gift is extremely rare. Now come. Let us get out of here and clear our heads of the Council stink." He went to lead her from the kitchen to the door outside. She stopped him.

"Council?"

He had turned back to her. "I will explain while we walk, and we will watch for eagles again." He had patted a pocket that held his old-fashioned telescope.

So with her feet shoved barefoot into her runners, and wearing her jeans and a blue flannel work shirt of Jack's with the cuffs rolled up to her wrists, she had followed him outside, enjoying the smooth play of the thigh muscles that Jack had healed. Each day since Vallon and Xavier left, she had done the same.

The day was one of those splendid fall days, with crisp air warmed by the sun and a light breeze that settled through the leaves of the poplar and cottonwood and sent them sifting down to freckle the green grass of the yard. The grey wood of the old shed that held Xavier's Porsche Cayenne gleamed rich tarnished silver and the air smelled sweet with corn stubble and garden patches all going fallow. A lone wild rose bush by the kitchen door held a few hardy pink blooms but swelled with livid rosehips ready for tea-making.

She could have inhaled the day, it was so beautiful. In the sunshine it was hard to remember her terror of not so many nights ago. And today she and Jack walked down the dikes beside the river, because somehow the treacly light, the cooling breezes, and Jack's constant presence made her feel like everything was going to be all right. They'd already spotted three eagles perched in the tall cottonwoods that verged the river.

"So how long do you think they'll be?" Fi asked as she kicked at the growing pile of fallen leaves on their path. The dike was tall—at least ten feet above the river's level—and sided with blackberry brambles that still carried a few of the sweet black fruit. It was hard to believe that the somnolent water so far below could rise far enough to pose a danger to the farmlands beyond.

Jack shrugged beside her. Today he wore a cream colored FairIsle sweater that set off the warm tones of his skin and the pale blond of his hair. "Who can say? The Council takes their own time, they say. Many of them have lived long enough that some say they have forgotten the rhythms that most people live by. There are some who say they are too old to rule, that they still live in old ways and refuse to see what the world has become."

She frowned. "How long-lived are you talking about?"

Another shrug. "Many of us live vigorously to well past a hundred and fifty, and we do it without falling into the same level of infirmity as nonCartos do—until close to the end of life. Old Victor of the Council: he is the oldest of them right now and is, I think, something like one hundred and sixty-five. But he fails. We do not know how much longer we will have him, and with his death, another of our bloodlines will be gone. That is the problem. Once Cartos bred like humans and spread their seed far and wide, but over the millennia since the great purge, we have become more—shall we say, discerning? At least the old ones have been. We must, after all preserve our race, and though we are more now than we were after the purge, still, our birthrates are not high—barely at replacement levels. If a new purge occurs, it may mean the end of us all."

He caught her hand and pulled her into his side to put his warm arm around her shoulders. "But that is too dark a thought for so light a day and in the company of such a lovely woman. We should talk of other things. Perhaps a lesson on the healing?"

Jack was just so easy to talk to. And since their discussion after Vallon and Xavier disappeared, he had never treated her like a child, only as a woman in every way. Here, in Canada, he was a country veterinarian and she had gone with him, helping to heal those creatures who could not tell what was injured: The cow with the prolapsed uterus. The horse with the broken coffin bone. The dog brought to him after it was hit by a car. Each, he had used to teach her of her talent.

She had a talent!

A useful talent!

It was the most wonderful thing in the world. She placed her hand over Jack's, where it hung on her shoulder, and couldn't help the smile on her face. The escape from Anacortes had been such a night of terror that she could barely believe it had brought her to this.

"You smile beautifully," Jack said.

"I was thinking of you, I guess. Of the last few days." And nights of bliss. He pulled her around to face him and leaned in for a kiss. Ooh, the man could kiss, with those soft-hard lips and skilled tongue. She could melt right into him.

But a raspy cry interrupted her bliss. Bird. Eagle. She never got tired of watching them soar overhead. Jack had pointed out an eagle's nest in one of the cottonwoods on one of their rambling walks. She pulled back from him, and Jack was already scanning the sky, his telescope in his hand. No eagle there. A soft, slapping sound and another cry had them both craning over the blackberries at the river.

Swirling, grey-brown water and the occasional log that coasted past. The fishing season was still on, according to Jack, at least for the Aboriginal people who lived along the river.

Another raspy cry, and this time the unmistakable sound of splashing.

"That's an eagle. I'm going down there." Jack started shoving through the brambles, but they snagged his sweater so badly he finally gave up.

"Take this. It'll work better. Fi yanked the flannel shirt off and stood there in her t-shirt until Jack traded his sweater with her and she pulled it on, inhaling his warm apple and cut-grass scent. He shoved through the blackberry bushes then, carefully crushing a path down the steep-sided dike toward the water. She stood there, shouting encouragements, but tight with concern. If he fell, not only would the brambles flay him, but he could get seriously hurt falling on the rocks that formed the base of the dike system. He shoved through another blackberry bush and the branches sprang shut behind him. She could hear him sloshing through water and then: "Fi! You better come down here. This's going to take more than one set of hands."

She hurriedly yanked the sweater off—no need to ruin Jack's nice sweater—and slipped-slid down the track he'd made, the thorns stabbing at her and ripping her shirt and her skin. She finally shoved through the last wall of brambles and stepped down into water. Her sneakers were inundated and so were the bottoms of her jeans.

"Where are you?"

"Here." She followed his voice and found him around an outcrop of old concrete, the water swirling around his knees while he fought to hold a panicked bald eagle almost cocooned in fishing line.

The poor bird's wicked beak kept stabbing at Jack and had already left a nasty score down the back of his hand. Fishing line wrapped the bird's neck and body and had snugged one wing so tightly to its side that there was blood on the feathers. The other wing beat weakly and the two taloned feet slashed dangerously at the air.

She held back for fear of those talons and for the way the water seemed to suck at her ankles. "What do you want me to do?"

"I need you to come beside me and hold the bird while I untangle him."

She looked at him doubtfully. "I'm not sure I'm strong enough."

Jack grinned. "Of course you are, as long as he stops fighting."

Fi dutifully waded through the chilling water, the wind cutting through her t-shirt. She came up beside him and Jack glanced down at her.

"You are shivering."

"I didn't want to hook your sweater on the blackberry bushes."

"So you will let yourself freeze. Bloody hell, woman. You're mad." He shook his head. "Now place a hand here, over mine. And the other here."

She copied him, and the warmth of his Cartos aura surged through her. Her mouth went dry and she swallowed. Nodded.

"Now reach into the earth."

She did, and the sweet warmth of the rose-scented ley lines flooded around her. Jack was like a shadow beside her.

"Draw the power in."

His voice sounded distant and hollow, almost secondhand, while her essence was half outside of her body. The last time she had done this on her own was in the back of the Cayenne with Vallon. She felt shaky and uncertain as she -reached- out to the flow.

The power current almost tore her away until she remembered to just catch a small tendril. Power fumed and plumed above the main flow. She caught one of the power plumes and rose-scented heat poured into her and melted her strength. She staggered. It was like when Vallon or her mother cycled power into her, but with a clarity she had never felt before. No licorice and burning brimstone of her mother. No ashes and roses of Vallon. This was—pure lightning, electric and beautiful that sparked through her veins. She opened her eyes and looked up at Jack and felt like crying.

"What? What is it?"

"It—it's such pure power." The day was a crystalline blue bowl around her.

Jack nodded. "It is powerful here. A great channel next to a great river."

The eagle rasped and began to struggle again, his beak flashing back and barely missing Jack and her hands.

"Send him to sleep, Fiona. You do it like this."

It was as if the warmth of his palm was at the small of her back, drawing her with him back to the power they had drawn from the ley line, using that power to reach into the eagle. The light turned red as if she shifted inside the bird's flesh.

[*Send warmth and ease and sleepiness.*]

She almost fell into the water at Jack's voice in her head, but she held on and did what he said. The straining muscle under the feathers went slack. When she opened her eyes, the bird hung in her grasp and Jack eased his hands from under hers.

"Hold him."

Then he swiftly set to unwinding the lines, pulling a jackknife out of his pocket and cutting what he couldn't simply pull free. When he was done with the eagle, he drew in the fishing line and wound it into a basketball-sized bundle as he ripped it from the reeds along the shoreline and then pulled it out of the water. Finally he thought he had all of it and turned back to her where she still gingerly held the bird.

He was big. Heavy. But in her arms like this, he had none of the grandeur of the great bald eagles that were the emblem of her country. The great beak hung open. The sides rose and fell rapidly. The black eyes seemed to stare up at her in fear.

"I'm sorry. We're trying to help," she said softly. "I think he's hurt pretty badly. His wing is broken and he's terrified and hungry and he'd fought for so long. He wishes he could just die."

Jack looked at her strangely. "You are still feeding him slumber?"

She frowned. "Not exactly."

Because she wasn't. Her gaze locked onto the eagle's black eyes. It was more like she was connected to the eagle and felt what he felt. She slowed her breathing and saw the bird's breathing steady out to match. "It's more like we're one. He knows I won't hurt him. So how do we help him, Jack? How do I fix him?"

Strong arms came around her from behind and large hands covered hers. Jack's heat and apple-scented aura settled around her like a balm.

"Follow me," he whispered into her ear and led her back into the red glow of eagle flesh.

She flowed through tunnels of veins and arteries, feeling the shadows of bones and organs, and following the flesh to where the light came brighter and patterned with feathers. The shadow that was Jack stopped. [*Examine everything. Where are the breaks?*]

She -reached-, and it felt as if the particles of her essence spread out and became one with the animal. Her left arm-wing throbbed painfully and she almost dropped the bird. Would have, if not for Jack's steadying hands.

Shifting, she focused in and was suddenly there, swirling around the broken bones, and Jack was there with her. [*Like this.*]

Heat poured from Jack into the bone, and as she watched the bone knitted itself back together. It was—it was just like creating something, like she had done in school!

[*Now you fix the torn muscles around the wing.*]

She reached out, and becoming one with the bird felt like second nature. Perhaps it was, after all the ways others had used her, but this time the pooled blood of bruises were all around her, telling of torn tissue and tattered cells. She poured the rose-scented power into them, erasing the extra blood, reforming the cells, the tissue, kept going, feeling the bird's returning health, wanting to go further to heal the parasites in the belly, the fading eyesight of age.

[*Enough!*]

Jack's voice cut through her concentration. She pulled back into herself and sagged back into Jack's waiting arms. The eagle stirred in her hands, turned its head to look at her with black intelligent eyes, almost as if the bird understood what she and Jack had done. Before she could set the eagle down, its huge wings unfurled.

They beat once, twice, as if in a test.

"Hold him up!" Jack helped her and together they tossed the bird aloft.

Great black wings caught the air. Caught the air again with each wing beat and the bird didn't fall. Instead it soared in, low over the water as if seeking, then found a current of air and it lifted aloft. Beat-beat of wings and then it soared above them, its rasping cry floating back on the breeze.

Fi burst out laughing and realized she'd been holding her breath. She clapped her hands and turned around to throw her arms around Jack's chest. "That was fantastic!"

He hooked a knuckle under her chin and brought her gaze up to his. "No. You were the fantastic one. I've not seen a young healer learn so quickly, nor so well. And you are Gifted, not Cartos. What else have we missed by refusing to make contact?" He leaned in to kiss her once, lightly, and then turned her back toward the dike, one arm around her shoulders, the other hand carrying the ball of fishing line.

The path up through the brambles wasn't easy. As blackberries seem able to do, the brambles had closed in around the trail that Jack had made. Thorns grabbed at their clothing and stabbed Fi's flesh, even though Jack did his best to save her from the worst of it. When they reached the top, both of them were bloodied.

They were also not alone.

Half-blinded by the sun, Fi stepped up beside Jack, sucking a thorn-wound on her knuckle. Someone stood there. Man. Familiar, but with the sun at his back, it was difficult to make out his features.

"Hello Fi," the man said, and features coalesced on the dark silhouette.

"Jason!"

CHAPTER 14 —DISCORD

Even from the train window, Venice rose like a swan from the glittering blue of the Venetian lagoon, the huge domes of the ancient churches and palaces more like something out of a Hollywood dream than anything Landon thought he would be facing when he followed Xavier de Varga halfway around the world. He'd thought of secret headquarters hidden in Corsican mountains. Or island retreats in the midst of an Alpine lake. Even a skyscraper in the midst of Berlin, but not this—not having to submerge himself in the slow eddy of tourists, arriving on the train from Mestre and Padua in the late afternoon.

It just didn't make sense. If Xavier de Varga was the agent of a dynamic civilization of powerful but hidden Gifted, why on earth would they be here? The water alone would be enough to discourage any Gifted. Water blocked access to the earth's power.

The causeway that allowed vehicles and trains to deposit tourists at the sinking city arched up over the lagoon and ended in a huge, multistory parking lot that was as out of place as he was whenever he went out with so-called normal people. But the train itself was slowing and finally chugged to a stop in the high-ceilinged Santa Lucia Station. He wrestled his daypack onto his shoulder and followed the other passengers off the train. The air smelled musty and humid after the air-conditioned recycled stuff of the train, and the sultry heat of late afternoon immediately plastered his white shirt to his chest. If it had been humid in New Madrid, this was worse, even though a faint Mediterranean breeze ruffled his thinning white hair when he stepped through the main front doors and out into the mayhem that was Venice's front porch.

Too many touts and tour guides, all plucking at his sleeves. Not to mention the pickpockets. Even with the water in the soil, a thrum came from the earth that sent his limited Gift humming, but he kept his head down and plunged through the tourists, who caught in shoals and eddies of hesitation. He stepped down into a boat and let it take him—he didn't care where. He would find a place to stay and then he would find his way to the little blinking light on his GPS system. At least, for the moment, he was out of the press of people by the train station.

The Grand Canal curved away from him, its ornately carved, four- and five-story palaces growing straight up from the crowded water's edge. Water taxis, called *vaporetto*, tour boats, and private boats with high-powered engines wove through the water, avoiding each other and the anachronistic, diminutive gondolas with their black-and-white clad boatmen like so many clowns. Reflected sunlight placed a lovely, golden patina on the ancient buildings, but even the mask of sunshine couldn't hide the cracks in the ancient stone, the yawning empty windows. Venice might be a lovely woman of a city, but she was a woman in her dotage, still wearing the wigs and powders of her much younger days.

Was that a metaphor for the Gifted he was looking for?

For so many years, he had dreamed of finding the powerful Others and convincing them to help him to understand what and who he was and why he was different. He didn't know why he had always known they would be out there. He didn't know how the idea had come to him except for the barest of memories from when he was a child and his mother had told him a story of how his family, too many generations back to name, had been split apart in a horrible war. During that war, half the family had stolen all the power and the rest of them had died one by one until there was only one. And that one woman had hidden amongst others and had kept the secret of what she was, except she had told this tale to her child. Who had passed the tale on, until it had come to him.

And would die with him, given he was the last of his bloodline. All of his family were dead, which was just as well, given he had nothing in common with a bunch of Midwestern farmers.

The water taxi bobbed and wove into a siding close by an arching bridge, teeming with more camera-toting tourists. So he would be a tourist as well. He paid and stepped out of the vessel and pressed into the crowd, vigilant for the feel of hands on his pockets or his pack. Voices carried across the water and from the restaurants and bars that lined the canal. After so long alone in his hideaway, even his time in airports hadn't prepared him for this press of people, nor for the humidity of the air, nor the smells of garlic and tobacco and tomato sauce and plain red wine that came from the restaurants and from so many people pressed so close together on such a small, perilously vulnerable bit of land. It would take nothing to wipe Venice away, given she was already sinking.

And yet, somewhere amidst this crowd of tourists and the people here to serve them, lived some of the most powerful people in the world. The sensation of power could almost stagger him. Perhaps the Others' presence should not be such a surprise, because by the feel of it, Gifted power might be all that kept the city above the waves. In the midst of human history with so many cities destroyed in so many ways, why preserve this one?

He pulled out the tourist booklet he had grabbed in the train station and set out toward Piazza San Marco. It was as good a place as any to find a hotel and take a breath before he made his final approach to the Others. He had the GPS, but he would not turn up on the Others' doorstep exhausted and jetlagged. No, he would check into a hotel, take a shower and a nap, and then find them.

The shifting lines of tourists took him through narrow streets, past crowded restaurants and expensive shops. He probably should have simply caught a water taxi directly to the piazza, but frankly, it felt good just to move after his long transit. The song of rapid Italian. The guttural German and English languages. The fluid grace of Middle Eastern and Arabic speakers. French, Dutch, Spanish, Japanese, Chinese all flowed around him.

He stopped, realizing this was actually the perfect city for the Others. Gifted men and women could come and go from all over the world and would never be remarked. Given Venice's history as a trading center and once home of Marco Polo, it had been like this forever. The ancient ruler, the Doge, and everyone else from the merchants, the soldiers, and the priesthood had been concerned with trade, exploration, and things foreign, and had written wonderful treatises on the role of maps in our understanding the world. Fra Mauro, the ancient monk, had even gone so far as to suggest that it was maps that formed the way men thought. Such comments could be a barely veiled reference to how the Gifted could rewrite not just the world, but people's knowledge of it.

Yes, Venice was looking more and more like the perfect place for the Others. He should have seen it before, but perhaps his vision had been clouded by what he knew of Francis Drake's exploits in Lisbon twenty-seven years ago.

He came back to himself when a female tourist jostled him right into the front window of a high-end designer dress shop. The tourist didn't even glance at him as Landon righted himself and ran his fingers through his hair. But someone else did. A man, casually propped against the white stone storefront across the narrow street, met Landon's gaze and nodded.

All the little hackles stood up on the back of Landon's neck. There was too much recognition in the man's dark gaze, and yet the man was a stranger. He had the olive skin, black eyes, and tousled dark hair of the southern Italian, and the slim, athletic build of someone who made a point of keeping himself in shape. He wore cream-colored trousers and a russet-colored shirt with an open collar that set off his features. He straightened and casually made his way through the tourists toward Landon. He was not tall, but still stood a good six inches over Landon's five foot four.

A tout? A criminal? Landon was reminded once more that he *was not* an agent for a reason. He had no desire to place his person in danger. He had just about decided to duck through the tourists and escape meeting the man when the stranger reached him.

"Ciao," the man said, his voice low and thick with the music of Italian. "You are lost, no? You look for something? Perhaps I can help. I am Erminio." He stuck out his hand and it was so unexpected it took a moment for Landon to decide how to respond.

He stuck his hand in his pocket. The man's name—meaning '*of the earth*'—if Landon's recollection of Italian was correct, and his approach, could mean something far more sinister. Did the Others watch for Gifted tourists to ensure they caught no sense of Gifted presence here? Had he erred by reaching out to sense the island? Had they sent this one after him? Had Xavier de Varga sensed him?

"I am fine, thank you," he said in Italian. He turned to go and a hand fell on his shoulder, flooding Gifted presence into him.

Landon whirled back to Erminio. "You! You are Gifted."

The man's gaze changed and his gaze narrowed as he scanned the crowd around them. "Not a good term to use these days. American?" He dropped into barely accented English.

Landon found himself nodding.

"Then come with me." He caught Landon's arm and began to tug him toward a side street.

Landon yanked loose. "No way. Not until I know who you are."

Erminio rolled his eyes and leaned in close. "Is it not enough to know that I am like you?"

An easy answer: "What do you want and who do you work for?"

That brought a sly, sidelong look from Erminio. "Could I not be working for myself? Or for your welfare?"

"Then there's no need to go anywhere and we can deal with each other right here. But I think there are Others and you are taking me to meet them. Tell me, do you approach every Gifted who comes to Venice?"

Lips quirking in a small smile, Erminio leaned in close. "Perhaps only those whose faces have shown up on Interpol."

Interpol. Amundson's work, no doubt. Probably every AGS agent still at liberty was a wanted person worldwide. "Interesting that you know Interpol's wanted list. Do you make a practice of it?"

Erminio gave an exaggerated bow of his tousled head. "For certain people, yes. And when we see them come to Venetia, we gently discourage them from staying, no? It is for everyone's good."

"So you plan to usher me back to the train station?"

A showy display of empty hands. "Non. Non. It is not like that. We never demand someone leave." He leaned in close enough Landon scented the garlic on his breath over top of the Gifted scent of oriental spices. "We push them out, little friend. And if they will not go willingly, well then, we deal with them, non?"

His hand closed on Landon's bicep like a vice and the pain brought him up on his toes.

"You will walk nicely with me until we reach my boat."

It was hard to breathe with the pain eating through him. Erminio's fingers had found painful pressure points and used them to keep Landon acquiescing. He could breathe, but the pain made it more like rapid panting.

This could not be happening. He had followed Xavier too far, had too many things he regretted, had waited too many years for his chance to meet the Others, to have this man take that chance from him. Around him the shadows of evening had begun to sift into the streets, the light globes flickering on in the light standards, highlighting the glitter and the brilliant plumes and colors of Venetian masks in closed shop windows and the ancient marble facades of the close-knit, shuttered houses. The waters darkened and swirled under the water taxi engines and, with the thick moist sea air and the slow slippery breeze, he felt like he was drowning.

He would not let this happen. With his free hand, he dug in his windbreaker pocket. Not much there, but there was no chance of him getting anything that was in his pack. His fingers closed around the map of Venice and the pen he had used to mark his route to Piazza San Marco.

He shoved the map aside and gripped the pen in his fist, glancing sideways at Erminio. The man's attention was on finding a way through the crowded street ahead of them. The scent of garlic, briny olives, and tomatoes enriched the air as they passed a tourist-packed pizzeria. They rounded a corner onto a narrow, empty street that ended in a small bridge over a smaller canal, and with every ounce of strength, he swung. And stabbed.

Across his body and into Erminio's abdomen, the pen like a knife, stabbing up under the ribcage and crunching through the diaphragm. Erminio stumbled and jerked Landon sideways against the wall.

Landon fought the flow of warm blood over his hand and forearm and felt the stone soften under his feet. Erminio was Gifted, all right. And he was trying to use the Gift. Landon ground the pen deeper into the other man's chest and the grip on his arm released. Erminio groaned and collapsed against the wall, his eyes huge with anger and shock.

And then they went dead, as if a light had been switched off and the aura of Gifted light collapsed in around him and disappeared.

§

The low-angled sunlight of late afternoon lay in a column of light across the headmaster's desk of the AGS Academy. Dust motes danced in the sunlight, while the rest of the office remained in shadows, like the rest of America was in shadows, given the media messaging being spread about the Gifted. The place reeked of old coffee and ink and the dust of too many student records and too many years. Francis Drake turned one more time and glanced out the windows. The circular driveway in front of the AGS Academy for the Gifted lay empty. So was the playing field, the parents and children having departed as the light fell toward evening. Their absence left him with an empty feeling in his chest.

That, and the news about Fitzsimmons. The Gifted were on their own.

Since the call, he'd paced the narrow space in front of his desk, fighting the tight anger that twisted in his chest. No, it did not bode well at all, and along with the anger, an uneasy feeling he'd fought all day solidified in his stomach. It left him anxious and irritable and, damn it, this should not be happening!

He kicked the phone that he had thrown against the bookshelves and left there as a point of pride, and the blow sent the idiot instrument skittering under the desk. He could have stomped the thing to pieces, but that seemed ill-advised. He might have a need for further phone contact with whoever was at the other end of the phone at some point. Perhaps just to gloat when the Gifted changed the face of America except in Washington.

Now wouldn't that be fun to watch: all those power brokers and politicians, suddenly no more potent than eunuchs and feeding on themselves because all of their power bases had been taken from them. Of course, none of them would remember the way it had been before, given none of them were Gifted. Too bad, really. He would have liked the opportunity to gloat most of all.

But while losing corporate partnerships meant he and his operation would have to dig into the reserves he had squirreled away against just such an eventuality, it also meant that he didn't have to wait for anyone's approval. They could move now, instead of holding back. Not that he'd waited so far, but he'd hoped they would understand the need for immediate positive action.

He fished under the desk for the fallen phone and stuffed it in his pocket, then went out into the reception area and used the school's announcement system. "All trained Gifted, all trained Gifted. Meet me in the cafeteria in five minutes."

He shoved out the main office door and into the school's main entrance, with its spiral staircase, worn marble floors, and echoing high ceiling. It was here that he could feel the ghosts of all the Gifted who had come before. The children lost at Anacortes, the faculty and staff murdered here, and all the other casualties of this war. Those he had caused, as well. The Gifted and partially Gifted lost in New Madrid. The destroyed minds of some of those like Morgan Hoptaler. But that was what war did—it left the injured and dead behind, casualties of a higher purpose. In this age of video games, where every character could be revived with a simple reboot, it was a lesson that seemed to have been forgotten.

The long hallway to the rear of the building was mostly empty, the few remaining Gifted children now kept close by their families like precious jewels. That was an attitude he'd never understood. He'd always thought of children as tools to take their parents' vision into the future, or as caregivers in his dotage. Not that Vallon had ever knowingly carried his vision forward or showed any sign of caring for him, but Vallon was an anomaly in so many ways.

Five ex-AGS agents joined him in the hallway and followed him into the cafeteria. Preparations for the evening meal placed a pall of hamburger grease and onions and the clatter of metal pans in the air. It set his clenched gut aching. Yes, something was definitely off. His own sense of certainty, or something more, he wasn't sure.

The cafeteria looked as any school cafeteria did, with rows of white-topped rectangular tables and a few round tables scattered to break up the institutional look. It didn't work. Not even the attempts by some of the mothers to normalize the place by putting table cloths over some of the tables. It was still a huge barn of a room, with rolling metal shutters over the feeding station and the stink of too many onions and meat and powdered potatoes.

But fifteen men and women stood waiting for him. Some, like Evan Carragio, had been amongst the disappeared from the ranks of the AGS, those that had followed him to advance *Gild the Lily*, the plan to advance the Gifted's place in the world. The younger ones amongst them were all recent AGS agents, products of the edifice they stood in. Drew Libernaum stood among them, his red hair in a mop about his face, his yellow polo shirt covered in expanding sweat blotches.

"There's something wrong," Libernaum burst out before Francis could even nod a greeting. Sweat placed a sheen on his brow, and his scent of old socks and honey hung cloying in the air.

Had the youngster been listening at his door? Had he told what he'd heard? Francis began to pace. Pacing always calmed him and those he spoke to, like a ticking clock or a metronome could get people thinking in a similar rhythm.

"It's a setback, nothing more. Our contact in Washington has been killed. It's nothing to worry about." Drake waved them all to sitting, but no one moved except to glance at each other.

"What are you talking about?" Libernaum asked.

Francis stopped. The question was echoed on all their faces. Clearly none of them had a clue what he was talking about.

"What did you mean when you said something was wrong?" Francis asked.

Libernaum, the little piss-ant, didn't even have the good grace to hide how he rolled his eyes. "I mean something is *wrong*. Haven't you felt it? It rips into my guts—as if all my innards have been pulled out—and when I reach for the earth, I can't find it. It's like it's not there."

The man had obviously gone over the edge. The currents in the earth were *always* there. They were the source of everything. But the others were nodding, including Carragio and his other long-time supporters.

Francis -reached-, and a void roared in as if the world were a hollowed-out husk. Blackness of soil all around him, the press of rocks, but there was no soft glow of the power he'd always been able to access, and no scent of roses. Instead, the darkness smelled of ozone and ether and decay. Hell, the small creatures of the soil were dead or dying. The cedar and oak roots were dying, too, they just didn't show it yet. What the hell had happened? A poison in the Academy air that shut down their ability to access the power? But that didn't explain the dying creatures beyond.

The worst part was that he couldn't seem to find an end to the darkness. He didn't know whether it was that he could not move through this dead area, or if the deadness stretched forever.

He yanked back and staggered, and Libernaum caught his arm. "You see? And it seems to suck the power out of us, as well."

"Everything's dying," Francis said, trying to comprehend what he'd seen and the terrifying implications. He inhaled and pulled loose of the young man's steadying grip. His own hands were shaking.

"Amundson. It has to be. Some new kind of weapon. We're only going to get weaker the longer we stay here. Get your families and warn the others. We're getting out of here."

The not-too-distant sound of rapid gunfire stopped his orders. More of Amundson's tactics. Had to be. He swung back to the agents. "How many of you have weapons?"

CHAPTER 15 — THE EDGE OF THE TRUTH

The ornate ceilings of the Venetian room pressed down on Vallon. The breeze through the open balcony door was a prison guard's taunt, and the bed was the worst part. The broad expanse of crisp Egyptian cotton was the place that she'd allowed herself to be distracted from what needed to be done. Seattle was dying, dammit!

The door had barely slammed shut and locked behind them when Vallon wheeled on Xavier.

"How *dare* you?" Her fingernails dug into her palms as she advanced on him. "How dare you put me in that position? Leave me ignorant of what those people were going to say—how they were going to react. You left me not knowing who and what I might be. How long have you known, Xavier? What other secrets are you keeping from me?" She stopped and held her hands up. "Of course. Stupid me. Your whole life is secrets and you tell me none of them, because I'm just another Gifted—too primitive to understand what you might tell me. Is that it?"

The anger boiling in her flesh was so powerful it could consume her. No matter what Xavier might think, her fury at him not having told her of her parentage wasn't simply going to go away. Cool evening air came through the open window, bringing a sea scent and the scent of spices, food, and coffee that sent her last meal roiling in her stomach. And this man had caused it. Her friend and lover. She could barely see him through the grey pall of her vision.

She closed her eyes against everything, but it didn't help.

The wizened old man who had claimed he might be her grandfather, reaching for her with twisted hands. The man who she had thought loved her, standing like an offending shadow amongst the shadows of the twilight-filled room. *His* guilty silence the worst of all.

"You got nothing to say? To hell with you." She turned from his silence and marched to the balcony window and leaned out over the stone railing. The scent of jasmine seemed to have increased as the shadows expanded. Now sunlight only highlighted the spire of a church far down the canal and the rooftops of some of the taller buildings. She should just jump into the canal and be gone, back to America to do what needed to be done. The rest—all this—was just a distraction, because the grey pall wasn't going away. Whatever was happening in Seattle hadn't stopped because she was here.

But to learn that everything she'd believed about herself might not be true—it was just too much to comprehend. And yet, deep inside, it made too much sense. Her father had never loved her—had found it so easy to leave her—because she was not his. Or maybe she was. Perhaps her father had found this Lianna and impregnated her in a plan to gain control over a half-breed Cartos child. It sounded like something he would do. The AGS files *had* indicated he was her father. Of course, Landon probably created that file and she didn't doubt that he knew the truth. But either way, it meant she wasn't who she thought she was. She felt strange and her skin felt foreign. Behind her, the lights came on in the room and her elongated shadow fell across the dark canal water and the building beyond. Another shadow joined hers as Xavier came up too close behind her, the heat of his presence too hot against her skin.

"How long have you known?" Keep her voice tightly controlled, because otherwise she might start crying or yelling and she was not going to be weak about this, because regardless of her parentage, she was Vallon. Maybe not Drake, but the Vallon was hers.

He must have known that to touch her would have made her furious. Instead he stood there, the steady pulse of his Gifted—make that Cartos—aura pulsing gently, comfortingly, against hers. She stepped away to the side, resenting the soothing he offered.

"Since I first saw you, I suspected. Lianna Reinel was like the reincarnation of her famous ancestor—fearless and powerful—just as you are. The original Lianna broke all the rules and, with Prince Henrique of Portugal—the man the west calls Prince Henry the Navigator—established the first school for Cartos that began to draw together the bits and pieces of the old knowledge. From their work, we now know our history better and have reclaimed some of our ancient powers. Your mother was as strong-willed as her ancestor, but she had found no place to focus her attention. She became like a wild thing held captive, and so she fell into the wrong crowd."

"You sound as if you knew her."

"I met her once, when I was quite young. She had a questing mind and a capacity for love and kindness, much like you. I was about eighteen and it was only a few years before she disappeared. I was out in the night, having been ridiculed by my peers after I broke into an unGifted home because I thought I loved the girl who lived there. Lianna came upon me as I skulked around the streets. She stopped me and showed me how to redraw the rooflines of the surrounding houses so that I could simply walk across and inside instead of breaking through the doorway. She told me that it is better to change the big things if the change will be unremarked, than to act directly on what you want. When she was done, she looked at me with such sad eyes. 'Now go to her,' she said. 'Go to her and be happy.'

"But she didn't look like she was. In fact, she looked like one of the unhappiest women I have ever seen. I wanted to help her but didn't know how. It was not long afterward that she disappeared. You have the same look about you now."

He caught her shoulders and gently eased her around. "You have her eyes, her jaw line, her mouth, though your hair is more blonde," he said softly. "That was what I saw when I first saw you at your Academy. And I recognized the power in your presence, but I could not say for sure whether you were her child or simply a miraculous accident that had somehow been created out of the disparate bloodlines flowing through Gifted veins. Then I met you and my suspicions increased, given the power you used, but how fair would it be to tell you of a parentage that it was not within my right to confirm? Would old Victor have accepted you if you had come claiming your heritage? No, better he claim you himself, when you have no knowledge."

His gaze was dark as the falling night, his dark hair like wings about his hawk face as he looked down at her.

"Truly, I did not wish to keep secrets from you, my *Bela*."

His voice was soft and it was as if the rest of the dreamscape that was Venice disappeared around them. Believe him? A part of her wanted to. But a part of her hurt too much to do so.

She sidled away from him and crossed her arms. "You call me *Bela*, but my *name* is Vallon. That's who I am." She looked him up and down.

"But you keep yourself secret from me. Hell, you keep my own past secret from me! That puts *you* in control, and if you truly knew me, you'd know I resent other people trying to control me most of all."

She turned her back and strode into the room, regardless of the wrench it was to leave him behind. *Xavier, how could you betray me like this? If you love me, how could you do this to me?* She slumped into one of the ornately carved chairs beside the empty fireplace. The white marble mantle was an overblown, grating froth of carved fruit and cupids, just like everything else about this room. She closed her eyes, every part of her bruised and tender.

What had her father done to get her? If he was *not* her kin, how had he come to raise her?

"After I saw you the first time, I was filled with questions. Everyone knew Lianna had disappeared, but that in itself was not so strange. It was a time when the younger Cartos expressed their dissatisfaction with the old ways of the Council. They wanted more say in decisions, but the Council would have none of it. And then they began to disappear—some said to form their own shadow society. So Lianna's disappearance was just one amongst a number. No one knew how or why, and certainly no one suspected she was with child. I began to investigate and I discovered that she had been married to an older man. I found a marriage license issued to them, but then suddenly both of them disappeared as if they were stolen from the face of the earth. But when I checked your birth certificate, your date of birth comes right from that time, as if your birth and your parent's disappearance were somehow connected."

Xavier settled in the chair across from her, his face carefully neutral.

"So you think Francis Drake is either my father and killed my mother and abducted me, or else he killed both my parents for me."

His throat worked, but finally he nodded. "The Lianna I knew would never stop looking for you if she were alive. Any man worth her love would have been the same."

"You loved her."

Xavier's low chuckle seemed to fill the room. "As a young man loves a goddess, I suppose I did. She was—memorable and I have a penchant for formidable women. But it is you that I love. You are the woman no one else could ever be. Stubborn, beautiful, quick to love and quicker to anger, and *mea culpa,* I am so sorry I have offended you."

The clenched fist in her chest eased a little, but she still couldn't meet his gaze. "So you know all my sordid past. What about you, Xavier? Who is Xavier de Varga?"

"The man who loves you?"

She shook her head, determined not to let him escape with some platitude. "Not good enough. Where are you from? Who are your family? What do you do for this Council and why?"

His sigh was audible. "I was born in the Algarve, that sunny part of Portugal where the original Lianna Reinel lived. From there you can see the end of Europe at Cabo San Joseph and the places where Prince Henrique first sent sailors around the capes of Africa. My village was a dry, inhospitable place of stone, as dry and hard as my father's heart. He was of Moorish decent, and thus his family, great landowners, were always resented. But the Moors were a great people who brought much culture to Iberia while they ruled there, and his family came from old Cartos blood. He ruled his household with an iron fist and had five wives in succession. Some say they each died of a broken heart, living with such a man; some whisper my father killed them, but none bore him children until my mother, and that was in the twilight of his life. He was not a gentle father, and a less gentle husband."

His voice faded to silence and darkness flooded into his features. He sat lost in thought and she realized that he had his ghosts, just as she did. But that was still no excuse for his silence. If anything, it should make him understand her need to *know*.

He looked up and met her gaze. "I left home as soon as I could and began to work for the Council. My father was a member, you see, and he was training Carlos to follow in his footsteps. Me? I was the extra son in case something happened to Carlos—but I so dreamed of his approval." He shook his head. "I stood up to him only once, for all the good it did. Funny how clearly you can see your foolishness when you are older. So, I began to wander. I spent many years with distant kin, wandering the deserts of North Africa. Then Hector, the same who is now the head of the Council, found me and asked me to work for *CartosNationele* and so I found you."

It was so much information and so little, but they were much the same for their sorry relationships with their fathers. Xavier might have known his father, but it did not sound like something anyone would wish to remember. Perhaps it would have been like that for her, if her father had raised her instead of leaving it to Landon and others.

Landon, who had to know her parentage, too.

Her chest clenched a ratchet tighter. She thought of Landon's frequent reference to the Others in the world. It hadn't been a theory. It had been the truth, and he was trying to prepare her for it. Not prepare. Perhaps set her in motion to go look for them.

The sluggish evening air didn't seem quite capable of filling her lungs and her stomach heaved.

She looked up and found Xavier watching her.

"Do you know how much this changes?" she asked.

His expression grew guarded and his hands gripped the chair arms. "I love you, *Bela*. Vallon. That has not changed—cannot change, ever."

But simple words changed nothing. Xavier had kept her origins a secret from her and that *meant* something. She needed to be up and doing, because action would let her brain work through just what that was. This room—this confinement—kept her a prisoner both of the Cartos Council and of her own emotions. At least if she were at home, she could go out for a run until she was too exhausted to think anymore. But here—here they stopped her from doing anything and things were happening that demanded action.

She abandoned the chair and started pacing. "We need to get out of here—or I do. These people are taking too long to act and something's happening back home. Something bad that I have to stop—because I'm not some Cartos royalty. I work for the AGS and someone's messing with Seattle." She turned back to Xavier, still sprawled in his chair, watching her with a hint of amusement in his gaze.

"What? So you think I'm funny, now?"

He clambered out of the chair. "Not funny. Amazing. How do you say it? The world has pulled the carpet out from under you, and yet you climb up and do not go after the carpet puller, you think of the others hurt by the loss of the carpet."

He approached, but she backed away. Her head hurt. Her heart hurt worse, but she had to do this.

"This isn't going to work, Xavier. I'm sorry. But it can't possibly work until I have things sorted in my head. Now will you help me get back to Seattle, or do I have to do it on my own?"

§

Fi's feet squelched in her sodden sneakers as she and Jack faced Jason Bryson on the dike trail. The blackberry brambles to either side oozed the scent of mildewed fruit, and the rushing river water suddenly just smelled cold and uninviting. The afternoon sunlight dappled Jason Bryson's hair, but something about his eyes stopped her from stepping forward to greet him.

They were black as pitch and brittle as old glass, but the weak sunlight didn't seem to catch in them. He wore a trench coat, open over dress trousers and an open-collar white shirt that looked like it had been slept in. So did his mussed hair, and his cheeks and jaws were shadowed by beard stubble. His mouth was set in a hard, unfriendly line that seemed to have forgotten how to smile.

"Is everything okay, Jason? Where've you been?" It had been a long time since she last saw him—since New Madrid, in fact, when she was sent off with Gregor Gleason to Washington and Jason had headed off to Seattle with Vallon to rescue the Gifted kids kidnapped from the AGS Academy. Somewhere along the way, Jason and Vallon had obviously gotten separated. In all the excitement of escaping Anacortes, she'd neglected to ask how.

"Where's Vallon?" he asked, a vein pulsing in his temple.

Fi eased in closer to Jack's side. "She's—with Xavier."

A shadow seemed to cross his face. "Of course she is. Where are *they*?"

All the hairs on her body prickled at Jason's presence. This wasn't the man she'd helped save from the Seattle underground. This wasn't the cop who had hounded Vallon and who seemed to have a bit of a love affair with Vallon's cat, Maggie. That man had carried an old grief like—like the last of a dying species. She'd seen it in New Madrid, too. But now the grief seemed transformed into something hard—and angry—like a piece of a void that could devour her.

"Who is this, Fiona?" Jack said softly.

"Oh. Sorry." She straightened and tried to put on her best 'friend' face. "Jack, this is Jason Bryson. He's an old friend of Vallon's and a Seattle Police detective. Jason, this is Jack Henry, an old friend of Xavier's and a veterinarian."

But her introduction didn't seem to ease the tension like it was supposed to. If anything, Jack eased closer to her. He put his arm around her. "Fiona has been staying with me while Vallon and Xavier are away for a short time. Vallon has been healing. She was quite badly injured."

Fi nodded. "She almost died, Jason."

A flicker of proprietary concern crossed Jason's gaze and the cool wind bit through her. She shivered.

"I'm glad she didn't," Jason said, but his voice didn't sound right. More like someone who was relieved a car door hadn't been dented. "You look cold, Fi. Does this belong to you then?" He toed the Fair Isle sweater she had doffed before rescuing the eagle.

"That is mine," Jack said and took off the flannel shirt and gave it to Fi. She slipped it on, but then noticed Jack had done nothing about retrieving the sweater. A question filled his gaze. "Perhaps we should head back to the house and get warmed up?"

Jason waved them past him and fell in behind, retrieving the sweater to toss to Jack. Jack pulled the sweater on, but Fi couldn't stop watching Jason. The way he moved, it was like he didn't want to get too close to them. As if he were trying to protect himself from a weapon.

Or had a weapon that he didn't want taken from him.

She stumbled and almost fell, but Jack caught her elbow. A surge of warmth ran through her and he didn't let go, just gave her a serious look that said he'd read the situation just as she had. Something was seriously off.

"So, Jason, how'd you find us? We took off from Anacortes to find Vallon a doctor. I didn't think anyone knew where we were."

She glanced back to see Jason shrug behind her. "I'm a cop. I've got my ways. You were in the black Porsche Cayenne that ran the border, right? I saw it in the garage or barn or whatever that building is."

She didn't know what to say at the fact he'd apparently searched Jack's place, so she nodded. "Xavier's car. The police were chasing us and he knew Vallon wouldn't make it unless we got her to a doctor fast. But how'd you find us on this side of the border?"

Another shrug. "A car like that with a broken headlight. It doesn't go unremarked. I asked around and a few gas station jockeys remembered seeing it come blasting through, headed north. So I came and parked and waited. I knew one of you freaks would have to use the Gift eventually. I wasn't wrong. So I tracked you here."

His hand slipped out from under his jacket, this time weighted with an ugly black gun. "So which one of you was it? I'm betting on ol' Jack here, because you were always a lightweight, Fi. No offence."

Jack stopped dead in his tracks and turned. "What is this all about, Jason? Fiona names you Vallon's friend, and yet you aim a weapon at us."

Jason just shook his head. "Shut up and keep going. Your place is just up ahead. We'll sort things out there."

"What's going on, Jason?" She clutched Jack's hand, but obeyed. Her knees wobbled and she couldn't seem to get enough air into her lungs. "You're Vallon's friend. Why are you acting like this?"

"Well maybe that's something you should talk to your little friend about. Seems Vallon Drake has a hell of a lot of Gift, but she's not about to share it." He shook his disheveled head. "No, she wants to keep it all to herself. Won't even do a service for a friend." He motioned down the dike embankment toward the house and Jack urged Fiona down ahead of him.

She felt Jack -reach- for the power and turned to warn him that Jason was not like other unGifted. The hard-packed soil of the dike softened under them. Jason took one look down at his feet and brought up the gun. He shot, and the air filled with thunder.

Jack stumbled back into her and went down to his knees, the left shoulder of his Fair Isle sweater blooming red.

"Jack!" She went to her knees beside him. "What do I do? How do I fix it?"

"You try anything more, and the next shot's a little more permanent," Jason said, all emotion drained from his voice.

"Jason! How could you?" She pressed her hands hard against the wound in the back of Jack's shoulder and fought back tears.

Jack blinked, his gaze dazed with shock. "How?"

"He can sense Change. We don't know why." She glanced up at Jason, who held the huge pistol ready. "Come on." She struggled up and hauled Jack to his feet. "We have to get you into the house."

He leaned on her, but there was no surge of warmth. Instead, all warmth seemed sucked from him, leaving behind a cold, cold world. She sent a small stream of power into him, praying it wasn't enough to set Jason off again.

The kitchen's warmth couldn't cut the cold that chilled her to the bone. She shoved inside and yanked out a chair for Jack. He collapsed, looking pale as milk, his blond hair tangled, his handsome face gaunt with pain. She got scissors out of the kitchen drawer and cut up the arm of the shredded sweater to expose the ruin of his shoulder.

"You didn't need to shoot him. He would have stopped if I'd asked him."

"Sure, Fiona. You're every bit as reliable as Vallon." Jason's sarcasm was heavy.

"Don't try to reason with him, Fiona." Jack murmured. "There is something wrong with him. A—vacancy?—I don't understand."

Jason stuck the gun in Jack's face. "Shut up, or I'll do it for you."

Jack's blood flowed down his shoulder and over his hand. Fi grabbed towels out of the drawer and wadded them against the wound, then dug the medical kit out from under the sink. Everything looked so foreign and so far away and her fingers were sausages, her hands clumsy lumps of ice. She fumbled everything. Didn't know what she was doing. Why couldn't she be more like Vallon?

Darn it, she was crying as she lay dressing over dressing over dressing. The trouble was they were drenched in blood as soon as she put them on the wound.

"I can't get it to stop bleeding," she sobbed and hated herself for crying.

"Fiona. Look at me. This way will only slow the bleeding. There is another way." He looked up at Jason. "She will help me with the Gift. This is no Change." Then he caught Fi's bloody hands with his own.

[*Fiona.*]

The voice in her head was clearly Jack. [*How?*]

[*Those with the healing Gift can do this. Now swiftly, Fiona, for I do not know how long he will let me live.*]

[*He'll let you live. I'll make him.*]

[*Fiona, listen. There is something about him. I am surprised Xavier did not notice, but it is a subtle thing. -Reach- for him, Fiona, and I will show you.*]

[*But I have to heal you first. Isn't it like with the eagle? I reach into you, like this.*]

She did and found herself in the midst of the apple- and cut-grass-scented presence of Jack, following the flow of blood as it swirled through arteries and veins to the heart and outward—pulled along and then suddenly she was amongst torn flesh and shattered bone.

[*I don't know how to do this.*]

[*You do not need to waste your power on this. Look at Jason. See how the edges of his aura are connected to the earth.*]

[*No! It's you who's hurt. Tell me what to do. Tell me how to help you!*] Because already his aura was showing grey streaks. If he kept losing this amount of blood, soon he'd be like Vallon had been. He'd die.

A bloody hand caught her chin and turned her face toward him. He held her firmly and forced her to look him in the eye. "I am not about to die just yet."

His gentle strength somehow calmed her panic. She swallowed. Nodded.

She turned to Jason and -reached- to look at his aura. Typical unGifted, it carried the usual rainbow shift of colors, but none of the heated red or golden glow of the Gift. In fact, the utter lack of any Gift was surprising, given most people had at least the faintest glimmer of it. But Jason had nothing except an aura as untainted by Gift as if he were some new kind of unicorn. Then she looked for what Jack had pointed out—Jason's aura shifted around him with part of it extending down into the ground. Not that most auras didn't form a bubble around the person, but instead of the crisp line of where the aura entered the earth, Jason's aura appeared to lift from the earth as if the earth itself extended up to surround him. Almost as if he was part of the earth.

She pulled back, blinking and turned back to Jack. Nodded and -reached- again into him.

[*I saw. Now what do I do to heal you?*]

A hand yanked her loose of Jack. "This's taking too long. Where's Vallon, Fi? When do you expect her back?"

She fought to hold onto her grip on Jack, while blinking up at Jason. "I don't know when she'll be back. She's gone off somewhere."

"Where?"

She had to get back to Jack. Healing him was everything. But Jason had her by the shoulder. He shook her like a rag doll, or some ill-behaved puppy.

"Tell me or I hurt him worse."

Not Jack. Not that. "I don't know. Somewhere in Europe. Venice, maybe."

"Venice?"

She yanked away and turned back to Jack. [*Tell me quickly. How do I do this?*]

[*It is like a jigsaw puzzle, Fiona. You must find the pieces and put them back together. Where there are no pieces, you must steal from elsewhere to form the pieces needed.*]

A soft pressure against her legs. Maggie had come into the room, probably to beg for food.

Then a low growl turned into an angry cat yowl and the sound of an attack.

Fi snapped back into herself in time to see a small black-and-white ball of fury, ears backed and spitting. Then the cat leapt at Jason and he brought up his gun.

"No!" she screamed.
Jack lunged and Jason's gun went off again.
Then everything went horribly still.

CHAPTER 16 —CORDITE AND FADING

Francis Drake and twenty other Gifted hunkered down at the AGS Academy's heavy wooden front doors and leaded windows, peering out at the armed men approaching the school. The Walther in Drake's hand felt weighted all wrong. His usual weapon for the past forty years had carried no more than the weight of a pen. But in this situation, with the void built beneath the school, the pen-and-vellum solution wasn't going to work for him. Getting free to do what needed to be done required a more direct approach. Thankfully he and the agents had had the foresight to also bring guns on their escape from Amundson and their retreat from Anacortes. Of course, it didn't mean that they liked to use them. The air stank of nervous sweat and fear.

The main entry of the AGS Academy, with its broad, unfettered expanse of floor and its open staircase and its open doors into hallways leading deeper into the school, felt like the most ridiculous place in the world to hunker down and try to stave off the attackers. Through the windows beside the door, he could see the two unfortunate AGS agents who had once patrolled the front driveway. Their bodies lay sprawled on the pristine green lawn between the arms of the circular driveway.

"The fact Amundson's men attack so openly doesn't bode well," Libernaum said. "It's like they want us to know because they know we can't beat them."

Drake nodded. Amundson's men could have attacked by surprise and killed any number of them before the Gifted could raise a response. He straightened and stepped back from where he'd crouched by the window. "So just what do they expect us to do in response, do you think?"

Libernaum eyed the scene beyond the window. "This is where the gunfire was. It's drawn us here with most of our weapons."

"And we have placed most of our women and children under limited guard in the cafeteria." It all became clear. "Your families. The gunfire here was a ruse. If they capture the families, they know most of you'll surrender."

At least that was what Amundson and his ilk would figure. Families as hostages meant the ex-agents, at least, would cooperate. "Libernaum, you and Carragio stay here and hold the door. If anything moves, shoot it."

He took off at a run, eighteen other agents behind him. Around him the long, linoleum-floored halls echoed the thunder of their footfall. Please don't let him be too late. If he was, he'd have lost the war. The Gifted rise to power would be over. If he was wrong in his assessment, he'd left Libernaum and Carragio to face an onslaught alone. Libernaum might stand a chance—if there were twenty of him. Carragio he had little faith in after the New Madrid affair.

Too many doubts that had never been there before. Doubts that would undermine his resolve.

He reached the junction that led to the dorm wing and cafeteria, or to the gymnasium. No one used the gym, given the slaughter that had occurred there. A sound stopped him and he held up his hand. A cry. Another. A crash. A scream. Something was happening in the cafeteria.

He motioned them back into the hallway. "Here's what we do. Five of us head for the Cafeteria doors and engage the attackers. The rest of us are going out the gymnasium doors and coming at them from the rear. Everyone got that?"

A series of nods from the men and women with him. He split the team, putting mostly his people on the frontal assault. They wouldn't be quite so caught up in saving the families, and thus were less likely to give up in the face of hostages. The agents, however, would be more than ready to assault the rear of Amundson's forces to save their children.

The double doors to the cavernous gymnasium swung open with barely a sound, revealing a gloom-filled, hardwood-floored cavern. The place still stank of death, even though he'd had a team of agents scrub the blood off. Something about the iron scent had seeped into the very soul of the space. Nothing moved in the darkness, but the Exit sign glowed like a beacon.

He led his team silently across the floor as gunfire suddenly broke out behind them. Good. Amundson's men might be trained, but that meant they'd probably move into the room to engage rather than risk the hostages. He hoped. If he got this lot killed, it was going to be very hard to hold the AGS agents. On the other hand, it might help them see the correctness of his vision a little more

He eased the exit door open and a whiff of cool autumn air met his nose. Afternoon light flooded into the dimness and illuminated thirteen anxious agent faces. He nodded and peered outside. The forest beyond the school grounds was silent, the tops of the cedars tossing in an afternoon breeze. Watery autumn sunlight placed a golden glow on everything. From the far end of the building came the sound of screams and gunfire.

He slid out the door and along the building, keeping an eye on the forest. When the others were outside, he motioned five of them into the woods to circle around where they would be less likely to be seen. Then he led his team along the wall toward the cafeteria and the sounds of mayhem.

The building was built like an H, with one upright deleted. The front entrance and the administration and teaching wing were the short central bar of the H, while the gymnasium and cafeteria sat at opposite ends of the remaining upright. He led them at a lope along the outer wall, knowing that if any of Amundson's men stepped outside, they'd be seen. They reached the half-way mark and the gunfire inside the room suddenly went quiet. Either his men were dead or they'd surrendered. He needed to be at the doors now!

He broke into a run, the others behind him, and reached the doors just as two black-clad armed men stepped out.

Without thought, Drake shot. The closest man collapsed. Amundson's other man swung his weapon toward them. Automatic machine gun. Before Francis could get his shot off, one of the AGS agents got him. Children's screams were muffled by the ringing in Drake's ears. The air felt like taffy around his limbs, slowing him down. He wasn't used to shooting people. But they needed to do this. It would solidify his hold over his agents, meld them together as a team.

Gunfire from the forest confirmed what he'd suspected. More of Amundson's men guarded the way they'd come in to the Academy. He could only hope that his five agents got the jump on whoever it was.

Children spilled out the door in front of him, panic-stricken women among them. Drake swung around the open door to face three more armed men, each with a hostage pressed to his body. One woman, two preteens who had been saved from Anacortes. Maybe they were just not meant to live. But it was a small force against them. Amundson had first sent in an extraction team. Get the families as hostages or experimental subjects, then bring in the big guns. His phone buzzed in his pocket and he figured he knew what Libernaum would tell him. More of Amundson's men coming in for clean-up.

Drake fell back as his team confronted the hostage takers. Two of the women were gathering the families back against the building.

Drake opened the phone.

"Three troop trucks just rolled up the driveway." Libernaum's crisp voice.

"Get the hell out of there and head for the cafeteria, but do it quietly. I need you to take out three men who'll have their backs to you."

He flipped the phone closed and stepped into the building between his agents. Let the agents see how hard he worked to save their children.

He holstered his gun and held his hands up. Beyond, on the floor, were the bodies of the four men and the woman he'd left guarding the families. Only one of them moved—the woman, with blood pulsing too quickly from a shattered leg. *Not going to make it, I'm afraid.* He turned back to the attackers.

"You can't win. Release them and we'll let you leave." Like hell.

"You surrender and we'll let these three live. They must be important to somebody."

Sure they were, but not directly to him. He didn't need families with children, even if children were the future. What he needed right now was hardened agents who wouldn't hesitate to do what was needed. This was just the kind of situation that would gel their cohesiveness.

"You might kill the hostages, but you'd be dead, too. There are too many of us for you to get past us."

"Not for long, ya Gifted mother-fucker."

As if that was supposed to frighten him. The agents beside him looked uneasily at each other.

"I repeat. Let them go. They're harmless women and children. They've hurt no one."

"Surrender or I'll shoot her." The black-clad man jabbed the barrel of his weapon up under the chin of his female hostage. She was young, brunette, pretty enough even though she was sobbing.

Drake said nothing. From behind the men, there was movement that he prayed was Libernaum. Then the kid slid in the door and two-handed his pistol up. Carragio eased in beside him and copied his stance. The first bullet took the gunman with the woman in the back. A second almost on top of the first took a second attacker. The woman and child they held ripped free as their captors crumpled. The third man swung his hostage around to stop the new attackers. But Drake and his team were ready. A bullet caught Amundson's man in the shoulder. Another found his neck. A third his head. His body shuddered under the impacts. The girl he held yanked free and fell to the ground, screaming and clutching her arm. She'd been hit, but it had gotten her free.

One of the agents scooped her up. Another went to check on the fallen agents.

"No time!" Drake roared. "There're reinforcements out front. Now move. Outside and into the forest. There's only one chance, and that's to reach the vehicles we stashed."

The agents shoved the still-sobbing woman and child out the door, leaving the gymnasium in silence except for a sound like the ocean's roar—running footfalls down the hallway behind them.

One chance, and that chance was fading.

§

Jack's kitchen filled with the roar of the gunshot. The whole scene went still and time shifted. Dust motes crept through the column of sunshine from the kitchen window. Fi watched the slow fall of the drip from the kitchen faucet, the expansion of smoke from the gun, out and out until the whole room reeked of its devastation. Then time shifted back to normal again.

"No!" she screamed and leapt for Jack. He collapsed in a heap by the kitchen door, Jason standing over him as if he shot innocent men every day. She turned Jack over and his blue eyes were wide as if with surprise, but he was still there, still alive.

"Jack. Jack, what do I do?"

A new bloom of red spread across Jack's chest and his breathing didn't sound right. It came in tight little gasps and red burbled at his lips. Oh God, Oh God, Oh God.

"What do I do? What do I do?" She -reached- and found Jack's aura stained black, too akin to what Fi had seen with Vallon. Oh, where was Vallon, she'd know what to do.

But she had to do this herself. She dove into Jack's body and found herself cloaked in red. Too much and flowing too swiftly. He was dying, would die unless she did something. What was it he said? Treat it like a jigsaw puzzle?

But she'd never been good at puzzles. In fact, they irritated her with their little misshapen pieces and the tedious work of putting them together because they just never fit. Nothing ever fit after her mother—just like she didn't fit.

But for Jack she would. Lungs. One whole, one torn to a bloody pulp. Bone like a shadow, shattered and not where it should be. All those pieces…

She had no time to put them all back together. Jack's heart was beating too fast and there wasn't enough blood in him to keep flowing like this. What should she do first? What *could* she do?

She placed her hands flat on his chest and felt the suck and release of each breath. "I need the medical kit. I do."

Jason stood above her, his gun at his side.

"I need the medical kit," she shrilled.

It was like she broke Jason out of a deep slumber. He grabbed the medical kit from the kitchen table and dropped it on the floor beside her. She fumbled through it, examining and discarding everything, it seemed. Then a firm hand closed on her wrist and she found herself looking into Jack's blue eyes. Not scared. At least there was that. He looked like he wanted to tell her something.

She -reached-. [*What do I do? What do I do?*]

[*The pieces. Heal the veins. The lung.*]

She felt like the eagle, beating useless wings. Where to begin when there was so much destruction? She patched whatever she could see. Shoved bone aside. Grabbed tattered flesh, drew power in a heated flash from her body to create new cells between the torn edges. It was working, but there was so much blood. Too much. Something was broken and she didn't know what to look for. Jack's blue gaze was fading.

[*Fiona.*]

The calm bell of his voice stopped her frantic work.

[*I'm trying.*] She sobbed. [*I just don't know how to stop it. Where you're bleeding.*]

[*Listen. You must listen because I am almost gone. This Jason. He is not like other men.*]

She gripped Jack's hand, squeezed his fingers back. [*I'm not letting you die.*]

She started to work again. This piece to this piece, the most important puzzle of her life. But she just wasn't fast enough. She -reached- for the earth power and drew it up, poured power into him. Just live. Just live.

Not enough. If anything, his Gifted aura blackened further. Its edges crumpled in toward him.

[*Fiona, listen. Jason…*]

[*I don't care about Jason! I have to save you!*] The first man, the first person who had treated her like an adult. A person who showed her that she could be more than some half-addled creature. A man she cared for and who cared for her.

From somewhere he drew strength and his fingers crushed hers, stopping her work and then he released her, his fingers gone abruptly lax. His presence faded in her head, as his aura collapsed in around him. [*Fiona. Listen. Tell. Xavier. Jason—he was made.*]

His intense blue eyes went flat.

CHAPTER 17 — TO TURN AWAY

In the murky Venetian twilight, Landon stood above Erminio's flaccid body that was half supported by the meeting of two walls and the pressure of Landon's bloody palm. He inhaled the dank air, ripe with copper, and yanked his hand away, but his fist, his wrist, and the cuff of his jacket were already red. With no other option, he wiped them off on Erminio's ruddy shirt and turned away from the dark backwater alley that led to a small dock and motorboat on a narrow canal. Instead of the boat, he stumbled back the way they'd come and stepped into the crowd that streamed down one of Venice's main streets toward Piazza San Marco.

He kept his head down, his bloody hand at his side. Surely anyone who looked at him would know that he had just killed someone. He yanked his jacket off his shoulder and tucked it inside out around his bloody hand as he scurried through the street, and suddenly, with the crowd, exploded out into the expanse of the Piazza.

The broad, white marble underfoot had turned grey and seemed to absorb the light from the shadowed storefronts and the light seeping from the ornate façade of Saint Mark's Basilica. Ranks of tables and chairs held troupes of tourists, absorbing the nighttime view of shoals of gondolas on the water and the Basilica di San Giorgio Maggiore across the water, layered over graduated shades of deep blue like a study in perspective. The crowds stopped him and he spun around, certain someone was watching him. No one stood out. No one met his gaze. Instead, shadows swept around him and stole his air.

He panned the Piazza and then strolled toward the water. Slowly. Calmly. The same as any other wandering tourist. Lagoon breezes found his face as he followed a shoal of tourists along the water. Restaurants leaked the clinking of cutlery, happy voices, and the scent of red wine and oregano. A terracotta building front oozed with the soft glow of gold light through windows and a slowly revolving wooden door. *Hotel Denali* read the discreet sign overhead, and the sound of soft music and voices came from what must be a restaurant terrace on the roof.

He needed to get off the street and this seemed as likely a spot as any—more likely actually, given how high-end the place looked. Who would expect a wanted man to choose such a place?

He plunged inside into a world of lush carpets over rich, multi-colored Italian marble floors. Scrolled and carved walls competed with richly-muraled lobby ceilings that gave onto staircases that climbed the pale yellow inside walls of a multistoried, interior courtyard. Graceful, arched openings gave onto the upper hallways. Beautiful. Medieval Venetian palace transformed into the epitome of luxury hotel. He stopped a moment, admiring and imagining whispers of Byzantium, then took a deep breath to reclaim the old Landon Snow confidence. He strode up to the front desk like someone who belonged there, instead of someone who had just killed a man.

It was a disquieting thought, but he set it away. Preserving himself was the order of the moment.

"A room, please," he said in his best haughty voice. If he could just get his heart to stop trembling.

"Have you a reservation, sir?" asked the neatly coiffed desk clerk. She wore a pristine navy jacket and white blouse, with a scarf carefully fluffed around her neck. Her hair was a sleeked-back black, the ends held in a bun and her face a lovely mask as perfect as the ones sold on the promenade outside.

"No. No I do not, but I had heard of the Denali and thought I would try it out."

She had the good grace to not look him up and down and instead check her computer screen. "Sir, there are no deluxe rooms available. I do have a luxury suite with lagoon view, if that would interest you."

She met his gaze then, as if it was a test. Ask for the room rate? He was sure that would give him less than a passing grade. And what was money for, other than to use it when you had need. All those years of living in the apartment on the AGS grounds, he'd had no need to spend money on much of anything until he bought the downtown apartment as an investment. A few lucky breaks with the stock market and he was not hurting for money.

He pulled his wallet out of the wad of his jacket and, with his clean hand, produced another credit card he had long had under an assumed name, but had never used. His other hand he kept wrapped in his jacket. Thank the creator he'd managed not to get more blood on his clothes. When the transaction was complete, he was ushered up to the room by a blue-uniformed young man who hovered too long after showing Landon the room. It took American dollars across the palm and then Landon almost had to shove him out the door.

He could finally breathe when the door shut and he was alone. He crossed to the open drapes and opened the sliding glass door out to the small, iron-grilled balcony. The illuminated spire of the Basilica di San Giorgio Maggiore shone on its island across the lagoon, the lights of boats shifting like wandering spirits across the waves. He looked down at his hand. Blood was caked under the nails and in the cuticles and in all the lines in the palm of his hand, and for a moment he felt like a wanderer, too. He had wandered so far from where all this was supposed to go and from his meditations.

He had only planned to question Xavier. Instead, he had used force. *Torture—name it for what it truly was.* When Xavier had been passed out, he had placed the tracking beacon deep in the man's injured forearm and then had doctored it as best he could before throwing up at what he had done.

And now he had killed a man.

A part of him felt shriveled and cold and ugly and old, like a dried and desiccated pea. Yes, that was what he felt like. His soul so old and shriveled, not even the beauty of Venice could reconstitute it. After all his years of purifying meditations, it had come to this.

Sighing, he turned back to the lovely suite, with its king-sized four-poster bed in the next room and the couches and chairs set up by the marble fireplace. He set up his computer on the breakfast table by the window and the screen sprang to life, this time with an aerial view of Venice with the snake-shaped Grand Canal, cutting through the center of the city. A red dot blinked north of the Piazza San Marco, close by the Rialto Bridge, where he had disembarked from the water taxi.

He closed his eyes and -reached-, and though the water-logged soil of Venice made sensing anything difficult, he could feel them there, like a volcanic fissure in the cool of the city.

"Well, I am here for you, my brothers. You cannot will me away so easily."

He left the computer open, the red light softly blinking its promise, as he went in search of a shower.

§

She was a flipping caged animal in a flipping luxury cage, that was what she was. Vallon paced the marble floor of the bedroom in the Cartos Council headquarters as the new day crept through the windows that gave onto the canal below. With her mind churning and the grey pall over everything, she hadn't slept at all last night. Xavier had sat up with her, trying repeatedly to justify his actions; she refused to listen. He had finally given up and gone to bed and still lay amid the tangle of the sheets, his head dark on the pristine white pillow.

She'd refused to join him even though his incense and cedar drew her. For a few hours, she'd curled on one of the chairs and dozed. Now lack of sleep placed gravel in her eyes, and a low-grade headache pulsed behind them.

It just couldn't be true. She was not the bastard daughter of some runaway Cartos woman, no matter that the old man had just about fainted when he saw her.

But he *had* just about fainted. And the way everyone else in the room had looked at her. But the look in Xavier's eyes said he *still* wasn't telling her everything. Something was going on, and the worst part of it was that it was stealing everyone's attention away from what was happening in Seattle.

None of this stuff about her parentage mattered. What did matter was stopping Amundson.

She leaned on the iron balcony railing, peering down into the murky canal water. Just like her life, murky and full of trouble, but calm looking on the surface. She practiced a smile down at the small reflection of her face, but a gust of sand from the pall made her close her eyes.

The old man, Victor, had tried to talk to her once since she'd been pushed back in this room, but she'd refused to see him. What did she need of another father figure who would disapprove of who she was and probably leave? No, she was nobody's daughter now, and her mother had always been dead. That was the one thing her father hadn't lied about.

A presence behind her and two warm arms came around her. The warm scent of incense and cedar filled her nose and she crossed her arms, her elbows feeling a little sharper as he leaned down to nuzzle her ear.

"You have not slept, *Bela*. Perhaps there is a way to lure you to the bed for just a brief time." His lips caught her earlobe and a part of her flared in response.

Instead, she tugged away. He was bare-chested and tousled and still flushed with sleep, his eyes heavy lidded and sensual, and oh, God, she loved him, but she could not trust him. Not when he would keep such an important truth from her.

"You expect me to just fall into your arms again? After you betray me like this?"

He opened his mouth as if he were going to try another of his lame excuses—protecting her, for the better, yadayadayada. She held up her hand.

He just threw up his hands and didn't try to touch her again. Instead, he turned away. Then he turned back. "You have the right to be angry—with me, with everyone—but you must deal and move on. Your parentage is ancient history. You are who you are, and that is all that matters. And I love you."

"Strong words, Xavier, but just who am I? What else aren't you telling me? Because when I look at you, all I see is a whole mess of secrets swarming in your eyes, and you're not telling me anything."

She glared at him, and wonder of wonders, Xavier looked away first. So she was right. He knew more and wasn't telling, and *that* just confirmed everything. She whirled away, back into the room. She had to get out of here. Went to the door, but when she opened it, Leticia's two Cartos guards were waiting. She slammed the door shut and turned back to Xavier and the claustrophobic room. The window, then. She could swim. The canal water was about the last thing she wanted touching her skin, but you did what you had to do, and right now she needed out.

She headed back to the balcony. Had swung one leg over the railing when Xavier grabbed her shoulders.

"What the hell do you think you are doing?" He pulled her back and she fought him. Punched his face, his stomach. He accepted her blows and still kept dragging her back as she pounded his shoulders. As she kicked him.

"Vallon, no." He pulled her into him, used his arms to imprison her even as she struggled.

Damn him for being so strong. Damn him for being so gentle when she wanted to kick and punch and fight.

His lips found her forehead. "You are as strong and honest and clear-sighted as your mother. You are also powerful like your father."

She stopped dead and looked up at him, hating that he was stronger than she was and could subdue her. "So?"

For a moment she thought she saw truth and honesty swimming up through his dark eyes, but they shuttered again as he shook his head. "You come from good stock, Vallon Drake. The very best. Your mother, almost Cartos royalty. Your father, strong and talented."

"Yeah. Sure. And he tried to kill me—more than once. So much for familial loyalty." The bitterness like aspirin in her mouth.

Strong, gentle hands stroked her hair and back. "What does Francis Drake matter, then? Or your mother? We each stand or fall on our own merits."

"Sure. I'll let that go when you let go of your relationship with your father."

She felt him stiffen and used the chance to pull away and step back. *Right back at you, buddy. Hit you where it hurts and I'm sorry, but… it doesn't take long in this world to forget how to trust.* She liked to think she was a quick study. No, her flesh might respond to this man, but he was no longer the person she'd thought she knew. She had to make plans on her own.

She retreated to the chair she'd occupied all night and slumped down in it, considering what to do. Leaving this place was top of her list.

Xavier slung himself in the chair across from her, his bare chest and delectable abs catching the light through the window. His large hands clenched the chair arms. God, she would like those hands on her, but that was over.

"I was wrong not to tell you, Vallon. I am truly sorry."

"I heard you the first time, but it doesn't stop you from still keeping secrets. Nothing will." Mexican standoff. She turned back to her thoughts and to the grey pall washing away the presence of the room.

They were still there when the urgent knock came at the door.

CHAPTER 18 —REVERBERATIONS OF DYING

A shower. A few hours of sleep. A clean shirt and his jacket, cuff still stained, but with the worst of the blood washed out of it and then blown dry with the complimentary hair drier provided in the suite. Breakfast of sublime espresso and jam-filled brioche on the terrace overlooking the gondola harbor, and now Landon pushed through the morning crowds, allowing his Gifted senses to lead him. He no longer needed the GPS to find what he sought. The auras of the Others glowed through the pale morning light like a beacon if one knew what to look for, and the hint of their mélange of scents came through the murky water and wafting odors from trattoria kitchens. The Others called him through the wandering crowds of retirees and newlyweds threading through the narrow streets, through the sound of voices over water, the clinks of metal housings, and the low rumble of the water taxis.

When he came to the spot where Erminio had died, Venetian carabinieres in black with bold white leather belts stood guard. Landon lowered his head and pushed past in the crowd in case anyone had seen him at the murder scene. No one yelled. No one grabbed him, but he still felt a target between his shoulders.

The narrow turns of uneven pavement guided him northward until he came out into the milling mass of people in the small square next to the Rialto Bridge. He kept his hand over his wallet and pushed through, still following the beacon of presence that waited a little further north. A small concrete bridge led him into a quieter area of restaurants and broader streets that looked more like places people might live, instead of a tourist area. He paused, lifted his head, and sniffed the air.

There. To his left. He threaded between two restaurants into a narrow alley that looked like it was only used to bring supplies to those establishments. Not exactly auspicious. Beyond them, the neat facades of the buildings had decayed to unexpected crumbling brick and graffiti.

There was no plastic feel of Change. Real age and disuse had done this. The few doors fronting the alley appeared boarded up and windows gaped empty from upper stories. Here and there foliage spilled through cracks in crumbling walls. Definitely unexpected. There was no hint of the opulence of the Denali or the faded grace of the moldering palaces on the Grand Canal. Broken grills jutted from windows. Graffiti covered walls like diseased murals. He came into what once had probably been a courtyard, but collapsed brick filled half the space. Ahead lay a dark thread of a canal, oozing with the stench of summer sewage. The tides didn't always manage to pull the effluence out to sea from these backwaters.

He stopped. This made no sense. The sense of the Others was so potent it was as if the morning light seemed to pulse in his eyes, but it made no sense that they would live in a place like this. With their power, they could own all of Venice. What did this place say about them? The ill-repair? The rotting buildings? A disguise? Were they so powerful they were beyond caring for the niceties of life? Or had he fooled himself about the power they wielded?

Clearly they had something to hide if they sent people like Erminio to every Gifted who came to the floating city. No, it made more sense that this was a disguise meant to ward off the usual tourist. What tourist would frequent such a place? It would be much easier to come and go unremarked without the crowds around you. It would also be much easier to get rid of unwelcome guests.

He needed to be very careful in what he did. But then, he *had* established contingencies. His hand came up to the cord around his neck and the device suspended from it. One push of the button and what he knew of the Others and their locations would be blasted out to the world's media. After the coverage of the Gifted in America, a group this secretive should be fairly tractable with that sort of threat hanging over their head.

There was no door in the derelict courtyard, but many of these old houses had only doors onto the water. He headed for the canal. This strip of water was barely eight feet across and dark and oily in the shadows of early morning. The pavement ended with three steps down to the oil-slicked liquid. To his left, a small, shadowed stone porch led to a gleaming black door, heavy with brass bolts and set into the stone. A circular mandala design eerily akin to some of his meditation guides was carved into the door with a small viewing port like a shuttered eye in its center. Situated as it was, the sun would mostly leave this spot in eternal shadows. And if that wasn't emblematic of the Others, what was? Beside the door stood a small brass plaque:

On this spot once stood the home of Marco Polo.

And that made perfect sense. Polo, with his great adventure from Europe to China and Southeast Asia, could easily have been one of them. Perhaps he was like Landon—searching for Others of his kind. A light mist rose from the darkling water.

Well, he was here. He knocked on the door and *felt* the regard of those in the building like a hot brand on his skin. They knew he was there and they were not happy. Well, to hell with them. He had committed too many sins to reach this place. He and Francis Drake had spent years of playing with his Pigeon's emotions and feeding her seeds of information in hopes that she would eventually lead him to this place.

The only part of *Gild the Lily* that was really important to him had finally come to fruition. Let Francis Drake keep his grandiose plans of world domination.

There were more important things in the world. Like finding those like him and gaining the knowledge that had eluded him all his life. Vallon, ripped from the arms of her dying mother, was part of it. Drake had wanted to raise the child to be his tool in advancing the Gifted in the world. Landon, had seen other possibilities, like the fact that any Other child was liable to get the Others' attention when she started using her Gift. *Gild the Lily* had been the plan to put Vallon into situations that required significant displays of power, both to test her and to force the Others to make contact. For there were different types of power in the world. The overt kind Francis Drake lusted for, and the more subtle power Landon had cultivated during his years of study.

A sharp click reverberated in the silence and the small viewing port opened, revealing bright, golden light and the darkness of a silhouette— man—woman—he couldn't say.

"Chi sei? Che cosavolete?" Who are you? What do you want?

A woman, then, with a voice rich and fluid and full of condescension. Landon drew himself taller. "I am Landon Snow from America. I wish to speak to your leader."

He saw the figure pause; knew the small window in the door was about to slam shut.

"Tell your leader I am prepared to tell the world what I know about you if he does not speak to me. And tell him that if I disappear, that information will also be distributed."

The port snapped closed and he stood in the shadows, still waiting. They would consider killing him. Perhaps they would even try, but he doubted it. A people that had lived in secrecy like this could not afford to take the chance of disclosure.

The sun rose above the city and became a single, angry eye in the sky, watching and waiting to see what he would do.

§

Vallon Drake had to be the most frustrating woman in the world and he was almost out of patience. Anger radiated off of her like a furnace in the room as she slouched in the chair across the empty hearth from him. A salt-scented morning breeze from the window stirred strands of her blonde hair across her face.

Stroke them back from her lips. Tell her his story and why he truly had kept the truth from her. The tension in her limbs even at rest reminded him so much of his mother sometimes it took his breath away. Always running off on some mission. Always stepping into danger. Unlike his father, who, through his actions, had almost sent his mother out into the world to die, when Vallon had thought he slept, he had kept vigil all night for fear Vallon would try something similar.

The knock at the door broke Xavier free of his ruminations.

Vallon roused to glance at the door while he rose to answer it.

The air off the canal was cool and moist and rustled the curtains around the balcony so a soft murmur seemed to fill the high-ceilinged room. Vallon hugged herself and rose to follow him. He pulled the door only partially open; Vallon had enough challenges without facing Leticia's venom.

But it wasn't Leticia. Hector Gonzales stood there.

"Si?" Xavier asked.

"I'm fine, Xavier. Let them in," Vallon said, as usual rejecting his protection.

Hector, looking less intimidating outside of the Council chamber, wore his new style of flowing cream trousers and tunic as if he'd lounged through the night. But the tell-tale pinch of lines between his eyes and the downturn of his lips said this wasn't the case.

"It seems we have a problem," he said, stepping into the room with a nod in Vallon's direction.

"Si. There is a growing one under the streets of Seattle. We need your aid to address it.

"No. You mistake me." Hector shook his head. "One of your Gifted has arrived at our doorstep."

"One of mine?" Xavier asked. "I have no Gifted."

"Who?" Vallon stepped past him. "Has someone brought news of Seattle? Have things gotten worse? Has the Council made a decision? We need to take action against Amundson quickly." For a moment fear flared through her aura, but then she controlled herself.

Hector's face was grim as he faced Xavier. "I thought your loyalties ran deep—aside from the woman. Your long refusal to help us on that other matter was understandable. I made allowances. But now this…."

Xavier shook his head. "*No entiendo.* What are you talking about? My loyalty will always be to Cartos-kind—except where Vallon is concerned."

But Vallon did not want his protection. She had always worked alone—always would. It was something he must accept—or not.

"The only people who know where we are, are Fi and Jack. Are they here?" she asked.

"That raises another matter. You endangered one of our most valuable assets in North America to come here. There are few enough healers as it is." Hector strode across to the window, his tunic and trousers flowing around him. Before he stepped onto the balcony, he stopped and pulled the double doors closed against the morning. "Who is this Fi?"

"My friend. A Gifted," Vallon said.

"Jack says she is a healer as well, though untrained. It seems there are potentialities amongst the Gifted that the Council has never foreseen," Xavier said. Another deficit in the growing list of holes in the Council's knowledge and actions.

Hector frowned. "But there have never been healers amongst the Gifted." His hands scrubbed his hair and he went to Vallon's chair and sank down. "Creation, what is happening? The Gifted do not heal, just as they do not arrive on our very doorstep. We have safeguards against it."

Xavier sighed. Hector had become as rigid and blind as Xavier's father had been, and Carlos—placed on the Council supposedly to ease the rift that had developed between young Cartos and their elders—had been nothing but a token. As long as their father was alive, Carlos was simply their father's puppet. "All the years of refusing to reach out to the world, or to listen to my and others' advice, and this is what happens. The world arrives on your doorstep. Who is it, Hector? Who do you think we have led here?"

Scrubbing his face wearily, Hector looked up at him. "A small albino man. He says if we do not let him in, he will send our location to the world's media. He says that if he dies the same will happen." Hector seemed dazed, as if he could not quite fathom everything that had happened. "He says his name is Landon Snow."

Xavier froze, then flexed his now-healed hand. "Snow. Now that is a score I would like to even."

"I can deal with Landon for you," Vallon said, stepping up to Hector.

"This is what it was all about," Xavier said, suddenly understanding. "This is why he interrogated me—to get to you."

Vallon's gaze met his and froze. She sank down in the chair Xavier had vacated. "It makes sense. *Gild the Lily* was about raising the Gifted— what better way than joining with the Cartos. He always called me his pigeon. *As in homing pigeon, maybe?* He knew what I was. He's always told me his theories of the Others—Gifted who have more power than our Gifted do. In other words, Cartos." She hugged herself, looking weak and confused, but then she took a deep breath and all of her masks fell into place, like a player in the Venetian passion play. She looked up, all cool and calculating.

"He's known all along. He's done this breeding program amongst the Gifted to increase the Gift, but what if that wasn't all? What if he traced bloodlines back and that was how he found my mother? He and my father." She scrubbed her face. "They found her and found out she was pregnant or got her pregnant. Then they held her prisoner until she had her child and then she either died as a result of childbirth, or—or they killed her. All those years, they waited for me to lead them to others like me. He knew eventually it would happen, or that you would find me." Her gaze locked on Xavier.

Her skin had taken on a greenish tinge, even though her mask was calm. She shook her head as if trying to accept this horrible news about men she had trusted. No, men she had *loved*. Betrayal by a father he could understand, and the cold, hard place it created in your heart. It was no wonder she did not trust him.

"It's about finding the Cartos and somehow controlling them, as well as the Gifted. Dad and Landon figured I'd do something to catch someone's attention because I have too much power. They were counting on me to either screw up or find my way here—to you." She met Hector's gaze. "Apparently they were right. I'm sorry."

"You did not tell them where we were, *Bela*. This is not at your feet."

"Either way, we can't leave Landon to do what he's threatening. We need to know what he wants."

Hector stood. "Will you meet him with us?"

"It is not a good idea, Vallon. Snow manipulates you too well," said Xavier.

She shook her head. "Not now, when I know it. You can stay here if you want. After what he did to you, I'd understand."

No way in hell. He -reached- for power through the sodden soil as he pulled on a black chamois shirt. He would immolate the little creature for what he had done—both to himself and to this woman. Vallon pulled on her Daytons and then they followed Hector to the Council Chamber. The comfortable grumble of the Venetian *vaporetto* reached them from the canal outside, and the familiar voices of shopkeepers came through the open balcony of the Chamber and echoed in the high painted ceilings; a salty harbor breeze stirred the dark tapestry draped behind the half-circle of Council chairs. Hector slumped into the horse-carved, high-backed chair, but the other eight chairs remained empty. Clearly they did not want to expose more people than necessary. The other Cartos waited below and would probably leave via the canal once Landon was brought to the floor above. His arrival had caught them by surprise. Hector waved Xavier and Vallon to a spot near the wall.

"The white one has the Gift. He will know they are escaping," Xavier said.

Vallon nodded beside him. "I doubt he'll allow it."

"Allow it! Who does he think he is?"

"The man who holds exposure over your heads?" Vallon asked sweetly and crossed her arms.

A single rap on the door and Leticia burst into the Chamber. She was clad in her usual spike heels and leather leggings, but wore a blood red, ruffled, sheer organza blouse with nothing underneath, leaving little to the imagination. Her dark hair was twisted up into a severe figure eight that was held at the back of her head by chopsticks. A single fire opal hung at the base of her neck, but there the cool dominatrix of Leticia ended. Her face was flushed with fury and a thick strand of hair had come loose. Xavier inserted himself between her and Vallon as she came to a stop in the center of the room.

"That damned little man will not come unless the others show themselves. He says he knows they plan to leave."

Hector slumped in his chair and sighed. "Then I suppose you must retrieve them."

Striding past the Council chairs, Leticia pushed through the tapestry.

Springing up to pace, Hector turned on Xavier. "Damn it, do you see what you've done to us? The danger you've placed us in?"

"It's me he's followed. Not Xavier." Vallon stepped up beside Xavier and it almost felt like she was with him again.

"But it was Xavier's infatuation that made it possible."

She glanced sideways at Xavier, conflict in her gaze. "It should never have happened."

And would never happen again, given what he read in her stance. It was over between them, and a hollow grief in his chest echoed a far older pain that had changed his life and led to the man he was.

The sound of returning footfalls came from beyond the curtain and Leticia and eight others returned. Last through were Victor of Lisboa and another man. Not Carlos, who filled the de Varga family seat from the Algarve.

Xavier froze.

His father.

Demetrio de Varga strode to the seat usually filled by Carlos. It had been years since Xavier had been face-to-face with him, and in truth, his father did not seem much changed. Still tall and straight, with black hair streaked with gray and a hawk nose that was quite possibly the only thing Xavier inherited from him. As always, he wore an immaculate sable-colored suit over immaculate white shirt and black tie. He crossed one slim ankle over his knee and radiated cardamom and pine scented power that overwhelmed the auras of the other Council members. Just like always. His father, a throwback to the old days of power of the Council.

His father's presence dared to invade Xavier's own, just as it had always invaded everyone he confronted, but Xavier braced himself against the pressure. Oh yes, the man was nothing if not consistent. Domination was all he knew and all he would propagate.

He felt, rather than saw, Vallon come up beside him.

"Your father?" she murmured.

He gave the barest of nods. His father's gaze had slipped to Vallon and he would not have the beast of a man harming her. He spread his presence across the room, hardening it into a barrier. His father's will slammed into him with the overpowering scents of cardamom and pine.

Vallon caught his hand. "I can take care of myself." Her aura flared.

[*No. You cannot. You do not know him. Demetrio de Varga holds levels of treachery you could never understand.*] He held his presence like a shield around them.

Then suddenly his father's pressure ended and Xavier took a deep breath. He still didn't lower his shields, for his father's face was too dark and dangerous. Well, let him be angry. Let him be as angry as his son had been for too many years.

[*What is it?*] Vallon asked.

[*He is not happy with his youngest son. He never has been.*] He focused on the man who had betrayed everything he had held dear so many years before.

[*He has a lot of power. A father like that—it must have been difficult growing up.*]

No one could understand. The memories of his childhood and youth were best locked away. Demetrio de Varga had disowned his youngest son years ago. Not that Xavier hadn't disowned his father first, but even now, all these years later, a part of him had hoped that his father would approve of his service to the Council. Apparently, that was not the case. He flexed his hands. Would prefer to be striking something, flesh on flesh. His father's face would be a good target.

But not here, not now. There were other matters to be dealt with. Like Landon Snow. Leticia left the Council chamber for him.

"You realize that by fully giving in, you have given Landon his first victory," Vallon said to the Council. The pressure on his aura eased and all conversation stopped as they turned to her. Unfriendly gazes, every one—except old Victor—and Demetrio inspected her as he would a strange insect that had had the ill grace to fall into his wine.

"May I suggest that at least a few of you step back behind the curtain?" she offered. "He may know you're there, but it shows that you don't just do as he tells you."

A suggestion he should have expected from Vallon, given she had never, to his knowledge, just acquiesced to any command. The council looked at each other. Then Voda stood, her luxuriant mane of black hair belying the age lines around her eyes. "She has a point. I will go."

"And I," old Victor said.

"I suggest you leave now," Vallon said.

"You presume a great deal, young woman," Xavier's father said. "Some may accept your parentage based on a cursory look." He cast a dismissive glance at Victor. "I, however, am a more cautious man. You may be no more than a Gifted trick—or that of some less loyal Cartos."

Xavier sent more power into his protective aura, but Hector waved a hand at Xavier's father. "Demetrio, it is this Landon Snow we must deal with. Leave your family bickering for another time." He suffered a glare from Demetrio that had sent many men cowering and sat back in his seat.

"I take it you believe this Snow will not expose us even though we do not fully comply." Victor paused at the black curtain.

Vallon nodded.

The old man considered a moment and then he nodded and caught Voda's arm. "Then we shall leave. Come, dear. Our water taxi awaits."

The curtain closed behind them, and none-too-soon, for the sharp *click-click-click* of Leticia's heels approached down the corridor. A single sharp rap on the door and the heavy wood swung open to admit the familiar, diminutive figure of Landon Snow and his wafting baby powder scent.

It was him: the same wispy, white hair that had spun a halo around his head at the same time as he dissected Xavier's living hand. The same man who, like a strip miner, had mined the secrets of Xavier's mind.

There were differences in Landon Snow, too. Instead of the usually pristine Landon, this one's jacket looked rumpled and even carried damp stains on one sleeve cuff when he usually exuded a sense of foppishness.

Xavier fought to steady himself when all he wanted was the little man's throat in his hands.

Snow turned a brief glance in Vallon's direction, then scanned the room like a hungry man at a banquet. A look of satisfaction filled his face.

"This? This is the danger?" Demetrio demanded with a snicker. "What do you want little man? Before we send you crawling back to the cave you crawled out of."

A slow smile formed on Snow's face as if he enjoyed the consternation he caused. Xavier worked his now-healed hand against the stiffness he doubted would ever leave. And here stood his tormentor, smiling, within easy reach.

Vallon laid a hand on his arm as if she knew what he was thinking.

"Mr. Snow," Hector said, breaking the tension in the room. "To what do we owe this pleasure?"

Snow scanned the council members, then stepped forward, hand outstretched. "I'd say well-met, but you have me at a disadvantage."

Leticia grabbed his shoulder.

The little man froze. His hand fumbling to his chest. "I suggest you have your viper unhand me."

Viper indeed—but the air vibrated with cardamom and pine as Demetrio tried power against Snow. For a moment Xavier couldn't decide who he would prefer to win any altercation. The air thickened around Snow, but he didn't change. His fine hair only lifted from his head.

Vallon stepped to his side. "Landon, this is the Council. They don't use names with people they don't know. What do you want? How did you get here?"

She placed herself between Demetrio and Snow, and Xavier froze. Would his father try something?

"Why, I followed you, of course," He said looking up at her.

"How? You weren't in Seattle when I was there. Nor in Canada."

"Actually it was your mysterious friend," he said casting a glance at Xavier. "I slipped a little something in his arm. A biological tracking device, as it were. I'd hoped it would withstand his teleportation, and it seems it did." He glanced back again. "How is the hand? I'm sorry that things came to that, but I needed the information." He nodded at Xavier's hand. "I tried to put it all back as I'd found it."

Xavier raised a fist.

"Very good." Snow nodded.

And turned back to Hector as if Xavier's anger was of little matter. Well, he would show the gnome what he thought of him. He would let him experience the pain firsthand.

"First, let me apologize for arriving unannounced. I would have sent my card before me, but it seems that your agents are determined to deter anyone Gifted from entering the city. I had a rather unfortunate meeting with a man named Erminio. Unfortunate for him, that is. So I thought it best that I come directly myself and advise you of the situation."

The council members glanced at each other.

Aziz of the coriander scent and the Arabic robes suddenly sat upright. "Erminio is gone."

Hector straightened. "Dead, then, I presume." His gaze raked Snow's small form with a deeper assessment and the other Council members stirred. "What do you want, then, Mr. Snow? What is worth the life of one of my men and potentially the safety of all Cartos people?"

"All?" Snow sniffed. "Do you truly presume to speak for all Cartos? According to Mr. de Varga, here, you've already broken into two factions."

Xavier leapt across the room and had Snow in a satisfying choke hold before Leticia could react. "You have no right to speak of things you learned by raiding my mind."

Then Leticia's stiletto was at his throat. The Cartos Council were on their feet, yelling—all except Xavier's father.

"Xavier, no!" Vallon's voice.

"You will unhand him," Leticia's voice in his ear.

Vallon grabbed Leticia and yanked her away. "Stop it! Stop it right now! There are Gifted dying as we stand here. The void eats at Seattle and you squabble like children."

Xavier released Snow because she was right. He'd seen. He'd felt.

She turned on her mentor. "All those years I thought you were my friend and protector, but you were just grooming me to lead you here, weren't you?"

A shrug was all the explanation she got, and that must hurt, for she had trusted and even loved this man growing up. But, as usual, Vallon rose above her circumstances. She stepped in close to Snow. "Answer them. With the truth, for once."

Finally he nodded and turned back to the Council.

"Let me apologize if my business seems nefarious. I assure you, it is not. As I said, I come to you only to meld pieces of the Cartos race back into one."

"Damnation, Xavier! Is that what this is?" Demetrio leapt to his feet. "Another of your idiot attempts to honor your mother's foolishness? There is no Cartos Alliance—only a ragtag scattering of disaffected runaways who play at make-believe. They've no more power and no more right to rule than you have."

"Or you, father," said Xavier. "Something you and your illustrious colleagues on this Council have failed to recognize. It is a new world out there. Yet you continue to rule in the same fashion as was used in the Middle Ages."

Demetrio waved his argument away. "Your mother's words, parroted. They're no more ready to rule than—than you are. Upstarts, rebels. Traitors. Terrorists."

"And I name you fools. All of you!" Xavier swung around to the Council. He did not want this argument now. Not ever. He'd done his best to hide his allegiances, to remain neutral in the tug-of-war between the generations. He'd tried to gently ease both factions toward understanding. "Human action threatens Pangea's very life and yet you refuse to act. Yes, there are old edicts we must live by, but someone has to preserve what remains of the world we knew."

"So, what?"Demetrio said. "We Change the earth to fit our vision of what it should be? But wait, who is to say that what we perceive as positive change is not destruction to someone else? So do we take a chance on the edict's destruction arising just because we disagree with what the humans are doing? I say we are Cartos—preservers. We do not invest our power in rampant Change!" He thumped down in his chair in disgust and turned to Hector and the Council. "It is a black day in Cartos history if you entertain this."

"You're the fool, father, if you think that is all we can do. We can undo the damage caused to the world. Replenish the coral reefs, clean the river beds, stop the mine runoff. Stop the desertification. But you refuse to act. Is that why you took back your chair, father? You did not trust your puppet to be your mouthpiece? Perhaps he expressed views similar to my own. Perhaps you've sent him on some task he will not come back from. Isn't that how you work? Push your problem loved ones out into the world to die? Isn't that what you did to your wives?" Xavier's chest clenched with old emotion. "I apologize for not being as obliging as my mother."

The room went silent and icy cold. Then Demetrio lunged to his feet and a blast of heat struck Xavier's aura. "Your mother was a fool— trying to protect the rainforest and its people. It was not my doing when the logging companies took her. No one knew there was a problem."

"And I name you liar. I heard her call. She screamed for your aid, for they took her unawares and asleep before she could save herself. You refused to answer or to help her."

"By then she'd no doubt been shot and was dead."

"You didn't even try to protect her. Not even to retrieve her body. I did that, and I was fifteen years old." His voice cracked and he hated himself for the weakness it showed. "You never loved her. You shut her out because you couldn't control her, so she was nothing to you."

"You are wrong." Demetrio had gone still as the dead.

"You never loved anyone but yourself."

"I loved your mother. I just couldn't stop her from destroying herself." The room went even more quiet, if that were possible.

Hate burned through Xavier's chest and he blasted power at his father. For a moment his father's pine and cardamom scent flickered and faded and Demetrio fell back a pace. Then his own aura steadied and flared as the two forces met.

"People. People. It appears I have opened old wounds, and for that I apologize, but I know nothing of these matters." The horrible little man stepped between them.

Vallon tugged Xavier around, forcing him to break the eye contact with his father that *he should never have allowed.* The man was a menace to everything because he cared only for himself and his power. Xavier ripped his hand out of Vallon's grasp, but he fought back his anger. He inhaled her ashes of roses and—for a moment, at least—let it calm him.

"If you are not speaking of the Alliance of young Cartos, then of whom are you speaking?" demanded tiny Norvanahpum of Southeast Asia. "We will not recognize the Gifted as our brethren because their blood cannot be traced back to specific Cartos lines."

"An odd logic, given the Gifted hold powers similar to yours, but no, no Gifted and no Alliance," said Snow. "I'm talking about the division of the Cartos race that occurred at the time of the great cataclysm." He held up his hands to stop the murmured protests. "Yes, I know your history and my own. Your own man confirmed my family's legends when I had him under my control."

All eyes in the room pointed accusations at Xavier. "When have I had a chance to inform you? You have kept us locked away."

"You're despicable. You destroyed his hand for information." Vallon said.

Snow only shrugged. "It was simple, really. Drugs for the pain of his wounds were easy to mix with something that would loosen his tongue. When that did not work, well, I had other means at my disposal."

"Torture, you mean," Vallon said.

Snow at least had the grace to color slightly, but he turned back to Hector. "I know that the cataclysm divided the Cartos people and many were lost. I know that some came together into small communities and you are their descendants. I know that there were others who survived on their own and interbred with nonCartos, spreading the blood out into the general population that has now coalesced again into the Gifted. And I know that there were individuals amongst the lost ones who were aware of their loss—their history and knowledge and their access to a hidden power. Throughout their lives they labored to find the secret of returning to that power, brewing potions, collecting the sacred dew and seeking to turn themselves into the *prima material—you*. Legends remember them as fools who attempted to create gold out of lead."

"Alchemists," Vallon breathed, and Xavier remembered the tales of strange men and women and secret texts that his mother had told him.

If anything, Snow stood up straighter as he scanned the room. "I am such lead, and I stand here to demand that you relinquish the secret you have hidden from us all these years."

The room again went still around them, the ubiquitous sound of the *vaporetto* on the canals a distant rumble. Then an apple and cut-grass scented wind flooded up from the floor. Xavier went rigid. Every Cartos in the room froze. The scent caught on a breeze from outside and disappeared as swiftly as it had come. He recognized the scent.

"Jack," said Norvanahpum from her seat in the half-circle.

Something had happened on the far side of the world.

CHAPTER 19 — THE EMPTINESS OF EVERYTHING

Jack's kitchen seemed to spin around Fi as she sought for signs of life in Jack's body. But the strong, clear aura was gone. His scent of apples faded as if sucked into the ground. Oh, God. Oh, God. She had to save him. Had to bring him back, because what did she know about what he'd said? What did it mean that Jason was made or that when Jason moved, his unGifted aura seemed to shift the fields of the earth, like a tiny moon in orbit.

A strong hand bit into her shoulder and yanked her up. "Too late, Fi. There's nothing you can do for him. If it's any consolation, I didn't mean for that to happen."

"He was my friend, damn you. My teacher. My lover. The first person who ever made me feel like I was worth something!"

She wheeled on him and swung. Her palm branded Jason's face and he stumbled back, releasing her. She leapt back to escape, but tripped over Jack. Before she could right herself, Jason had her shoved against the counter, his snarl right next to her face.

This was no Jason she knew. Instead of spicy aftershave, he smelled of sour sweat and bile.

"Try that again and you'll pay, Fi. Do as you're told and you might actually live. Understand?"

Then he dragged her toward the door, his fingers biting into her arm.

"Please." Tears blinded her. "Please." She twisted in his grip. "We can't leave Jack like this. He doesn't deserve that. He doesn't."

"He's dead, Fi. Nothing you can do for him now."

He dragged her roughly out the door into the cool, lunchtime air. The smell of wet soil, of moldering leaves, filled the chill breeze. The sound of a train rumbled in the distance. He dragged her to the nondescript brown car that had been purchased when they were all in New Madrid. So long ago. Everything had seemed so normal then. Happy, even though they had been so concerned about what was happening in Seattle. Everyone had treated her as a child then. But now she was an adult.

She jerked in Jason's grasp. "Where are we going? What are you going to do to me?"

Jason's face was mottled red and ugly and his fingers dug so hard into her arm she knew she'd be bruised.

"You, Fi, are going to help me show Vallon what happens to people who aren't my friend."

He shoved her up against the car and dragged her arms behind her.

"Jason, no. Please. I won't try anything. Please." The quicksand of fear sucked down her resolve.

In answer, he applied too-tight plastic cuffs and shoved her in the passenger side. He seat-belted her in, effectively trapping her hands behind her.

"Where are you taking me?" she tried again as he slid into the driver's seat.

"Back where we should be. Where Vallon should be. I left a business card on the table. She'll know what that means."

The car started and he aimed them out of the pot-holed driveway of the little house that had seemed like such a paradise. Now, it just filled her with sorrow. Jack. He had helped them and look what it had got him. But then, not much good came to those who were around Vallon and the AGS.

"Vallon won't come for me. She doesn't care about me anymore." A lie, but it might work.

Jason just guided the car onto the pavement and accelerated, back toward the highway. When he finally did look at her, the feral light in his eyes sent her heart racing even faster.

"She'll come, because either she does, or I kill you."

§

The afternoon sunlight on the AGS Academy playing field seemed too bright, the running figures of his people too exposed as Francis pounded after them toward the trees beyond the Academy. Young Derrick

Brown led the way and others of his trained ex-agents held a loose formation around him, guarding the flanks of the hurrying women and children. They were sitting ducks. Entirely too vulnerable, and that was impossible.

They were Gifted. They held more power in their little fingers than any unGifted had in their entire body. The Gifted power should be able to deal with the armed men coming through the school like the proverbial hot knife through butter, just as they had dealt with the National Guard troops at Anacortes. Except this time they couldn't.

Something had inserted a straw in his chest and sucked him dry. His bones, his chest felt almost hollow and his shoulders itched, waiting for the bullet that could come if they weren't in the trees by the time Amundson's men reached the back of the school.

Damn it, he was stronger than this. He was the predator, the tiger in the brush, never the prey. But this time the hunters were out after him. He was *not* going to stand for it—would find a way to turn the tables again.

"Faster," he hissed and tucked two lagging children under his arms. He loped along and the group seemed to pick up speed. Then the trees were around them, cloaking them in shadows and the strong scent of cedar and moldering earth.

None too soon. When he looked back over his shoulder, a black-clad man appeared in the open door of the cafeteria. He spoke into a radio.

"Gone," came his voice over the playing field. "We've got six bodies inside, all from gunshot wounds."

Drake realized he was holding his breath as the figure disappeared again, presumably to continue the search of the building. That gave them a bare few minutes of reprieve.

"Keep going," he said to Derrick Brown, and the runner-built, brown-haired ex-agent gave a nod and led off into the forest like he knew where he was going, but then, he should. Brown had disappeared right out of these very halls in his senior year only a few years before. Some of the mothers and fathers groaned, but they urged their children on, trying to maintain the quiet. Everyone understood what was at stake. Even the children.

The forest was a mess of low huckleberry brush, tangled willow, fern, and fungus between the moss-covered trunks of the huge cedars. Late afternoon sunlight leaked sideways from the playing fields, but gradually disappeared behind them. The three Gifted Drake had sent to clear the forest materialized out of the gloom and joined them. The forest filled with the wind in the treetops, the occasional bird call, and the over-loud snap and crack of breaking underbrush from their passage. Each time a branch broke he glanced over his shoulder. So far so good.

The earth cut away under them down into a gulley, following a narrow path that traversed down the steep ravine toward a narrow runnel of water. The earth was soft and crumbly underfoot, as if the last few weeks of no rain had left the area parched. But that wasn't it.

Drake -reached-, and the forest soil felt as empty as his chest. Trees were weakly flickering candles around them. Dying. But he could only sense the trees closest to him. The rest was darkness, as if the whole place were dead. Because of whatever denied him access to the ley lines? How was that possible? How did one cut off the earth's power?

The cool of the forest turned a little colder. What had Amundson done? How could he, Francis Drake, be like a blind man, stumbling through an ill-kept suburban forest?

From the top of the ravine came a shout and gunfire that exploded into the soil beside him. The time for silence was over.

"Move!" he shouted.

Derrick ran, leading their small party across the soft floor of the gulley, the small stream, and along the gulley wall on the far side. There were no more gunshots, presumably because they were out of range. This side of the ravine was too steep to climb—a near-vertical drop of about fifty feet. If they didn't find the way out, they'd be sitting ducks for Amundson's men from the gulley edge and all the vehicles they'd secreted in the area would be worth exactly nothing to their escape.

Another shout from behind, and a figure on the gulley edge said that was exactly what was going to happen.

"Go. Go. Go!" He shoved the two children he'd helped at two other agents and caught what must have been a five-year-old girl who labored behind her mother. He scooped her up. Her mother had a toddler in her arms. The little girl sobbed into his shoulder, her arms wrapped around his neck. She smelled like baby shampoo and fresh soap that reminded him of Vallon as a small child.

Damn it, he was *responsible* for these people. They, and the few other AGS agents who might have escaped, held the entire hope of the Gifted race. If he got them killed, not only would his plans be over, he would have killed any possibility of ever fighting against Amundson.

Amundson's future promised a world of constant purging of anyone who showed signs of the Gift.

He could not allow that to happen. He would not.

Derrick Brown fell back beside him as the others spilled down the length of the gully.

"What is this thing, Drake? How the hell do we stop it?"

"You know as much as I do. We just have to hope it doesn't extend too far."

"You think he could do this over the entire country?" Derrick's face had paled.

"How am I supposed to know what Amundson has up his sleeve?" But what if that was the case? What if other governments bought the technology or developed it themselves?

He glanced back over his shoulder. The figure had disappeared from the gulley edge. The fact they hadn't just mowed his party down with machine gun fire suggested Amundson wanted them alive. That gave them a chance. The little girl whimpered in his arms.

"It's all right. We're going to get you to safety." He hurried after the others, Derrick racing to catch up with the front-runners just as a shout suggested that someone had found the trail up their side of the gulley.

They had. It was a steep, unforgiving trail almost straight up this side of the ravine. The mother ahead of him slipped and slid as she struggled to climb with the little one in her arms.

"Sweetheart, can you climb on your own? I need to help your mom."

The little girl looked up at him for the first time. Heart-faced with loose brown curls, she nodded.

"Good girl." He set her down, quickly relieved the woman of the toddler. "Now climb."

The little girl scooted up the trail like an unlikely mountain goat. Her mother, now able to use her hands, pulled herself up using brush to the sides of the trail. Drake labored behind, fighting the slippery soil one-handed.

Voices behind said Amundson's men were too close. He lunged up the last few feet of trail and found the rest of the Gifted waiting for him.

"Move. They're right behind us."

"Where are we aiming for?"

"Our vehicles. Then the industrial park beyond the housing development." Beyond that he wasn't sure. Just out of this dead zone.

They kept going. Women with children sobbed quietly. Male and female agents slung their weapons and picked up the smallest children to increase their speed. The forest thinned and the back fences of semi-rural properties sprang up on their left. Then the trees ended on a huge tract of new homes and playgrounds placed cheek by jowl in an area where every tree had been razed.

Derrick stopped at the tree-edge, clearly not trusting the openness. Understandable, but they had no choice. Francis felt naked and exposed when he stepped past the others and out of the forest. But there was only the sound of a lawnmower, cutting end-of-the-season lawn. He nodded back at his people.

"Hide your weapons. If anyone asks, you were on a nature trek to show the children what lives in their backyard." He scanned the faces, reading their fear, gauging their resolve. "Given we're east of town, they'll probably expect us to head east. I suggest we surprise them and head somewhere else. Oregon. The coast. Lincoln City."

"But the ocean…" Derrick said.

"Yes, the ocean masks the power, but I'm also hoping it will make it harder for Amundson to do whatever it is he's done here. We'll know better when we reach the edge of whatever this is. If it gradually subsides, then it suggests that it comes from a central source and that may be a problem. But if it ends suddenly, it probably means that they had to set up a perimeter. That'll be harder for them to do on a coast line." He hoped. "Everyone okay?"

A ragged set of nods.

"Good. Then I suggest we break up into family groups and head for our vehicles as swiftly as we can, because Amundson's men are coming fast behind us. I'll see you on the Oregon coast." He handed the toddler back to his mother and walked away, leaving them to copy him. He glanced once over his shoulder.

They did.

CHAPTER 20 — STORM WATCH

Shocked silence replaced the rush of apple and cut-grass scent in the opulently furnished Cartos Council chamber. Landon stood transfixed as it faded. He had never experienced something like this.

From outside the broad balcony doors came the distant hum of music and raucous water taxi engines, carrying tourists to their daily pleasures, but everything here was still. Not even the angry dark one moved from his seat at the end of the council chairs, and neither did Vallon or Xavier.

"Jack?" Landon chose to break the tableau. "And who is Jack?"

Everyone started talking at once, but not anything that he wanted to hear about. The Council members, this motley bunch of secret-hoarders, used whatever had just happened to ignore his demand.

"Stop it! Silence!" He shouted into the din. He dragged the small button on the neck chain out of his shirt. "Silence, or I send this information to the media!"

All conversation cut off like a knife. He peered around until he was sure he had everyone's attention. Even the snarling man who could only be Xavier's relative—father, perhaps?—sat slit-eyed and angry, but silent. So they could be cowed. Good.

"Now that I have your undivided attention, I'll ask again: what was that?"

"Jack," Vallon echoed the name the small, golden-skinned woman had mentioned. "What can have happened? What about Fi?"

"Who is Jack?" he continued, determined to get his answer.

The nameless man who had greeted him when he'd entered the chamber motioned everyone to silence from his seat in the center of the half-circle of chairs. "One of our people. A great man in his own right. That was his death knell, his essence returning to Pangea."

Interesting. The dead man must have held a great deal of power, indeed.

The council members bowed their heads. The small woman who had first spoken wiped at her eyes.

"Because of this one's betrayal," said the dark man he suspected of being Xavier's father. He glared at Xavier. So there truly was no love lost between Xavier and his father. Xavier had been more truthful than he'd realized during interrogation. Interesting.

"He brought nonCartos into our midst. He is most likely to blame for Jack's demise," the dark man continued.

"That is no business of Landon Snow," commanded the Council spokesman. "Would you bare our soul to an interloper?"

Interloper. *Interloper!*

"I am no interloper. Nor am I just what you call Gifted. I am your kin by blood and passion. I demand access to your knowledge. This one," he pointed to Xavier. "He says my kind were killed in the witch hunts. That it was your kind that left them to die. But they can't have gotten everyone. I want to know where their decedents are. I want to know the secret of how to commune with the Creator. I want to know how to access my power." They were looking at him as if he were a mad man. As if they would lock him away and deny him. Well, he would see about that. "You have one choice: tell me, or I release this information."

He raised the button on the chain. Please let them believe him. For all his threats, he did not want to destroy such an ancient institution. It would surely be destroyed if the world got wind of its existence. He could imagine the secrets locked in the brains of these men and women and in this moldering building, and what would be lost should it go up in flames. But he would do it, if they left him no choice. He had lived his entire life searching for answers, and now that he finally was face-to-face with the people who had them, he would not take no for an answer.

"Well?" he asked.

It wasn't defiance that faced him from the Council members. Instead, the tiny woman and the man in eastern robes would not meet his gaze—almost as if they were ashamed. Xavier's father lounged thoughtfully back in his chair, and the Council leader looked at him with a mix of emotions that shifted into—pity.

Landon froze, his finger tight on the button.

Pity, he remembered too well from his childhood. Even Sylvia, the first and last woman he had ever loved, looked at his scrawny frame and his pale, white, sun-vulnerable skin and eyes with such an expression as they grew from childhood into adolescence.

"I *will* do this."

The Council leader nodded. "We see that you will, but we have no secrets to give you, brother. Your people were lost to us long ago. Through the years, they chose a different path. They dared not use their meager powers, and over the years—with generations of intermarriage with nonCartos—the possibility of those powers dwindled and was gone from our knowledge. We have not met a true Alchemist in many generations."

"A lie." It had to be. His mother would not have lied to him all those years before. He had been only ten, and mightily scrawny, an outcast from all the other children. It had been only a year before his father died in a car accident. On a warm evening outside Tabor, Iowa, seated on the front porch; the maple trees had been doing their hushed sighing as the last of the sun dappled their leaves, and barbeque coal and lighter fluid had tanged the air. His mother had sat down beside him and explained why their family was different from others. They had a *history,* a secret one that involved a relationship to a greater power. His mother had taken him down to a forbidden locked room in the basement and had introduced him that day to his past and his future and the story of how their people were lost to their main civilization. All Landon had to do was to find those of their kind who had survived, and he could regain the secret of their power.

To a small albino boy who was regularly ridiculed in school, the thought of gaining power for himself became a heady brew that had motivated him all his life. When he met Francis Drake and the other Gifted, he had thought he had found his secret race; but that was not so. So he had continued to seek with Francis's help, and then Francis had happened upon a young pregnant woman in the south of France. Vallon had been the result, and his hope to lead him to those greater people. His homing pigeon, he had always hoped. His *Gild the Lily* that would bond him and the Gifted to these Others of power.

But the leader of the Council only shook his head. Pity again.

Landon's gut twisted into a tight knot of denial. They lied. They were a lying bunch of bickering has-beens who would not give up their secret.

"With each generation, your blood was diluted, Mr. Snow. And as your blood diluted, it spread out into the unGifted and gave rise to something else that may be similar to us, but is not the same."

"With each rise, a fall," he whispered part of the ancient dichotomy. Man-woman, hot-cold, soft-hard, dark-light, lead-gold, impurity-purity. The lessons of Alchemy. His people—for all their efforts to raise themselves to the perfection that would once more reunite them with the power—had just, through procreating, apparently diminished themselves.

The irony left his legs weak. His fingers went limp on the button. It could not be true. His mother had been a proud woman with a proud history.

But she had not truly known their history—not as well as Landon did now. Certainly not as well as these ancient ones might, even if they were far less than he had built them up to be.

"It can't be true." His voice sounded weak and querulous as an old man's. An entire people wiped out. But then, genocide was an established part of human history that went right back to Neanderthals. Wolf Amundson was practicing it right now in America.

All his plans, and all the years, weighted his shoulders and left him old. He had done such horrible things to get here. To follow Vallon here….

He glanced in her direction.

She wasn't there.

And then the dark man bowled him over.

§

Vallon ran. Down the gallery corridor. Down the stairs. Around a corner that she prayed would get her out this decadent prison of a Cartos palace. All the marble floors, gilt furnishings, and mural-painted walls and ceilings couldn't hide the place's true purpose. A physical prison for her. A prison of purpose to the Cartos Council, *that they chose to live in.* Blind fools. They were tied up in worthless minutia, and preferred to gloat over Landon rather than deal with the fact that Amundson threatened everything.

Because aside from the grey pall that still warped her vision, something more immediate had happened to Jack. And if Jack had just died, then what had happened to Fi?

She reached the open courtyard, with its tall potted palms and banks of snow-white bougainvillea, and started across the sun-heated paving stones, but Xavier's hand on her arm swung her around.

"Where do you go, *Bela?*" He loomed over her like a shadow and blocked the sun.

"Where do you think? I'm going home. If Jack's dead, then Fi's in trouble and I'm what? Five thousand miles away, standing around, twiddling my thumbs in some Venetian palace? I was a fool to come here and a bigger fool for letting you convince me to stay."

Her chest felt clenched tight, and standing here just made it worse.

She pulled loose, ignoring his protests. The damned door to outside had to be here somewhere. She wasn't quite sure how she was going to get home, but she'd do it somehow.

"Then we will transmute together."

She turned back to look at him. His hawkish face lay open to her. Concern. Love. Guilt. A little anger. As if he had the right to be angry with her. *She* was an open book.

"You have to stay here and get the Council to take heed of what has happened."

He shook his head. "I doubt that is possible. Not with—Demetrio de Varga here. There was a chance with Carlos on the Council, but if Demetrio has taken back his seat…. He is more rigid than the rest."

So he could not even call him his father. Even she could do that with Francis Drake.

"We have many things in common, Vallon, beyond difficult fathers. Like the need to make this world a better place. Like the desire to rest together at Pangea's breast." He pulled her into his chest and for a moment all the worry, all the fear for Fi disappeared. But that was a lie, just like he'd lied to her. Well, perhaps his failure was the lie of omission.

She pulled loose and shook her head, though she missed his arms. "Pangea's at risk, Xavier. You have to get them to understand. Hector saw. Make the others see, too. You have to make them check."

"America is too dangerous for you to go alone."

"Damn it, Xavier. Someone has to go and someone has to stay. There's no other way." He might want to protect her, but…. "Xavier, I know you want to protect me, but I'm not like your mother. Your father let her go into danger and never was there for her. You—you're not like that. You've been there for me over and over." She placed her palm on his chest and felt the strong surge and pause of his heart. "You always have been. But you have to let me go. Someone has to go *now*."

If eyes were the windows of the soul, his gave onto a dark pit. He pulled her into him, and his incense and cedar of Lebanon burned into her as his arms came around her.

I love you, she almost said. But was it love or lust or simply the result of being thrown together through so many trials? If she did love him, she should leave him behind for safety. Let him have his life back. Because if Amundson had gotten Fi, she would hunt the man down. She would quite likely be killed in the process and deserved nothing less for how she'd used her power to kill.

He tilted her face up to him as the *clippity-clip-clip* of Leticia's heels sounded from the stairs behind them. "Vallon! Xavier! Come!"

"Xavier, I have to go."

"Yes. You do."

He pulled her into him again, his palm cradling the back of her skull. The air crackled around them and then the floor geysered up with a stink of ozone and ether and she came apart. Her essence tore down through the floor and the sodden Venetian island. Down through silken lagoon mud to the heated, rose-scented ley lines, under the sea bed, and then deeper still through the pressures of the earth far under the oceans.

She exploded up through clay and fertile soil and came back to herself tasting muddy silt on the back of her tongue. She staggered against Xavier's naked, broad chest. His arms tightened around her as late afternoon sunlight poured through a gingham-curtained window.

Yellow walls. Dust motes turned golden. Double bed. The bedroom they had used in Jack's house in Canada.

"Dammit, all to hell, Xavier! You were supposed to stay in Venice." She ripped away and almost fell onto the bed. The damn transit. She looked up at his nakedness and afterburn flared. Xavier could deal with that quite nicely, thank you very much. Instead, she staggered up and searched for clothes. She was not going to let Xavier stop her and she wasn't going to soften. She needed to get him back to Venice.

There were clothes in the closet, all cleaned and hung up. Fi's doing, probably, in preparation for her return. She pulled out jeans and a red t-shirt and bulky fair isle cardigan because her leather jacket was back home in her house in Redmond.

Socks and her boots and she stood and looked around at Xavier, still gloriously naked. She tossed a plaid robe at him. "Cover yourself or I'll get distracted."

"*Bela*, we need to talk."

"There's no time. You need to get back before your father has the Council deciding to side with Amundson or some such idiocy. You need to deal with Landon. Don't let him bully the Council."

His lips downturned. He stood there, robe in his hand, a magnificent animal, his aura crackling around him. Correction: an angry animal.

"What's the matter now?" she asked as she buttoned the top of the jeans.

"You avoid dealing with what must be dealt with."

She sighed and pulled on her t-shirt. "Is this really the time to discuss this? I just need time, okay? I need to sort out how I feel about everything."

"About us, you mean. *Bela*, you have avoided this discussion since you learned of your parentage."

She closed her eyes, seeking for the words. "Then perhaps it can wait a little longer. Please? I know I love you, but I hate the fact that you aren't honest with me. You keep secrets, and the only way I found out anything about you was because your father turned up and you argued. That's not the kind of trust I want in a relationship."

There. She'd said it. She held her breath as Xavier looked down at the robe he held as if it was the most fascinating thing in the world. Finally he shook his head and met her gaze.

"Sometimes—some things are too intertwined. Secrets upon secrets. There is a secret society of other Cartos outside the Council." He shook his head.

"And you swore an oath not to talk about it."

He nodded his shaggy head. "A blood oath. I hold it more important than my service to the Council. They do not know, but they suspect, for I have refused to investigate the rumors they have heard."

A secret society within a secret society. These people were worse than Landon. She met his gaze. "A while back, you said to me that we are all strangers in this world. How am I supposed to trust a stranger who will not trust me?" Her heart felt tight and her shoulders stiff. Her hands had somewhere along the line become fists. "I think you'd better go, Xavier. Maybe we can sort this all out later, but for now, I work better alone."

A sound like a small cry came from down the hallway. She spun around and Xavier startled. The cry came again, and a small, black-and-white cat zoomed down the hall, puffy black tail held high. Maggie let loose a steady stream of anxious meows.

She skittered into the room and practically leapt into Vallon's arms. Her small pink nose head-butted Vallon's face and that seriously was not like her.

She met Xavier's gaze as she cradled Maggie against her.

"Go," she said. "I can take care of myself and Maggie."

Xavier just pulled on the ridiculous robe and padded out into the hallway. She followed him to the kitchen, where he stopped at the door.

Through the grey pall of her vision, the room was like she remembered. Sun-filled, with its yellow counter tiles and wood cupboards, the butcher-block table filling the center of the room, the small T.V. on the counter. But the room was cold and reeked of copper and death. The back door stood slightly open so that a cool wind sent brown leaves skittering like cat playthings across the floor to snag on the body at the base of the table.

Jack lay on his back, his blue eyes milking over, blood gone dark brown on what looked like gunshot wounds on his chest and shoulder.

Xavier knelt beside him. Shaking his head, he closed Jack's eyes. "He was a good friend over many years." His voice thickened, Xavier glanced up at her. "I shall miss him. But now his essence has returned to Pangea. May he be at rest forever in her bosom."

"He wouldn't be dead if you hadn't brought me to him." It was the truth. Too many people paid the ultimate price for associating with her. The whole problem with Amundson started with her discovery of her dead partner.

Maggie snugged a little tighter into her side and purred like an outboard motor.

"You cannot know that."

She shook her head. The fresh wind and copper had dispersed most other scent in the room, but there was still something. Along with the faint remains of Fi's anise and mint, there was something that made her think of storm-tossed ocean on the darkest morning and spice.

She scooped up an official-looking business card left alone on the butcher block table. Seattle PD.

"Jason."

CHAPTER 21 —IRON-SCENTED FEAR

The black Subaru Impreza STI purred under her as she wound her way out of the small farming community. The afternoon sunlight had turned the gold of evening and gilded the leaves of the cottonwoods and poplar across the corn-stubbled, muddy fields. Overhead the first V of geese she'd seen headed south ahead of her.

It was Jack's vehicle and still smelled new, kept stored unused in a second outbuilding on the small acreage, while Jack had driven a well-used pickup truck for the veterinary work that had been his cover. Maggie complained from a carry case beside her, and a small bag carried the few bits of clothing she'd accumulated at Jack's, along with a few things of Fi's. She had a new passport in her pocket that declared her to be Veronique Beaumont, provided from a cache of emergency Canadian passports that Jack had kept secreted about the place and the work of a Canadian forger Xavier had known.

Xavier had returned to Venice, but not without further argument, and not without him holding her in a final embrace that had gone on too long. He had left with the final admonishment to stay safe and that he would find her—that he would always find her. It should have left her feeling relieved that he *would* come after her. But did she want him to, given that everyone who came in contact with her ended up dead? Did she even deserve his help, given what she had done and what she planned to do now? Killing someone wasn't exactly something to be proud of or a task to drag others into.

It was sad, but it was better like this, just as all her previous break-ups had been. Vallon Drake was alone now and always would be. Doing this fell to her.

The Subaru rumbled under her as the day slowly faded from the sky, the déjà vu of driving through the rain to find a parking garage where a two-story blue house was supposed to sit came so strongly it almost left her breathless. But it felt like the same kind of thing—a return to the scene of a previous crime. This time it was the crime of what had happened between her and Jason, because the few hours she had been at Jack's house while the passport was readied had made her sure of her destination. Jason had taken Fi to Vallon's house in Redmond.

The border proved no problem. The border guards were expecting Gifted to be trying to get *out* of America—that was why they had roadblocks set up just south of the Canadian side of the border—not that they'd be able to tell a Gifted when they saw one, but that was another story. But heading south, there were the usual questions—where was she headed, for how long, was she bringing anything into the country other than her cat? They didn't even ask for Maggie's papers, something else that Xavier had spent time perfecting. Who knew he had those talents?

She sighed in relief when they waved her through, even though this was far more dangerous than staying in Canada. But this was her home. It was worth fighting for.

The drive south—two hours, driving a carefully gauged amount over the speed limit—got her south of Everett just as the last streaks of sunlight left the sky. In Venice, they would be waiting for dawn. She wondered what Landon was doing, now that his ultimate dream seemed to have gone awry, and whether Xavier had been able to convince the Council of the danger in Seattle. She wondered about the man who claimed he was her grandfather. Who was he, who was his daughter, her mother? Most of all, she thought of what little she knew of Xavier. Cartos. Watcher. Disowned by father and brother, ex-lover of Leticia. A man of deep passions, who had gone into danger for her. Did she need to know more than that?

Unfortunately, yes. She'd been betrayed and abandoned too many times by men she'd thought loved her. Being in a relationship was about trust. Could she ever do that?

At Lynnwood, the road filled with light evening traffic. The sky had purpled around the edges and become a bowl of indigo blue when she slammed through an invisible wall. Her hands went numb and she lost control. The car careened into the next lane. And the next. Horns blared around her until she somehow fought the car to the road's shoulder and sat there panting. Like stepping through a door from spring rains to desert.

Outside the car, the trees and grass were still green. There were people in the passing cars and birds overhead, but she felt *nothing*. No power. No feel of the earth. She checked the traffic, then opened her door and climbed out cautiously, hoping it was simply a matter of needing to be grounded.

Still nothing. Absolutely nothing, except the chill wind of the passing traffic, the beads of sweat on her skin as she -reached- for something, anything, but there was nothing there except void and being trapped between gravity on her shoulders and soil and concrete pressing up against her soles. No sense of the life around her. No sense of the life that was the globe. She -reached- further, and something caught her, and— pulled, or tried to. She staggered against the car and clung there, fighting back the sense that something was out there, waiting to devour her. The sweat chilled on her skin and left her freezing. She felt sick and shaky, her sight grayed through with the desolate vision. This was what she'd felt happening in Seattle. Whatever it was, the gray was getting worse—as if the normal world were fading.

Fumbling her way back inside the car, she fought to clear her vision. How the heck was she going to drive like this? She sat there, blinking and trying to stop the shaking that had taken over her hands. Gradually she got control of herself. From the carry box beside her, Maggie meowed her displeasure.

"I know you don't like car rides and I know it's past your dinner, but it can't be helped. We'll be home soon and then you can eat."

If she dared bring Maggie into the house, with Jason there.

A deep, steadying breath and she dropped the car in gear and pulled out into traffic.

It grew almost bumper to bumper as she got closer to Seattle, and just north of the bridge over Lake Union, she took her exit and threaded her way down into Fremont. The maple trees were turning yellow over Fremont Avenue as she turned off into the neighborhood where her rental house stood. She found a parking spot three doors down, pulled in, and sat with her window rolled down. Usually the evening would be alive with the sounds of the people who lived here, and the gardens and houses would be alight with the life force of living things.

But tonight everything was unnaturally quiet. She -reached- and the sickening vertigo lanced into her again, but not before she glimpsed fading candles of trees, her neighbor's flames stripping away like candle flames in high wind. The whole area was in a slow process of dying.

It had to be stopped, but first she had to free Fi.

She looked over the seat at Maggie. "So, little girl. Do I take you in with me, or leave you hungry out here?" Maggie mewed plaintively, clearly preferring the former option. "All right, then. We'll take our chances together, but if things look bad, you get out of there, hear? I know things haven't been perfect between us, but I've tried, okay? I've just tried to keep your weight down so that you could live a long time."

And clearly she'd lost her mind, talking to her cat. She climbed out into the cool of a fall evening. A mist haloed the house porch lights and softened the line of vehicles parked along the street as she hefted Maggie's carry cage out of the car and locked the vehicle. Hopefully she'd be back in the Subaru quickly with Fi and headed elsewhere.

The blue light of televisions leaked out of neighbor's windows, and from somewhere not far off, a dog barked and then subsided. Leaves drooped on branches, and maybe that was because it was fall, but the whole scene felt exhausted. It made sense, given the way the absence of power seemed to suck at her as if trying to fill the absence below.

Well, she'd fix it, once she had Fi and Maggie to safety. She stopped at the gate to her little brown house. Same overgrown rhododendron bush. Fi's bright garden fading into autumn. Were Amundson's men watching? She doubted Jason would have brought Fi anywhere he thought he might be stopped from doing what he wanted, but she wouldn't put it past Amundson to keep an eye on her house.

Well, she was blind at the moment and there was nothing she could do about it now. She'd have to talk Jason out of his madness or else use the weapon she'd brought from Jack's place—a small pistol that Xavier had produced out of the same cache that had held her passport. It was stuck in the back of her jeans under her bulky sweater.

Through the gate, she pushed past the rhododendron and around the house to the backyard. No need to be totally predictable and go in the front. She pulled her keys from her pocket, but before she could use them, the kitchen door opened.

Light spilled out onto the porch stairs and silhouetted Jason Bryson. "'Bout time you got here. I was beginning to think you didn't care about your friend." He motioned her inside.

She obeyed, but she'd blast him into the earth if she could—or at least knock him out. Her kitchen looked the same. Strange, when it felt like she'd been gone for years. Same rough linoleum. Same worn counters and chipped, painted cupboards. Same blue glass bottles on the window shelves by the sink. She set Maggie down and set about feeding her, then turned to face Jason.

"Where's Fi?"

"Wouldn't you like to know?"

It was Jason, but barely. His cheeks and eye sockets hollowed out his skull so his gaze came from dark pits. His brown hair lay matted and greasy and stuck to his skull. His trousers, white shirt, and trench coat hung on a scarecrow frame. But his gun looked the same—dull metal and ugly and far too big, with its business end pointed at her.

She swallowed. "I'll ask it again. Where's Fi? Is she okay?"

What might pass for a smile spasmed his face. "You really don't get it, do you? That won't get you any further than the first time you asked it. Fi's stashed somewhere safe. I'll tell you where, when you do what I want. Of course you could refuse, but then you won't learn where Fi is." He shrugged. "Your choice."

Automatically, she -reached- for Fi, but the void blasted in. She slammed back into herself and clung to the counter, her heart beating a tattoo. Then she took a deep breath and she met Jason's half-dead gaze.

"I told you before. I can't bring Cheryl back. I tried. It didn't work. I know you don't believe me, but I gave it all I had."

"Liar."

He moved across the room—so fast she barely saw him—and had her backed up against the counter. His breath smelled like metal and his body reeked of sweat.

"I was there. Remember? You brought Cheryl back and then you destroyed her. I saw. You did to her what almost happened to me that night I was here."

His fingers dug into her biceps. His gaze said he wanted to hurt her, but was waiting for the final reason to do it. One hand came around her neck and it was almost a caress until his fingers closed hard around her windpipe. Squeezed as he leaned in to whisper in her ear.

"Fi's not happy, Vallon. In fact, she was terrified when I left her. Think about it. Poor little Fi, all tied up in the dark and alone." He pulled back with mock surprise on his face. "Oops. Shouldn't have let that slip, should I?"

Then he flipped her around and twisted her arms behind her back and up until her shoulders screamed in protest. She went up on her toes.

It didn't help. He forced her around and aimed her at the door to the basement, flicked on the lights, and she tried to resist, but he marched her down into her work room. Into the scent of moisture and a shimmering emptiness.

Chill air cut into her when usually the basement was warm. The yawning emptiness threatened to swallow her. Her workbench lay at one side of the room, covered in cupboard contents. Baggies of herbs and powdered stone and bottles of ink that someone had spilled out onto the bench as if searching for something. Jason, most likely.

At the side of the basement lay her practice sandbox, new, heavy-leather shackles bolted into each corner. She slowed until he jerked her arms up her back again. If she let him shackle her there, she'd be helpless and she wouldn't be able to rescue Fi, because there was no way she could do what Jason wanted.

"Don't do this, Jason. There's no way I can help you. Not here. Not now. Amundson has blocked the power from the area around Seattle. No power means I can't do anything."

"Now who's lying?" He shoved her, stumbling, down the last few stairs, but she yanked loose and scrambled across the sandbox to face him.

"It *is* possible. Right now I'm no different from you or the people who live in the houses around here. I have no Gift. There *is* no Gift. Amundson erased it somehow, and the question is how? Now why don't we just go get Fi and stop him?"

Maybe she could convince him. Hell, maybe he'd even help her again, like he had before. He had a vested interest in wanting her to have power, and if she had power, she could overpower him. A way better plan than trying to get past him and up the stairs before he could use the gun. The way he looked at her, he wouldn't hesitate to use it. *Pull her weapon?* He hadn't searched her yet.

His face seemed to rework itself as if he were listening, but it settled back into the same skeletal lines.

"You know I'm right, don't you? You know what Amundson has done!"

"All I know is you're a liar and a cock tease. You led me on—first with your body and then with your power. Well, I'm doing the leading now." He motioned with his gun. "Turn around. Hands against the wall."

Pull her gun and fight it out? In a firefight, there wasn't much question but that she'd lose.

"Get your hands up on the wall!" he roared.

She made as if to turn—slowly—and yanked out her pistol. She pointed it at Jason, her heart pounding so hard it seemed to echo in the basement.

"It's your turn to listen, Jason. I know you're angry and I know you think I can do great things, but you're wrong. Sure, I can Change the landscape, I even made that stupid castle here in the basement, but they didn't last. They fade out over time. Cheryl—I tried to make her like you wanted, even though it's an evil thing to do. But I tried. And I didn't destroy her. The thing is, just wanting her isn't enough to hold her into being. So you had to go through losing her again.

"And now things are even worse, because whatever Amundson has done blocks the power that runs under Seattle, and that means I don't have any power here, either. And the thing is, it might make unGifted feel safe, but who knows what its effect will be? Things are changing as we speak."

Jason shook his head. "You're lying again. Everything's fine."

His fanatical gaze said conversation was hopeless.

"You're wrong." She kept her voice steady, even though everything else was shaking. The unfamiliar gun felt heavy and wrong. She wanted a pen and vellum, not this instrument of violence. She wanted the feel of the power in her veins. "The trees might look okay, but I think without the power they might be dying. The people and animals, too. It's just a matter of time. Amundson's wiping out everything he's trying to protect—or he will, if he extends what he's doing any farther."

His gaze skittering around the room like a set of caged mice, but the gun muzzle wavered. *Was he going to shoot her or believe her?*

"You know something's off, don't you? You can feel it, just like you can feel when the power's being used!"

The gun steadied on her. "What I know is that you're trying your tricks on me again. Now drop the gun and up against the wall." Deadly calm.

She swallowed and stayed facing him. He knew. He just didn't want to believe it.

"Amundson told you, didn't he? You were working with him. So you know he's blocking the power somehow. That's the only way he'd let you out of his sight again. He let you go because he didn't need you as long as he stayed inside the perimeter he created. So he let you go to find me and that brought us here.

"Tell me what Amundson did, Jason. It's dangerous. More dangerous than anything. Think of it like cutting off the blood supply to a part of the brain. You do that and the starved part dies. Well, that's what's happening to Seattle."

His gun still held steady on her while hers was shaking. It was far more likely he'd kill her than she would even injure him.

"Jason, we can't leave the city this way. People are going to start dying soon. Look at yourself. You're not well."

His skin was grey, and little drops of sweat glittered on his forehead in the single, bare light bulb. Did his gun lower just a little? Was he listening to her?

"Put your weapon down, Vallon."

"I will if you will."

"Damn it, put the fucking gun down!" His pistol roared and she jerked back as she felt rather than saw the bullet pass right next to her arm in a little puff of heated air. The stench of cordite flavored the air.

"Are you nuts?"

He launched himself and slammed her back against the wall, his gun hot between them. He crushed her arms between them. His hot breath smelled like iron.

"Drop the gun, Vallon," he growled into her ear. "Drop it and we'll get Fi and we'll get out of here."

She couldn't believe him, and yet she had no choice.

She nodded and let him yank the gun from her fingers. Then Jason expertly flipped her around and confined her hands in plastic cuffs. He dragged her from the wall and shoved her toward the stairs with a last, regretful look at the cuffs attached to the practice pit.

"This's no victory, Vallon. I can set something up elsewhere. Amundson's still winning. And so am I."

He drove her up the stairs and into the kitchen, where Maggie still had her pink nose buried in her plate of food. She looked up and licked her whiskers, just as Jason caught her. Maggie backed her ears and yowled. She swiped at Jason's face and he dropped her, but she was too quick. Blood flowed from four bright red lines across his cheek as she leapt into bite his leg.

"Fuck!" He reached for his gun. Vallon turned and kicked him in the chest. It sent him toppling. The gun flew out of his hand and went off. Maggie ran for the cat door, every hair on end. Jason rolled for the gun, but Vallon leapt over him. She kicked it away.

"Everyone on the floor! Homeland Security!" came a voice through the door.

§

To Landon, the holding room could have been much worse. It was small, with a single grilled window that let in the watery reflections of morning light and the sound of life from out on the canals, but the walls were of wood, shiny with the patina of age, there was a small Persian carpet under his feet, worn with years, and he sat in a cushioned chair with carved arms and legs. Not quite freedom, but not exactly the place you would put a man sentenced to death, either.

At least that was what he kept telling himself. It was cold comfort, given the emptiness he felt. All those years of scheming and it was for nothing. All those years of believing, and now that the belief had crumbled—what did that leave?

Not much, except anger. He felt old and his bones ached, just sitting in the damp air. He spread his fingers on his thighs and sighed. The things these hands had done, all for plans that had come to naught. All these years he'd been certain the Others held the secret to him regaining his power. All these years, with his delusions of grandeur that had given him license to do so much, and all it left him with, now, was feeling small, very old, and a little guilty.

He looked up at the man who slouched silently across the room from him. Tall, dark, his shaggy black hair hanging lank around his hawkish features. Strong arms, crossed over his black-clad chest, but the sleeves of his shirt were rolled up to reveal solid forearms and the right hand and arm that Landon had tortured.

Landon cleared his throat. "I—I am sorry. For what I did to you. And to Vallon. I tried to watch out for her." Apologizing felt exceedingly strange.

Xavier de Varga straightened and unfurled his arms. He flexed the fingers of his apparently fully-healed hand and made an exceedingly deadly looking fist. "You and Drake stripped her from her family. Her heritage. She may never forgive you for that."

The way he said it, he'd like to avenge it, along with his own complaints.

"We took care of her. Her mother was too wild. She wouldn't have been good for Vallon."

Xavier turned a baleful black gaze in Landon's direction, and the cool air of the room seemed even more chill and damp. Xavier's heady incense and cedar scent burned Landon's nostrils. "And you are a seer, now? You know how Lianna would have parented? She was Vallon's mother, but you took away her chance—her choice."

Landon shook his head. "I've seen other wild mothers. Rebecca Murdoch was one, and look how well she did for her daughter. It sounds like you had one, as well. Just how well did she serve you?"

"My parentage has nothing to do with this. This is not about me. Or Fiona, or anyone else. It is about Vallon."

Then he sighed. "Lianna might not have been good for Vallon, but I tell myself that Lianna would have found calm with a child to care for. I understand why Lianna did as she did. The Cartos Council and its families are too old-fashioned, too restrictive." He looked away to the small window, far up on the wall, that let in the rare strains of a gondolier's song.

"So the young Cartos have split from the Council and are trying a different way that you support."

The big man only shifted around the room, seemingly uncomfortable that Landon knew this about him.

A shadow Council of young Cartos, not so set in their ways. Made up of youngsters, who might need the help of someone who had years of experience working under the radar. Xavier stopped and rested his forehead against the stone wall. His scent of cedar spiked into the room.

"You're worried for Vallon," Landon said.

Xavier didn't move. "She goes into danger. Always she does that to help others and Pangea. I should be at her side, not here awaiting the judgment of the Council regarding addressing the danger."

His Cartos presence sparked and flared in agitation. Clearly his return had not been at his choosing, but then Vallon had always been a lone wolf operative.

"If it's any consolation, that's the way she's always been. I doubt she'll change."

Xavier turned a haunted gaze on him that could almost make Landon smile. Yes, his barb had struck deep.

Landon had been about to be escorted out of the Council Chamber when Xavier had suddenly materialized out of a spout of ozone-scented power. He had ignored his shocking nakedness and told the Council that they must take action. That the entire world was at risk. The Council had apparently not listened, for they had marched them both out of the room together after telling Xavier that his request was under consideration.

"So Amundson really has found a way to block the power?" Change the subject after he'd hooked the man and see how far he could make him run.

Xavier seemed to shudder. "Yes. And what it leaves behind dies. That entire city does not have much time. A year at most, by what I felt when I reached there. Vallon worries that Amundson will spread his field across the country." He cocked his head. "So now you scheme how to use this to your favor?"

Landon shrugged. "In the past I would have used anything I discovered, because everything was about getting what I wanted—into the presence of the Others to demand my birthright. Foolish of me, because those men and women are fools, and apparently I already had all that my birthright could give me." He sighed pointedly. "Do you know what it is like to spend your whole life thinking others have denied you something important? How it can twist you into something you do not even know you have become until suddenly—someday—somehow—something makes you visible to yourself? We each want to be the hero of our life stories, but right now I feel like Rumplestiltskin, who trades in the misfortune of others. I'll say it again: I'm sorry about your hand. Does it pain you much?"

He kept his head down, watched Xavier out of the corner of his eye.

Xavier balled his once-injured hand into a dangerous fist, then held it up for consideration. "Not so bad. Jack healed it." He looked at Landon and smiled as if prepared for a little demonstration.

A threat to his body was the least of his concerns. What he needed was to get Xavier talking. Build rapport.

"So your people heal, as well." Could a healer heal *him*? At times his heart felt shriveled and shrunken, like a character in a fairy story. "So much power in your blood. And in Vallon's, but not enough to undo whatever Amundson has set in motion. But Vallon has gone to try, as is her nature. My question is: why are you not with her?"

Xavier jerked as if struck. The fierce flare of anger in the gaze he turned on Landon almost made Landon reconsider his words. But he wanted out of this gentle prison, because it was only a matter of time before the Cartos Council decided to rid themselves of a certain researcher who had researched too well and knew too much. Xavier presented the only way out of here.

"Let me guess. You came and you stay because Vallon asked you to. You came, and right now, while your woman is walking into danger, your father is counseling them against helping—and against you and your questionable loyalties.”

“Shut up, little man. You think I don’t know that?” Xavier turned away and paced the room.

“Strange you let her.”

“Shut up! Not strange at all. I’ve the bloodline for it.” Xavier said bitterly and turned back to him. “But then, you know my history, don’t you? How my father let my mother go into danger and was never there for her. How the worst happened and she asked for his help. How my father refused and I allowed myself to be convinced not to help either. Until it was too late.” His throat worked.

“And yet you let another woman go into danger, too.” Landon shook his head and stood. He did not bother to mention love. Xavier could fill in the blanks himself. He crossed to the window and a gust of fresh air refreshed him. Now was the time to set the hook. “You—all of you—you think I have no power, but you’re wrong. I might not have a Gift like yours, but I have this.” He touched forefinger to head. “If Amundson has done something, I would lay money on it being based on research I did for the AGS.”

Xavier’s gaze narrowed. “So we should blame you for what has happened.”

“Until I see and understand what has happened, I won’t be able to tell, will I?”

Xavier considered. “What the unGifted have done leaves a dead and dying zone under Seattle, though those who live there and those who caused it do not recognize it. Unless they leave that area, they will die, just as everything else will without the power of the ley lines.”

The fresh air turned icy. His research *had* looked at the many factors that might contribute to the Gift. One area he had considered years back was the supposedly pseudo-science of ley lines. Homeland Security had dug deep if they’d found the old files that referenced them. What else might they have found? “And Vallon has gone to stop it?”

Xavier jerked in a nod. “She has. She will. But her first priority was to rescue her friend, Fiona, from Jason Bryson. It seems he has killed my friend Jack and abducted Fiona.”

That news took a moment to digest. “The detective? But he was with us in New Madrid.”

A nod, but the dark man's worry was clear. "According to Vallon, it was because he knew of her powers and wanted her to bring his wife back from the dead."

Madness—and yet—was such a thing possible? The permutations of the news churned in his brain. His Pigeon. Was she capable of such a thing? She *was* his creation—the greatest weapon he'd ever created through all his years of subtle manipulation. He scrubbed his fingers up through his hair and peered up at Xavier. "So she's gone into this dead zone to rescue her friend, without any access to her powers, and you worry for her."

He took a chance and laid his hand on Xavier's arm and felt the big man stiffen.

Xavier's slow nod was like watching an executioner's axe fall. "Even though I could not sense her in New Madrid, I was sure she still lived because they wanted her power. With Jason, I am not so sure. Vallon claimed that he tried to kill her and that he wants his revenge. And now she has gone into that dead place, and I can no longer find her."

Landon met his gaze and knew the time was right.

"Then let me help you save her."

CHAPTER 22 — A WARM SURGE OF POWER

The first shots echoed through the subdivision, just as Francis Drake reached the dark blue S.U.V. that he had driven from Anacortes. The late afternoon light had faded to evening and the front yards were vacant of children as families came together for dinner in front of the television. The squawks and canned laughter of sit-coms wafted out open windows as Francis Drake led Derrick Brown and Evan Carragio through the neighborhood. So did the scent of fried onions.

At the gunfire, Francis whirled, his hand going for his weapon. Derrick matched his motion, but ever-helpful Carragio froze.

More shots, like small explosions in his nervous system, but they came from the next block over. He tried to remember who had parked in that area, while he fumbled for the SUV's keys. Libernaum, maybe, but it didn't matter. What did was that Amundson's men were now among the Gifted.

"Get in." He used the key fob to unlock the vehicle doors.

"Shouldn't we help the others?" Derrick asked.

Carragio had already slid into the rear seat.

Francis shook his head and pulled open his door. "Everyone's on their own, now."

But Derrick still hesitated.

"Get your ass in the car, or you're on your own, too." Damn it, didn't he know what was good for him?

Derrick relented and Francis leapt in, started the SUV, and accelerated down the road. This was going to be tight. Amundson could have this whole neighborhood cordoned off.

He turned west, headed back to Redmond. Through the rearview mirror, he watched a few other cars burst free of the housing subdivision and follow. Maybe it wasn't as bad as he'd feared. Maybe more of his people had made it out ahead of him. Maybe.

The tall cedars steeped the road in almost continuous shadow. Just let them reach I-520 and they'd be up and away southward, and hopefully out of whatever it was Amundson had done to the landscape. The yawning emptiness made concentration difficult. It seemed to suck his strength away. Even the cedars seemed to feel it. They'd lost their deep, glossy green, and the air through the car's vents carried an undertang that sat on his tongue like he'd eaten something unpleasant.

"They must not have had cars on this side of the school. They probably didn't think we'd make it this far," Carragio said, stating the obvious.

"So they'll be calling for roadblocks in town. I'm thinking at the 520 entrance. They'll figure we'll try for that," Francis said. Of course, maybe they'd get lucky. Maybe Amundson wasn't quite as farsighted as it was beginning to seem. Every time Francis had taken action, Amundson had been ready for him and turned the situation to his advantage. And now here he was, *running for his life*. It was unnerving as hell.

He tromped the gas harder and the car careened around the last tight curve in the road before settling down for the last straight run toward the highway entrance, the other vehicles—three, four, five of them—hot on his heels.

"I think there're seven cars behind us," Carragio said from where he sat peering out of the rear window. "I caught a glimpse of a couple more before we went around that last corner."

Was that all that had gotten free? There had been ten cars, all full, when they left Anacortes.

A sinking feeling filled his stomach. He was losing too many, too fast. Sure, he could fight against Amundson, but to accomplish what he had set out to do would be far more difficult with this few Gifted. In the war of attrition, Amundson's tactics were working. And the empty feeling of the landscape was still there.

Just how big an area had Amundson quarantined?

Flashing red and blue lights ahead as they neared the junction. Amundson either hadn't been as assumptive as he'd thought or else he'd reacted quickly. And aside from the small arms he and his men had, they were defenseless.

A street came up on his left and he swung the SUV wide onto it. The other cars followed.

"No reason to drive right up and ask to be arrested," he said.

The buildings around them were light industrial, sitting dark and sullen on either side of the road. The elevated I-520 beckoned, just a few blocks over. He took the next right and flashed under the highway, ending up on Redmond Way, the major thoroughfare through town. The warehouses were replaced by family restaurants and shopping areas and stoplights he plowed through to a chorus of horns.

"Jesus, Drake. You trying to get us killed?" Carragio said.

"I'm trying to save your skinny ass, and all of us, so shut the fuck up."

He wound through traffic. The other vehicles fell behind, perhaps not so sure of his tactics to get through the traffic unscathed. Well, they were all on their own. He'd told them that. If they didn't believe how serious Amundson was, then they were fools and he didn't need them. He reached the next major road and turned left and I-520 soared ahead. They were going to make it. Two of the Gifted cars swung in behind him. Please let the others make it through. He needed their power.

He breathed deep as he swung onto the on-ramp and up into the highway traffic. Redmond fell away behind him. Now just get out of the dead zone before Amundson brought a new tactic against them.

They took the 520 to the 405 southbound, praying Amundson would think they'd make a run northward for the border. The SUV settled into cruising speed and he matched the speed of the traffic around him. Tight coils of tension still compressed his chest.

"Can you tell how many are with us?"

"I counted four cars made it onto the highway. The others are probably farther behind because of traffic," Carragio said.

"If I was Amundson, I'd shut the whole town down," the youngster, Brown, said.

"Then let's hope that Amundson doesn't think like you do." But Amundson had proven himself a far more worthy adversary than Francis had expected.

The concrete highway hummed under them as the light faded further from the sky. The lights of Renton held back the coming darkness, but it was twilight when they hit the I-5 junction, and swept up onto the eight-lane highway south.

The blast of heated power almost sent him off the road. Power flowed over him like a sneaker wave. It blinded him to the road. He fought the SUV as his skin burned. Then his vision cleared as the blast of power subsided. For the first time since the Academy, he could truly fill his lungs.

"Halleluiah," Carragio said.

"We're out of it." Brown sighed and slumped back in his seat, loosening his collar. "What the hell has Amundson got that can do that?"

Behind them was an empty, dark space, surrounded by a cascade of seething blocked power. A black hole of death that was slowly sucking the life out of everything. And the poor slobs had no idea. He looked at the vehicles driving northward. Hell they were going *into* it of their own volition.

"He's got to have some sort of perimeter devices, given the abruptness of the edge. But we're not going to deal with that now. Let's get our people safe first."

"And just how safe is that?" Carragio murmured from the back seat. He'd turned back to see who followed. So far they'd been lucky. If Amundson had had helicopter support ready, they really wouldn't have stood a chance. Their vehicle descriptions would have been broadcast and the state troopers would be gunning for them. Not that a state trooper could take them down when they were free of the dead zone.

The darkness yawned behind them as night took the sky. It was really too bad that everything was dying back there. He'd always been fond of the Emerald City.

§

The huge, silent map in the center of the room provided a constant reminder of what Amundson and his men were up against. The map pit was dark, blank, the nanites at its heart having gone dead when Amundson's researchers had switched on the grid that protected Seattle as far north as Lynnwood. The grid extended as far east as the old AGS school, as far south as SeaTac, and as far west as Puget Sound. No one could use that profane power against him or anyone else in Seattle.

Around the infernal pit, Page and the cadre of agents he'd surrounded himself with were busy listening to and directing the take down of the Academy, as well as another small operation. Amundson paced behind them ready to give orders, but Page and his men had years of experience in Iraq and Afghanistan. He had to trust they knew their business and could successfully resolve both operations.

Wolf closed his eyes.

Two simultaneous operations. If they pulled them both off, then the overt war against the Gifted would be over. Then operations would enter the more difficult phase of rounding up the partially Gifted that Landon Snow's research indicated were a plague spread across North America. Once that was done, the human race would be safe from these lethal mutants.

The call from the watcher on Vallon Drake's house had reported the arrival of Jason Bryson. The fact that the good detective had not reported in to Amundson did not bode well, and he'd contemplated having Bryson picked up, but planning the take down of the Gifted at the AGS Academy had taken his attention. Then the significance of Bryson's appearance had leapt when one of the primary subjects had turned up.

Vallon Drake, problem child AGS agent, was back in the city. Given she was without her powers, it was a golden opportunity to show her who was boss.

Two operations, and it would all be over.

"We're going in," came the tiny voice over the speakers, just as Crater, Page's man overseeing the Academy operation, swore and started talking rapidly into his headset.

"What is it? What's happening?" Wolf demanded.

A flurry of hurried conversations between Crater and Page, and then Page turned his bald, bullet head in Amundson's direction.

"They must have had warning. They escaped out the back of the school. We've got men in pursuit."

Wolf swore. The plan had been based on taking the Gifted unaware. They'd cut off their power, so how could they know Amundson's plan? A moot point, now. Now it was pursue and clean up the mess before the damned Gifted could make it to places where they could do more mischief.

The sound of shattered glass and broken wood came over the speakers and Amundson swung around to the other operation.

"We're in. We're in," came the disembodied voice.

They were going to do this. They had the damned house surrounded. There was no way Drake or the good detective could weasel away this time. Not that Jason had been a problem—his usefulness had just ended now that Amundson had a technological solution.

"Kitchen clear. No!" A shot. "Fuck. It's a cat."

"Living room clear."

Pounding footfall spoke of someone heading up the stairs.

"Basement door is locked. I repeat, basement door is locked." More pounding feet, more splintering wood, and the hollow sound of feet on stairs.

"Fuck. There's an open window. Repeat, open window. Target's in the wind. Repeat: target in the wind."

Fighting back the need to swear, Amundson wheeled on Page, who barked commands at Crater, who repeated them through the computer console. Page's pate showed a sheen of sweat that bespoke the seriousness of this failure. Crater just looked panicked, because failing at the take down of the AGS Academy was one thing, but losing the girl was another altogether.

Vallon Drake was a problem. She'd been a thorn in his side for too long. She needed to be locked up, helpless and begging to do what he commanded.

"What. The fuck. Is happening?" he growled.

Page glanced up from the console. "Fucking team apparently didn't realize there were windows hidden behind an overgrown rhododendron bush in the yard. Subjects escaped out them while our men searched the house. They can't have gotten far. I've got men scouring the neighborhood."

Page was fighting to maintain the bravado that had always encouraged Wolf to keep him around.

"You couldn't check the schematics of the house or keep a simple perimeter while the others went in?"

"We did. But the damned bush blocked sight of the window, and somehow they got past the man we posted in the backyard. The men stationed out front didn't see a thing."

"And where was this window?"

Page bit his lip, then smoothed his face of expression. "Apparently on the side, next to the neighbor's fence. It was the only window on that side of the house, and we didn't know it was there."

"Fuck. Fuck me." Wolf stomped over to the small office that was now his only office. The door slammed behind him and he fell back against it, fighting to slow his heartbeat and his breathing. "Fuck!" He kicked the huge desk that took up most of the miniscule space. The place was a dingy, fucking hole with its windowless walls. He should be—should be where? In an office in downtown Seattle, with a million-dollar view of the water and the Olympic Mountains—at least that was what Jason had said he'd had as an office before the damned Gifted wiped out the building and all its contents. It had been wiped away so completely he never would have remembered, except for what Jason had told him. Fucking Gifted. Fucking Change. Just who or what was he, now that he'd been Changed? He couldn't even trust his memories anymore. Who knew how many times some fucking Gifted like fucking Vallon Drake had done something that changed how he saw the world?

He ground his fists into his thighs. He would not let it happen again. Not to himself, not to the people of America. He crossed to the phone and stabbed a button. The speakerphone buzzed in the office, but finally the connection clicked complete.

"Sandhu." The researcher's voice filled the office.

Wolf took a deep breath to steady himself. "The grid. How's it holding up?" He spoke of the perimeter of installations that together blocked the power the Gifted needed to access their Gift. At least his voice was steady.

"Sir? The grid continues to operate within acceptable limits."

"Good. Good. And you've been readying the additional units as I requested?"

"Of course." Sandhu's voice suggested he was surprised Wolf asked. Sukh Sandhu was a leader's dream, brilliant as a researcher, but he rarely showed the propensity for questioning command decisions. Wolf appreciated that at this particular moment, given Sandhu himself had recommended that they limit the use of the installations to this area until such time as they were certain that there were no side effects.

Wolf scrubbed his eyes. A low-grade headache had been bothering him the last few days as if he had a cold coming on. "I want you to extend the grid across the continental US immediately. Get your teams out there on the borders north and south and then working down the seaboards. That should give us some coverage, right? Until we can get the entire grid settled in place?"

Sandhu's pause went on overlong. "Sir, I'm not certain we're ready to do that yet. We haven't completed our preliminary observations of the effect on the Seattle area."

Wolf glared at the phone. So Sandhu was going to let him down. "That'd be all well and good if this was a time of peace, Sukh. But we've got a war on our hands and a bunch of enemy agents on the run, probably aiming to get outside our perimeter so that they can access their power.

Who knows what they'll do if they get there? The only way to keep the country safe is to get the grid in place."

Another pause on the line. "All right. But we have a problem, sir. I will need more men to make this happen. The team I have is needed here to monitor the Seattle grid, now that it's functioning."

"How many men?" Wolf could strip a few away from other functions. He could make this happen.

"How quickly do you want this done?"

Now. Yesterday. A month ago. Wolf settled in the uncomfortable chair he had inherited from Gregor Gleason. He could replace the chair, but the damned thing had become a trophy of war, the symbol of Wolf's ascendancy. "Immediately."

There was a brief pause as if Sandhu did mental calculations. "I'd say, at minimum, fifty."

His fingers drummed the desktop as he considered. Fifty was huge. Fifty was more than he could possibly raise by pulling in all favors that might be owed by Loadstone or any other Homeland Security connection.

"You'll have your men." He tapped the phone off and held his finger over the speed dial as he took a deep breath. It was time to take on Homeland Security head on.

CHAPTER 23 —MUSTY DARKNESS, LAVENDER LIGHT

Vallon's breath burned in her lungs. Her boots pounded on the concrete as she sprinted downhill toward Lake Union through the gloom of the evening neighborhood. Jason ran beside her through the cool air, silent and sleek as a hungry hound and just as deadly, given he was the one who held the only gun during their mad, silent retreat to the basement after the Homeland Security command had come through her kitchen door.

How they'd both known to just go silent, to just return to the basement, she wasn't sure. But he'd freed her hands and they'd worked together using hand signals and whispers and fought the window open and then helped each other out into the thick cover of the rhododendron bush as if they'd done it a thousand times before. In the darkness of the side of the house, they'd both scaled the tall fence into the neighbor's yard and left, silent as ghosts, Vallon helping them avoid the houses with dogs. They'd cut across the yards to the next street over and then set out at a run to get as far away as they could before the alarm went out.

Roaring car engines behind them said it wasn't as far as she'd like. In unison, they dove behind the bushes of the house they were passing. A vehicle sped past down the hill.

"That means the Fremont Bridge is blocked," she whispered to Jason.

"The Aurora?" Jason's face was almost invisible in the shadows. Not seeing his gaunt features made it almost possible to believe he was the man he'd once been instead of an enemy.

The north end of the Aurora Bridge was the actual home of the Fremont troll; it was also east and slightly uphill from where they were. But if the Fremont Bridge was closed to them, they had to get across somehow. Staying in the Fremont area was a trap that Amundson's men would be happy to spring on them.

"Fine."

They struck out, loping together back uphill and eastward and ducking into cover when they heard someone coming. They crossed Fremont Avenue into a quiet neighborhood, where the explosive sounds of television and hushed strains of music came from the surrounding houses. She started trying car doors.

"What the hell are you doing?" Jason demanded when she fell behind him.

"We need a car."

He looked at her a moment, his haggard face made more so by the overhead streetlight. "I'm in enough shit as it is. Do we really need to add a charge of grand theft auto?"

She rolled her eyes. "After kidnapping and murder, I think auto theft is the least of your worries. Besides, we'll need a car eventually, so the three of us can get the hell out of these dead lands."

His gaze narrowed. "You're serious. Amundson's really done it."

"I don't talk to feel my lips flap. We've got one hell of a problem. I would have expected you to feel it, given you can sense Change." She closed her eyes. She was just so damned tired of all the running and how everything felt so out of control.

She felt Jason's gaze and opened her eyes. She couldn't afford to be tired. Not with so much at stake.

"We need a car to get the hell outta Dodge, because I'm not sure how long I'm going to be able to carry on, running like this. Whatever this is, it's sucking my strength. Given how you look, I'd say it's affecting you, too."

They finally found an older Ford Focus with a dented fender. Not exactly undistinguishable and not exactly a high performance vehicle either, but it would have to do. They slid inside and Jason made short work of jump-starting the engine.

"And you said you hadn't done this before."

"Shut up." But he tossed her a grimace that probably passed for a smile.

The little car rumbled as they headed uphill. They avoided the Aurora Bridge, too, and instead turned eastward back to I-5. They reached the on-ramp with no problem and crossed over into Seattle. The city lights glimmered in the gathering darkness. Car lights formed a never-ending necklace north and south that glimmered in the waters of Lake Union where the last pontoon planes were coming in for the night.

"Where to?" Jason asked.

"Wherever you've got Fi stashed. We aren't leaving her here to die with the rest of them."

Jason's glanced at her, his gaze assessing.

"If you're wondering if I'm going to try to escape again, you're most likely right. But I can give you this assurance: I can't and won't do a flipping thing to help you unless you get Fi and me out of this city. Your choice."

His jaw settled into a hard line, but he swung the car off the highway and down into the downtown core, then farther south to Pioneer Square and the tourist areas around iconic Elliott Bay Books.

"The underground," she guessed, as he pulled into a parking spot not too far from where she and Fi and Jason had escaped from that very place. "You fucking left her in the underground!"

She slammed her fist into his shoulder. "How could you do that?" Another punch. "Don't you know what she's been through? The poor kid'll be terrified—and you left her there! Do you know what harm that could do to her mental state? She's barely recovered from what her mother did to her, and now you do this?"

But it made sense. It wouldn't have been the first place she looked, and the egress of the sea water in the soil made it hard to detect anything down there even when she had her full power.

He fended off her blows and grabbed her wrists. "*I* wanted her some place safe. *She* is. Now are *we* going to get her, or do *I* handcuff *you* to the car?"

He produced a set of plastic cuffs and her jaw snapped shut.

Jason was an oddity. An asshole. A flipping wild card, who was just delaying her battle against Amundson. She really should be dealing with that, but she would not leave her best friend in Jason's hands. He'd already killed once.

She followed him into an alley behind the Seattle Underground tour company. The Seattle Underground was the linked tunnels that remained of what had once been the ground level of the city. After the great Seattle fire, the city had decided that all buildings must be of stone and that the streets would be filled in one to two stories to deal with the tidal flooding that regularly occurred in Pioneer Square. This left a series of tunnels, walkways, and rooms beneath the newly established ground level that became a thriving society of speakeasies, opium dens, and flophouses.

Now it was all long abandoned and condemned, but a small area had been reinforced for safety and gave tourists insight into a lost Seattle past. That left a number of tunnels largely abandoned to rats and the homeless.

Jason led her to a small metal door in a brick-walled building. The door seemed locked, but a solid yank dragged the metal door open. Scrapes on the door frame showed that this had been done many times.

"I found this years ago when I was still in uniform."

The opening yawned onto darkness and released a fetid odor of urine and old mud. Jason fished a key ring out of his pocket and displayed a small maglight. The narrow beam of light exposed brick walls around a steep staircase that led into darkness. He handed her the flashlight and ushered her forward.

Cold, musty air surrounded her as she started down. From somewhere came the *drip-drip-drip* of water and the repulsive sound of scurrying.

"You left Fi in this? You really are an asshole, you know." Her voice echoed back at her. Hell, *she'd* be panicked if she were left in darkness in a place like this. If Fi had somehow gotten loose, she could be lost in this maze of darkness.

She reached the bottom of the stairs and flashed the light around her. A narrow walkway between the building and another wall in the street, with a glimmering ceiling of glass blocks that had been paved over long ago. Underfoot was the original sidewalk. The street-side wall showed where the road had been built up about eighteen feet. She flashed the light over the ceiling and the pale mauve skylights reflected back at her.

Jason came up behind her. "That way."

Vallon followed the narrow beam of light into the utter darkness, carefully counting the number of paces she took. Thankfully there weren't a lot of corners. The last time she'd been in these tunnels she'd had no light at all, and had fumbled her way along, following the walls. Having the light might be worse because she caught glimpses of movement, disappearing rat tails, and perhaps other, bigger, things. That was the trouble with an active imagination.

"Here." Jason stopped her beside a closed wooden door that once had been painted red. The wood groaned and hinges squealed as he forced it open onto more darkness. A whimper and the sound of breathing. The scent of anise and mint.

"Fi?"

"Vallon?" Soft, almost disbelieving.

Vallon shoved Jason aside and flashed the light around the room. Dust and cobwebs everywhere. Debris of beer cans and an old mattress spoke of previous denizens, but chained in a corner, a pale figure caught the light.

"Fi!" Vallon was at her side in an instant, arms thrown around her. Sobbing, Fi collapsed in her arms, slight and trembling. Her fine-spun blonde hair smelled of fear-sweat and grit.

"Vallon, I'm so sorry. But he came and he killed Jack and forced me to come with him. How did you find me?"

"Easy. Jason brought me."

Fi jerked away. "He brought you?"

Vallon nodded back into the darkness and Jason materialized. He stood over them, gun ready. "Hello, Fi. How're you doing?" Like he'd just bumped into her on a sunny Seattle afternoon.

In this setting, with gun drawn, his companionable attitude upped the creepy quotient by about fifteen fold. Fi cringed against Vallon and she fumbled the light down to the chains restraining Fi's ankles. Solid-looking metal-and-leather shackles were held closed by matching padlocks. These were connected by solid links to chains that were shackled to the wall. It didn't look like a place that had been set up on the spur of the moment. More like the kind of out-of-the-way place Jason would expect to bring her.

When she flashed the light in his face, she knew she was right. He could decide to keep them both here and then where would they be? Somewhere no one would hear them scream and where she didn't stand a hope of doing what he wanted even if she wanted to. She pulled Fi into her side and glared up at him.

"Unchain her. Now."

Jason only shrugged and motioned to the keys on the maglight. Vallon fumbled them until she found the right one and the locks clicked open. She pulled a wobbly Fi to her feet.

"Get us out of here," Vallon demanded and prayed her command would work. The guy looked like shit, and if anything, it was getting worse. An undertone of rot marred his spice and oceans scent.

His weapon wavered—almost as if he contemplated shooting—but then he motioned them toward the open doorway.

"Are you okay?" she asked Fi. Her voice echoed back at her. There'd be no conspiratorial whispers here, but if she could just get Fi to understand…

She gripped Fi's hand and motioned at the door. Fi's gaze flickered up to her and she nodded, then eased a little ahead.

Fi stepped through the doorway, holding the maglight. Vallon hesitated, listening for Jason behind her. She half-turned.

Just push off with her feet and drive her shoulder into Jason. Then back to the door and drag it shut behind her. Hopefully it would leave Jason disoriented for the few seconds they needed.

"Don't even think about it." His voice came through the darkness. Then a strong hand caught her arm and he swung her to face him. "You think I don't know you well enough to know you'd try something?" He shoved her at the door.

She stumbled through and up against Fi. God, she was getting too weak too fast. He never would have been able to do that before. They had to get out of this dead zone.

Ten minutes later, the metal door to street level gave with a groan and they stepped out into the briny wind running through the Seattle streets. The traffic on I-5 was a low, distant rumble. A siren wailed somewhere up toward Swedish Hospital. Fi leaned, panting, against the wall, as if she'd just climbed a mountain, and Vallon could empathize. Movement that had always been easy was becoming harder. Whatever Amundson had done, its effects were coming faster. Even Jason was puffing, as he trained his weapon on them.

"I'm almost starting to believe you," he said. "A single set of stairs shouldn't leave me so winded."

"Good." She nodded. "Then let's get the hell out of here." She limped back down the alley toward the stolen car, but reflected red and blue strobes stopped her. Police. They must have found the car.

She crept the rest of the length of the alley and peered down the street, just as a black sedan oiled its way around the corner. It stopped and two men climbed out. One was big, bald-headed with a cold mercenary look to him. The other one she knew.

Tall, blond, and cold-eyed as a predator in his custom tailored suit, Wolf Amundson stood there.

§

It was time to leave.

The infernal albino's question kept playing over and over in his ears. Why was he here, when Vallon was in danger and needed him?

Because you told her you would bring aid from the Council. As if that would happen. He had been a fool to ever believe it might happen.

The Cartos Council's unhurried discussion was an abomination that could drive him to howling, given the danger that lurked on the far side of the world. Snow was right when he called them old fools. They were fools who had cut themselves off from the world, and now that the world was in danger, they did not know what to do.

"I still say America is not our responsibility," Wark said, with a shake of his cold, northern Europerean head. He sat back in his chair as if that was all to be said.

Damned Demetrio sat with his long legs stretched before him, his hands draped on the chair arms, but he said nothing. It was as if he waited to see which way the winds blew before he'd take control. And he could assume control. He had been the Council voice for many years until he decided to control the Council from outside the room.

"It is not America or the Gifted that are the issue," Xavier said, taking a deep breath to calm himself. "If you will just read the landscape— try to touch Seattle. You will see that it has, for all intents, ceased to exist. At least, Pangea's power no longer runs there."

The heavy tapestry behind the council chairs seemed to swallow his arguments. If only he could just grab their hands and show them, as Vallon had shown him and Hector. But the Council would never agree to his touch, and Leticia would stop him if he tried to do it by force. Besides, Hector had seen and he was not helping, either. He had fallen back on his role of tiebreaker for the Council and would not add to the debate until his counsel was needed.

The florid murals on the walls and ceiling seemed akin to something overripe and rotting—a rotting disease of the mind, and all who joined the Council caught it. Even Hector. But then that was likely why Hector had been selected—and approved by Demetrio—to maintain the old ways of secrecy.

Amongst this Council, the only hope appeared to be the oldest amongst them. Old Victor spoke with power, but he had missed the point of Pangea's possible destruction and spoke endlessly about the need to save his new-found granddaughter.

Damnation and Creation! Xavier slammed his palm against the marble wall. The resounding boom silenced the room as he rounded on them.

"While you dither, the world is in jeopardy! You act like old men who refuse to face facts!"

Why are you not with Vallon?

He felt the weight of the Council's glares. Sensed Snow stirring by the wall and Leticia, like a harpy waiting to pounce, guarding him. The gnome of a man was like an insidious parasite that had lodged its offspring in Xavier's brain.

Why are you not with Vallon?

"Don't you see? Cut through all your arguments of secrecy and the fact remains that our mother, Pangea, is in danger. The blight upon North America is only the beginning. The Americans may block the power in America, but do you think they are the only ones who will not want beings like us to hold our power? What if the European powers decide to do the same? And the others? How much desolation can Pangea sustain?"

"They would not dare do that to Pangea!" Demetrio said.

"The Europeans are wiser than these fool Americans," Wark asserted.

"Listen to yourselves! What have you become? Once we were a proud people, who could claim responsibility for all the world. What are we now? Men and women who refuse to stick our heads up for fear we might be found and so we let the world die around us!"

Xavier turreted toward Snow. "Well, you are too late! We have been found. He proves it. For years you have discounted these people. You have laughed at them as upstart cousins who are too beneath you to acknowledge. You discourage or kill those who find their way to you, though they seem to be drawn here from around the world. You ignore an entire continent, where the blood has coalesced again into something powerful enough to cause volcanoes to move and major earthquakes to erupt. You saw the devastation of the Indian Ocean tsunami, and yet you convinced yourselves that it was an accident, caused by beings who are no more than children. These same *children* have found ways to perform works that our ancestors would have found taxing, whether for good or ill. To me, that says they are less children and more our equals. And now the unGifted want to wipe them out by damaging our mother, Pangea. Surely that should concern us. First and foremost because without Pangea everything will die. But in our own selfish self-interest, surely anything that can kill those who call themselves the Gifted can also be used against us. What will you do when you are cut off from Pangea, father?"

Demetrio sat like a cliff face that resisted the strongest dynamite. With his father here, there was little chance that the Council would take action. Just go himself? Take Snow? Of course, Leticia would try to stop them. The Council had yet to decide the little man's fate.

Hector raised his hand for silence. Perhaps he would finally do something. Today, dressed in a business suit of darkest blue silk with a tie of subtle gold and red on a white button-down shirt, he at least looked the part of their leader. "Brothers and sisters. We have known for generations how the blood spreads across the population. The blood that was diluted for millennia, Pangea has seen fit to return to strength. Already we must be careful in our use of power, because more and more of the population notice the Change and remember. We must decide whether that natural distillation of the blood is worth saving."

Murmurs started in the room, because at last someone had listened to what Xavier had said. Someone had heard.

Hector held up his hand again. "We must also preserve our Great Mother."

Praise, Pangea, he was going to speak in favor of taking action!

Hector nodded to the room. "At present, the small blemish of Seattle is like a pimple on the face of a beautiful woman, and we all know such can heal themselves. I say this is not devastating, and perhaps we would be better off waiting to see if the dangers Xavier speaks of ever materialize. It would seem unwise to expose ourselves for a mere momentary imperfection."

He sat down as the Council nodded. Nodded!

Idiots! Fools! They would risk everything. They would wait until it might be too late. If they did, they did not deserve to live. But Vallon did. He spun on his heel, strode to Snow, and shoved Leticia to her knees. He placed his hand on the little man's shoulder and turned back to the Council.

"I lost one mother to the likes of you. I will not lose Pangea."

He -reached- for Venice's deep-buried ley lines. As the rose and lavender geysered up around them, he heard Leticia screeching.

CHAPTER 24 — A SLOW PATH TO DYING

After an hour's drive, Francis Drake turned off of the highway at Kelso. I-5 was too dangerous to travel. There was too much chance that a description of their vehicles had somehow been cobbled together. He drove down the off-ramp and into the small town, with its strip mall and fast food restaurants gleaming with evening neon, and pulled into a service station. Two cars followed him. Where the other two had gone, he didn't know.

The service station was one of those big, modern ones with twelve pumps and a roof high enough to allow a motorhome easy passage. At this time of night it was empty, except for one car pulling out. Bright neon lights chased away the night and the red, white, and blue convenience store was lit up from within, the lone attendant at the cash register. No one who would notice his group arriving, but the security cameras above the pumps would.

He climbed out, keeping his face averted, and inhaled the diesel and kitchen-grease scents overlaid on the scent of cedar and running water. The hum of I-5 came from just up the hill through the fir trees, and the cowboy country of a local radio station came from a passing car. The Columbia River ran just south of them on its last 80 miles to the Pacific Ocean. They'd take the Ocean Highway that followed the north side of the river to that relative safety and hopefully meet up with the others in along the Oregon coast as planned. He had to hold to the hope that the others had won free, because two vehicles of Gifted was barely enough to protect themselves, let alone mount an attack.

His heart sank further when the door opened on one of the vehicles and out stepped Toby Watts, his unGifted liaison with Loadstone.

The man's dirty-blond hair was askew, but he looked as if he was enjoying himself. He strolled over to Francis.

"Hey Boss. Nice run from Seattle. You figure we gas up here and run straight through to Lincoln City?"

"Who's with you?" Francis asked.

"With me?" Toby shrugged. "That'd be no one. The others fell behind when we were heading for the cars. When I heard shots, I scrammed outta there."

The cool breeze with its hints of ocean suddenly turned frozen. "You mean you have no Gifted with you? Who's in the other car?"

They both turned to the other sedan that was as dark blue as a bruise and suddenly menacing. Francis -reached- to check, something he stupidly hadn't done since he escaped the dead zone. He was slipping, and that was totally unacceptable, but Gifted flame flickered and danced around the vehicle. The sudden alarm faded as swiftly as it had come.

He crossed to the car and yanked open the door. A pale woman looked up at him, her face in tears. Beyond her, crowded in the rear seat and with two children crowded onto the passenger seat, were a total of six teenagers, who appeared to be twelve or thirteen. Survivors from the warehouse. Too young to be any good to him.

The woman struggled to undo her seatbelt and climbed out, only to sag like a rag doll into Francis' arms. He hesitated a moment, not enjoying the woman's sodden breath and her pungent scent of charcoal, nor the way she clung like a limpet.

"There, there." He managed the obligatories and patted her back before shoving her into Toby's arms. "Everything's all right. You're safe."

She shook her head. She was middle-aged, with a sleek Latino look that was fading into matronly, and without the level of Gift he'd expect in an agent, but still more Gifted than most of the population. Someone's wife, he supposed, unless Gleason and company had been scraping the bottom of the barrel. Administrative staff, perhaps? Keep them in the fold and watch how their offspring develop?

She swiped at her eyes. "They—they got Matt—Matthew—when Toby turned back to help him. Matt had told me to just get in the car and drive. When I heard the gunfire, I shoved the kids in and did just that. I left them."

The tears filled her eyes again and threatened to overflow.

"You did fine. Toby's here." But Matthew was not, and Matthew was the one with the trained use of the Gift. He glanced over at the blond man. Toby Watts had thrown in his lot with the Gifted since New Madrid, probably due to the sizeable paycheck Francis provided to the mercenary Mr. Watts. After they'd both miraculously escaped the black hole that was all that was left of the New Madrid installation, Toby'd said he had some unfinished business to attend to with Francis' ersatz daughter. But a man with Toby's skills and intelligence wasn't to be turned away lightly. Francis had taken him amongst the survivors of New Madrid on their cross-country mission to destroy Amundson.

If only he'd done that first. But instead, he'd gotten too cute for his own good. Instead of taking the direct approach to rid America of Amundson, he'd thought he could use Amundson's imprisonment of the school children as a justification for rewriting the nation as he saw fit. Unfortunately, he'd underestimated his adversary.

Being wrong left him feeling a little sick.

He looked back at the still-sniffling woman. Untrained, she'd still managed to get more people out than Toby had, or himself. "You did well. You got the children out. That's excellent work." Just not excellent enough. "Now you've got to fill your gas tank, pay with cash, and continue on to the coast. Do you have the money?"

Her passengers climbed out and stretched as she fumbled in her purse, nodded, and went to obey. Derrick and Toby filled their vehicles. Just how and why had Toby made it alone? What had happened to the Gifted he was supposedly aiding? Strange that the one unGifted among them had managed to get free. A little worm of doubt formed in Francis' gut. But in New Madrid, Toby Watts had lived while many Gifted had not. Sometimes life made no sense—or perhaps it did. If Toby wasn't a friend....

But that made no sense, given all they had been through together.

Still, he'd hoped that between the three vehicles there'd be at least four or five former AGS agents and some of his rogues. Instead, he had next to nothing. Derrick, the near useless Carragio, himself, and half a dozen barely pubescent teenagers, who would barely have two years of Gifted training behind them. He -reached- out beyond the slumbering town, back along the highway, seeking the blaze of light that was Gifted. They had to be following him. There was no way they could have passed him.

The unremitting darkness did not bode well.

Was this all that remained of his team? Of his hope? For a moment he felt like the last hunted rat on a sinking ship as Amundson extended the perimeter that would make the Gift impossible. He -reached- farther north and came up against the emptiness that was all he could sense of Seattle. Along I-5, blips of unGifted and partially-Gifted light either ceased to exist or popped into existence as they crossed the unseen barrier that confined the city. Around the perimeter, power frothed and foamed like waves around a stone jetty. Where it went he didn't know. Here, he felt alive, could scent the life around him on the river and cedar-scented wind.

In Redmond, everything died; and that was what Amundson had in store for the rest of the country. *His* country.

"Toby, I want you to escort this lot to the rendezvous. Wait for the others. Derrick, Carragio, and I have some business to take care of."

Toby's pale blue gaze measured him and finally he nodded. "You're going back, aren't you?"

Francis didn't even acknowledge the question. Instead, he returned to the car and nodded to Carragio and Derrick to climb in. He pulled out ahead of everyone and turned back to the highway.

He might have started all this years ago by abandoning Seattle and the AGS. He wasn't going to do it again.

§

"What the hell's happening?" Jason asked.

Vallon and Fi were indistinct shadows against the alley wall as Vallon peered out into the Seattle street. The stink of tidal mud clung to the wind and mixed with ship diesel and car exhaust this close to the harbor. From up the hill behind him came the sound of sirens, heading toward Swedish Hospital and Harborview Medical Center. The strobe of blue and red police lights caught in Vallon's eyes as she glared back at him.

Vallon nodded toward the street where he'd parked the car they'd stolen. He edged toward the end of the alley and peered out of the shadows. The sedan was boxed in by two Seattle PD cruisers and a dark sedan that seemed to absorb the street light. He tensed and his stomach felt like he'd just ingested a boulder. Along with the uniformed officers stood a man in a custom-fitted black suit with white-blond hair that gleamed like chrome in the street light.

Wolf Amundson here, as usual barging in to take control. This time of the vehicle. By the way the two officers stood back with crossed arms, it was clear he'd already pissed off Seattle's finest.

Jason looked back at Vallon. "How the hell did he get here so fast?"

With her hands on her hips, she looked like she could tear his throat out with her teeth. "My question, exactly. So what is this, Jason? Decide your little personal project wasn't going to work so you hand us over to him?"

Her glare could have reduced a lesser man to ash, but he knew Vallon Drake and knew that regardless of her bravado, she was probably just as scared shitless as the rest of them. He waved them farther back into the alley with his pistol. "I had nothing to do with it. He's probably monitoring scanners and heard the report of the car and its registered owner's address. He could easily have put two and two together."

The glare held on him a few moments more. "So what do we do now, Mr. Man with the Gun?"

He looked down at the pistol in his hand as more sirens echoed amongst the downtown towers. He'd worked this area in a uniform for years before becoming a detective. All those years he'd had the feeling that he was protected because he worked the 'right' end of a gun—the police end. Now he was likely going to meet the wrong end. Jeezus, what was he doing? Everything was going to hell and just didn't make sense anymore. Amundson had promised him Vallon and yet now he seemed to be hunting the two of them. But if Amundson had technology that could block the Gift, he might decide he didn't need Jason anymore—except as another research project.

"We need to blow this area as fast as we can. If Amundson decides it's us, he'll have this area cordoned off in no time." A wave of fatigue ran through him and he closed his eyes as he motioned the two women back up the alley.

"Why not just turn us in? Amundson'd be pleased, I'm sure." Damn it, she was goading him.

"Just shut up and don't tempt me." He checked over his shoulder. No sign of a search *yet*. That was one thing in their favor. But he wasn't going to tell Vallon he was working on his own, now.

He scrubbed at his face. He was just so damned tired—as if something had just scooped him out. Did his face show the same exhaustion he saw in the dark circles under both women's eyes, and in the way they seemed to move as if they had weights tied to their limbs? The toes of his shoes kept catching on the concrete, and even his windbreaker weighed down his shoulders.

Like maybe all the shit stories Vallon had been feeding him since he nabbed her in Fremont were true. If that were the case, then she probably couldn't help him with what he wanted here in Seattle, anyway. Hell, if that were the case, just what was this technology of Amundson's doing to the rest of the people who lived in Seattle? Were they all feeling like he did? The wail of sirens suddenly took on a different meaning. Could people die from it?

The hospital wouldn't have a clue what they were dealing with. They wouldn't believe him if he told them. But for years, people had been talking about the harm of radio towers placed near schools and homes. What if the opposite were true for whatever power it was that fuelled Vallon and the Gifted? Maybe what fuelled the Gift fuelled everything.

If he was fucked for having gone all woo-woo before, well, he was really off his rocker now.

At the other end of the alley, Vallon took a careful scan of the next street. He came up beside her, scenting her faint ashes of roses scent.

The street was mostly dark, with widely spaced streetlights and broad, older trees that added to the shadows. The buildings were older two-story conversions to small trendy shops and lofts. At this hour there wasn't a lot of activity on the street, which could be good for them, or which could make them stand out. Vallon looked a question at him.

"That way." He pointed them up the hill and back toward James Street. "We'll head uphill to Broadway. They won't expect that." Back to the place he'd first met Vallon.

Something shifted in Vallon's gaze, but she moved out briskly, tugging Fi with her. Fi stumbled behind as if she were in a daze or had fallen back into the semi-incoherent woman he and Vallon had rescued from a burning building not too far from here only a few months ago. Too bad.

At Broadway they'd steal another car, and then get the hell out of Seattle. He'd find some quiet spot and force Vallon to do what he wanted. He'd kill Fi if he had to.

He would.

He caught Fi's arm when she stumbled and she looked up at him with huge, frightened eyes like a puppy.

He would. He could.

They reached James Street, angled up the steep hill from the water, and cut under the ever-rumbling lanes of I-5. He turned them up toward the hospital and urged them faster up the steep climb. Even Vallon was panting by the time they reached the top. Fi was sobbing as the ground flattened out around Swedish Hospital. He ordered them to stop and she collapsed on the curb.

Normally, the neighborhood should be quiet, with closed offices and quiet residences. He should know. He'd spent enough time here. But tonight tail and headlights glowed as lines of cars circled the area, looking for parking. A crowd milled around the emergency entrance.

"What's going on?" Fi asked, her breath still hitching.

"It's gotta be the barrier and the blockage. More people are feeling it." Vallon's gaze met Jason's. "It's like I said. Everything's dying here, just like we are."

Her gaze dared him to admit it, dared him to do something about it, and he fucking just didn't know what to do. That was it, wasn't it? The way he'd been feeling ever since Cheryl died? Helpless and hopeless and as if his will to go on had been stretched so thin it didn't exist anymore.

Until he met Vallon and grasped at the fantastical hope that she might be able to bring him and Cheryl together again.

But that only happened in movies, didn't it. Someplace where simply wanting something enough could make it happen. And here he stood, before the medical facility where he'd watched Cheryl die, no matter how hard both of them had wanted her to live. Just like all those people around the emergency doorway would die.

Unless he and Vallon fixed things.

He sighed and scrubbed at his face again, putting all his thoughts in order. "You really were telling the truth, weren't you? Amundson's technology is going to kill us all unless we do something." He glanced back down the hill. "Maybe I should just head back down that hill and kill him."

"That would just get you killed," Fi said.

A surprisingly coherent assessment.

"Fi? You're okay?" Vallon knelt down beside her.

Fi shoved her fine hair back off her face. "Course, I'm okay. Being left in the dark was no fun, but I survived—no thanks to you!" She glared up at him, then shoved up to standing. "So what do we do to stop the blockage?"

"We need to find whatever it is that Amundson has ringing the Seattle area. When I drove into the City, it was like I crossed a boundary. That suggests that there's something out there like a fence, blocking the power, instead of a single installation disrupting outward."

Jason thought a moment. "That's tough. That means whatever's causing the field could be anywhere on the perimeter. It'll be like searching for the proverbial needle in the haystack."

Streetlights caught in Fi's furrowed brow. "Yeah, but it also means the technology is harder to guard, right? There's a bunch of installations instead of just one."

"She's right," Vallon said. "A single installation would be almost impossible to break into to destroy, but a chain of installations around the perimeter might be possible to break. We can hope that if one link is broken, the whole thing goes down, just like a power grid. So do we split up to search, or what?" She eyed him, eyed the gun he still held.

So what's it going to be, slick? You gonna carry on, burning bridges with your crazy ways, or you gonna do the right thing? He could almost imagine his old Seattle PD partner, Clint, standing before him. But then Clint wouldn't want to have much to do with him if he knew what Jason had done in the past few days.

Did he really have a choice? He holstered his gun, and all the tension seemed to run out of him. He staggered, but caught himself. "We stay together, but only because we have more chance of making things happen if we're together. I can't imagine Amundson'd leave whatever he's got out there completely unguarded. We just need a way to find it and get there."

And he had just the way to get that ride—one that Amundson wouldn't be watching for.

CHAPTER 25 —OPACITY

Ozone and lightning overwhelmed the stink of mud flats, tidal water, and diesel as Xavier stepped free of the geyser of power that filled the Everett boathouse with brilliant white light. The geyser died out and the building was in darkness again, the unheated air cool on his naked skin. He -reached-, but everything was the same in his little hideaway. The tiny candles of birds roosting in the eaves. A brace of mice. No sign of anything human or Cartos.

That was the reason he'd come here.

Beside him in the darkness were the bulk of the sailboat he supposedly worked on and the shape of the Audi he and Vallon had escaped in from her house. The car was stolen, but was better than nothing, and he could always change its appearance if need be. A moan turned him around to a doubled-over form beside him, scented of baby's breath.

"What the hell was that?" mumbled Landon Snow between dry heaves.

The little man's naked white skin seemed to glow in the darkness.

"My personal form of travel." Xavier stepped past Landon to the stairs up to the small living area. "One you apparently are not well suited for. Come. I have food and clothing up here."

Landon groaned, but he staggered after, banging into equipment and sending something clattering across the floor. Not exactly stealthy, this Snow. But then, he had never seen Landon Snow look positively vulnerable before, either. Even in Venice, when he was truly in danger of being killed, Snow had acted like he still had power. Now he moved like a frightened dog—or one that was seriously ill.

Upstairs, Xavier turned on a low light and dug out black trousers and a shirt for himself and a pair of shorts and a tattered, sweat-stained t-shirt for Landon that he kept for when he took the appearance of a boat owner. Landon just looked from him to the clothing, like he was mad.

Xavier shook his head. "It's all I have. I don't keep a store here, just clothing for myself. Unless you'd prefer to leave here naked?" It was difficult not to smile at the little man's discomfort, given this was the merest payback for what Snow had done.

Finally Landon sighed and yanked on the t-shirt and shorts—many sizes too big around the waist. A piece of nylon cord to hold up the shorts completed the ridiculous ensemble, but somehow the diminutive man retained a simple dignity. His pale eyes blinked and watered in the weak light as he studied his surroundings. Just how much could he learn without his glasses?

Snow turned down the energy bar Xavier offered and was forced to wear a set of oversized flip-flops because all of Xavier's shoes were too big.

"So now that you've finished outfitting me for Halloween, what are your plans? I take it we are no longer in Venice."

"Just north of Everett," Xavier said around a mouthful of granola and peanut butter. Energy began to course through his body in a gentle counterpoint to the throb of afterburn from their transit.

"Can all Cartos do such teleportation?" Snow was picking at a thread on the '*Save the Sound*' t-shirt he wore, as if it were an off-hand question. But nothing with Landon Snow was off-hand, and exposing anything to this little man was never a good idea. He already knew too much, and though he appeared to have acquiesced to the fact that he would never be Gifted or Cartos, giving in like that did not seem to be Landon Snow's true nature.

"Transmutation. It is managed by very few."

"But you don't get ill from the transit?"

Xavier just kept eating. Let that be his answer.

Snow took the opportunity to wander around the small living space. He stopped by the cot and looked up at Xavier. "Vallon has been here." As if he could sniff her presence, their sex.

"We came here on our way to Anacortes."

"So you were there."

Xavier nodded and closed his eyes. She had bolted inside that installation without waiting for him, just as she'd gone against his wishes in

New Madrid. And now she was gone again, against his better judgment. She never listened—just went off in her headlong rush to do what she thought was right. On the one hand, he could admire her determination. On the other—his fingers tightened around the granola bar and it crumbled to pieces.

He opened his eyes to find Snow looking at him. "You must be a very strong man, to let the woman you love go into danger all the time."

The bar's foil wrapper crumpled in his fist and he banked it off the edge of the counter and into the garbage. "Vallon will go where she will go. She is fearless."

A nod, and Snow wandered over to the rail of the little loft area to peer down into the darkness of the boathouse. "Perhaps she reminds you of your mother."

The remains of the granola bar turned to lead in his stomach. Turning the little man to a pulp for his goading would be a pleasure, but he would *not* give Landon Snow the satisfaction of knowing there was too much truth to Snow's words, and too much truth to the twisted frustration that coiled through his chest and gnawed at his heart.

"I think that Vallon is her own woman."

Snow swung back to him with an expression akin to scientific interest over a dissection. "But I gather your mother was, too. It seems you've chosen the same kind of woman."

"What I choose is no business of yours." He grabbed a leather jacket from the closet and a packet of tools from a side bench and headed for the stairs. Vallon was *not* like his mother and what he was feeling—the helpless protectiveness—was nothing his father had ever felt, because his father never loved anything, regardless of what he'd said. He turned back to Landon. "Are you coming or staying here?"

"Coming, of course."

Xavier thundered down the stairs and into the car. At the front of the car, he brought power up from the earth and used it to unbond the molecules of the license plate. At the rear he reached down, touched the metal, and the numbers rearranged themselves.

"Very neat," Snow said.

Xavier ignored him and climbed in, into fading pine air freshener scent. The wires from hot wiring the car still hung loose. Snow climbed in the passenger side. "I'm sorry if I've upset you, Xavier. I was just providing an observation."

"I think we will find whatever installation causes the perimeter around Seattle and then destroy it." He kept his hands clasped around the steering wheel and refused to look in Snow's direction. If he did, he just might use his fists. "I need you to open the boathouse door. Now."

Creation be praised, the infernal little man obeyed. A slice of orange-tinted darkness appeared behind him, illuminating Snow in his ridiculous getup. Just start the car and leave him behind, or better still, run him over? It was a satisfying option that would just cause him more problems. He touched the wires together and the engine cranked over and caught, then he backed outside into the burning orange of the marina's streetlights. Snow secured the door and climbed back in.

"Where to?" he asked.

The gravel road led through the crowded lines of dry-docked boats and the marina—silent now in the night—then met up with paved roads that led eventually back to I-5 South. Moonlight showed small whitecaps on the Snohomish River and groups of gulls roosting on its banks for the night, sheltered from the stiff breeze off Tulalip Bay. Xavier -reached-southward through the darkness, past the glittering city of Everett, and slammed into the void that was what the American's called the Emerald City. Vallon was there, somewhere. Alive or dead. If she were alive, she was most certainly dying, just as everything would be dying in that zone.

Not a good thought. He shivered. Vallon was working her usual magic in the heart of the city to rescue her friend and deal with Jason Bryson. She was safe. He had to believe that.

"We will seek the perimeter edge and follow it until we find an installation. If we do not find one, then we will have to surmise that whatever causes the void exists somewhere inside the field itself."

"We're going to have to be careful. Amundson doesn't care about the casualties. The research I think they're basing this technology on clearly indicated potential side effects, but either someone didn't bother to warn Amundson or he doesn't give a damn." The dash lights tattooed Snow's features blue and green as he faced Xavier. "So how do we help Vallon?"

Xavier guided the car along the river and then back toward I-5. "We bring down your Amundson's installation. Then we deal with him."

The blue-pink gaze seemed to study him for a moment, but then Snow shook his head and turned away.

"A bit sketchy, don't you think? I'd have thought you more a stickler for details."

"And I'd have thought you'd know when to keep your mouth shut." Xavier stomped the gas and the white car leapt forward, throwing Snow back against his seat. "Things move too fast for concrete plans. We must find these perimeter installations. Then we can plan."

Their headlights swept the empty roads as they followed the back routes back to the highway and then turned south. Vallon and the blockage loomed ahead, and he felt like one of the ancient mariners as the edge of the earth loomed ahead. *Here abide monsters, indeed.*

Snow sat silently beside him. Perhaps the monsters were closer than he liked to think.

§

The stolen vehicle with the Freemont address taunted Wolf Amundson. It sat in front of a heritage brick building, its blue faintly yellowed in the street lights, refusing to reveal its secrets. The wind off the water ran salt-scented, icy fingers through his hair and made him wish he'd worn his trenchcoat. Confirmation of who had taken the vehicle, where its occupants had gone, and why they had come to downtown Seattle all eluded him. But he suspected he knew the answer to at least two of the questions.

He turned back to Page, whose pate gleamed faintly in the amber street lights. The wind off the harbor rustled the tree branches and the first leaves of fall skittered down the street.

"We need a search of this area. Over to the stadiums, the harbor, over to Pike's Place."

Page nodded and spoke into his bluetooth. "What about up the hill?"

What, indeed? He turned and looked up past the lanes of I-5 traffic toward the towers of Harborview Medical Center and Swedish Hospital. Broadway was there. A lot of residential area. There was no reason for Drake or Detective Jason Bryson to go in that direction. South was more likely, trying to get out of the city and away from Amundson. The harbor ferries were easy to check if they tried that way. North was just back toward where they'd been, but then that could be a ruse, too. But up the hill… less likely and yet….

"Get a team up there stat. Drake's last major case started in a parking lot up there."

§

Vallon allowed Jason to draw her and Fi off James Street and into the dimness of the surrounding medical office buildings. The night was cool, the wind a little cooler up here where it had a clear path in from the water. Trees rustled around them as Jason pulled a phone out of his pocket. He punched in a number and waited a moment.

The area they stood in, near Swedish hospital, was alive with vehicles and people limping their way toward the emergency entrance. The crowd there had grown just in the few minutes they'd been standing there. Elderly people. Parents carrying children. All probably sensitive to the effects of Amundson's 'protective' field, because she sure enough felt like hell. How many of these people were partially Gifted? Seattle, with its preponderance of ley lines that attracted so many Gifted and partially Gifted, suggested a lot.

The effects of Amundson's field ached like a body-sized toothache that wore you down. These people would see the increasing weakness and depression and the loss of coordination, and this was the early stages. It was pretty likely people would just start dying. They really needed to get the hell out of town.

"Caught your breath yet?" she asked.

Fi nodded, but her tangled, fine hair and gaunt face made her look like she'd been through hell and back. Something dark, like blood, stained the front of her shirt.

Vallon pulled her into a hug. "I'm so sorry about Jack."

Fi nodded into her shoulder, but then pulled away. Her blue eyes were huge pools of grey. "Jason did it. I don't think he meant to, but something's not right with him."

He had his back turned and was talking to someone on the phone, presumably not Amundson, given he was giving directions to their location.

Vallon leaned into Fi. "I think he's gone crazy," she whispered. "Really bat-shit crazy. We're going to have to be very, very careful."

"Well, duh." Fi rolled her eyes and wrapped her arms around herself. She looked exhausted, and sorrow burned darkness under her eyes.

If they could just fade back into the crowd, they might escape Jason. They could get a vehicle on their own. She grabbed Fi's hand and started to ease back and away.

Jason turned back to her and she froze. Change of plans.

He gave her a thumbs-up as he finished talking. "Thanks, old buddy. I owe you. Again."

He hung up. "My old partner, Clint, is coming to pick us up. He says he's got a car we can borrow."

"Are you sure we can trust him?" she asked.

"He's been riding my ass hard that I need to walk away from you. But he'll come through. Leastwise, he always has."

Hiking his head for them to follow, he pushed through the groups of people clotting around the hospital. Vallon bumped into a young couple both carrying children.

"What's going on? I've never seen so many people here," she said.

The man's smooth, ebony skin gleamed in the streetlight. He carried a groggy toddler. The woman had features that could have belonged to a model. She carried an infant in a Snuggie, cradled protectively in her arms. The woman looked up at her husband.

"That's just it: we don't know. The kids were fine a few days ago, and then they started to fail. Jackson went quiet and started to sleep all the time, and Katina won't wake up even to breast feed." He hiked the toddler farther up on his shoulder and the little guy moaned.

The woman started crying, and the man placed an arm around her. The tiny baby in the woman's arms had cheeks faded an unhealthy gray.

Vallon swallowed. "You know…. There's such a long lineup here, you might be better off to head to one of the hospitals out of the city. Say, in Tacoma. Or Vancouver. Or Bellingham." Just get away from the city and the blockage area and she'd bet money that the children would be fine.

The man's eyes narrowed like he suspected something. "Just what are you saying?"

Vallon shrugged. "Just what I said. You're going to be waiting hours here." She nodded at the crowd. "Two little ones hit like that at the same time—maybe there's something going around. Something in the air. Maybe you need to try a change of scenery."

It was all she could say, and probably made no sense. She left them, following Jason up the sidewalk, but a glance back showed the couple were talking. Maybe they'd take her advice.

They made it to Broadway and Jason led them across to the Seattle University campus. "Clint said he'd meet us at the Campion House parking lot." He nodded at a twelve story building that looked like a dormitory. They circled the building until they came to a courtyard at the front door and then huddled in shadows, listening to the sirens, all apparently headed toward the hospitals.

"It's getting worse," Jason said as he peered into the dark. His eyes were fever-bright.

"It is. It will. We have to stop it."

Jason turned a bleak gaze on her. "I've arranged to get us the hell out of here. Isn't that enough?"

It would be a start, if she could be sure he wasn't going to just take them outside the field area and then hold them hostage to force her to do the impossible. She hunkered down on a stone bench beside Fi to wait.

The sound of a car engine brought all of them to their feet again as a set of headlights split the darkness of the driveway to the Campion Tower. The vehicle, a pristine, mid-90s, black Impala, pulled up and the passenger side window rolled down.

"So you going to stand there, Slick, or you getting in?" said the driver, a big burly cop she remembered from a certain episode at a parking garage that should never have existed.

Jason slid in the passenger front seat and Vallon and Fi climbed in the back into a litter of comic books and crumpled loose leaf papers and the combined reek of gym strip and fast food meals not quite defeated by over-the-top floral potpourri.

Vallon coughed and covered her nose.

From the rearview mirror dangled what looked like a chandelier crystal that caught and fractured the street light. It placed shivering rainbows over the two men's profiles. Clint's face had gone rigid the moment he saw her.

"Carol's car," Jason stated. He grabbed his old partner's hand. "Sorry to drag you out like this, buddy. I know I told you Vallon wasn't involved, but, well, things have changed. The whole city's in danger, and Vallon may be the only one who can fix it."

Clint just shrugged and eased the car away from the courtyard, "No problem, Slick. It's all good. Carol's good with you using her car. I'm good with it, too. Whatever you want to do."

But she felt his unfriendly glances through the rearview mirror. A stink of iron came off his skin that spoke of tension.

Vallon leaned forward. "We'll get out of your hair as soon as possible."

"Sure you will."

He turned the car out of the Seattle University grounds and onto James Street just as a large SUV pulled out from the curb and blocked their lane. Vallon jerked upright in alarm. Jason did likewise.

"Backup," Vallon ordered.

Two sedans jerked away from the curb behind them. They blocked any chance of escape in that direction.

"Fuck," Jason yelled. "You set me up." He slammed a fist at Clint and then opened his door.

Vallon leapt out and dragged Fi with her. Too late. Dark clad figures faced them, weapons ready.

Amundson's own private Homeland Security army.

CHAPTER 26 —CEDAR SCENTED REVIVAL

After an hour of driving through the long tracts of darkened farm land and undeveloped areas, Francis Drake had left the illuminated dome of Olympia's state legislature behind him. He cruised through the constellation of military bases just south of Tacoma.

An hour of driving, and he and the two men traveling with him had seen no sign of any other Gifted. With each mile, his blood felt colder and his anger flared brighter until he felt like a bonfire about to light a forest aflame.

The Gifted did not deserve this. The Gifted were the hope of the future. Amundson was the monster and must be stopped at all costs. Had he simply mown down all those people in Redmond? But there had been no reports on the news—not even of the shots fired that Toby and the Gifted woman had said they'd heard. Homeland Security was keeping a lid on the whole situation. He could kill Fitzsimmons for this if the man weren't already dead. The National Homeland Security head had totally fucked up by not taking action against Amundson. It had allowed him to consolidate his power and had left the Gifted of Seattle and environs at his mercy.

His fingers tightened around the steering wheel as the fury built. Over the years, he'd set aside emotion and tried to focus on cold logic to make things happen. It seemed he'd missed out on the pleasures of hate.

The highway wound down to the casino and car dealership strip of Tacoma harbor and then up into the last, long dash toward Seattle.

"Derrick. Carragio. Wake the hell up. We're getting close."

Derrick stirred beside him from where he'd slumped against the passenger door. He scrubbed at his eyes and ran a palm back over his skull. "I'd kill for a coffee."

"Sorry. Coffee joints are behind us. We'll get coffee in Seattle when we've done this job."

Derrick nodded and fished a TicTac out of his pocket, offered one in Drake's direction. Drake shook his head.

In the back seat, Carragio's narrow face and tousled head poked up from where he'd lain down on the seat. His bad breath and oversweet scent of pomegranates was too pungent. "Where the heck are we?"

Drake sighed. A good agent would look around and figure it out. But then, Carragio had never been a good agent.

"Just coming up on Federal Way. I want you two to study the barrier. Look for whether there are places where it seems less or more pronounced. It might help us to pinpoint a weakness."

Or strength. It might also point out where they needed to root out Amundson's men, or whatever it was that caused the blocking effect.

Derrick nodded and closed his eyes. He could have dozed off, except for the froth of power use. Carragio, on the other hand, sat forward between them, like a bobble-headed half-moon moron. Not even seat belted in. *Just slam on the brakes and let the idiot go flying.* Except he had too few agents, so Carragio was worth something.

"You searching?" Francis asked.

"Just getting my bearings. Federal Way, right?"

Drake clenched his jaw and nodded.

"Okay then. Let's get busy." Carragio made a show of leaning back in his seat, his hands palm up on his thighs as if meditating.

Give me strength. He could have already scanned the barrier six ways from Sunday and this fool was making a show of getting settled. They cruised closer to the point where the barrier had ended when they'd headed south. He pulled onto the shoulder and stopped. Derrick's brown eyes flickered open and caught the dashboard light.

"Anything?" Francis asked.

Derrick only closed his eyes again.

"Nothing here, boss." Carragio's nasal voice.

He turned off the car, leaned back, and -reached-.

The early hour had people at home, groups of small, human candles huddled together before they left for their daily Diaspora. Sprinkled among them were the brighter flames of partially Gifted that had gathered like shoals in certain neighborhoods where the powerful ley lines ran closer to the surface.

Northward, the blank of Amundson's barrier cut like a knife across the landscape. It wasn't an electric shock, or a mist arising from the ground, or even a dome that had clamped down around Seattle. This was—*nothing!* As if the Emerald City had been swallowed by a black hole.

It was an abrupt barrier, not something you eased into, and yet….

He stretched his senses. There was a little spill-over, a small residual area just outside the barrier. In that area, amidst the seething power, he was able to get shadowy sensations as if he were half-remembering something.

He followed the residual area. It bisected neighborhoods and city blocks. Half of Renton was inside the boundary, all of Bellevue and Redmond, then north as far as Lynnwood.

Just east of Lynnwood, the flare of a Gifted radiated so brightly Francis yanked back. Gifted. Immensely so. He -reached- again, and caught a powerful whiff of cedar and—baby's breath. Pulled back again. Not one, but two Gifted, and one he recognized, too well.

"Landon Snow. Well, well, well."

"Sir?" Derrick glanced at him.

"It appears we may have allies. Look northeastward along the perimeter. Tell me what you see."

Landon Snow, the puppet master of so much that had happened over the years, but too subtle to allow anyone to see him pull the strings. And now he was with someone whose flare of the Gift was beyond anything Drake had ever seen—save one. Had Landon done what he'd set out to do so many years before? They'd confirmed long ago that there were greater Gifted out there, but they'd never been able to prove Landon's greater hypothesis that there would be a secret society of them. Vallon's mother had gone to her grave with secrets never revealed and had left them with nothing except a squalling infant. Where Vallon was in all this was another question.

"Holy shit," Derrick said and looked over at Francis. "Who the hell *is* that?"

Carragio was still seeking northward—as usual, behind the eight ball.

"It seems friend Snow has brought in the cavalry, though I'm not sure how much help it will be against what we're facing. If our power doesn't work, I doubt theirs will, either."

A slight exclamation of surprise, and then Carragio's narrow face came between them. "Theirs? Are you talking about the Others? I thought that was only a fairytale?"

Beyond the windshield, the stream of taillights, all headed toward the Emerald City and the darkness that surrounded it. "They're as real as the three of us. They just don't want anything to do with us. I tried sending agents overseas to make contact. A lot of them didn't come back."

But now one of the Others was here, with Landon Snow. Strange, but good to know. He stirred.

"So did either of you notice the shape of the edge of the blockage? There are areas that seem to bulge, as if whatever is creating the blockage spills over slightly, so the edge isn't completely clean."

Derrick nodded. "There's one of the anomalies not too far from here. Maybe around South Center."

Francis keyed on the car and thought a moment. The blockage was only part of the problem. "Change of plans. If Landon and one of the Others are going after the blockage, then I say let them deal with it. We've all got weapons, correct?"

The two men nodded.

"Then I suggest that we get inside the perimeter and pick our spot. We're going after Amundson."

§

"All secured." The radio crackled.

Wolf drew in a breath of the chill air of the main map room of what had been the AGS and felt like he could breathe again. In the past, the room's temperature had teetered toward warm, but without the heat created by the workings of the multi-million dollar central map, the desk area around the rim of the room was as chill as the heritage district down by the harbor had been.

He'd just arrived back at the installation after he'd ordered the search of the Elliott Bay area when matters had taken a different turn.

"That's it then. They've got her—them," Page said.

Cheers came from a few of the agents, but Wolf couldn't quite find the energy to join them. The whole operation was beginning to wear. When he thought about the breadth of the task ahead—creating a perimeter for the United States and then rounding up the Gifted—all he felt was exhausted. He cracked his neck and nodded at the cheering agents and the others surrounding him, Loadstone agents most of them. Fitzsimmons had pulled out as many HS agents as he dared before he died, while Loadstone had never abandoned him. It made sense. Fitzsimmons had played both sides in a not-so-valiant effort to save his ass, while Loadstone was in it for the money, and the potential for money came from harnessing the Gifted talents. They wouldn't have walked away without finishing their mining of the AGS data even if the government had pulled the funding.

And now they had Vallon Drake and Jason Bryson, all thanks to Bryson's old partner. Seemed the poor man was concerned about Bryson's erratic behavior and was hoping Amundson could get him help. Of course he could. In spades.

"Estimated arrival?" he asked.

"Twenty minutes," Page said.

"Then I suggest we be ready. We need holding facilities first."

"Sir, the makeshift setup we've got here is already full of prisoners from the Academy and the others we arrested."

"Then move them. Double them up in the cages. There's got to be space in some of the old apartments on the grounds." He held up his hands against the protests. "I know it means moving the I.T. research team, but what choice do we have? Take the spouses and children. Leave the agents secure, but give me space for these three."

He left them to sort it out and headed down the long corridor to what had once been Landon Snow's research facility. He knocked once, ran his hand up over his face and through his hair, hoping to wipe the fatigue away, and then opened the door. What a difference a few months made. As Snow's domain, the large, single room had been filled with shadows that stank of strange concoctions. Weirder books and drawings had gathered dust on the wall like some place out of a historical movie.

A new wall now split the large space into two, with the space he entered positively gleaming with the latest in chrome and enamel equipment and pristine counters and cupboards and examination tables complete with the latest in restraints. A set of huge, brilliant lights over the tables allowed the space to double as an operating room, and a single door led beyond the research area into the holding facility. Amazing what a few days and unlimited corporate funds could do.

Sukh Sandhu perched on a stool next to a computer and looked up from what appeared to be a deep conversation over the phone. He waved Wolf over and pointed to a stool similar to his own, then signed off the call saying someone had come in.

"That was Sharp, from Loadstone. They've come across further data they think might improve the range of the perimeter installations. It should cut the number of pylons we need by half."

Wolf blew a breath up over his face. "Good news. I've got some more for you. We've got the Drake woman and Bryson coming in. You should be able to up your research into detecting the Gifted."

"Good news, indeed. If we can find a way to replicate Bryson's talents, it will be much easier than manufacturing portable units of the installations we're proposing for all airports."

The installations, though still theoretical at this time, proposed to use the same electromagnetic frequency as the blockage pylons, but in such an intense blast it should—theoretically—knock out anyone with even a partial Gift. All good. All exactly according to plan, in fact.

But if everything was going so well, then why did he feel like this?

"Is something the matter?"Sukh asked. From the look of the man, dark circles under his eyes and a gray pall to his golden skin, Wolf could have asked him the same.

Wolf took a deep breath and scrubbed his hands through his hair. "No. I'm fine. Just fine. This has been such a long time coming, it's almost a letdown when it happens."

"Sir, it's only been a little over a month—less than six months if you count it from the time HS took over the AGS."

Wolf closed his eyes a moment, because even that time frame seemed incredibly long and he was just so tired of the whole thing. Stretched—and at the moment he felt stretched thin. He shook himself upright. *What the hell was wrong with him? He'd run longer operations than this.* "Guess I haven't been getting enough sleep, thinking about everything that needs to be done."

He stood up, swayed slightly, and hoped that Sandhu didn't notice. "You'll be ready when they arrive?"

"Sir, there's a slight problem. As long as the field is in place, there'll be no way to have a Gifted make Change, and thus nothing for Bryson to detect."

Damnation. He should have thought of that. Why hadn't he thought of it? Something was definitely wrong with him. He needed to get out of here. Needed to get back to his office.

"Do what you can and let me know what you need. We'll figure out something."

Then he fled, with his usual steady gait—he hoped. Out the research room door and down to the exit. He shoved outside into predawn grey and the amber illumination of the lights set around the parking lot. The cedars surrounding the campus seemed to whisper in the last of the night breeze, and overhead the stars slowly faded as the sky turned from darkest black to deep blue.

Just like the Gifted would fade when he was done with them.

He stood there, just breathing as the minutes ticked past, but still couldn't seem to fully catch his breath. Until the sound of vehicle engines reached him from the long drive up the hill to the AGS campus. They were finally here.

The dew-drenched air filled his lungs.

CHAPTER 27 —THE SCENT OF EARTH AND MORNINGS

Vallon swayed as the SUV took a curve in the road too fast and she bumped her shoulder on the locked door beside her. If she could just get her hands free, she'd try the door handle. Duck and roll wasn't beyond her, but then there was Fi… She worked her wrists in their plastic cuffs, but they were expertly trussed behind her. Jason and Fi had had the same treatment before being marched into separate vehicles.

All because Jason had trusted his partner. Clint Blacklock hadn't even been apologetic when he climbed out of the car behind Jason, cast Vallon an unfriendly glare, and said: "I did this for you, Slick. Something's gone wrong in your head. You need a chance to fix it. I'm giving you that chance."

He'd just stood there, cross-armed, as the three of them were arrested. Then he'd shaken his head, climbed back in the old Impala, and driven away. Another prime example of why you should never trust anyone but yourself. Depending on anyone was a good way to get them or yourself killed. It was a good lesson, considering she'd almost trusted Jason again—at least to get them out of the city.

All history now, and she, Fi, and Jason were in a heap of trouble, and so were the people of Seattle. When they'd pulled out from Seattle University, there'd been a traffic jam around the entry to the medical facilities. Things were getting worse and Amundson didn't have a clue what he was doing.

"The perimeter's killing everything," she said to the two men in the front seat. "You saw at the hospital. People are sick. We're sick, too. Can't you feel it? We need the ley lines to live. All of us do. Amundson has to turn off the perimeter."

The driver barely glanced in her direction. She kicked the rear of the front seat and thumped back in hers. The idiots were choosing to be obtuse.

On the familiar, long, straight stretch of the floating bridge over Lake Washington, the water reflected the lightening sky. The clouds caught new sunlight, just as the car entered the trees again and wound up and over toward Redmond, past home of the AGS and the AGS Academy. All gone now. The past she knew was wiped out as surely as the news of her parentage in Venice had wiped her history.

Vallon Drake, Cartos. Fat lot of good it did her. She kicked the back of the seat again and heard a satisfying grunt from the man riding shotgun.

Kicked again and let the anger blossom. Brought her knees up and slammed both feet against the front seat in unison. The seat jerked forward. The passenger jerked around.

"Listen, Bitch," said the bald-headed bruiser—*just where did Amundson get these clones?* "Do that again and I'll…"

She let fly again. Higher this time and almost caught him in the face. For a big man, he was fast. He grabbed her foot and twisted until she almost screamed. Her body arced, trying to follow the direction of the twist, but he just kept going—was going to break her ankle.

Then he let go and shoved her foot back over the seat. She collapsed, her ankle throbbing, and lay staring up at the SUV's vinyl ceiling. Give her the power back and the bastard would pay. Oh yes, he'd pay.

Like the researchers in Anacortes?

She clamped her eyes closed against that memory. Was she becoming the dangerous wild card Landon had always warned her of in school? The kind of agent the AGS would quietly remove and contain, never to be seen again, like a rabid dog?

Sure, all her life she'd been a problem child, but she'd never *tried* to hurt anyone. Until Anacortes, when it was like something got away from her. She'd *intended* to kill those researchers. And now here she *wanted* to murder again.

She pushed herself upright. Perfect. She couldn't trust anyone else and didn't trust herself. Just what was she supposed to do with that revelation?

She shivered.

The convoy of vehicles wound off the highway and into a hilly, wooded neighborhood that told her where they were likely headed. The AGS complex sat on a hilltop, surrounded by an area of expensive houses.

This area was famed for its high-tech companies, and the neighbors thought the AGS was just another one—the high-tech portion of the U.S. Geological Survey. No one at the AGS had ever disabused them of that misconception.

She straightened when they pulled into the AGS parking lot in front of the bunker-style building. It hunkered in the late September sunlight under the palest blue morning sky. Apricot streamers caught in wispy clouds that a brisk wind sent swirling. Unlike the old days, the parking lot was full of vehicles right up to the edge of the tall cedars, and standing by the glass door to the building was a phalanx of burly male agents she'd come to associate with the man who stood at their head. Wolf Amundson: only slightly diminished by his agents' size.

His white-blond hair caught the sunlight like a blade. His square jaw was set and his blue eyes set back under jutting, pale brows.

The SUV pulled up in front of him and the big man who had twisted her leg climbed out. The open door refreshed the SUV's air with the heady scent of cedar. Maybe this was her chance. Maybe she could get Amundson to understand what he was doing and he would turn off his infernal device. *Fat chance.*

The big man and Amundson talked for a moment, but Amundson's gaze was locked on her window and his mouth slanted in a Cheshire Cat smile. He was enjoying all this a little too much. Then the big man opened the car's rear door and Vallon met Amundson's predatory glare.

She might be a killer in the making, and if she were, this man would be one of her victims. She slid her legs out the door and stood in the cool morning air, shrugging off the big man's guiding hand. She held her head high as she faced down Amundson.

"Your goons said you wanted to see me. You could have just called, you know. I needed to talk to you."

Amundson's face barely twitched, like a wolf surprised when the rabbit it caught fought back. He'd try to take her head off about now.

"Vallon Drake. About time you were in cuffs for all the damage you've done."

She just snorted. No use bothering to tell this unGifted what she'd actually done. Like stop the unzipping of the New Madrid fault. Like maybe slowing down her adopted father's attempt to take over the United States. No, she needed to flipping stop this man from killing every man, woman, and child in Seattle and environs.

Behind the SUV, a sedan pulled up and disgorged a hissing, spitting Fi, her hair gone wild, her pale, blue gaze wilder as one of her escorts dragged her over beside Vallon.

Fi jerked loose of their hold and worked her thin shoulders before grinning up at Vallon with a surprising clarity. "Bastards. I hate fucking cops."

"This isn't cops, Fi. This is Homeland Security."

She glanced at the men facing her. "Then I hate them worse."

It had been a long time since Vallon had seen such fight in Fi, right back to when they were two teenage girls at school and Fi was right there with Vallon in defiance.

"And who is this charming woman? Gifted, I presume?" Amundson scanned her. "I don't recall seeing her in the files." His gaze rose to Vallon and met hers. "Part of Gleason's secret army?"

"Gleason's dead. Your goons shot him in Las Vegas. He didn't make it."

The damn man barely reacted. It was like he was a cipher, or a block of flipping ice. His brows rose the barest fraction. "That *is* good news. But you did not answer my question."

"What I'll tell you is that your perimeter isn't just blocking the Gifted from the ley lines. It's killing the people of Seattle. Ask your man, here. He saw. The hospitals are being inundated with unGifted, who are starting to fail. You probably feel it yourself—fatigue, depression, loss of appetite."

It was like he didn't even hear her. Amundson's gaze roamed over her as if she were a prize heifer come to slaughter and he was figuring out the best cuts of meat. Then his attention came to rest where the warmth of Fi's shoulder pressed into hers.

"I would say this isn't just another Gifted. I would say this is a friend. Someone special."

The cool of the morning suddenly went cold and she wanted to shoulder Fi behind her.

The last vehicle pulled up and Jason was dragged out beside her. His face was haggard, but he also faced Amundson shoulder to shoulder with her.

"You're killing us all," she tried again. "Look at Jason. He's not Gifted, but he feels the lack of the ley lines. It's weakening all of us."

At that, Wolf actually smiled. "If you think your little lies will work, you're wrong." He turned to Page. "Let Dr. Sandhu know his new subjects are here."

She *had* to get him to listen. "Are you fucking deaf? I'm talking about the protective field you put around Seattle. It's killing all of us—slowly enough maybe you haven't noticed yet, but others have. I'll bet you're feeling exhausted—maybe overwhelmed. Maybe your coordination's gone a tad wonky. These are all signs I'm telling you the truth!"

He just turned to Jason.

"Mr. Bryson. I thought our deal was that you would bring Ms. Drake to me."

Jason stood straight and defiant, but the twitch of Jason's head said there was truth to what Amundson said.

"I had my own business to attend to first. You knew that."

So all her worst suspicions about him were confirmed.

"And yet I had to receive a call from your old partner to know you had returned to Seattle. Things like that make me think that you might be working against me. Is that true in this case?"

He stepped up to Jason and looked him eye to eye, one man's perfect hair blazing white in the growing sunlight, the other dark and rumpled like the fading night. Jason was the first to look away, down to the earth.

"You should listen to Vallon. There's something happening. Can't you feel it? The weakness? It's like a worm, eating you from the inside out."

Amundson's gaze swung to her. "So you've poisoned him too, have you? At least his mind?" But there were dark smudges under Amundson's eyes that said he was probably feeling the perimeter's effects, too.

"You've poisoned the minds of a nation against the very people who were trying to protect them."

"Yes, yes. The poor, benighted AGS. Well, it is no more." He nodded at the big man from her car. "Take them to the holding facility."

He turned to leave them, but she had to make him understand the seriousness of the situation.

"Check the hospitals, Amundson. Don't listen to me. Check them, and you'll see I'm telling the truth. You need to turn off whatever you've got shielding the city. If you don't, you'll kill everyone and everything."

But the column of Amundson's back said there was no way he was listening. He just entered the building as the bruiser's meaty hand gripped her shoulder.

§

Ozone and the last of the season's wild roses overwhelmed the early morning air, dripping with cedar-scented dew. The moisture dampened

Xavier's shoulders as he stood amidst the trees and watched the small, single-story, wood-sided house. It was painted dark green and a thin line of chimney smoke trailed up between the tall spruce and cedar. A single porch light glowed through the shadows that still clung to the earth here in the forest. The scene was peaceful and pastoral and a total lie, given a miasma of energy radiated off the place that left him half-blind and swaying.

This was one of the node points. Amundson's men had placed an installation here that was part of the Seattle perimeter. Ten feet back, the trees burned with living flame, and Landon Snow's presence beside him was perhaps not as brilliant as a Cartos, but certainly branded him one of the blood. Here, though, everything was dampened. Snow was barely a glow beside him and the trees and small insect flames had winked out, though birds occasionally flew by overhead like firework traceries on a dark night. When he -reached- down into Pangea's breast, the ley lines, which were supposed to flow through Seattle, geysered and sprayed as if they had been severed. The power churned and frothed and sent up jets of spume, like waves blocked by cliffs.

Beyond the house there was nothing. Yes, trees grew there, and southward there was Seattle, but it felt like a sickening void, as if by stepping into that place, he was about to leap off a cliff. Self-preservation said to turn and walk away, but he could not. His *Bela* was in there somewhere, battling whatever demons Jason Bryson had turned on her. And Pangea needed him, for the mother of all things would certainly die if places like this proliferated around the world. Even this wound could drain the ley lines eventually.

"You are certain that if we break the circle of installations it will allow power back into the city?" he asked Snow.

Landon Snow stirred, looking even more ridiculous with Xavier's black leather jacket on top of the shorts, t-shirt, and flip-flops. A child playing dress-up was the impression one got, until you glimpsed Snow's rheumy little eyes. Calculations on calculations as if life was a poker game and Snow the card shark intending to end up on top. Yes, Snow may have aligned himself with Xavier, but he had no illusions that Snow would stay that way.

"I am certain of nothing until I see what we've got."

Normally he could sense how many men waited in that house and whether there were other watchers in the woods, but in this situation he could tell nothing except what his eyes and ears reported. The trees around the house that sat east of Lynnwood rustled in the wind, but otherwise all was silent except for Snow's rapid breathing. Light grew slowly under the trees, exposing the grey trunks and the low foliage of fern and, in sunnier spots, berry bushes that had long ago given up their bounty.

"I think we go now. Quietly. There is the shed to one side of the house. I believe the field comes from there."

The shed in question was low and of the same green as the house, but looked more like a combination well-house and storage shed—likely of garden implements, given the plot of meager-looking turned earth behind the house.

He eased between the trees. The light was increasing and he had probably hesitated too long. They should have come under cover of darkness, but Snow had been virtually blind in the dark and he was the one who needed to see the most. The compromise had been to come in the grey dawn, and then Xavier had wanted to observe, first.

The soft cedar debris underfoot cushioned his footfall and Snow moved as silently as some magical forest creature, even in the oversized flip-flops. They shifted around to the side of the house, which brought them closer to the shed. The rumble of voices came from inside the house. Men. More than one.

He just had to hope that they were occupied inside. He nodded to Snow and stepped beyond the trees, ducked low, and loped the few strides to the shed. A stout combination padlock kept the door closed. Damnation. Normally he could blast such hindrances out of existence, but now the field of nothingness flowed like ants up his legs. He glanced at the house and knelt beside the lock. Long ago he'd practiced on locks, for surreptitious entries and exits went with his work, but as someone Gifted with transmutation, it was a skill he had rarely used.

He breathed in deeply and closed his eyes, then exhaled and let all his tension go. Loose in the shoulders and hands, he spun the face of the lock, getting the feel of the piece, then began to turn the face slowly, listening to the tone of each click. Time slowed. The air grew thick and warm.

"It's getting pretty light out here, Xavier. How much longer?" Snow's whisper right behind him jarred him out of his work.

"Damnation, be quiet. I am just about to finalize the combination." He shrugged off Snow's presence and bent over the lock. His careful turning had already given up the first two numbers. It was the third that he had been carefully counting off when Snow interrupted.

Sighing, he spun the wheel and started again. Left to twenty-one. He felt rather than heard the soft click through his palm. Right all the way around to fifty-four, and another click. Now left again, this time taking each number slowly, waiting to see just what number would click. He passed zero and kept on going. *Click. Click. Click. Click.* The sound of voices suddenly escalated as the front door of the house opened.

Xavier heard Snow's weak squeak of alarm, but he kept his wits around him and slipped around the shed corner.

Xavier didn't move. Luckily, the angle of the sun came from the other side of the shed. It left the door side bathed in darkness that, clad as he was all in black, acted on his behalf.

Click. Click. Click. He kept turning the padlock face, because he didn't know if they'd get another chance.

CLICK.

The faint sound of the last of the tumblers falling into place came through his fingers as well as his ears. He straightened slowly and wiped the sweat from his eyes, then gently pulled the lock down from the haft. He'd done it.

He glanced over at the house. Lone man. Big. Lean. Smoking. Staring at the apricot-tinged sky and the mare's tail clouds dyed gold by the sun's light. He looked relaxed, but alert enough he'd catch any swift movement from the side of the house.

Xavier eased up to standing and looked at the unlocked padlock in his hand. If he left it on the door unlocked, they'd notice. He gently clicked it closed and then shifted sideways around the shed's corner.

Snow stood there, his pale gaze wide. Xavier motioned him to absolute quiet. The way the sunlight was increasing, they'd lost the advantage of the shadows around the shed. He crouched to chance a look around the base of the shed. The sound of gravel shifting stopped him. Someone was there, just around the corner. In the silence, their breathing was a quiet rush and flow.

Xavier had to do something or they'd lose all chance to break the perimeter. He grabbed Snow's hand and swiftly used his finger to write the combination in Landon's palm. He looked at the little man and Snow nodded. He'd understood.

Xavier swept his hair back and stepped around the corner of the shed to meet whoever was there.

CHAPTER 28 —THE MONKEY HOUSE

The cage was exactly that, a hurriedly built square of metal bars, set in a corner of what had once been the rear of the cavernous space of Landon's research facility in the AGS. No beds, no toilets. Just cold bars under Vallon's hands and barred walls looking out onto huddled Gifted in other square cages, like a monkey house at a zoo.

Like a monkey house, the open sides allowed the smell of too many bodies that had been in too small a space for too many days. The reek of human waste—urine and feces—overlaid the mélange of Gifted scents so it was difficult to separate them—apple running into lime, into urine, into cinnamon and clove, into burned leaves and ocean breeze and feces in a most unfortunate way. Overlaid on that was the copper stink of fear, powerful enough to send her shivering.

She clutched the bars a little harder.

"What's the matter with them?" Fi whispered, staring out at the other, strangely silent, cages. She crouched in a corner of the cell beside Vallon.

"They look half-dead," Jason said. He slumped in the farthest corner from them, his long legs stretched in front of him. The exhaustion on his face mirrored her own.

"They do," she said.

When they'd first been marched into the room, there'd been no reaction from the captive agents. After they'd been locked up, she'd tried to make contact with the agents in the next cage. Agent James Dean and Gleason's ex-EA, Moore. Dean had always been a crew-cut, razor-pleat-in-the-pants kind of guy, with no imagination. Moore, a sleek Eurasian woman who had once worked *for* Amundson, looked like a broken china doll. They and five other agents in their cage huddled against the barred walls as if they didn't want to touch each other. They wouldn't even acknowledge her when she spoke to them.

"Moore, damn it! What the hell's the matter with you? I need to know what we're up against."

Moore didn't stir. The usually inscrutable woman didn't even push the tangle of her normally sleek, dark hair out of her face, and Moore *never* had a hair out of place. If anything, she and the others buried their faces further into their knees or curled tighter into fetal balls. Moore's green-tea scent seemed tarnished and faded, like a tea bag wrung dry and flavorless.

Could drugs do that? Could blood-letting? She had to know.

She reached through the bars and grabbed Moore's shoulder.

The woman started and froze. Then her head twisted like a doll's, until her dark gaze met Vallon's. Pain filled her gaze and defeat and loathing—not of Vallon—of herself. Then her gaze fell away and her body went limp again.

"Moore! Work with me. What the hell have they done to you?"

A shudder ran through the Eurasian woman. Her hair fell forward and covered her face.

"Moore! Gleason would so not be proud. Now, what have they done? We need to be prepared."

She shook her head. "Nothing you can do against it," she said, and went silent.

"Dammit, Moore. You never act like this. You've been the above-it-all bitch goddess for all the years I've known you. Now snap out of it and help us!"

Pale hands shoved black hair off of a pale face. Tears ran down her cheeks. "Can't you tell? They ended me. I'm not Gifted anymore. None of us are, I think."

The woman seemed to fade away, and that was the most terrifying thing of all. Moore had been a truly terrifying figure in her role in the AGS. Vallon grabbed her shoulder again. "How, Moore? How."

"Perhaps I can answer that," a too-smooth voice said.

Moore jerked loose and cowered back in her cell. Vallon spun around to face a tall, thin man, with thick black hair and soft, golden skin that didn't look like he'd ever worked outside with his hands. He stood just outside her cage and wore a white coat like Landon had always affected. Scientist, then. Two large men in black flanked him. Obviously not scientists.

"Who the hell are you?" she demanded, hands on her hips.

A small smile stitched its way across his features. "Vallon Drake. I see why Amundson has been obsessed with capturing you. It's the attitude."

A light South Asian accent still lingered in his speech.

"You seem to have me at a disadvantage." She crossed her arms over her chest and gave him her best defiant look.

"Dr. Sukh Sandhu, at your service."

A doctor. That didn't bode well.

"What have you done to them?" Because it had to be something physical. Moore's words suggested something far more permanent than drugs or bloodletting.

The doctor shrugged. "Simple, really, when you think of it. All Snow's research pointed to the Gift being blood born. A disease, if you will, similar to leukemia. We have yet to detect the difference in the blood, but there is one way to deal with such a disease."

She knew she should get it, but at the moment she was tired enough she just wasn't tracking. "Spell it out for me."

He shrugged. "We destroy the bone marrow as they do for leukemia. It's a simple matter, really, when you're not bound by the ethical limitations placed on typical medical practices. A series of injections. Painful, yes, but simple to do. A form of chemotherapy to wipe out the Gift. We'll do marrow transplants from unGifted as we get the donors, but we haven't had time yet."

The room seemed to empty of air. Leastways there was none for her lungs. Her gaze swept over the room. All these Gifted. Moore's defeated gaze. All accomplished so quickly. Truly terrifying.

Sandhu's smile widened and waved his two companions forward. "I believe, Ms. Drake, you are next on our agenda."

§

"What the fuck? Hold it right there, bud," came an unknown voice from beyond the edge of the shed.

Landon huddled back against the shed's wooden side and prayed. Xavier's long shadow said his hands were raised.

"I mean no trouble," Xavier said, but the shadow and a thump said the newcomer had Xavier spread-eagled against the shed door. The *pat, pat, pat* of clothing, and then the shadows showed Xavier yanked around.

"What the fuck at you doing here?"

"I wanted to borrow some gardening instruments."

"Like hell. Get going. Toward the house."

Landon chanced a glance around the corner. A broad-shouldered man in plaid shirt and jeans jabbed the business end of a rifle at Xavier. Xavier crossed the yard and was marched up the porch and inside.

Which meant that dealing with the installation fell to him. He swallowed and the earth felt unsteady. But then, maybe that was just the effects of the perimeter field. After all, he'd proved he had skills when he dealt with the agent in Venice. And an electronic installation wouldn't fight him.

He counted to ten to make sure the man from the house stayed inside and then slipped around the end of the shed, the ridiculous flip-flops softly slapping his feet. Ridiculous foot coverings to go with ridiculous clothes. He couldn't imagine the dark-clad de Varga dressing in them anymore than he could imagine himself. And yet here he was.

The padlock rattled on the hasp when he picked it up and applied the numbers Xavier had given him. A soft click and the lock opened.

A glance over his shoulder and he quickly opened the door and stepped inside. Darkness and energy were his first impressions. Anyone trying to work in here would either need to use a flashlight or to leave the door opened. A low hum and the scent of heated metal and roses filled the space, but that didn't explain the sense of energy. He fumbled in the pocket of Xavier's jacket and pulled out the set of tools. Inside was a small flashlight. He flashed it around.

The shed was small, maybe six by eight feet. In front of him stood a dust-covered well pump that was the source of the humming. Shovels and rakes stood against the wall beside the door. Old cardboard boxes stood against another wall. It didn't leave much floor space. Nothing here that would cause the perimeter around Seattle, and yet the shed's air positively set his hair on end.

He stepped cautiously up to the well and -reached-. The sensation of void slammed into him and he stumbled against the wall, but the air around him transformed into seething masses of energy. Overpowering scents of roses, lavender, and something deeper, darker, almost nameless but filled with spice almost sent him to his knees. He caught himself on the pump and burned his hand, jerked back, dropped the flashlight, and stood there panting. He clamped down on the Gifted vision while he nursed his injured palm.

Okay. *Not* the way to go about dealing with this. Inhaling to steady himself, he scooped up the flashlight and keys and flashed the light beyond the pump.

Something silver and white reflected back at him. He stood on tiptoe to see better. Pylon, it looked like. Almost missile-shaped. When he tried -reaching-, the streams of power seemed to break around whatever it was. He closed off his Gift and carefully edged around the pump.

A white, lozenge-shaped pylon had been planted into the earth so it protruded two feet out of the ground like a mutant carrot without the greenery. He reached a hand out hesitantly, but there didn't seem to be anything preventing him from touching it, so he crouched beside it, flashing the light over its side. The good news was, a simple metal panel appeared to be all that guarded the inside. The bad news was, if anyone discovered him here, there was no way out.

Well, every soldier had his part to play, although ending up a prisoner of Wolf Amundson was not any future he'd envisioned for himself. Still, one must take chances if one is to contribute to the greater good.

He pulled out the packet of tools and selected a screwdriver, then fumbled trying to slot the tool into the screws. His prescription glasses were probably garbage at a certain Venetian palace, and all he'd managed to get was a pair of 4+ pharmacy reading glasses. It left him more than half blind. Sweat stung his eyes and dampened his shirt by the time he managed to remove the screws and carefully pulled the panel. He sat back, panting.

Amundson's men had obviously been moving fast to get the perimeter set up. They hadn't had time for the niceties of booby traps, for the panel came away cleanly. He set the panel down and eased his shoulders, then squinted through the glasses. A tangle of wires led down into the body of the pylon that was buried in the earth. Barely opening his Gift, vibrations came through the earth like a physical assault.

At the panel level, the wires seemed to connect to a power source. Made sense. Though the lower end of the pylon might hold the more interesting gadgetry, the power source was the part of the installation most likely to need servicing. A single green light seemed to indicate that all was in order. Well, he would see about that.

Clip the wires? Unscrew the connections? What would happen if there was no draw on the energy source while it kept working? That could be the booby trap all by itself. So perhaps the best way to dispose of the perimeter was to stop the power source.

He swiped at the sweat threatening his eyes and shifted closer and farther away trying to find an optimal focal length for the infernal glasses.

Fingers weaseled through the wires and the power source hummed under his hand. No intake wires, so the power source was self-contained. No battery, either, at least not that he could see. Interesting.

His hands shook as he unscrewed the screws that held the power source in position, then eased it out of the pylon. Then he sat back on his heels, examining what he held, the wires straining against their connections. The back of the power source had another small access panel.

Russian dolls came to mind. Almost impossibly small screws resisted opening, but finally he pulled the panel open. Yes. Mundane power source of something that looked like an over-large battery, with coils of metal wire that suggested someone had determined how to multiply and sustain the charge. Interesting.

He really should study this, but the sound of muffled shouts from beyond the shed said Xavier's time to distract them might be running out.

Pity. This really bore more study, but…

He pulled a set of wire cutters from Xavier's tools, reached in, and snipped.

CHAPTER 29 —OZONE AND POWER

The reek of cigarette smoke and blood filled the main front room of the small, isolated house just north of Lynnwood. The smoke rose in thick columns from the three cigarette-smoking men playing cards at the scarred wooden kitchen table, and coalesced into a cloud that currents of air churned along the ceiling. The blood came from Xavier, where he sagged in a chair against a fly-spotted grey wall: the men's oh-so-gentle ministrations had opened a cut on his temple. It bled profusely down his forehead and into his eyes and placed vivid crimson spots on the worn white linoleum. It was little enough payment to keep the men occupied if Snow could take care of the pylon.

He blinked his eyes free of blood and peered out at the men from behind his long hair. If these idiots thought a few blows to the belly had cowed him, they did not know who they dealt with. Leticia and her helpers had done far worse. Snow had as well, in his secretive, subversive way. But these…

They talked and laughed while he worked at the bonds that twisted his arms behind his back. Tight nylon rope confined his wrists. He held his awareness split between the low voices of the men and the ropes. If the infernal little man would just do his job, he could deal with the men and the restraints in one swift moment.

Between one breath and the next, currents of air in the room went still. The men looked up from their cards as if they felt it, too. Silence fell. This had to be it. Snow had done what was asked of him.

Xavier -reached-.

Pangea's power exploded up around him in a miasma of rose, lavender, and saffron.

No flow of ley lines. No order to the power. Just a seething stew of lavender-rose-saffron and something darker and full of spice.

His body seared to ash. The ropes that held him disappeared. The room flickered around him and melted. He felt-heard Snow's scream and the screams of others as the pylons fell, useless, like a cascade of dominoes around the Seattle area, and the blocked power surged into the void.

He went to his knees on rough gravel. House gone. Blinded by blazing light all around and inside him. Had to hold it away or it would consume him, just as it had consumed the house, the guards. He struggled to standing as the landscape transformed to rolling prairie. Change. Hopefully the power would sort itself out into the ley lines.

He shoved against the headwind of streaming power and started walking. Landon had to be this way. The landscape changed again, this time to towering rainforest, and the power burned like fire through his veins and muscles.

The sudden release of the barrier had sent Pangea's power surging like a volcano's pyroclastic cloud down over Seattle. He stumbled across the shifting earth toward where the shed had been. Not there now. A stump. A boulder. The landscape shifted sickeningly around him, reality streaming past him like leaves on hurricane winds. He waded through a river, through sand, and finally stumbled over Snow, curled into a ball, his arms wrapped around something metallic shaped like a lozenge, its base still buried in the ground. The source of the barrier. Was the little man dead? Dying? Didn't matter.

Xavier grabbed him by the shoulder. "What the hell did you do?"

The little man stirred and looked up at him through weirdly magnified rheumy eyes. "What you asked me to, what do you think?"

"We need to stop this," Xavier said, as reality twitched again and they stood in a vast expanse of shallow, salt lake, sunlight reflecting blindingly around them.

"We need to get out of here and figure things out," Landon said, sitting up. But he still held onto the pylon like his life depended on it. "I need your help to carry this."

There was no sign that the streaming power was sorting itself out into coherent ley lines. He dared to -reach-, and the screams and clamors of too many Gifted and partially Gifted slammed into him. He understood them. The power was caustic and ate at his flesh almost faster than his Cartos blood could fend it off. It was being drawn into the space that had previously been blocked, but the drawing didn't seem about to end.

[*Bela?*] He sent his seeking, like a spear through the wilderness of Change. Where was Vallon? Her powerful presence should be a beacon. But through the turmoil of presences, he caught only whiffs of ashes and roses that could be anything. Was she dead?

"Leave it." He grabbed Snow's shoulder. "We're done here. We have to go."

"Not without the pylon." He shook his head. "We leave it, there's too much chance of them fixing it."

"Not if we destroy it." Xavier -reached-to send power surging up through the ground.

"No!" Snow threw his arms around it. "The technology is too valuable."

The surging power was an uneasy landscape. In that sea of Change, Snow and the pylon were nothing to him. The immense power would surely eventually destroy them if they stayed here. Snow was not the issue. Vallon's absence was.

"Then get it out of here yourself."

He abandoned Snow, striding through the blizzard of landscape. Forest. Swamp. Rocky desert, again. Reedy lakeshore. Badlands. The power ate at his essence, but Vallon was out there, somewhere, in that seething caustic mass.

Could she withstand it? If so, where was she?

The earth bubbled under him and the shallow lake disappeared, leaving behind a fetid, sulfur scent and the steam of geysers. The landscape stabilized—at least for a moment.

A pulse of immense pain stabbed his brain and he grabbed his head. The pain ratcheted up and he went to his knees, his whole body trembling. The earth rumbled under him and heated water shot out of the earth. Scalding water poured on his head and shoulders. He lurched up— away—and came up against a boulder that might once have been a house. It might have been a forest, too. Or a person? Snow perhaps? No, Landon Snow was behind him.

Sweat ran down his scalded face. His brain was on fire. He gasped and his throat burned from the sulfur and heat. Breath hitched in his chest. His lungs refused to work.

Then the sending winked out and he collapsed against the stone. Drew in deep droughts of the still-fetid air, and ashes of roses clung to his tongue.

Vallon. It could only be. He pushed himself upright.

The world twisted again.

[*Bela. I am coming.*]

§

Under the midmorning blue sky, the tall cedar trees flanked the road leading up to the crown of the hill and creaked lightly in the late morning wind. The sun made that narrow concrete road a taunting tongue, and shot angled beams to spotlight pieces of woodland. From behind Francis Drake came the sound of a lone lawnmower, doggedly doing its job in the yard of one of the nearby oversized, post-modern, heritage-style monster homes, while closer in came the inane humming of Carragio. He played with his smart phone and studied the map that Francis had memorized. But across the street was the forest that masked the place he had abandoned and planned on never returning to, except now he was.

The entry to the AGS campus loomed before him, much like standing before a piece of history, except instead of the Arc de Triomphe or the Washington Monument, he was standing before his own history. A depressing thought, given he normally focused on the future, but the steady drain of Amundson's perimeter field was taking its toll. If driving through the dead zone of Seattle left him feeling like he was struggling to find enough air to breathe, standing on the soil left him drowning.

He'd come to raze the place. *Then he would breathe again.*

Something moved under the trees and a figure materialized out of the shadows. Derrick Brown stepped down onto pavement and trotted across the street, looking younger and more fit than Francis doubted he had ever been.

"So?" he asked.

Derrick shook his head, his skin a deep chocolate in the sunlight. "I couldn't get close enough. I'm pretty sure they had motion detectors set up in the trees. I didn't chance blowing our cover." He looked back the way he'd come. "The path's clear, though. It looks like the neighborhood kids use the lower slope as a play area. Lots of little forts and signs of a squatter or two—gone now, probably at Amundson's insistence. But I don't think we'll be sneaking up on them through the trees."

Francis ground his fingers into fists and drew in a deep breath. Not what he wanted to hear. "How the hell are we going to take that bastard down?"

"Go up by road?" Carragio offered from where he stood by the car.

Derrick frowned, considering. "Could work. If they don't expect it."

Francis was about to wave Carragio's idea off, then stopped. He'd hoped to go up through the trees and take Amundson by surprise in payback for the artillery barrage at Anacortes. Well, that and many other things.

On the way up through Seattle, they'd waited overnight to use some of Carragio's connections and made a stop for equipment. The back of the car held two long, black, plastic cases with the perfect blunt-nosed weapons for what he planned to do.

He looked up at Carragio, who fished an automatic weapon from under the front seat and handed it to him. The oily smoothness of the metal was almost sensual.

Yes. He would relieve the world of the burden of Wolf Amundson, and he'd do it head on. He nodded. "Okay. Let's do this thing. Carragio, you're driving. Derrick, take one of rocket launchers. I'll take the other.

"Carragio, your job is get us into position, so Derrick and I can get our shots off while you still have the car running. It won't slow us down." And Carragio wouldn't kill them all with an ill-timed shot. "When you stop, use the automatic."

They checked each other out one last time on the rocket operations and climbed into the car. The sun was rising into a heated blue sky, with marine clouds flowing in like errant thoughts from the ocean. The breeze through the open windows smelled of cut grass and cedar.

Carragio eased the car away from the curb and drove slowly into the curving road up the AGS's hill. He kept glancing at the rocket launchers, as if he were afraid that simply driving might set them off. Doubly good that Francis hadn't entrusted him with operating one of the damn things. It was awkward and unfamiliar in his hands, but there was a certain thrill, knowing what it could do.

"Move, Carragio. We want to get there today."

The car barely sped up.

"The weapon is secure, Mister. Now drive!"

The car picked up speed, following the shadowed driveway upward.

Just a few strategic impacts should do it. Sure, the AGS bunker was built to withstand earthquakes, but that didn't mean it was built to withstand direct hits with weapons. The map room where Amundson's office would be. The research lab once occupied by Landon. That should hit Amundson where it hurt and hopefully kill the man. Without him at the head, this vendetta against the Gifted would end and he could move forward with his plans.

He'd have his agents back, then, though he might lose a few in the battle. Casualties, unfortunately, were inevitable.

"Speed up. We want to be going a good rate of speed. They're not just going to let us waltz right in. Aim for the building's front door and stop there a moment. Derrick and I will take our shots. You'll wait and get us out of there. Understand? If need be, you'll use your weapon." He patted the automatic weapon on Carragio's lap.

The engine roared and tires squealed as Carragio obeyed, and they careened wide around the last curve, throwing them against the side of the car.

The parking lot came into view—almost full. Maybe more men to fight back. Maybe more collateral damage. Good. He could wipe the bastards out with a couple of full-on blasts.

The low building hunkered beyond the cars, like a concrete blemish on the hill. Well, he'd pop the damned thing right open.

The car burst into the parking lot and bullets shattered the rear window. More slammed into the passenger door. Francis ducked as the car slewed to the side.

Carragio held to the wheel and tromped on the gas. His face was white. Something red spread across his chest.

"You've been hit."

Barely a nod, but the man showed more fortitude than Francis would have thought. The building came up fast, but Evan showed no sign of slowing. Bullets slammed the vehicle. Another bloom of red on Evan's chest.

"I've been hit. I've been hit!" Derrick screamed from the back.

"Stop, damn you!" Francis lunged for Carragio.

"There's no way you can get the shots off fast enough." The car sped up.

"Stop the damned car."

Carragio shook his narrow head.

Francis rammed the end of the rocket launcher down past Carragio's legs and into the brake pedal.

The car's tires squealed and the car slewed sideways to a lurching stop that threw Francis against the dash. It was an instant before he moved. Derrick was already out the door, his launcher up and aiming.

Francis rolled out of his door and headed in the other direction, then took cover between two vehicles. Get the map room and Amundson. He raised the launcher to his shoulder.

The front door of the bunker slammed open and armed men flooded out, spraying the parking lot. Derrick went down just as he got a shot off. Carragio had already hit the gas and the taillights of the car turned the scene red.

Francis toggled the weapon on and focused on the end of the building that held the map room. Hit the release and the explosion of force almost sent him sprawling just as one of Amundson's men came around the vehicle. He raised his gun and Francis fumbled for his own. Not fast enough. Cordite in his nostrils and pain exploded through his chest.

He fell.

A burst of ozone surged up from the earth and power scoured the parking lot, the shooter, and Francis away.

§

Cold, white light blinded her. Cold. So cold. Hard steel under Vallon's back, where the bastard doctor had strapped her down on his table after his two henchmen had fought her out of the cage. Cold where they'd slit her t-shirt up and left her with only a thin, surgical gown, tied in the front, and more cold where they'd stabbed a needle into her chest and injected her with something.

She lay in another part of what had been Landon's research space and, unlike when her father had held her prisoner in New Madrid, she could breathe, she could move, but most terrifying of all—she could feel—everything. The cold, circulating air on her skin. The metal needle too near her heart. The gazes of the six scientists, the dark-haired man who called himself Dr. Sukh Sandhu among them, because she didn't believe there was a medical person among them. And she was their guinea pig. Or just their latest victim in Amundson's desire to cleanse America of the Gifted.

Keira, the girl Vallon had fought to rescue from the Anacortes research station, had lain almost exactly like this at the hands of Amundson's researchers. *Until she let the girl die. Was it her turn this time?*

Sandhu looked down at her like she was a piece of meat. Beside him, someone rolled up a tray that carried an array of syringes.

She wrestled back fear, but she could smell it in the air. Be clinical, Drake, pay attention to what's happening, because Jeezus, this was really going to happen. He was really going to do to her whatever he'd done to Moore and the others. She twisted in her bonds, but the leather cuffs held at ankle and wrist. The thick band over her middle kept her from bucking.

"You shouldn't do this." Her words came out slurred around the punky-tasting teeth guard they'd fitted in her mouth. Sandhu didn't show any sign that he'd heard. She *was* a piece of meat to him. That was all. A piece of meat that he was about to inject with some horrendous marinade, and all she could do was plead and shiver. *Not a nice picture of who she was: frightened little girl again. An orphan, alone.*

Alone doesn't matter. Vallon Drake always works alone.

Sandhu inserted the syringe into the line of fluids that fed into her body. He pressed the plunger down and she watched in fascination as the pale green fluid wound its way toward her. Down to the line that fed directly into the needle that plunged deep in her chest.

Heat.

Then pain burned through her body. Her jaw locked. Her head flew back. Her arms rigid, muscles straining, as the pain burned white-hot through them. Muffled screaming that went on and on and on. Her own. Vision charred away. Then everything went black. She collapsed on the table, her body shut down.

Ozone.

Ozone burned in her nostrils and she opened her eyes. Still too-bright lights, too many faces, and Sandhu leaning over her, stethoscope in hand as he checked her vitals.

But that didn't explain the ozone stench. It was as if lightning filled the room.

First came the explosion. The building shuddered and dust poured from the ceiling. Sandhu staggered against the table. The bunker shuddered again and one of the other researcher's went to his knees.

"What the hell was that? What the hell was that?" Sandhu yelled.

The door to the room shoved open and a coughing man fell inside in a cloud of smoke. Another of Sandhu's researchers, only this one was bleeding and cradling his arm. "Help me! They're attacking the building."

Attacking could only mean the Gifted. Her father.

The ozone.

Power exploded up around her, and Sandhu, the table, the room, the world, flickered and burned like old negatives.

Then came the second explosion.

CHAPTER 30 —MADE

Ozone burned her nostrils and gagged her throat. Power blasted around Vallon, up from the earth and through her, as if she were a sieve. Through her flesh, searing nerve endings and pulling her apart—launching her up—to fall: *nothing in nothingness.* She slammed into something, curled in on herself, and covered her head. Cold and heat so intense it branded her soul.

Power thrummed under her cheek like an engine on overdrive. Then it faded. Faded more. *Not as if the power dwindled.* As if she were going *deaf.*

She should be reveling in the power, feeding on it and using it to blast her way free. Instead she lay cold and hot and sweating, her eyes clamped shut and unable to move. Maybe she didn't *want* to move. The burning in her bones could only get worse if she moved.

The stench of ozone all around and copper fear came off her skin. She shouldn't be here like this, she should be—

—where?

A table in a room? In a cage? With—Xavier? Yes that was his name. Someone she'd loved once, lost to her now, probably still trying to do—something—in—Venice. Yes, that was right.

Thoughts were so hard to pull together when the power pulled them apart. An image of a female face. Blond-haired.

Kiera? Lost in an explosion. *This explosion?* But Kiera didn't have blonde hair.

Fi.

She clung to the name. Yes, Fi. Fi in a dark room. Fi with her, running. Fi in a cage—with—with—Jason!

Fi screaming and Jason fighting when they tore Vallon out of the cage.

The cage.

The Gifted. The AGS. Amundson. The blockage under Seattle.

But the blockage was gone. Power seethed like worms over her skin, even if she sensed it through a gathering fog.

[*Fi?*] she called. Her query bounced back at her, like a blue-bottle fly caught against a window.

She -reached-, but the blooming power was beyond her. She was helpless and tied and Amundson's doctors would continue to do whatever it was they were going to do to burn the Gift from her.

They already have. If you don't realize it, you're a fool.

The plastic mouth guard muffled her groan. She grabbed the damn thing and tore it out. Well, maybe not tore, maybe more like eased it out with shaking fingers. Shoved it away from her across the damp earth. *Earth?*

She opened her eyes.

Tree trunks and ferns. A phalanx of pale white mushrooms grew delicately up the side of a fallen log. Then the scene trembled around her and a shimmer brought a new scene of endless desert, and a cold wind blew, stealing the heat from the sand and from her body. She shivered and pulled her arms in around her.

So hard to move, like her muscles belonged to someone else. She fumbled up to sitting. Swayed and choked on ozone.

She sat alone on a hilltop, with desert sand and boulders and cactus silhouetted against a fading umber sunset. Downhill from her, a line of figures supported each other as they made their way away from her. *Gifted.* She wasn't sure how she knew it. She -reached-, but her senses bounced right back at her. Even the burning sensation of power faded away, like a car disappearing down a tunnel.

Something horribly wrong inside her.

The scent of ozone spiked again and walls formed around her. Gleaming chrome room. She fumbled with a counter and pulled herself up; Sandhu's large needle still impaled her chest. Another shiver of ozone and she stood in a forest, her hand planted against a cedar trunk for balance as her stomach rebelled against the movement. She ripped the needle from her chest and the pain was nothing compared to the burn consuming her bones, the python unleashed and consuming her from within. Consuming her Gift and leaving her empty. Far worse than the hollow feeling she'd had when she used Fi to deal with the afterburn. Now she was empty and weak and she wanted to curl up and cry.

But she had to find Fi. At least Fi hadn't yet faced Sandhu's needle. Together they could get away and find a way to deal with whatever had happened under Seattle.

She shoved off the tree and stumbled through the forest, clinging to rough-barked pine and cedar trunks to keep to her feet. The ozone pulsed around her and built beneath her feet. At least there was that. She could feel *that*. An unGifted *wouldn't* feel it. So maybe it wasn't as bad as she thought. Maybe Sandhu hadn't managed to finish the job. Maybe this would all pass.

Maybe.

The trees flickered under her fingers and the bark faded away, leaving her staggering through a hillside of boulders. Where were the people she'd seen? Were Fi and Jason among them? Were Amundson and his people wiped out by the Changes, or were they out here somewhere? And where were her father and his army?

Dammit, pigeon, cut it with the questions, just go find out.

"Fuck you, Landon Snow. What'd'you think I'm doing?" But she brushed her hair out of her eyes and frowned out at the landscape and then down at herself. Long, bare feet on cold, sharp stone. "You know, Pangea, the least you coulda done in all that Change was give me some decent clothes to wear. And shoes. Shoes would be really nice."

A thin hospital gown, tied in the front, and barefoot was *not* the way to be covering this patch of ground. She kept going, but a sound stopped her beside a bus-sized boulder. Soft sounds of gravel shifting, of—breathing?

She looked around her for a weapon and claimed a sharp-edged stone that filled her palm. *So we're going stone-aged here. So much for being her father's next step in human evolution.* So avoid whoever or whatever it was, or check it out? Given her pitiful physical state, avoiding would be the better, low-risk choice, but since when had she ever been about low-risk? She was Vallon Drake, dammit. Even if she lost her Gift, it wouldn't change her nature.

Weapon ready, she crept around the boulder.

§

Xavier grabbed the power streaming under him and let it burn up through him, then he *twisted* his essence, and his matter came apart into a stream of consciousness that could flow anywhere around the world. Plunge into the ley lines and let them draw him away through Pangea's veins until he leapt for the surface and *twisted* into being again.

At least that was how it was supposed to work. It had, every time since he'd discovered that skill as a young man, desperate to go to his mother's aid. Then, he had arrived only in time to find a body.

He would do better this time. He would.

He plunged into the earth, but there was no ley line to follow. The world was a maelstrom that tore at his flesh, that yanked him down to where the stone darkness filled with flashes of red, blue, gold, as *kata, heret,* and *platiqua* tore apart and mixed together with a greater darkness.

Somat.

Great Pangea, no. The great, dark rivers that were Pangea's deepest power—they, too, had been torn apart by Amundson's barrier; and if the *platiqua* was caustic, the s*omat—the mother power*—was the dreadful power that all Cartos returned to upon their death. Once the great Cartos race might have used it, but today none dared its power but the most foolhardy of Cartos.

And now it was loose to consume the landscape.

Pangea consumed herself? But that made no sense. If anything, the Great Mother was about balance. The lighter powers of *kata, heret,* and *platiqua* balancing off this darker power, this power of death.

The faint scent of ashes of roses bloomed in his nose. Vallon. He needed to find her. But there was something here. Whispers brushed his awareness. Something that needed to be understood if it were to be dealt with.

He -reached- and let the maelstrom take him, plunging down toward its core. The flashes of color streamed around him, became a swirling, spiraling mass that he followed. The heat of the *somat* tore at his essence. If he carried on here, it would tear him apart.

Downward toward the core of the earth. Downward toward Pangea's heart.

[...*ending*...] A whisper suddenly clear.

[...*grief*...]

[...*made-unmade*...]

The whispers were all around him, like brushes on skin. The dead. Something—something they were trying to tell him. A horrible sense of urgency and the *somat* flayed him. The colors around him had been flayed into bare drops torn through the darkness, consumed in the never-satiated death power.

But he needed to understand what was happening. What drew the power down? What stopped the ley lines from reforming? Surely in all the eons of Pangea's existence, cataclysms had broken the ley lines before. They had healed. Why not heal now?

He drove lower, through the whispers into almost total darkness, but he had to stop. Any farther and he would be torn apart and consumed, just like the colors.

Just a little farther. Just a little.

[*Xavier, no! Stop!*] The voice of his mother almost stopped him cold, but overlaid on it was another voice.

[...*made, made, made*...] like a song, like a chant, like the rhythm of blood.

And then the darkness parted, revealing, below him—

A space. A gap in Pangea's substance. And beyond it, a void.

CHAPTER 31 — A CAUL OF DUST

Fi huddled in the corner of the cage she shared with Jason. The large room was dimly lit, but it couldn't hide the misery of those relegated to the room's shadows. The room was almost silent except for the rustle of cloth, the occasional gasp of breath, or a soft sob. The agents still wouldn't talk, and after what they'd been through, she could understand their pain. But the place stank of too many people in too small a space, the sour scent of fear, and the competition of coriander, ashes, vanilla, strawberries, cherries, dung, lime, and cut grass made it seem like her head might explode. Too much was happening. Had happened. And now Vallon, the strongest person in the world, was gone.

Not just taken from the cage and from her presence, but really gone. The horrible barrier that Vallon's boss, Wolf Amundson, had placed around Seattle made it seem like she was not only gone, but like she had never been. That meant that Fi not only had to be strong, she really did need to be like Vallon—strong, resourceful, smart.

Terrifyingly smart and powerful. Was it even possible?

She swallowed. Who else was there? If they did to Vallon what they'd done to these other Gifted, she might be the only truly Gifted left here. Not that having the Gift was an advantage at the moment. But if the barrier fell....

Time to get over being a little girl, Fi. She could almost hear Vallon's voice.

She shifted, and Jason jerked upright from his doze beside her and turned a miserable expression to her. His spice and licorice scent faded in a burst of ozone.

Ozone? She sat up straighter. Ozone only happened when power was being used. At least she'd always smelled it when her mother used her to help with the afterburn.

She shoved her tangled hair behind her ears and scrambled to her feet.

"What is it?" Jason looked up at her.

"Something's happening. Can't you smell it?"

He inhaled and his face screwed up. "Noooo. Just—them." He nodded at the other cages.

But the stink of urine and feces still couldn't stop the tang of ozone. She reached through the cage bars and grabbed the shoulder of the woman Vallon had talked to.

"Moore."

The dark woman yanked away, but Fi caught her arm again. "Listen to me. Something's happening. Can't you smell the ozone?"

The other woman didn't move. Then her head came up and she sniffed. Sniffed again. She turned a haunted gaze to Fi. "I think I do. I smell ozone." She nudged the leg of the man next to her. "Dean. Do you smell it—the ozone?"

He turned dull eyes on Moore and Fi. "Why? I can't do anything anyway."

"But it means someone's doing something. Maybe someone's coming for us?"

"We need to be ready in case anything happens," Fi said. She looked back at Jason. "Right? Isn't that what Vallon would say?"

"Probably. But I still don't smell anything." He leaned against the cage bars across from her, arms crossed over his chest.

A distant, high-pitched whine came through the ceiling and Jason came upright. Then he grabbed Fi. "Down! Everybody down."

He threw himself on top of her.

The room exploded. The cage was thrown—somewhere. They tumbled together, Jason scrambling to cover her as pieces of concrete ceiling thundered down. Dust filled her nose. Something pinned her legs, and Jason's weight held her down.

The roaring stopped. A wall lay just outside the barred cage. Ozone—more powerful—up her nose. Concrete continued to shower down and someone started screaming. A brilliant light cut through the dust and illuminated the wall behind them.

"Jason? Get off me. It's over." But wasn't because the ozone....

Jason didn't move. More moans from nearby, and would someone please stop the screaming? She grabbed Jason's hand. It lay limp in her grasp.

"Jason?" her voice ratcheted up.

Not how Vallon would sound. Not how Fi should sound either, given she might be the only hope for any of them. She shoved up from the floor and coughed. Jason—so heavy—slipped from her shoulders with a heavy thump, but her legs were still caught under something—cage. Bars twisted and blown inward, leaving a gap to freedom. Whatever had exploded had blown out the far wall of the room, too. It allowed in a brilliant stream of sunlight that laced through the settling dust that filled the room.

The bars that had bent inward pinned her legs, but she slid along the bars and freed them. Jason still hadn't moved. Beside him lay a breadbox-sized chunk of concrete. If it had hit him...

She went to her knees beside him. But that wasn't the worst of it. The bars that had pinned her legs and had impaled his thigh, and a concrete chunk as big as a desk had crushed his legs. Bright blood pulsed in a growing pool on the dusty floor.

Just run. Just close your eyes. You can see your way to freedom.

"No. No. No. No." She put her shaking hands on the wound and felt the pulse of the blood. Like a heartbeat, and though that said he was alive, the pulse couldn't be good. Something major like an artery or vein broken. "Help. Help me, please!" she called. I need a doctor here!"

No one came, though she could hear people stirring. Moans came from behind her. The screaming had finally stopped. Over her shoulder, figures stirred in the dust. No one came to help. They staggered for the sunlight, climbed through the hole, and disappeared.

She had to do something.

The ozone... Something happening...

Maybe... She opened herself—and power ripped up through the floor and blew off the ceiling.

§

The harsh, white light of the sun couldn't warm the cold places inside Vallon as she leaned against the huge, blood-red boulder on the hilltop where the AGS bunker once stood. The ozone scent built around her again, so another Change was imminent, and the earth began to tremble. Quake, then, too. The scraping sound came again and she tightened her grip on the sharp-edge stone that was the closest thing she had to a weapon. A hot breeze blew harsh sand against her bare arms and legs, and the sharp gravel cut her bare feet. Being dressed in a hospital gown didn't exactly leave her ready to defend herself, even if she'd tied it as tightly closed as she could.

Defense was never her way, anyway. She shoved off the boulder and came around its edge in a crouch that stuck her bare ass out into the sunlight. Couldn't be helped.

A figure was collapsed on the ground. Red snail-trail on the earth and chest said he'd likely been crawling. Suppurating wound. Gun shot, by the look of it. Her gaze trailed up to the face.

"Dad?"

Francis Drake's blue eyes flickered open.

She went to her knees beside him, trying to shield him from the terrible white sun as the vibrations in the earth increased. "Dad, it's me." She caught one of his searching hands.

"Vallon." Barely a whisper as his gaze locked on her. His face was so pale. All the rigid lines she'd come to know as her father seemed to have melted away into a man who might have had smile lines around his eyes.

She felt a sensation like feathers trailing over her face and then he frowned. Tears formed in his eyes.

"What have they done to you?" A hand came up and retraced the feathers.

"What Amundson apparently plans for all the Gifted. Chemotherapy or something to destroy the bone marrow."

"No—"

"Dad, I'm fine. I'll live, even without the Gift. It's you we've got to help." She fumbled with her hospital gown and tore a strip off the bottom that she wadded up and applied to his chest. Too little, far too late. Blood swelled up and around her fingers.

He closed his eyes and shook his head. "Too late for me."

His gaze flashed open again and he caught her hand as the earth gave a wet-dog shudder. "You have to stop it—whatever is underneath us."

"Working with the power might be a little beyond me right now, Dad. Besides, I need to get you help." The boulders held around them like a fence holding out the world. There could an entire hospital nearby and she wouldn't know it. "Help! If there's anyone out there, we need help here!"

A single shake of his head and he caught her hand. "Never beyond you. You—you're Vallon Drake."

Was that actual pride in his voice? What did that mean? That he was her father?

"Sure I am, Dad. But somehow I'm also apparently the long-lost granddaughter of some Portuguese nobleman. Know anything about that, Dad?"

His hold tightened on her hand and blood burbled out of his lips as he strained to speak. With strength she hadn't expected, he hauled her down to him. "Not—Dad. I made—what you are."

She jerked back and away. "*You* didn't make me. Neither did Landon. *I* made me. I'm who *I* decided to be."

His blood-rouged lips curved, then formed the word. "Strong. Strong now, too."

That was a laugh. She felt hollow as a straw.

Her not-father closed his eyes and he caught her hand again. Almond-scented power surged from his grip up through her arm.

"What the hell are you doing?"

She tried to wrestle away, but somehow he held on. His determined blue gaze held hers, too.

"Power. Use it," he gasped. His body arched. The oversweet almond almost made her gag, but power swelled in her bloodstream and her flesh seemed to plump, her skin sparked in the sunlight.

And then his hand went limp. His body collapsed. The spark in his gaze still held her, as everything about him went dark, and then his eyes did, too. The wind caught in his gray-blond hair and blew a caul of sand over his face. It left behind barely a trace of almond amid the ozone as she closed his eyes and bowed her head.

"Why do I feel so sad for you, when you caused so much damage? Why do I grieve, when you hurt me even when you die?" Her voice sounded thick. Ridiculous tears clotted her eyes. She shouldn't be feeling this, given that all Francis Drake had ever been was a problem and a source of pain.

"He was your father. At least, the only father you ever knew."

She leapt to her feet to face the speaker—naked as a god. "Xavier!"

Dark and dangerously handsome, he stood before her but seemed to hesitate.

She threw herself into his arms.

CHAPTER 32 — DOOM AND DESTINY

The world exploded around Fi, the power pluming through her in a pyrotechnic heat like a child's kaleidoscope gone mad. She was thrown out of her body, into a morass of churning power like a riptide.

What? How? Where?

She floundered in rancid ozone, but rose-scented power poured into her. Power to do something if she could just figure out what. Just figure out where she was. Just get back to her body.

Her body—she -reached-, but couldn't find it. Had the power wiped it away? Was she trapped forever in—*this?*

She floundered for something to grab hold of, but there was nothing there. She tumbled head over heels again and again, as if she'd been thrown into space. Couldn't breathe. Couldn't think. Couldn't live like this.

Was going to die.

Or she was dead already.

The dreadful churn of panic stopped. If she was dead, nothing mattered anymore. The churning mass of color was beautiful, really. Below her lay a field, a garden that faded away, its form melting to join the stream of lovely colors. There was a forest, the trees bending sideways under the force of the flow, their branches dissolving to green and brown streamers. Beautiful and terrifying. Was that what had happened to her? Would it happen to *everything?*

She shivered.

And were those *voices?*

Angels?

Leastwise there were sounds like whispers all around her. *Listen, listen, listen, mine, mine, mine,* they seemed to say. Nothing that made any sense. Her racing pulse slowed.

Shivered? Pulse? But a shiver required skin and a pulse required a heart and a heart required a body. Where?

A thread of connection reached out through the colors. She still had a body. She followed the cord through colors streaming past like iron shavings drawn to a magnet. She flowed through them like an eel and came up gasping as if she'd swum through deep water.

She wiped sweat and grime-matted hair from her eyes and pushed up to sitting. Cage and fallen concrete gone. The stench of ozone almost overpowering. What the heck was going on? The earth trembled and she lay on top of Jason on a shuddering stone hillside. His legs were trapped under a mountain of stone. His blood drained into the gravel and his café au lait skin had gone plaster white. She ripped the hem off her t-shirt and hurriedly tied a tourniquet around his thigh.

She had to help him. She could heal him. She could. That was what Jack would do, and she had the talent.

She placed her hands on his chest, took a deep breath, and -reached -.

His heart still beat. Blood still flowed in his veins. But he didn't feel like Jack had, or even like the eagle or the other animals. There was something strange about Jason. The perfect way his veins lay. None of the twists and redundancy she'd noticed in the eagle's wings.

Even his licorice and spice scent seemed almost like a perfect blend to draw women to him.

She yanked back and frowned. It didn't make sense. She -reached-again, and spread her awareness through him like Jack had shown her. Flowed down into his legs. Crushed and broken. So many fractures, like Humpty Dumpty; she didn't know if she could put the pieces together again. Flesh crushed. She could rebuild it, but the weight of the concrete would just crush anything she healed.

The world shuddered around her and the ozone stench was so great it burned—her skin, her nose, her eyes. The earth shuddered again and the shaking continued. The rock heap shifted above Jason and threatened to topple, became sand—the hillside disappeared into a series of dunes that shifted and moved and threatened to swallow him, but the bar impaling his leg was there and his legs were buried in sand. It could catch her, as well, if she wasn't careful.

She needed to get Jason out of the sand before she could heal him. She began to dig, but the sand filled the hole she made as fast as she dug it. The ground swayed under her and the ozone stench increased. The sand poured faster.

The world wrenched again and the sand faded around her. She knelt in light-dappled darkness. A scent of cedar and mud and copper, a jumble of logs, and Jason, pale as a ghost under them. A long metal rod pierced through his thigh and impaled the floor, trapping him there.

Fresh blood glimmered on the floor. Yes, floor. Wooden. She was in a room of some kind, or what had once been a room. The ceiling and walls had collapsed all around her except for the small space around her and Jason. Almost as if her Gifted presence had held the ceiling away. Jason hadn't been so lucky.

She went to her knees beside him and fought with the tourniquet again. The blood flow slowed, but something was strange. It was like she was going through the same motions again and again.

With the roof collapsed on the weight of logs, there was no way she was going to get him out of here herself.

She had to do something. The question was what. Vallon was the one who would figure this out. She—she was just Fi.

She caught Jason's hand and held on, flowing power into him to keep him alive.

His dark eyes flashed open. "Fi?" he groaned.

She nodded. "We're someplace that's collapsed on you. The cage got broken. And then there were stones, and Jason, I can't heal you and I can't get you free, and I'm so sorry. I am."

She was crying, darn it.

She closed her eyes. "Help! Help us, please!" she cried.

In the confined space of the crushed room, her words echoed back at her. Wherever they were, no one could hear them.

§

The warmth of his *Bela* in his arms was the most wonderful sensation, even though the hospital gown she wore filled him with dismay. Her presence filled him up after the fight to get free of what existed under Seattle. He buried his face in her hair and stole a moment to inhale her ashes of roses, but there was something different about her—a scent of almonds, but also something bitter and acrid and—burning.

Something was wrong with her.

He looked up from her as more ozone spewed up around them, and the boulders shimmered a moment and became—desert. They stood at the side of a dry pan, a ridge of hard red stone beside them, towering into the sky. The body of Francis Drake was gone.

"You're cold," Vallon said and looked up at him, her eyes glassy with unshed tears.

Whether for her father or for him, he wasn't sure. He nodded. "There is trouble below us. Amundson's barrier has destroyed the ley lines. When the barrier let go, it released the power, and without the channels, the power has pooled under the city."

How could he tell her what had happened? How could he tell her the possible consequences when he was not sure he understood himself? How could he load this problem on the one person who looked like she had just been through hell and back?

She swallowed, pulled away, and scrubbed the pain out of her gaze. "What is it? What's happened?" She staggered and he caught her arm to steady her. Her flesh fizzled with power, that was *wrong—not her.*

"What has happened to *you*?"

She shook her head in the infuriating way she had, as if what she had experienced did not matter. "What's happening under Seattle?" she demanded.

Vallon, his Vallon, would know. Would feel.

"The fact you have to ask says whatever has happened to you is serious. Now tell me." He caught her arms.

She shrugged. "Amundson happened. He caught us. He tried a little procedure on me. It doesn't matter." Shrugged again, but everything about her was grey and defeated—haunted, as if the vision she had shown him was now embodied in her flesh.

"What kind of procedure?"

Her throat worked. "Chemotherapy of some kind. Something to burn out the bone marrow. Unfortunately, it seems to work."

The chill of his venture into the chaos under the city was nothing to the winter he felt at her words. The bone marrow produced the Creator's blood that ran in Cartos veins. If the marrow was ruined.... It was the most horrific thing he had ever heard. An abomination, and yet Vallon stood before him almost as if she apologized. *Like his mother had apologized as she died in his arms?*

Damnation, no!

He tried to pull her into his chest, but she yanked away. "I don't need your pity. It's happened. There's nothing to be done for it now. My father just died, and his last gift was giving me the last of his power." She flexed her fingers. "So I'm not done yet. Not yet. What needs to be done?"

"No. This is beyond you. Amundson's barrier ripped apart the ley lines of Pangea's deepest power, and that caustic power has ripped apart Pangea's flesh. There is a void below the city and it draws the power into it. With it, it draws the matter that makes up the city. It is as if the absence of power that your Amundson created with his barrier has provided a template for something greater, but without the barrier, now the void feeds. It feels like a ravening beast down there on the substance and power of Pangea. If it is not stopped it will consume everything."

"All the more reason to act quickly, then." She faced him, shoulders back, and fair, as the wind blew her fair hair around her face and the silly, pale green hospital gown around her legs. She looked thin and wan and like she needed to be abed, not planning to save her city again.

"*Bela*, please. The thing is too powerful. I am not sure if the entire Cartos Council could deal with it."

Her gaze went dark and she shoved him away when he tried to take her in his arms.

"Don't treat me like a child, Xavier. I know what I'm capable of— or not capable of, as the case may be. I also know that I and my people caused this and that I've dragged you into too much danger as it is."

"Pangea preserve me from stiff-necked women!" The words exploded out of him before he could stop them. "You plan to go off alone! You would rather die than accept my help or admit you are at the end of your strength."

Was this what his father had faced with his mother? Was this what he was doomed to face over and over and over and over if he could keep her alive this time? Was he prepared to do that?

His hands closed into fists as she glared up at him. That was it, then. She would have him walk away.

Do it or stay? Either way he was doomed.

Like his father? Was that the man he was destined to become?

The ozone stench filled his nose again and the world rainbow shimmered and wrenched around them. When it settled, they stood in muddy shallows as small waves lapped at their ankles. Tall cedar and pine trees ran right down to a lakeshore, except for a small slope of grass behind them and a dock that led out onto the water. A log cabin stood back in the trees.

Vallon's frowned and scanned the lakeshore. "I know this place."

"Help! Help us, please!" came a muffled cry from the cabin.

CHAPTER 33 —CAUSTIC SLITHER

The voice from the cabin could only be Fi's. Vallon knew the voice. Knew the fear, and knew she couldn't leave her. At the same time, she knew something had to be done about the maelstrom under Seattle.

Xavier stood across from her, his nakedness blushed by the sun. The wind off the small lake lifted his hair off his neck and brushed against her nearly-naked skin with a mountain chill that spelled fall was coming. The stand of forest sloped away upward, and over their tops stood the heights of the mountain. Mount Rainier. So either the horrible Change under Seattle had grown with the falling of the barriers, or something or someone with considerable power had sent them here—to the place she had escaped from once before: Jason's cabin in the woods where he had tried to force her to bring his wife back from the dead. Something else was in play here.

Using her father's power, she tried to -reach- just as the earth heaved underneath them. Miraculously, she could feel as the ley lines contorted and writhed like a snakes, glowing sparks running their lengths. Her father's last gift had given her borrowed access to the Gift. What the hell was going on? Northwestward, she felt the growing darkness of Seattle. If it hadn't already, the city would soon cease to exist. Then the darkness would begin to feed more broadly. Xavier was right. Even from this distance, the sense of ravenous hunger was immense.

So do something about that, or help Fi.

She looked up at Xavier. His dark hair hung in his eyes and anger flickered in his gaze. The force of his presence seemed to have sucked in on itself, as if he held himself in check and away.

"We need to help Fi and then we can decide about Seattle." She started for the cabin, wading out of the waves. She stopped and turned when she realized Xavier wasn't with her.

"Aren't you coming?"

He just stood there a moment, as if surprised she would ask him, then shook his head and followed with the grace of a panther. She loved that about him: The way he moved. The way the light struck his body, the wind shifted his hair. Sexy as hell and with an intensity that seemingly matched her own.

"What would you have us do?" he asked.

Something wasn't right between them, but there was no time to figure it out. "Come on."

The front porch of the cabin was as she remembered. Five wood stairs led up to a broad front porch, complete with two Adirondack chairs. The solid wood front door swung open at her touch and gave onto the single main room, with its worn brown couch and chairs and side kitchen. The scent of beer and dust filled her nose, but that was as far as the familiarity went. The roof sagged at the rear of the room and the door to the rear of the cabin had been crushed in half by the weight of a beam that had collapsed on the door frame.

"Fi?" She -reached- at the same time as she called.

Fi's brilliant flame blazed from the rear of the structure. With her was a much fainter flame that tasted of oceans and spice. Jason.

"Fi! Fi!"

"Vallon?" A quavering voice that could only be her friend.

"I'm here. Just hang on." She wrestled with the broken door and Xavier came to her aid. "So you are going to help me."

He shook his head and said, "I do this for Fiona. You never need anyone's help. Not really. It is always your plan you throw yourself into. If the rest of us happen to fit in, that is fine, but otherwise you will just go alone, without thinking of how the rest of us feel. We—I—wish to help, *Bela,* to work *with* you—but you will not accept it. And so I think that my energies are better spent dealing with Seattle. That is where I am most needed now."

"If you can wait a few minutes, I'll come with you." She fought with the other half of the door, and with his help, yanked it free.

He stepped back from her. "No. You are on your own, now. You say you wish to always be together, and yet you leave me so many times to throw yourself into danger. My mother did that. My father became the man he is because of her. I see that now. I do not want to become the reason you die. I do not want to end up hating you and everything that reminds me of you. Is it not better to leave you while we still love? And there are dangers that must be dealt with."

It couldn't be, and yet it was. His face was the most serious she had ever seen. The end. Of them. Of the world. "Are you giving me an ultimatum?"

His lips curved. "I would never do that. You are Vallon Drake, an immutable force of nature."

The room shook around them and Xavier looked westward. "It is getting worse. If the void isn't stopped, it will destroy everything. Goodbye, *Bela*." The power geysered up around him and then he was gone.

Her legs almost gave. *What had just happened? What had she done?* The building ozone scent erased even the hint that Xavier's cedar and incense had ever been, and she was alone. Like she was meant to be.

She pushed away the tight feeling in her throat and chest and turned back to the shattered doorway. Fi needed her now.

The ceiling had collapsed into the hallway that led to the rear of the house, leaving barely a foot of space between it and the floor. She clambered through the remains of the doorway, got down on her stomach, and began to crawl.

"I'm coming, Fi."

Dammit, her vision was all blurry and her eyes wouldn't stop watering. She had no business crying.

After the Murdoch affair, she'd been so concerned that Xavier wasn't coming back that when he had, she'd held him away. When he tried to protect and help her, she'd still gone her own way and left him to deal and to pick up the pieces.

Not a nice place to be, given how she'd felt those long months when she hadn't known if he was alive or dead. A sickening weight formed in the pit of her stomach. Xavier had a right to be mad.

A surge of ozone flowed up from the earth and the mountainside vibrated. The wood cabin groaned and the beams overhead shifted. She froze. Her body blocked the light behind her and ahead laid only darkness. She used some of her father's—no, Francis Drake's—precious power and -reached-.

Fi's brilliance flared ahead. How long the gift of power would last, she didn't know. She needed to conserve it. She hiked herself forward on her elbows and knees, the stupid gown hiked up until her bare butt ran against the collapsed boards above until finally the darkness lightened a little.

"Fi?" For some reason she whispered.

"Here!" And suddenly there were hands on her wrists, dragging her forward, and Fi was there, her arms around her. "Vallon. Oh God, Vallon, I was so afraid when they took you from the cage. But you're all right. You're all right." Fi's hands traced her face, her arms, her hands.

Then she stopped. "You smell funny. What did they do to you?"

"And you're a regular bouquet of roses, my friend. Now show me what's going on with Jason." There was enough light through gaps in the collapsed beams and roof that rested just above their heads that she could actually see something. Fi was a mess of dust-matted hair, tearstains, and sweat, but she looked like she'd escaped the collapse mostly unscathed, and her blue eyes might be wide, but they held none of the dazed, child-like fear Vallon expected. In fact, they looked determined.

Fi shifted in the small open space to reveal Jason, comatose on the floor, his legs trapped under beams heavy enough they had to have crushed everything, and one long metal rod impaling his thigh. A thin band of cloth was tied tight around his leg above the wound, but it didn't completely stop the flow of blood.

She crawled over to his side and checked the tourniquet. "You did good, Fi. He'd be dead if you hadn't acted so fast."

"But I can't heal him with his legs under the beams and that thing in his leg. If I disappear the beams, I'm scared I won't have the power to heal him."

"How about if I disappear the beams and you heal him?" She checked Jason's pulse: thready and thin. His face no longer held the gleam of health, nor even the gaunt skeletal anger. She stroked his hair back from his forehead. "He looks like a wax copy of the man I knew."

Fi came up beside her. "Jack said he was made."

"What?" She craned around to look at Fi. "What the hell does that mean?"

Fi shrugged. "I don't have a clue. I just know that's what Jack said. It was practically the last thing he said before he died. And there's something weird about his essence. It's like the earth's magnetic field moves with him. See?"

She grabbed Vallon's hand to show her, but a burst of power came up through the floor, carrying with it the stink of ozone and incense and cedar. Xavier, trying to do what she should be doing right now. Well, it would have to wait a little longer. She couldn't leave Fi and Jason like this. Afterward she would go. She would.

"It doesn't matter. You get ready to stop the bleeding. Let's start with the puncture in his leg." She grabbed hold of the rod and Fi scrambled around her to place her hands on his leg. She got a faraway look in her eyes. "Ready?"

A slight nod.

She could yank the rod out, but the process would likely cause more trauma. Better to simply use the matter to help rebuild the leg. She placed one hand on the back of Fi's and -reached- for the wood.

A churning darkness consumed everything northwestward. A single, brilliant, flash of power that was surely Xavier. So none of the Cartos Council had come to his aid. She needed to go to him. Needed to help him. It might be over between them, but the world was a safer place with him in it.

But first this. Save Jason.

Long cords of metal bound together in chains. She sent power surging into the steel and destroyed the chemical bonds that held electron to electron and grabbed the matter and sent it to Fi. Felt her startle as she kept up the surge of power.

[*To use to heal.*]

Her hands shook. The room grayed around her. Her feet began to tingle and then burn as if they turned to ash. She couldn't sustain the power use for long. Not if she hoped to have anything left to use under Seattle. She yanked back into herself and barely sagged next to Jason. But the wound on his leg was closing. Flesh knitted together, skin formed, and then Fi took a long stuttering breath and was suddenly present in her gaze again.

She looked down at Jason's leg and then up to Vallon. "I did it."

"You did."

"I really did it!" Power fountained up around her as if the use of power had just filled her up, not depleted her. She looked at her hands and then at Vallon. "I could heal you!"

A possibility, but Vallon shook her head. "A waste of power, I think. Amundson's chemicals burned me out. And there are other things that need your help." Because the horrible burning in her bones suggested she might never hold power again. She cringed at the thought, but pushed it away and caught Fi's hand. "Things are bad. When the barrier came down, the power didn't go back into ley lines. Instead it became this huge vortex of power that's devouring the landscape—at least, that's what Xavier said."

Fi nodded. "I felt it. It's bad."

"It's eating its way outward from the city. It could destroy everything. Xavier's trying to stop it, but something that powerful—I doubt he can do it alone, and no one from the Cartos Council is coming." She met Fi's gaze and it came out in a rush. "You can heal. Maybe—maybe you can figure out a way to heal this, too."

It was a bad idea. Fi was untrained. She was in some ways no more than a child. She didn't have Vallon's skills, and damn it, this should be *her* job. See this through and over. But the throb in her bones and the flicker of her flame said the potential for her to come back from such a venture was slim and none. And Fi had power. She had grown a lot—had helped in each crisis along the way.

Fi's blue gaze had gone huge. "Me? You want me to heal what's down there?" She nodded to the floor underneath her.

"Well, not exactly here, but under Seattle, yes. You're the only one I know who can do it, Fi. You know how to knit matter back together. I—don't. I jury-rig things back together, but this requires healing of the ley lines. I don't think Xavier can do it, either. He said Jack's talents were rare, but you have them." She squeezed Fi's hands. "I think you can do this."

The funny thing was, she actually believed it. If Fi could just believe in herself, it was possible.

Fi frowned, and for a moment, fear crossed her face and she looked like she might curl into a fetal position, but then she took a deep breath. Her shoulders straightened. She sat up and brushed her wild hair back from her face.

"Okay. I'll try—no—I'll do it." A big nod. "I will. But what about Jason?"

He still lay unconscious between them, his legs still crushed under the roof beams.

"There's no way I can remove the beams—not without risking bringing the whole house down on us—and I don't have the power to remove the whole house."

"And I can't do it and be there to heal his legs, too. If I take the house off, the shock of the release of pressure will kill him before I can heal him. I learned that much from Jack."

Ozone flooded up around them, but the ozone stench was from Seattle, fifty miles north of here. And just how had they gotten here? When the barrier had come down, things had Changed around them, but the shape of the land had still largely been like Redmond.

An oddity, but the danger sat under Seattle. "We'll have to leave him like this for a little while. At least unconscious, he doesn't feel the pain. I'll come with you for as long as the power holds. We'll all come back here to help Jason once the danger's dealt with." Or Xavier and Fi would come back, because she really didn't see herself lasting long in this fight. And if they didn't succeed in fixing Seattle, well then, Jason would die just like everything else, because if Xavier was right and there was a void under Seattle that was draining the ley lines, it was just a matter of time before Pangea was emptied. No wonder she'd had a vision of the world empty of life. She held out her hands for Fi's.

"Let's get this show on the road."

Holding Fi's warm hands, she -reached- and followed the ozone down to Xavier.

To help him. To help him live.

§

Darkness. Whirling darkness, darker than the darkest night in the desert. Darker than the dangerous tunnels under Seattle. Darker than the decision to leave Vallon that had seemed to freeze Xavier's heart, and yet the darkness sang to him. Not so much in words, though there were whispers in the soft waves of sound that ran counterpoint to the roar of destruction that battered him. It was more like a hum of yearning that seemed strange and yet fitting in the destruction he hung in. The darkness churned like a hurricane, the faint streaks of red, blue, and gold—*kata, heret,* and *platiqua*—being consumed in the caustic black of the dreaded *somat.*

It came from the deepest reaches of the earth, and no Cartos in his right mind would try to use it. It held the greatest power and, according to legend, the source of the cataclysm that had destroyed Cartos civilization millennia before. And now Amundson's infernal device had broken its ley line and the darkest power of all consumed Seattle. And he hung at its heart.

Hung. It was a lie, really, for it took all his strength for his essence to stop here and not be stripped away into the greater darkness. The trouble was, he needed to deal with what rested below.

The void caused this cycloning power that stopped the ley lines from reforming. The trouble was the caustic *somat* destroyed anything that power created, so how did one create matter to fill a void, when it burned away as swiftly as it was made? He could waste himself on such a task.

But he needed to try something. He went lower, the *somat* slithering over him like snake skin. It reeked of vanilla and spices like frankincense until he sickened at it. His essence flickered like a flame in the wind, matter wisped away in a constant, painful stream.

But he needed to know. What did it matter if the loss of his essence meant a loss of part of himself? He had already lost the most important part in Vallon, even if he had walked away for all the right reasons.

He sank lower. The many-mile-wide circle of destruction around what had once been the jewel of the Puget Sound, at these depths had narrowed down, the vortex more powerful than he could withstand if he went any lower.

The darkness slicked across his skin in a caustic burn that he knew he should care about. How much of himself had been torn away into the darkness? How much more could he afford to lose?

[*Xavier!*] The presence of ashes of roses coalesced beside him, as did the fainter scent of mint and licorice. [*Xavier. We need to get out of here. The power's too great.*]

[*We need to understand what this void is. There is a force, a will, here. Can you not feel it? Can you not hear its song?*]

[*Xavier, I've got Fi with me. With her skills, we might be able to heal the surface and ley lines.*]

So many words, but there *were* words in the vortex's song. He'd heard the faint whispers before. [*I don't think this is just a result of the barrier. Something has created this thing. But why would someone create a hole in Pangea and then demand that all creation fill it?*]

The song hummed in his ears, hummed in his essence, and if he could just let go of his ridiculous fight to always save people and places— the world—he could be part of that comforting music.

[*Xavier! Listen to me. You've got to get out of here. We all do. The power here's too great. I—I don't think I can last much longer.*]

[*The song it sings is—sad. So sad. And so much longing.*] Fiona's soft waif's voice came out of the darkness.

[*Exactly.*] And the power of the song had momentarily caught him, and if Vallon and her friend had not appeared beside him, he would have had his wish and become part of it.

He shuddered. That was not his wish.

Beside him, power stripped from Vallon in a red-gold plume. Fiona's power was a multi-hued haze around her.

[*We must get out of here.*] He -reached- for the surface.

Far easier said than done.

CHAPTER 34 —POWERSTORM AND DARKNESS

The caustic darkness ate everything. From outside the whirling black, power flayed Vallon's presence until she felt skinless in a sandstorm. The worst part was that the empty places Amundson's scientists had burned inside her seemed to draw the darkness inside her and there was nothing she could do to stop it. It coated her insides in a sickening mélange of vanilla and spices that made it hard to think or move.

Yes, there was pain and longing in the song, but there was too much dark power, too many churning howls of anger and pain and—hunger. Ravening hunger that would devour her if it did not get what it wanted.

Wanted?

[*There* is *something here. Something with intent.*]

The dark power made it so hard to think. It was like parts of her were dissolving—like a river shoreline, collapsing in flood. She had to get out of here, like Xavier said, but she didn't seem able to move. Something *held* her and it wasn't just the vortex. Something in the groans-moans-hums-and-song called to the echoing places inside her. Something she *knew*.

Xavier lifted from beside her—slowly at first. Fiona, too. But something held her where she was, moment by moment, her power depleting.

[*Vallon. Come.*] Weary-voiced, so this wasn't easy for him, either.

[*I—I don't think I can.*]

In an instant he was beside her, though she could feel the weakening the caustic darkness caused in his cedar and incense.

[*No. You have to go. You've been down here too long.*]

[*Bela....*]

There was such love in that single word. And regret and fear.

[*Xavier. I know. I don't want to be here, either, but you were right. There's something here, something we need to understand if we're to fix this thing. But you two have to go. Work together and get the hole under Seattle healed. I'll do what I can here. Anything I learn, I'll send to you to help you.*]

[*You are talking suicide, Bela. This I will not let you do.*] His sending was a tight stream that flooded into her, mingling their awareness. His incense and cedar enveloped her and began to haul her up from the darkness.

But their ascent was slow. Too slow, and the caustic darkness burned away their essences, further depleting the meager power she had left. It ate at Xavier, too. It was like she could feel bones under the skin of an emaciated child. Surely he felt it, as well.

[*Stop this, Xavier. Look what you do to yourself! You help me, and you'll have no strength to do what must be done to help Fiona heal this. She's our only hope, and she doesn't have your power. She'll need your help if you're going to do this.*]

A tremor ran through him, like a chill up the back. [*You expect me to just leave you here? To let you die? Bela, I will not become my father. I will not abandon the woman I love!*] He struggled to carry her higher.

And she wanted to go with him. Did not want to lose him. She pulled him to a halt, the darkness flooding around them. [*Xavier, please. Listen. I don't want you to leave me, just like I haven't wanted to leave you. But this is more important than me. Or us. This is Pangea. Not just Seattle. We need someone down here and someone to help Fi. I can't help Fi, so that task falls to you—just like the battle with Rebecca Murdoch fell to you. Remember?*]

He went still in the darkness, his presence vibrating, and she pressed into his warmth, spread herself through him, hoping he could see that she did not want to die, that with her whole heart she wanted to live to be with him. That he would understand.

The vibration stopped. [*We have no choice.*]

[*That's the way I read it.*] Don't let him see how terrified she was, or how much she wanted things to be different. [*We work as a team, each doing what they can do best. Right now, the best hope of Fi succeeding is you. I can last long enough to try to get the information to help stop whatever or whoever has caused this.*]

With a last caress that sent her trembling, he unfolded his warmth from around her and she hung alone in the cyclone. Power ripped from her like blood from a wound. From above, the cedar and incense and mint and anise reached her, torn from the two people who meant the most to her in the world.

[*I love you. I love you both.*] Then she shut herself off from any sending that might weaken her resolve and let the dark currents of power suck her down.

Down through the vortex. *Painful to be alone, though she had been alone all her life.*

Power screamed past her, through her. Ripping her apart.

Perhaps she'd only fooled herself, for there had always been people around her.

Soon there would be nothing left. *Atonement for what she had done in the warehouse.*

The funnel of power twisted and turned above whatever anchor point was at the bottom. She caught glimpses of it as the darkness flooded into her.

Darkness and brilliance like brittle starlight, but there was a shape to the thing she couldn't quite fathom. She needed to see, *because it would mean something.*

Where the certainty came from, she wasn't sure. The darkness—like a wave in her mind—burning and cold at the same time. The stench of licorice and spice was so ripe *it was a lover's scent permanently tattooed inside her nose.* No scent of cedar and incense. Xavier lost, above.

But that didn't matter. She needed to do what she'd set out to do. She needed to understand the vacancy below. What vacancy could fuel this maelstrom—*this ravenous hunger!*

The darkness ate through her father's meager power and tore her down to what waited.

Ending. To be together again. Just one more time.

No that wasn't it.

Just once for all time!

Whose thoughts were these? They could be hers. She had hung in Xavier's arms in Pangea's presence and knew the transcendent pleasure.

Grieved for it.

For all time.

The funnel of tormented power narrowed. Darkness coalesced beneath her into a rift in Pangea, and the stench of spices burned through her like lightning and blood and—*she knew that scent.*

Oceans and mornings and a hint of spice.

She recognized it as power ripped her through the rift. Knew who and what would destroy her out of grief and madness.

[*Cheryl?*]

§

It was the only way. His *Bela* was right, but the decision left his heart like a stone, weighing him down. It made it difficult to follow little Fiona, up through the cycloning power, when his heart was tied below.

The streaming mélange of golden *kata*, the red-gold of *heret*, the blue-gold of *platiqua,* and the bold mix of rosewater, lavender, and saffron said they neared the surface, but his *Bela* disappeared below as if she willfully took the death spiral downward. Or as if she had no power to resist.

He should never have left her, except she was right.

This time she was right and there was no help for it. Unlike his parents, he and Vallon had agreed to a course of action, no matter the consequences. He had to follow through, had to trust that if there were any way through this, Vallon would find it. She always had.

Above them, the blue light of day said they had reached the surface of the destruction. He found the fountaining end of a *kata* ley line and dragged Fi into it. Power geysered up around him as he returned to his body and -reached- in for Fi, tore her body through the ley lines, and she collapsed naked beside him.

"Holy heck, what was that?" she said. Then she looked up at him and her eyes widened. "Uh—you realize you're naked, right?" Then she realized her own condition and her delicate hands flickered futilely over her body.

"We lost our clothing in the transmutation. It is nothing to worry about."

Her face screwed up a minute. "Yeah. Sure. But the afterburn itches like heck when I look at you." She twitched an eyebrow at him.

"Not now, Fiona. We have work to do." He caught her arms and helped her to stand.

They stood in a mud-and-diesel-scented, lightly wooded area, with white-trunked poplar dropping golden leaves around them. Underfoot was rough grass and patches of thistle, gone to seed with the fall. From not too far away came the sound of traffic and construction hammering. A vacant lot in the Seattle metro area and civilization was not far away, but then neither was the edge of the growing wound of destruction. The terrifying thing was that, as with all Change, the unGifted didn't notice what was happening. They would be consumed like the landscape.

"How do you plan to heal that thing?" he asked.

Fiona looked up at him, her blue eyes ridiculously wide. To trust the healing of Seattle to this slip of a girl—and yet Vallon had done so. Jack had said she had talent.

"Fiona? Are you with me? I can feed you power, but you must have a plan…."

She tugged loose from him and held up a hand. "Hold on a moment. I'm thinking."

Her eyes took on the faraway look of a Cartos or Gifted, working. Her scent of anise and mint rose in a heady cloud, but then she was back. Nodded.

"I think it's a lot like trying to heal a person. I have to pull together the ends of the ley lines. That'll stop the power from draining down into whatever that is. If the power isn't pooled like that and eating the landscape away, it should be easy to heal, right?" She rocked on the balls of her feet like a diminutive fighter ready to brawl.

"You truly think you can do such a thing?"

She met his gaze and sighed. "Do I have any choice? Is there any word from Vallon?"

He -reached-, but there was only a distant sense of Vallon's distracted awareness, focused elsewhere. He would not disturb her, no matter what it cost him. "Not yet. Let us get on with this effort then."

Fiona curled her legs under her to sit on the grass, looking like a modern day wood nymph, with her pale skin glowing the same white as the tree boles. She patted the grass in front of her, but Xavier shook his head. "I prefer to pace."

The girl spread her hands on the earth, took a deep breath, and closed her eyes.

How could she appear so calm when Vallon was trapped in the depths of this thing? He should never have listened to Vallon. Fi was not powerful enough to do this thing. She was a child in mind, if not in body. But he and Vallon had agreed that this was the best course of action. He had been a fool.

No, they had decided it in consultation. Vallon had not run off on her own; they had decided rationally to use each person's abilities.

And Vallon was probably dying as a result.

He cracked his knuckles and closed his eyes. He would not let that happen. But first Fiona.

The scent of mint and anise filled the copse of wood, and the frown on her delicate face and the corded muscle of her neck spoke of effort. He laid his hand on her shoulder, and followed her down into the earth.

Power hummed in the ley lines as it neared their ruptured ends. The soil vibrated around them as Fiona spread her essence around a pulsing kata line.

[*What do you do?*]

[*I can't make new ley lines in that.*] She indicated the whirling mass of power, stripping away the earth. [*I thought about the way old-fashioned telescope tubes fit inside each other. Maybe I make something that telescopes out to the other end of the ley line.*]

A surprisingly reasonable idea. He sent power into her in a gentle stream and felt her brief acknowledgement. Then she set to work.

The earth was warm with vibration, as if the soil were coming apart under them. Either Fiona would need to work fast or they would need to move again. Already the construction noises had cut off, that part of the landscape taken. The thing was growing too fast.

He increased the flow into her from a trickle to a river. Surely she would feel his urgency.

She ignored him. Damnation, she ignored him and kept on with what seemed like a slow, exacting examination. Damnation, what did she need to examine? It was a ley line. Create a sheathe around it and then shove it across the maelstrom. He could do it himself.

He would.

[*Ready.*] A glimmer in the soil that surrounded the *kata* line she examined, and the scent of rosewater and mint filled his awareness. [*It probably won't be long enough, so I'll keep adding to it if you'll drag it across to the other end.*]

All his life he had thought of the ley lines as swift-flowing rivers, no more, no less. When he needed the power, he reached into the river and drew it forth. What Fiona had done showed he was wrong. The ley lines were not just rivers. Indeed, just as blood flowed in human and Cartos bodies, these were Pangea's veins, complete with the finest of membranes that he had broken through how many times as he accessed the power?

The golden *kata* pulsed within the fine membrane that glimmered with Fiona's additional layer. Her sensitivity and skill could not be denied, for just to recognize and replicate the membrane would have been beyond him.

He caught the tingling end of the membrane and then stepped back into the maelstrom. It drained the power spewing from the end of the ley line and added it to the roaring maelstrom around him. The force tore him sideways and he nearly lost the ley line. The smooth membrane bucked in his hands like a fire hose. He barely held on as the dark *somat* burned him and the membrane right out of his hand. He held nothing but tatters.

[Fiona, you must send the membrane faster.] He told her why, and the membrane seemed to feed faster. Like being caught in a whirlpool, he would have one chance to catch the end of a ley line on the far side of Seattle and cauterize the ends together before the darkness sucked him down.

There! The collapsed end of a ley line, its tattered end waved like a flag at the end of battle. He lunged for it, dragging the spewing membrane with him. Slammed the two ends together, and poured power into cauterizing the ends together.

The *somat* burned holes in the fine membrane.

He fixed them.

The *somat* burned more. And more.

And more.

Too many for all his futile repairs. The healed ley line came apart like mist under sun, until only the dark *somat* cyclone remained.

The gold *kata* power swirled down the vortex's drain toward Vallon.

Damnation and Creation, he was failing her!

[*It must be stronger, Fiona. Strong enough to withstand this power.*]

No answer.

[*Fiona?*] Still no answer, and what, by all Creation, had happened to the girl? He loosed himself to return to her, and a blast of power stunned him with heat and tore him away.

Vallon's ashes of roses scent burned through him. *Pain. Longing so great it was both hers and another's.*

[*Vallon!* Bela!]

[*Cheryl.*] Vallon's voice faded as if it came down an immense corridor.

Then her scent, her voice, were gone.

CHAPTER 35 —LEY LINES

The *somat* burned around Xavier like a magna vortex, sucking him down into a dark, sunless place, pulling him toward where he wanted to go. Vallon. Something had gone horribly wrong, because he couldn't feel her anymore, like an absence in his heart.

[*Fiona, something has happened to Vallon. I have to help her.*] He plunged down through the burning darkness, but Fiona still did not answer.

Something had happened to Fiona, too. Either the task had been too great and she'd collapsed, or something else had happened to her.

He would worry about her later. First he had to find Vallon.

No. They had *agreed* he would help Fiona heal the wound in Pangea's face. Fiona was his task.

But Vallon was his beloved. He would never stop loving her. As a man for a woman, as a man for a fearless agent he could work alongside. A leader, and he was man enough to let her lead—in some ventures.

Unlike his father, who had resented his mother for her passion and her prowess.

[*Viver, Bela. Viver para nós.*] Live, *Bela.* Live for us. He sent his desire out into the maelstrom, let it tumble down into the darkness, praying it would reach her.

Then he turned and tore through the darkness, fighting to do what they had agreed.

He came up, staggering, where he had left Fi amidst the copse of gold-leaved poplar trees. No sound of construction or traffic. Most of the trees were gone. Instead, the yawning mouth of destruction stretched like an oily, shimmering, grey ocean toward the Puget Sound.

Vibrations ran up his legs and the stench of ozone and spice was overwhelming.

"Fi!"

His voice seemed lost in the hum of lawnmowers in the unsuspecting subdivision just beyond the vacant lot.

Power depletion placed an ache in his bones and a knife blade behind his eyes. A frost of trembling lights hung over his vision. This was worse than after the last venture into the vortex—much worse. Each time he went in, there was less chance of coming out.

He braced his hands against his knees and -reached- into the soil to replenish himself. The rose-scented *kata* streamed into him, but the soil misted around his ankles. It would not last much longer before it became the next chunk of landscape devoured by the *somat.*

But he would live. He could fill his lungs again, and with careful nurturing, he would be fine. The trouble was, there was no time for careful nurturing.

[*Fi!*] By all that was holy to Pangea, surely the *somat* hadn't undone Fi so easily. The girl was Gifted—she had Cartos blood, for the Gifted were truly the children of Cartos blood, spread wide and then distilled again over the years—and if she had the power to heal, then she was not too limited. Her attempt to heal the ley lines would have worked except for the caustic *somat.* So where *was* she?

He -reached- and sought for mint and anise.

In the subdivision, there were only flickering, unGifted flames. That left the vortex.

A whiff, a hint, came from the seething darkness. It could just be the remains of the healed ley line, but….

He had no time to ponder.

He stepped back from the infirm earth and -reached- for the *platiqua.* Filled himself with the saffron-scented power and felt almost whole again. Who was he kidding? His flesh felt riddled with holes from his long time in the vortex.

It could not be helped.

[*Fi, I am coming.*]

The blue-gold *platiqua* geysered up around him and he joined it, swept down into the earth. He followed the *platiqua* to where it sprayed out into the whirlwind of *somat.*

No mint. No anise. Wherever Fi was, she was not this deep. He started upward, though his beloved was beneath.

If she still lived.

She would.

A faint hint of mint reached him and he fought against the spinning power that flayed bits of him away. Where? If it reached him here, she must be up above. Surely she could not be torn apart already.

He raced up through the darkness, and the flickering streaks of *kata* and *heret* glowed around him. Fi's scent increased so she had to be here, somewhere.

[*Fiona! Fiona Murdoch, answer me!*]

[*Here.*]

So faint, but from above. He fought his way up, the slick oil of the *somat* like acid on his skin. He shut the pain away, because this had to be done.

[*Fiona.*]

And she was there, clinging to what looked like the end of a *heret* ley line that waved partway out into the maelstrom. Her essence flickered away from her in a relentless flow that would be her undoing.

[*Take hold and I'll get you to safety.*]

[*No. I have to hold this ley line. I'm learning how to do it, Xavier. I've held this one since the first one fell apart. I just haven't the power to make it any longer. I need your help.*]

[*My power could not hold the last one, Fiona. We need to get you out of here, if you are to survive.*]

[*No.*] Her stubbornness surprised him.[*Vallon said I have to heal this. I've figured out how; I just need enough power.*]

Stupid, foolish, brave girl. Yet her heroics should not surprise him, given who her best friend was. Perhaps healing this thing was meant to be the end of them all. It would be better than living, if Vallon were gone. He would never be his father, because he would always help the woman he loved. He would accept who and what she was, for wasn't it her passionate desire to fix things, to make them better, that was the very essence of the Vallon that he loved? Wasn't that what he also fought for—why they were such a formidable team? And now Fiona.

His Vallon set an example it was easy for others to follow.

[*I will help as long as I can.*]

[*I figure if we can get some of these ley lines sealed, it will make it easier to take on the darkness.*]

[*The somat, yes.*]

[*Is that what it's called?*]

[*Once it almost destroyed the world.*]

He felt her nod. [*I guess this is just another one of those times.*]

The eroding *somat* had stripped so much power from her that he wondered that she could still converse. And yet she held on like a stubborn limpet, feeding her strength by consuming her own body.

[*Hold on.*] He spread himself through her and fed her his remaining *platiqua*. The dark *somat* pulsed against him like a stone weight on his chest at the same time as the whirling acidic power burned his essence away. He could block it if he held onto the *platiqua*, but Fiona needed it more than he did. The ley line advanced inch by inch, the end flailing in the maelstrom, but this time there was no *somat* destruction. This time, whatever it was that Fi was doing, the damned ley line would stand against the infernal darkness.

They could see the collapsed other end of the *heret* ley line when he depleted the last of the *platiqua* he held. In normal circumstances, he might draw from the *heret* ley line, but he doubted that level of power could withstand the *somat*, and he dared not puncture the ley line's membrane. It could undo everything Fiona had done.

That left the *somat*. Was there a way to use it? Could he transform or tame the power enough?

Allowing in the *somat* in could destroy him from the inside out, like a child drinking caustic liquid. But there was nothing more he could do. Fiona rested against him and he had fed her essence enough that she might be whole, but he would not have her consume herself again and he had already drawn on his reserves as much as he dared.

He felt her draw on him again and he felt like a flattened straw. She faltered.

[*Hold on. I must try something*] he sent to her.

The smallest stream of *somat;* barely a thread. Surely he could manage that and transform it enough that she could use it. A chance he would have to take.

He opened himself.

Dark, acrid power flooded in.

CHAPTER 36 — FRAGRANT SWEET

Darkness and blessed silence surrounded Vallon after the roar of the vortex, while above her and the keyhole-shaped rift, the whirling power spun madly. The awful brew of Pangea's power spewed into this place and went calm, like a frozen cloud. Calm, and both hot and cold at the same time, as it spread around her. The ozone-scent of active power was gone. A good thing, considering only the barest dregs of her father's last gift still clung to her bones.

She hung there, afraid to move, the darkness and whispers like insect wings, brushing through her. She shivered and wanted to brush the sensations away, but what would happen if she moved? She hung in nothingness. Would a movement like that send her floating away as if she were in space?

It did look like space—the darkness, the distant pinpricks of light—as if she'd fallen through the earth and out into space on the other side. She didn't want to get too far from the rift, because that was her only way home. The scent of oceans and spice faded and were replaced by the unmistakable scent of apples and wine-rich vineyards that Jason had described when he spoke of Cheryl. A vibration through the frozen cloud of *somat* carried a sense of grief and loss that somehow matched the hollow place she'd sensed in Jason—as if loss of him were a vacancy in Cheryl, just as Cheryl's death caused a vacancy in him.

[*Cheryl?*] she asked again, because there was no question in her mind that the presence that rested around her was the long-dead wife of Jason Bryson.

No answer, but the *somat* hummed around her with a woman's half-heard voice. Hadn't Xavier said that Cartos dead returned to Pangea? Were those the whispers she had heard? Was there something about Cheryl and Jason that had a role in what had happened—was happening—above?

[*What do you want? Why are you doing this?*]

The humming surged and faded as if it were muffled words. If what Xavier had said were true, then this could be Cheryl, reaching out from beyond the grave. If that were the case….

[*You didn't plan this, did you? You took advantage of the release of the barrier to create this vortex. You—this is all about Jason, isn't it?*]

Jason, trapped in a cabin they had all, strangely, been transported to.

Jason, who so pined for his wife he would do anything to get her back.

Jason who—what was it Fi had told her?—what was the word she said Jack had used?—that Jason was *made?*

Made?

Had Cheryl Bryson done the unthinkable and *made* her mate? Who the hell had the power to do that?

But it made sense in so many ways—the way Jason could sense Change and remember it. If he were part of the earth, then why wouldn't he? His love for his wife and his absolute mania to get her back. It would mean that Cheryl was a Gifted of incredible power and that she had dipped into terrifying forces—like the *somat* that was destroying Seattle. It also explained why Jason had been so drawn to Vallon right from the start—almost as if he recognized what she was—because he had been with Cheryl.

Because both of them had the power to use deadly forces, Cheryl the *somat*, while Vallon had used the power to kill. Ruthless in getting what they wanted, no matter the cost.

It was a trait she would have to work on, but…

[*I understand, Cheryl. I can help. I just need to get back to Jason.*] And to feel a little less queasy. Cheryl had obviously been alone, and she had created the perfect man—for her. And then she had died, leaving both herself and Jason trapped and more alone than they had ever been, the uneasy line of life and death between them.

Like she was. The grief bloomed through her and she wanted to cry, but it was Cheryl's grief. She wasn't going to feel sorry for herself. Yes, she was alone, and she was probably dead, but she had lived a good life. She had loved with all her heart. She had helped others. She hadn't gone to her grave thinking only of herself. But while she hung in the stillness, the world was being destroyed above her.

[*Cheryl, I can help you—will help you—but I need to get free. I need the power to do it. To get out of here and through the vortex. Help me! Better still, stop the vortex destruction and then I can help. Jason wants you. He'll do anything to be reunited.*]

The humming stopped, leaving an aching silence behind.

Was the problem that Cheryl couldn't help her, or wouldn't? Or was this whole situation so whacked that her own mind had gone and the reality was that she was lost in the last craziness before absolute death? She'd read somewhere that the neurons kept firing for awhile after dying.

She had to do something; if nothing else but to prove whether she were dead or alive.

Her body might have been burned out of power, but she had been tossed through a centrifuge of *somat,* and that darkness had infused through her. Surely that was a source of power in its purest form, if she could just figure out how to use it.

The vortex's power poured through the rift and she hung immediately under the torn edges of the opening. No, not torn. The edges were an outline. Not a keyhole, a silhouette, actually, and she'd lay money on knowing whose silhouette it was. Jason had been made out of a piece of Pangea's flesh, and that was the hole that had created the vortex. Perhaps it had existed since his creation, but had not posed a problem until the power was loosed from the ley lines. Or perhaps Cheryl had used the opportunity of the vortex to demand back that which she most desired.

So to close the rift, she required Jason. [*I will bring him here.*]

The void around her shivered.

Darkness, but maybe not so complete. Pinpricks of light, but instead of starlight, it was more like weak sunlight through holes. The scent of dust and fear and blood and something soft underneath her.

What the hell?

Vallon pushed herself upright and banged her head on a fallen beam. Her hands. She could see her hands. *She had hands, again!* And arms and legs and a bump on her head and bones that ached like hollow flutes and before her in the darkness lay—Jason.

Dust covered his face, and he shivered violently, but his chest still rose and fell. He looked shrunken and oh, so vulnerable, with his legs trapped beneath the crushing log beams of the cabin's rear wall.

"Jason!" She stroked his face. "Jason, wake up. I need to talk to you." It felt so strange to say it, almost as if it weren't her. Almost as if another came through her. *Cheryl, what are you doing?*

"Jason. You have to wake up." *Beloved, I need you.*

Not beloved. Xavier is *my* beloved.

"Jason, Cheryl wants you. Cheryl is here." Light taps of her fingers on his haggard, stubble-bound cheeks

Was that a flicker of his eyelids and slight movement of his head? She placed her hand on his chest and fed him the last of her father's gift of power.

Jason's dark eyes flickered open and he lay there, blinking up at the fallen ceiling.

"So it wasn't a dream." It came out the barest whisper. "I dreamt I was trapped and Cheryl was screaming for me and I couldn't get free to get back to her." Tears made his eyes luminous stars in a thin beam of sunlight through a chink in the wrecked ceiling. "I'm not going to get out of this one alive, am I?"

"I—I'm not sure that's an option, but Jason, I think I have an answer for you—why you've been so desperate for Cheryl. It might sound crazy, but I think it builds on what you've known all along. She was one of us, wasn't she? A Gifted?"

He closed his eyes and gave a nod. "I think so. I've thought so since I saw what you could do, though when I was with her, I don't think I ever noticed. Whatever happened, just was."

"Jason, did you ever think it was too good to be true—the way you met her, the perfect love—almost like something out a fairytale?"

Another nod, still with his eyes closed. "Almost too good to be true. No one should be so happy. When she died, it ripped my soul apart."

It made so much sense because they were part of one being—Pangea. Cartos and Gifted were part of her, and therefore they returned to her upon their deaths; but Jason had also been created of Pangea's soil, leaving a hole in the earth's essence that all the power and matter in Pangea could not fill. All because Cheryl desperately needed to love someone, so she loved *him*.

"Jason, I can give you your soul back. Cheryl wants you. She wants you so badly that she caused the rupture under Seattle. She took what Amundson had done and made it worse, once the barrier came down, all because she wants you back." She caught Jason's hand. "I think she was so lonely she *made* you, Jason—her perfect mate. Now she misses you intensely. I can take you back to her—if you want."

His strong fingers laced in hers and squeezed. "After all I've done, you'd do that?" His voice was stronger now, his haunted gaze steadier. A small smile. "Or are you just trying to get rid of me one more time?"

She could almost smile. "A little of both, actually. You've been a regular pain in the ass, my friend." She did smile, then, but it hurt. It hurt to say goodbye to this man, who had once been her friend. After all that he had done—all the betrayal and pain—she still cared about him, just as she'd cared enough to save him when Rebecca Murdoch tried to destroy Seattle.

She swallowed back the lump in her throat. "I can take you to her, if you'd like, but you need to understand that you won't—exist—like this anymore."

His dark, pain-filled gaze locked on hers and he nodded. He trusted her.

"Then take my hands and hold on tight."

§

Darkness burned Xavier from without and within. He couldn't breathe. Couldn't see. Couldn't exist for long. There was no small stream of *somat,* regardless of what he'd told himself. He'd opened himself for a trickle and the *somat* surged like a river in never-ending flood. He was a flag caught in a hurricane wind.

Hard to think. Hard to exist. He was part of the darkness.

No. There was a reason he had opened himself to this devastation. No one but a fool would do this otherwise.

[*Xavier! I need more power. We're almost there.*] Demanding voice.

Fiona.

Awareness returned. Around him the shattered remains of the *kata, heret,* and *platiqua,* like the colors in a child's kaleidoscope, wisped away in the whirlpool of darkness. In the massive motion, there hung one point of stillness. Fiona, like a glimmering ghost at the point of a pulsating ley line that threatened to tear her away and spew more power into the maelstrom.

The power ripped past them and tore apart more of the Pacific Northwest landscape. It ate at the end of the ley lines and—that was why he was here. What little Fiona was trying to do with his help. The ley lines. Heal them and stop the mad swirling of power. With nothing to feed it, the maelstrom would die.

That was why he had done the dangerous and drawn on the *somat*.

He poured the power into Fi and felt her stagger, but then the ley line she formed almost seemed to leap from her, and the broken ley line ends met, glowed, and joined. Red-gold power pulsed through the membrane and the colored streaks reduced in the darkness.

They hung there a moment, waiting to see if the line held. The line pulsed like a living pipeline, red-gold sparked on its surface, but none of the tell-tale holes appeared.

[*You did it.*]

[*We did! It was your power. Now for the next one, and the next.*] She looked up above them. [*Start there?*]

The power. Yes. The power that pounded in his blood like a second pulse. The power that burrowed through his flesh like invading nematodes. It filled him up. There was no room for anything else. He was hollow, burned out, an ash-lined balloon, and filling it was *somat*.

Above were the *kata* lines, but they were not the problem. It was the severing of a *somat* ley line far below that caused the destruction. It had to be, because it was the dark power that consumed the others and the landscape.

[*The* somat. *We must stop that. If we do, the rest will be easy.*] He knew he was right.

[*But we barely got out of there last time…*]

He dragged her down, regardless of her protests. Down to the churning depths, where none of the light streams of blue and gold remained. The stench of vanilla and sweet spices would have been cloying except it was his scent now. All around him and in him. Universal. He *was* the *somat,* the slithering darkness that coiled in his brain.

Darkness swirled around them like water, coiling down a drain, but the power had to come from somewhere. From somewhere it exploded outward to tear the rest of the world apart. One side of the dark tornado bulged slightly.

He dragged Fi with him.

Dragged more power into him to continue the search and protect Fiona, but it ate at his essence. Memories of childhood wisped away. Memories of friends and family. Memories of his tasks as an agent of the Council. Memories of who and what kept him in Seattle.

No. He grasped for that. Vallon. Vallon was why he was here. Vallon was everything. But the darkness stripped the layers of her meaning away, away. No. He would hold on. He would not let it.

The darkness tore them around and down toward the utter darkness of destruction. No. He was here for a reason and the reason was Fiona. Help her heal the ley line. Hold to that thought.

He drove them through the bulge of power. It went on forever, as if the *somat* had consumed a huge cavern. Surely there had to be an end to it soon. A wall, an end to the ley line.

It was as if they stumbled through a door. Suddenly they were not in the whirling *somat* anymore. Around them was heated, dark sediment and granite, the substrate of the Pacific Northwest, and above them hung the open end of a massive ley line that must be at least a hundred meters across.

The cut end of the ley line was smooth, the dark stream of power spewed like a fire hose. They hung in a small arc of matter left untouched underneath.

[*This is the one we need to heal. Can you do it?*]

[*It—it's so huge!*]

[*Do it.*] He sent power slamming into her, felt her quake, but it could not be helped. The ley line must be healed. He felt her focus, and above them, the ends of the ley line began to glow.

He -reached- for the darkness and let it fill him up. It flowed like a river and he and Fiona were the conduit. A river of heat and power so great nothing—no *platiqua*—could ever compare. This was true power. This was great power no one would ever dare stand against.

The end of the ley line extended out into the maelstrom, and as it grew, the maelstrom shifted shape, grew narrower, tighter, the winds more intense so that little Fiona was almost torn apart. He steadied her, using the power against itself. Yes, in this way he could even control the *somat*. A method he should have tried against his father years ago.

The ley line stretched across the face of the rift, resisting the ravenous hunger that bent the ley line toward it. Then they were across and plunging into the other wall of the swirling vortex. But moving the source of the *somat* changed the current of dark power. The vortex wavered around them, and through the currents of power, they faced a wall of black stone and earth, seared smooth by the acrid *somat*. They had reached the far wall of the cavern! The other end of the ley line waited like an open wound in the earth as the whirlwind slowed around them.

The ley line they nursed spewed its ink-dark power that ate into the wall of earth before them, but some of it also entered the other end of the severed ley line.

The dark vortex stopped, and with it, the vibration through his bones. Then a new rumbling came from above them and the maelstrom collapsed like a towering mountain. A dark mudslide of caustic power caught Fiona as she tried to join the two ends of the ley line together and slammed her away. Xavier grabbed for her as the wave ripped her past. Missed, and she disappeared into the thundering darkness.

[*Fiona!*] He leapt after her, leaving the end of the *somat* line loose and spraying the acrid power in a wide arc that ate into the earth that underpinned what remained of the landscape above.

If he left it to spray, it could do so much damage. The new length Fi had created could only widen the circle of destruction. The infernal ley line swept around like a fire hose on full pressure and burned out the rocky depth of the earth. Landscape crashed down and wisped away in the maelstrom. He didn't dare leave it, and yet...

[*Fiona, where are you?*]

[*???*]

She didn't know, and all he could tell was that she moved somewhere below him. If she were pulled through the rift, they had no hope of healing the ley line. He left the wildly spewing ley line and dove deeper into the darkness.

The *somat* no longer burned quite so much. Instead it settled in his flesh and bones and frothed in his blood. With this power he could find Fiona, and with this power they could heal anything.

There. A flailing presence. Fiona, fighting to right herself, but without his aid, her lesser being burned away. She was caught in the flow of power that poured through the rift, and the rift swallowed the gouts of *somat* just below her.

[*Keep fighting, Fiona.*] He plunged toward her.

But a dark comet ripped through the power like a dagger through flesh. Concussion waves threw him back against the stone walls and the roiling darkness suddenly went still, except for currents caused by the still-spewing *somat* line.

Then the perfumed mélange of apples and vineyards, oceans and fragrant sweet spices reached him. Ashes of roses and a sensation of old hunger, finally satiated.

And everlasting love.

CHAPTER 37 — ALABASTER SKIN

Jason's hands firmly in hers, Vallon knelt in the darkness above him in the horrible rubble of the Mount Rainier cabin. She -reached- for him, remembering how strong he once was. Now he was a shadow of the man he had been. Crushed limbs. Loss of so much blood, but still there was the sense of his difference.

Made, Fiona had said. It made so much sense.

The earth rumbled under them and the collapsed roof groaned and shook, sending a shower of pine and bat-guano-scented dust down over them. Just what they needed: an earthquake now. No way that was good, and there was no AGS to minimize the damage. There was no way this place could last under a serious trembler.

"Ready?" she asked.

He gave a small nod, his dark gaze locked on hers in a desperate belief. Please let this work. Please give her the strength to make this happen. There'd be no hope at all if not for the burning darkness Cheryl had poured into her.

"Here goes…"

Her hands trembled in his and she held on tighter as she poured power into him. All matter was just a collection of bonded atoms. With the power, she broke those bonds, and Jason's body collapsed into the finest of dust motes that eddied on currents of air in the room. Still, he was not gone. She held his essence to her and absorbed the dust, then plunged down into the darkness of the maelstrom toward the rift.

The power's caustic burn threatened what remained of her flesh, but she had to protect Jason and get him to the rift.

There was no safety in a slow descent.

She stopped resisting the currents and—fell.

As if she'd stepped off a cliff. As if the world had fled from beneath her feet. She fell, enfolding Jason within her core. Fell long and far, past the torn ends of the *kata* ley lines. Down past a pulsing whole *heret* line—so Fi and Xavier had done something. Down past the still-broken *platiqua*, gushing glittering power around her. Down into the darkness of the *somat* that waited like a glistening pool, a ley line spewing power that burned her.

She slammed into the slithering-smooth pool and through it, sending tidal waves of darkness surging against the solid stone walls. The earth rumbled around her. The whispering voices rose and thrummed.

Down through rushing currents that led further down, and then it hung below her.

The rift and the emptiness beyond. She spread herself wide to slow herself, but the action only stripped away more of her essence.

The fall had built up too much speed; there was no way she could stop in time.

So this was the end. She straightened and dove like an arrow down.

[*Xavier! I love you.*]

The rift closed around her.

§

Like hanging in honey, the void's sticky presence held her in place. All that momentum suddenly gone and all the physics she had learned in school said this just wasn't possible, and yet here she was: stopped and hanging amid the swirling scent of vineyards and apple-blossoms as if the world was new made. Cheryl.

Around her the darkness was still unending and filled with the distant light of stars.

And not so distant. Like bees around a hive, bright flecks of light cycloned around her, carrying with them the scent of spice. They lifted from her essence to whirl around her head and then rose further above her. She looked up and followed the swirling mass of sparks.

The rift was still a rough tear in the earth, the ley line power gushing through to disperse. But the force of whatever came through the rift had no effect on that cloud of sparks. They swirled toward the rift like a cloud, reached it, and hovered a moment.

And then were gone. A wave of rich spice and ocean mornings and absolute bliss washed over her, and a bell seemed to peal through the darkness and send it shuddering. When she looked up again, the rift and what had been Jason were gone.

But the darkness continued to shudder around her. Different now. No longer like hanging in infinity's void. The stars were gone. She hung in a darkness of granite and clay, and the shuddering changed to a violent wrench sideways. Another. She -reached-.

Stone trembled and flaked around her. Granite crumbled. She spread herself wider and saw the horrible slide of the Pacific tectonic plate against the crumbling plates that edged North America. Ancient stone seals that had held the plates in place for over three hundred years, and that the AGS had preserved, gave like matchsticks from Alaska down western Canadian and U.S. coasts. The Juan de Fuca plate *moved*. The Pacific plate shifted. Inch by inch and picking up speed—and power. The earth shuddered around her, more violently this time.

Stone ground against stone and exploded. Soil liquefied above her. Under the ocean, a massive uplift of stone against stone mirrored the quake that had caused the Indian Ocean Tsunami. Ocean waters receded and rose. Rolled back toward the coast of Washington, Oregon, and British Columbia. Farther south, the San Andreas fault came alive, and magma surged into the slumbering chambers of the volcanoes that rimmed the Pacific Northwest. The earth groaned and shook itself like a wet dog, and steam ran through the faults.

Shook itself again, and the earth tore around her, the force stretching her thin, twisting until it would tear her limb from limb.

This massive a quake would devastate what remained of the Seattle landscape. It would devastate everything in western North America.

She spread herself out through the magma, the stench of brimstone like iron all around. It seethed and ran like blood and she -reached- for it. *Coalesce. Harden to stone.* She drew in the heat and -reached- for *platiqua*. The blue-gold burned and reeked of saffron, but ran right through her. Her bones. The damage Amundson's researcher had done still left her unable to work with the power.

There had to be something she could do. She was Vallon Drake. She was never totally helpless. Once, with her father, she had called on Fi to create a distraction.

Who was there, now? Amundson's scientists had destroyed every AGS agent they caught. Fiona and Xavier had their own work to do. Were there other AGS agents Amundson hadn't caught?

[*Help me!*] she called. [*I am Vallon Drake of the AGS. The Pacific and North American tectonic plates have come unzipped. Stop the destruction.*]

The call traveled out from her like a laser beam, but no one responded. Had Amundson's work been so complete?

The thought was devastating.

Or was she so weakened no one could hear her cry for help? Or was it that no one cared anymore?

[*Bela!*]

So distant she could barely hear, and it came with a sense of frantic work and too much depletion. She dared not ask him for help when he and Fi had so much they were responsible for.

But whatever they healed would be devastated in the upcoming quake. It built under her, with a stench of sulfur and iron. The stone glowed around her and her essence sizzled like water on a heated griddle. When she had been trapped under the ocean, Xavier's family had answered. When she had dealt with the destruction of New Madrid, there had been voices that had warned her against the power she tried to dissipate under the oceans. That meant that they were out there. The Council. Other Cartos. The other young Cartos who no longer believed in the Cartos Council. Presumably innumerable Gifted, scattered over the world.

The earth's shuddering increased and the stone began to bubble and boil. She had to do something soon because she would not last much longer. The power depletion left her like a hollow sail that the currents of the earth were blowing. Much longer and the sail would be gone, too, in this gale-force of power that was Pangea's ultimate power of creation.

She rallied the meager power remaining in her fragile bones and flesh and cried out.

[*Help us. Help Pangea. The entire Ring of Fire may cut loose.*] It went out like a searchlight, with images of the unzipping tectonic plates. A laser so brilliant she had to close her eyes from the ersatz sunlight.

[*How?*]

[*Que?*]

[*Jak?*]

[چگونہ؟]

A thousand languages answered her out of the darkness, so many she had to hold them away.

[*Like this.*] She -reached- for the liquefying soil. [*Hold.*]

Power streamed past her in a smooth scent of magnolia and the soil solidified again.

[*And this.*] She showed them where the heat built between the plates.

A confusion of essences swirled around her—baby's breath, cut grass, coriander, nutmeg, cinnamon, ocean waves, tidal pools, lemon, clean leather, cardamom and pine, and so many more she could not define them.

One combination she recognized, or thought she did. Her essence went cold as cardamom and pine coalesced around her.

[*Demetrio de Varga,*] she acknowledged.

His scent burnt her nose, still tainted with disdain, but the scale of the imminent disaster apparently prepared him to listen. [*What is it* you want?]

[*Take the heat in. Disperse it.*]

[*One alone cannot do that.*] As if he spoke to an imbecile child.

[*Do you think I don't know that? There are thousands of you out there. Hundreds of thousands. Do it* together.]

His presence disappeared and she knew all was lost. The Cartos Council would never help her. She tried to gather the heat herself, but could not.

A scent of coriander and mint suddenly surrounded her and she recognized the owner. Smooth-skinned South Asian woman from the Council—Voda.

[*Use me.*]

A smooth coil of power streamed in from the woman and Vallon reached for the heat and drew it in. Felt Voda shudder, but she still shared her power. Vallon reached through Voda to connect to others. Lemon grass. Mint. Melon. Dust. Poured the heat out into them and felt them fall back, but she would not let them be afraid. Reached beyond them for others, fed the heat to them, and beyond to others.

The earth groaned under them, but it was not enough. The fault lines had been set free of everything that held them in place. The earth still rumbled. The plates slipped past each other. If the Pacific Plate moved too swiftly under the North American one, what would it do to the plate actions deep under the ocean? It could rip the Pacific plate in two and cause massive volcanoes that would heat the ocean. The heat under North America as the Pacific Plate plunged underneath was already heating the deep magma under the super volcano of Yellowstone. The entire stability of Pangea's face was in question. At least it was for North America and the Pacific basin. And if Yellowstone exploded, it would cast the entire world into a new ice age.

[*Like this!*] She tore power from Voda, would not let her go even when the woman tried to pull away. Through Voda she reached Hector and the dismissive presence of Demetrio and his cardamom and pine. She ripped power from them and sent it out into the earth, created cracks and crevasses. Joined plates together in places.

The strain of too much pressure broke her new bonds into pieces. Voda and Hector and Demetrio tore loose.

[*No! Don't you see? We must work together to recreate the bonds!*]

Nothing happened. In a sea of awareness, she was alone; the least in power among them. If they wanted to, they could destroy her. She felt the hesitation, sensed their argument, and felt Demetrio's dark presence like doom.

Then the scent of coriander swept through her again. Tidal pools and leather said Hector was there. And more. Lemon grass and lime leaves and fresh cut licorice basil. Burnt toast and burning rubber and eucalyptus. And more. And more.

Power all around her. Power running through her until a web of connections reached round the world, with the power flowing under her guidance. The heat dispelled. Yellowstone gentled—at least for a while. The tectonic plates quieted, new bonds molded in place. The ring of fire put to bed.

She hung there in the midst of their presences, so weak, so depleted there was nothing left, but she had done it—stopped the destruction. That was what mattered.

The scent of cardamom and pine flooded around her.

[*Perhaps my son and old Victor are correct and you truly are more than you seem—a lost Cartos child or a throwback to the old days. You've done well to preserve Pangea.*]

She wanted to say he was wrong to think poorly of Xavier. She wanted to say that she chose to believe that she was her father's daughter, given what he had done before he died.

[*Xavier?*] It was all she could manage. Did he live? Did Fi?

Demetrio's dark presence went silent a moment. [*You cannot tell?*]

In answer, she opened herself to him. Let him see the destruction Amundson had wrought.

[*And yet you did what you did!*] Quiet. Thoughtful. And then his cardamom and pine flooded inside her and was joined by Voda's coriander and others' scents she did not know. Like parents with a new-born child, they lifted her up through the cooling bedrock, up through the living soil, until suddenly a breeze caught her.

It blew her away.

§

Xavier found Fiona, unconscious and drifting in *somat,* as the last of the whirlpool of power collapsed around them. The rift beneath them had closed, leaving a slight rise of stone where she lay. The half-healed ley line spewed *somat* over them, but the raging maelstrom was gone. They were deep in a pit in the earth that must be all that was left of Seattle and environs. Towering grey stone and clay walls rose around them, so that the blue sky was a distant dot above. Blue and gold power poured down the eastern side in falls of incredible glory to mix with the growing pool of *somat* below.

Now was their chance. Vallon had given her life to somehow close the rift. He had lost her, so he must not waste her gift. The earth shuddered around them. Shuddered again, and the rock walls began to crumble and rain house-sized boulders around them, sending the sea of *somat* like a wall toward them.

[*Fiona. We need to finish the task we started.*] He sent a bolt of power into her.

[*Is it over?*] Weak with exhaustion.

[*Not yet. Almost. We must finish healing the ley lines. It should be easier now.*] Unless the whole world was coming apart. The violent shaking grew worse.

Her attention was on him. [*What's happening?*]

That sounded more like Fiona. [*An earthquake. That is all.*] He hoped. [*Now, I will feed you power and you will fix the ley lines.*]

A tidal wave of *somat* deluged them, and Fiona moaned. [*How do you stand it?*]

[*Because it must be withstood.*] But in truth, the dark power had ceased to burn him. Instead it ran though him, slick and oily, with a faint sound of high-pitched ringing and scented of vanilla and frankincense. Not unpleasant; just different, the way it filled him up so completely.

He sent power into her, then lifted her up to the spewing ley line. Together they wrestled it in place to the cauterized other end. Fiona worked her magic and the spewing ley line grew, its surface slick with green sparks of power. Then the two ends of the ley line met and it was as if they had been seeking each other. The line locked into place. Fiona fed power into it until the line pulsed just as it always had.

The roar of the *somat* ley line went silent. The roar of the earth rose around them. Quake. Big one, and he had no time to deal with it. This first, then the quake.

Fiona's essence danced around him like a firefly. [*We did it! I did it! What's next?*] An image of Fiona rubbing her hands together.

[*We get out of here and heal this cavern and the other ley lines.*]

He used the *somat,* pooled at the base of the cavern, and wove new stone and clay. The base of the cavern filled and lifted them upward. He poured more of the darkness into creation. New stone, new ley lines. A city above it. The emerald city grew up from its center, the forested hills around it, and in the epicenter of the new earth stood a low, square, concrete bunker of a building with tall cedars swaying around a parking lot out front.

The earth wrenched under them as he geysered up and stepped naked amid the trees, Fiona beside him. He frowned. The trees whipped in a mad wind. Stone groaned. A crashing sound said a tree had toppled. The air filled with the scent of torn cedar.

Quake—far bigger than he'd imagined. He -reached- and saw the unzipping ley lines, saw the lone, small light amid the darkness of the land become a web of light, of Cartos—both Council and others—and Gifted, that spread like ley lines across the landscape—across the world.

The shaking stopped. The treed hilltop stood silent around him until finally a lone sparrow sang and a black crow coasted between the verdant green treetops.

He hadn't intended to come here. He'd thought more of returning to Vallon's house. He'd never been here before, though he had seen pictures of the AGS headquarters. The place Vallon had worked before everything had happened. A whiff of cardamom and pine froze him, and then swirled away on the breeze.

His father? Here? So there were other forces still at play.

He -reached- into the earth for the power to fill himself but, oddly, none of the *kata* or *heret* answered. Instead, a slithering darkness filled his core, tasting of dust and nightshade.

Fi swayed where she stood, then stumbled a few feet and fell to her knees beside a stand of ferns. "Vallon? Oh, Vallon, are you okay?"

Bela! His *Bela!* She lay unconscious, her naked flesh, blue-tinged and pale as an early morning alabaster sky and in places almost translucent.

"Does she breathe? Is she alive?" He brushed Fiona aside and scooped Vallon into his arms. She was, at least, warm. That must mean something. But her scent of ashes of roses was tarnished with the faint scent of cardamom.

He stiffened, but his father was nowhere to be seen. He kissed her forehead, her eyes, her lips. Oh, her precious lips. [*Live! You must live.*] He sent power into her, but it seemed to reflect off her body.

Her lips moved, but her breath was so shallow her chest barely rose and fell.

"Xavier, put her down and let me help her." Fiona tugged on his arm and he almost backhanded her away. This was Vallon, *his* precious *Bela,* whom *he* needed to protect.

No, this was Vallon, his forever partner. He could stand at her side, but he could never totally shield her, just as she could not shield him. And right now, the best person to help Vallon was Fiona.

A shadow seemed to pass over the morning sun as he relinquished her into Fiona's care. Together they laid Vallon back amongst the ferns, and Fiona placed her hands on Vallon's chest and belly and her eyes took on the glittering black stare of the Gifted, seeking.

"She's alive and strong," Fiona said. She went silent a moment and frowned. "Whatever she's been through, it's like half of her flesh has ceased to exist." She swayed where she was and a shimmer of sparks seemed to crawl over her hands. Then she sagged next to her friend. "It's done. I healed her."

She looked up and her eyes shone with excitement as if a light had finally gone on inside her. She no longer looked like she doubted herself all the time. "I really healed her. I did something good."

A groan and then: "You did better than good. You and Xavier—you healed it, didn't you? There's no longer a gap under Seattle."

The most beautiful sight in the world as Vallon groaned and struggled to shove herself up to sitting. She shook her tousled blonde head. Then her gaze snagged Xavier's and a slow, shy smile bloomed on her face and a warm scent of ashes of roses reached him. But there was still that cardamom tarnish to her.

"My father…." He fought a surge of anger.

"Your father helped me, Xavier. Everyone else had used all their power to stop the quake. He—he had enough left to bring me to where you would find me."

It made no sense. His father was no friend of his—or Vallon's. And yet—did he not want his son to experience the same loss he had? An impossibility. His father was—relentless—heartless. But he had said he once loved Xavier's mother....

He bent to help her to her feet and pulled her into his chest, then buried his face in her hair. Cardamom yes, but it could not hide her ashes of roses. By all Creation, she was with him finally. "You see what can be done when we work together?"

"All of us? We can save a world. I'm sorry I've run off on my own before."

He tucked a finger under her chin and lifted her lips to his. Tasted.

"Guys? Uh… There's someone coming." Fiona interrupted and Vallon pulled free of his arms.

Another surge of anger that she could so easily step away from him. No. Not him—the *somat,* it flared. He smoothed it down. Surely it would wear off, so he could use the other powers again.

Across the sunlit parking lot, a phalanx of seven men approached from the AGS headquarters. A white-blond man stalked like a white wolf at their head. The other six loomed larger than their leader, and all were armed. Xavier stepped forward and pushed Vallon behind him.

"Together. Remember?" She stepped up beside him and clasped his hand as Fiona scrambled to her feet on her other side. An acrid aftershave of light citrus preceded the pale man and cut through the scent of the cedar trees.

"Drake. I'm placing you and these Gifted under arrest."

This clown. This unGifted thought he could just order them around? Xavier growled deep in his chest and clenched his fists as the power fizzled up through his veins.

"It's over, Wolf," Vallon said. "Over and done. You did your best to destroy the Gifted, and in the process you nearly destroyed everything, including yourself."

"Ridiculous." The white-haired man pulled himself even more upright. He was as broad-shouldered and square-jawed as a Teutonic god, with a gaze as unyielding as the thickest ice. "I'm standing right here."

Vallon smiled. "Yes. You are. Courtesy of my friends here. They can just as easily undo that small token of forgiveness."

The unyielding ice shifted as he looked from Fiona to Xavier, met his gaze, and stayed. "You're the foreigner. The one Bryson said was a danger. A terrorist." He nodded at Xavier. "Arrest him."

Xavier nudged dark power through the earth. Get it under the men and swallow them up. Get this over with. They had been through enough.

"No!" It was Fiona who stepped forward.

CHAPTER 38 —FLEDGLING POWER

"Enough is enough," Fi said, and Vallon turned to her, surprised at her friend. Since when had Fi ever taken charge of anything? But this was a different Fiona, with her shoulders thrown back and a defiant gaze, regardless of the fact she stood there naked as a jaybird in the morning sun's rays. She even threw a warning gaze in Xavier's direction.

Vallon blinked back the feeling of distortion in her world. Xavier with her, though something was different about him. Amundson before her with his men, after everything had been destroyed. Jason returned to the void he was made from. Even just being in the AGS parking lot after all this time. The scene looked so flipping normal after everything that had happened.

But Amundson had to be dealt with, even though she just couldn't find the wherewithal to end him. It might be what he deserved, but she was never going to do that again.

A gold glimmer sketched across Fiona's skin and through the soil to Amundson and the men. Gold swirled up over their feet, unnoticed, and briefly shone through their skin. Then it was gone. Amundson staggered and blinked.

"It is about time you got back here, Drake. Hell of a way to run an operation. I know, I know, you'll have an explanation. I'll expect a full report at my office by the end of the day." Amundson turned on his heel and then stopped and turned back. "For God's sake, get some clothes on." He marched away, his guards at his heels like trained pack animals.

When they were out of hearing range, she turned to her friend. "What the heck just happened, Fi?"

She gave a simple shrug. "I healed him. Maybe Changed him a little. All that fear and anger had to be eating him from the inside out. Not healthy at all." She inhaled and crossed her arms over her chest. "I think Jack would approve."

Vallon glanced back at Amundson, who, with his men, climbed into three low-slung sedans.

"Anyone have any idea what Amundson meant when he said something about running an operation?"

Fi flushed a comely pink and stepped out into the sunshine. She twirled in the September warmth, much as she had done eons before when she had mischievously repainted her bedroom walls a gut-churning aubergine and chartreuse.

"Easy," she said. "With Gleason gone, someone had to be around to lead the AGS. You fixed things this time, so I put you in charge."

EPILOGUE

The lineup for SeaTac's airport security was far too slow for Landon's taste, so he chewed the inside of his mouth and gentled the roller suitcase along beside him, trying to still the nervous desire to yell at someone. Instead, he took a deep breath of the coffee-and cinnamon-bun-scented air and smoothed his hair and jacket. The last thing he needed was to draw unnecessary attention. SeaTac airport bustled around him, the loudspeaker spewing sounds that echoed in the high ceilings and glass panels into barely intelligible announcements. The place was busier than he'd expected, given it had barely resumed its existence. Most likely due to his pigeon's good work. Vallon was always efficient.

For a while there, he'd actually lost her in the slew of forces storming under the Pacific Northwest. He'd feared that this time it really was the end of everything. He'd been caught, trying to lug the precious pylon through the woods to the road, but then, there hadn't really been a road anymore. Or a forest. He'd ended up simply trying to make sure the pylon and he continued to exist as long as possible as things came apart around him. It had been rather ignominious, opening his eyes when the whole thing ended and realizing he was lying in someone's back garden with his arms and legs wrapped around the Pylon as if it were his lover. But his pigeon had come through, though he'd sensed other forces were also involved. Something huge had happened under Seattle. He'd figure out what at some point, but first he had to get to safety, for whoever came out on top in the battle between Gifted and unGifted would be coming for those pylons, either to destroy or reactivate them.

His palm stroked the suitcase beside him. He'd broken the precious piece of equipment down; most of it was packed in his checked-in luggage, but this case carried the heart, the technology that made the whole infernal thing work. He just had to hope that it would pass the scanners okay. A new kind of circuit board, he was prepared lie. Given he had no explosives, they couldn't be too concerned.

Sure enough, the airport security scanner paused for a moment to review the contents of Landon's bag, and he had to endure a white-gloved woman poking amongst the perfectly folded private contents of his suitcase and using an explosives detection wand. But she finally nodded and he futilely tried to straighten his messed clothing, then zipped the suitcase and trundled off as fast as he could to his gate, given the lineup had already made him late.

The fight to Las Vegas wouldn't be a long one and the drive into the desert was usually uneventful. Thankfully, his installation was still unknown to anyone but Xavier, and Xavier, well, hopefully their brief time together in Venice had eased the dark man's rancor some. Unfortunately, Vallon's lover seemed to have dealt with the tracking device so there was nothing he could do to track him. If he came looking, well, then he would deal with it, wouldn't he? He had dealt with everything up to now.

At his Nevada hideaway would come the careful examination of the pylon technology and determining just what he might use the technology for. After all, there was a lot of potential in something like this, and a lot of potential to avenge old wrongs. Like the annihilation of the Alchemist people.

He smiled as the first of the boarding announcements began.

The Cartos Council would be hearing from him.

ABOUT THE AUTHOR

Author of the unique Cartographer Universe series, Karen L. Abrahamson writes poetry, short fiction, and fantasy, romance and mystery novels, as well as non-fiction for newspapers and magazines. In her words, "a bad day of writing is still better than the best day working for a living."

A born wanderer, she currently lives in the Metro Vancouver area of Canada with two Bengal cats who channel James Dean's attitude. When she isn't writing she can be found with a camera and backpack in fabulous locations around the world.

If you would like to get an automatic e-mail when Karen's next book is released, sign up at her website, www.karenlabrahamson.com. Your email address will never be shared and you can unsubscribe at any time.

A Special Request from the Author:

Word-of-mouth is crucial for any author to succeed. If you enjoyed this book and the series, please consider leaving a review at Amazon, Barnes and Noble, or any other e-tailer, or on Goodreads; even if it's only a line or two, it would make all the difference and would be very much appreciated.

To find more of Karen's writing, visit www.twistedrootpublishing.com.

ALSO BY KAREN L. ABRAHAMSON

The Cartographer Universe (in chronological order)
The Warden of Power

The Cartographer's Daughter

The American Geological Survey Series:
Afterburn
Aftershock
Aftermath
Afterimage

Terra Incognita
Terra Infirma
Terra Nueva

Other Novels by Karen L. Abrahamson
Ice Dragon
Emberstone
Mutable Things
The Crystal Courtesan

Novels by Karen L. Abrahamson writing as Karen L. McKee
Ashes and Light
Shades of Moonlight
Judas Kiss
Second Spring
A Different Nightmusic
Shadow Play

TERRA INCOGNITA

If you'd like to read more about the Cartos and their descendents, attached are the opening chapters of *Terra Incognita,* Book one of the Terra Trilogy.

Chapter 1—Foretold

Ravi: 2073, the Rajasthani Desert, India

How could he undo the future? Could karma be overwritten as easily as his chalk writing tablet—or a map?

The twin rows of fading-to-gold poplar leaned over the dusty road like exhausted Sikh warriors—or like when Ravi's mother used to lean over his bed before he told her how she was going to die. The memory hunched him further into the hard wooden seat at the front of the camel cart his father drove towards the heap of stone that baked in the sun. A Villa, his father had said, though from this angle through the wavering heat, it did not look like it. Ravi rode the rumbling camel cart out of the last of the trees' shadows and into the dust and the unforgiving sun towards the villa gate. His mother's eyes had been unforgiving, too—so hurt that he would say such a thing.

But now her predicted death had come to pass and had forced him to come here. His stomach threatened to rebel as he inhaled the dust the camel raised and it coated his mouth and nose and eyes. His mother, dead, and he had told her how it would happen a full two years before she died. It was unfair. It was unkind that he should have this power.

The cart rumbled forward and the heap of stone grew until finally a grand white villa stood like a fallen jewel on the dusty plateau that had risen like a mirage out of the Rajasthani desert. How had his father even known this was here? He wanted to ask, but his father had told him to ask no questions. Only tell the truth. Climbing the switchback road up to the plateau had only reinforced how alone they were in the midst of desolation. Each tight turn had revealed expanding vistas of brown, heat-laden sand in every direction, when once, according to his father, this had been a golden land of wheat all the way to the horizon. Before the end times.

But it did not explain why someone would build a villa so far from civilization. The building's heavy wooden gate hung open like a mouth to swallow him and the dread flooded in once more. If only the dreams would stop coming. If only his dreams were wrong. The gate's shadow ran cool fingers across his skin and then they were inside, in a heated courtyard unlike any he had ever seen. The camel stopped and the quiet almost overwhelmed him.

Wind caught in the corners of the high walls and raised small dust devils. Brown palm fronds rattled, but did nothing to dispel the blaze of blinding white marble. It was as if he had passed from his world to the next. Dust swirled around the camel's hooves and the cart's heavy wood wheels, filling the courtyard with a brown haze. The dust did not bode well. In most homes the courtyard would be swept.

The cracks in the white marble suggested no good could come from this place. By the dark arch of the villa door, even the grand mosaic of India had precious stones pried out. This did not look like a prosperous place of a historical and majestic past. It did not even look like anyone lived here.

"Look. The Council is waiting." His father lifted his chin at four fine horses tied in the shadow of a palm, roofed lean-to. One had a hooded falcon perched on its saddle, and that straightened Ravi's shoulders. Such a bird could only be the property of a wealthy man and there were few enough of those in this falling down world. But it was the ancient automobile lined up against the farthest wall that was the marvel. The horses were a fortune in themselves when meat was scarce, but the gleaming, chrome-covered automobile…he had only seen them in books before.

He swallowed and started towards it. To touch it. To see what such smooth metal would feel like.

"Ravinder. No. This way," his father said.

The automobile would go untouched, but he craned around as he followed his father, trying to place the vehicle indelibly in his mind. The unreachably wealthy owner of this miraculous thing had come to this desolate place—for him.

They stepped into the darkened arch of a door. No one greeted them. Ravi went to take off his shoes, but his father stopped him. There were no other shoes on the ground and voices and the sound of trickling water echoed down the shadowed corridor. Perhaps the speakers would provide him with water to quell the dust in his throat and coating his tongue. He started to hurry, but his father stopped him with a hand on his shoulder.

"Ravinder, you remember what we spoke about?"His father's brown eyes were more serious than he remembered ever seeing.

His father was a tall, strong man, a copper smith who made the best copper pots in all Delhi. Ravi nodded.

"Good. Now remember that I am to talk. You are not to foretell these men of their deaths or anything like that. Just the dream—you understand? They will have enough challenge listening to that."

Ravi nodded. He understood perfectly what his father told him. He'd learned that after he told his mother her future and she had stopped loving him. She had been too afraid of her strange son and, against all natural custom, had returned to her people. He *knew* how to guard his tongue.

Ravi had never spoken of his father's future.

His father batted the worst of the road dust off his clothing and Ravi copied him, then went with him down the empty corridor, following the spectral voices.

The shadowed passage went on too long, but finally ended at a beaded curtain that gave onto a large audience chamber. A single, blinding beam of light came through the center of the ceiling and the curtain broke the light into a million shifting pieces when his father pushed past. Ravi swallowed and followed.

In the chamber the light through the roof caught in a silver basin of burbling water set in the floor. His throat ached at the sound of it. His tongue was thick and unwieldy. The light reflected up to a silver mosaic that covered the ceiling, filling the room with light from more stars than he had ever seen in the night sky. And half-masked by the darkness at the edge of the room were five people seated in heavy black chairs. Four men and a woman, all terrifyingly old.

The man slouched in the center chair might even be ancient by the look of his snowy full beard and the heavy lines on the skeletal face under his golden turban. His twisted gnarled hands looked old enough that he might remember the days before the change—when India and the world prospered and Pangea had not demanded retribution for all the ills wrought by human and Cartos.

The four others looked like ambassadors from all areas of India. The woman on the left wore a ruby-colored sari, and under her snake-coiled gray hair had the round dark features of the south; the man between her and the ancient man still wore rough riding boots and a heavy purple silk brocade coat that would have been a burden to wear in the day's insufferable heat. He had the almost slanted eyes of the mountain people and his gaze was so deep Ravi stepped back behind his father. To the ancient's other side sat a man Ravi recognized: the Sultan of Delhi, in a blue Nehru jacket with the huge diamond of his office on his right hand. The final man wore something strange and elegant. Deep blue as a the sky just before all light stole away. A *suit and tie* were the words, and he wore his long black hair tied back with a simple leather thong like an ancient warrior.

He was the one that looked most admirable, and must be the driver of the automobile from Mumbai, where such things still existed. Ravi smoothed his rough-shorn hair and regretted its length as his father stepped further into the chamber and bowed like a beggar before these great ones.

The most-ancient straightened.

"Good, Sanghera. You have brought him, then?" At least he was all business.

"He is here," his father said.

Ravi scrubbed the sweat from his palms and stepped up beside his father. Around the room, braziers trailed spicy incense that couldn't quite dispel an under note of bat guano. The room had not been used for a long time and he wanted to sneeze.

He bowed, uncertain what to do with his hands. He fumbled with his pockets. This was worse than facing an exam at school or doing the math for his father in their shop.

"Your name, son?" asked the ancient.

"Ravi—Ravinder, sir." He tried to meet the old man's gaze and found himself lost in the darkness. Too many years sat behind the man's eyes. Ravi ripped his gaze away, but caught the man's hint of smile.

"And how old are you, Ravinder?"

"Fifteen, sir." In the old one's presence it was the briefest of existence, a mere moment of time in which he had seen barely nothing of the world.

"And how did you find your journey to our villa?"

Ravi thought a moment, knowing they would judge his answer. Simple was best to get your point across, his father always said. "Long. Hot. Thirsty."

That brought out the old one's smile, and he nodded at his compatriots.

"I think the boy lessons us in manners. Would you like a drink, boy?"

Ravi nodded and the old one motioned at the woman. She stood and produced a goblet and flask out of the darkness behind them.

"My father would like a drink, too," Ravi added, and expected his father's cuff. It didn't come. This conversation was his, now.

The old one sat back in his chair, fingering his beard. "Would he? Then he shall have one."

The woman nodded and brought them each a goblet filled with a bitter liquid. Wine—at least that was what Ravi thought it was called. He would have preferred water, but thought requesting something different would have pushed his luck. So he nursed the wine.

The old man glanced at the others in their chairs. They inclined their heads at something unspoken.

"Your father tells us you have dreams of the future."

Ravi nodded and covered his nervousness with another bitter swallow.

"He tells us your dreams come true."

Another nod. He gulped the last of the wine and his thoughts swirled uneasily. He had to be careful.

"Tell us of a dream that has come true."

Ravi looked at his father. What was he to do? Ravi wasn't the one supposed to be doing the talking, but his father only motioned his assent. Ravi licked his lips.

"I dreamed of fire destroying Varanasi. It came to pass."

"Varanasi burns with amazing regularity," the suited man said. "Tell us something not every holy man in the country could have foretold."

Ravi closed his eyes. There were many small dreams—of chickens escaping and being found. Of wells failing. Of children's deaths. All of these were too common for these men.

He opened his eyes and looked regretfully at his father. "When I was very young I dreamed my mother would be killed by a tiger. It so frightened her that she abandoned my father and I, and returned to her family in Calcutta. She thought she would be safe so far from the wilderness where all tigers live. A year ago an earthquake rocked Calcutta and many buildings were destroyed—the Calcutta zoo among them. A tiger got loose and killed his keepers. And my mother. It was shot as it fed on her."

The old man stayed unmoving, but his story had brought other four forward in their chairs.

It was the one from the north who broke the silence. His high leather boots scraped across grit on the floor. "Your father sent us word of another dream and that is why you are here. He told us the tale, but we would hear it in your words."

Ravi glanced at his father again. The tale of Ravi's mother's death had weighed his father's shoulders. His face had gone pale as butter. He had so loved Ravi's mother that he had never taken a new wife in hopes she would someday return. Ravi had always known it would never happen.

He sighed. For all his father's directions and attempt to control this meeting, for all it had been his father who had informed the Council of Ravi's dreams, this telling fell to Ravi. He had known it, just as he knew what was going to happen, when all he wanted to do was go back to the copper shop and school.

"I have dreamed this dream many times, sir. As long as I can remember. I dream of the end of the world. I see a shadow of a person spread over the land. I cannot tell if it is man or woman, but I feel their power and taste its spice, and know he or she is one of us—Cartos. I see clouds covering everything. I see great mountains falling, and cities ending, and the world coming apart into pieces. This person has done it."

"Pangea ending? How can that be?" the Sultan of Delhi interrupted the telling. "There has not been a Cartos of that power since the first times."

Ravi shook his head, though the question might not have been for him. "I do not know, sir. But it is a true dream. I know the difference. My father says that Cartos blood runs truer in some people and that sometimes chance bloodlines come together and produce powerful throwbacks. He says the question is how to stop the destruction from happening."

If it was possible. Great Brahma, please make it possible. Let these great ones find a way. He did not want to live in the end times.

The sultan shook his head and sat back in his chair.

The others looked thoughtful—looked at each other in a way Ravi had seen in dreams. He couldn't look at his father.

The old one stirred. "Your father is a wise man, boy. You should listen to him always."

Ravi nodded.

The old one looked at his Council members and raised his hand in the way Ravi had seen. His legs started to tremble.

"We have thought on this since we heard from your father. His words were compelling then; just as they make sense to you, they made sense to us. Someone must stop this from happening. Long have Cartos been content to stay hidden out of fear of another purge by the humans if our power was discovered."

They were the words Ravi had dreamed the ancient man would say and he had to stop it—had to make them different before the horrible future occured.

"Sir?" he blurted and could not let himself think or stop, because to do that would make the future as he'd foreseen. "What of the maps? Could not the Council create a map of power that would preserve the world, just as the ancients drew the boundaries of the world? Would that not stop the shadow I see?"

Ravi hoped. But when he looked from face to face of the council members, they would not meet his gaze.

Finally the old one sighed and the sound ran round the room and seemed to multiply until the marble itself wept sympathy.

"A fine hope, young man, but not to be," the old one said. "We preserve our old maps in the vaults, but the talent to make new maps of power was lost with the plagues. No, there is only one thing we can do. Your father told us you dreamed this destroyer lives far away in what was once North America. Someone must go there and destroy the destroyer."

The burble of the water filled the pause in the old man's words, but already the water sounded like waves, storms, winds in sails, and screams. The incense disappeared into the stench of death.

The great wheel of creation turned and his knees almost gave. Great Vishnu, preserve him.

"The Council has decided the task falls to you, Ravinder Sanghera. And to your father."

Chapter 2—Hanging

Terra: Two Years Later, Near the Independent City of Couver

Some people tell me I do stupid things. I can hear Aunt Kirsten now: "Terra, don't you ever think what you're doing? You're old enough to know better."

But, at seventeen, what I knew was she was wrong this time. I'd been thinking about this all day and on the long paddle from Grandfather Island.

Ahead, through the darkness, the bulk of Melani Island lay low on the water of Indian Arm, the coastline ragged, dying spruce and fir illuminated by a weird glow that made my stomach lurch. Not what I wanted to see. Everything should be dark; the frigging light meant my work would be that much harder.

I stopped, resting the carefully muffled paddle across the cockpit of my mud-daubed kayak to prepare for what came. This was the future: night dark and the wind barely breathing, but the scent of the oily stench of diesel, tidal pools, and seaweed on the barely visible shoreline ahead were gone.

Instead, the copper-bright scent of blood joined the fuel stink and turned my blood cold. The beast inside me growled, but the image of a circle of moons kept him chained. You know the beast—we all have them—those angry parts of us we keep under such tight control it feels like it's caged inside you.

But the Melanis couldn't have done it yet, surely.

All the hairs on my forearms stood on end as I reached out with my Awareness—a sense other than the usual five, but the damned water blocked me even this close to shore. Still, danger lurked ahead, I knew.

Hell, I was *making* my own danger doing what I'd planned, but it had to be done. The slaughter of the last porpoise pod in the Georgia Strait couldn't be allowed.

I inhaled. Exhaled in a growl. Calmed the angry rush of blood in my ears and the litany of "too late, too late." I went over my plan one last time.

Get in close, slide into the water, and cut the nets one-eared Melani and his family had put up to hold the porpoises while they killed them for meat. Help the animals find the hole and then vanish into the night with them.

Easy, like falling off a log, even though this was a tad bigger operation than simply destroying people's traps or sabotaging a *deepee* attempt to build a new camp that would tear up even more of the landscape. But that was what I did. Protected the animals and the wilderness from the city and the displaced people known as *deepee*.

If I was caught, old man Melani and his brood weren't likely to turn me over to the authorities. Like me, they'd take justice into their hands. But someone had to do right by the animals.

Aah, justice. A little rope. A little knife. A lotta blood.

I stopped my brain from following that happy thought to the screaming.

In the darkness I hung suspended between black, glass-still water and sky filled with the heaving, never-ending cloud that was illuminated above the mountains. Probably from another ant-hill *deepee* camp up in flames in one of their ongoing squabbles over who owned what square meter of land. We'd be better off without the lot of 'em.

Floating here most people would feel lonely—and frightened—but to me this was hope and promise. A place without people. A place before endings and beginnings and all the pain and destruction that went on between. A place where there might be a possibility of something better—instead of what we'd created.

Ahead, the slight white line and the gentle hiss of gravel betrayed where the water ended and the little bit of land that was Melani Island began. The smooth water was like an invitation in.

"You're procrastinating, Terra," I said and then wished I hadn't. The words seemed to rush out across the water.

I picked up the paddle, but a sound stopped me from the stroke.

Slight gurgle. A muffled, hollow thump and I strained to see into the darkness. Dammit, now was the time I needed my Awareness, because that sound could only spell a boat and any boat traveling as quietly as me could only be up to no good.

Who was out there and what did they want?

No one knew what I had planned tonight. Better not to involve anyone in something that could get you banished from Couver.

So whoever came wouldn't bode well for me and my plan.

I hunkered low in the cockpit and waited, hoping to be unseen or, better yet, mistaken for a log. I smeared muck from my kayak over my face and arms again in case my pale skin gave away my presence.

A slight splash said they were close.

So what was I going to say? What excuse did I have for being out here so far from home in the middle of the night? Visiting friends? A lover?

Me?

Both were nothing anyone would believe.

Chapter 3—Black Water and Blood

The chill off the water sank into my veins as the clouds seethed overhead. The slight, syncopated plop-plop-plop of dipping paddle-blades came too clearly across the water, and the sweat of my long paddle chilled on my skin and made my leather wrist guards itch. The splashes said two paddlers but I prayed I was wrong.

Then, through the darkness, two darker forms coalesced like shark fins and I knew I was screwed.

If I could see them, they could see me suspended against the white line of the shore and that weird-assed glow. They'd know I didn't belong anymore than the diesel that slicked the water.

I could make for the glowing island for cover, but whoever it was could sound an alarm and then I was screwed again. Totally screwed, unless I was smarter than them and I had to think I was.

I eased up in the kayak and grabbed the comforting length of the paddle. If worst came to worst, it was a weapon, even with all the seaweed I'd tied on to hide the flash and flick of each stroke.

Behind me the splashing stopped and the world went silent. I took a deep, diesel and blood-tainted breath and eased my shoulders. A few quick strokes I'd be on the shore. Then I'd be up and out and running. Even if I was caught, if I could free the porpoises it would be worth it.

I drove the paddle in.

"Terra!"

The familiar, harsh whisper hissed across the water and seemed to echo my name louder than it should.

Not good.

I back-bladed with too much splash to stop my forward momentum, and then two more mud-darkened kayaks flanked mine with Serena and Jo Peters at the helms. They were twins, both with an aristocratic, fine-boned look that spoke of their Native heritage and belied their strong muscles. They were the nearest thing to friends I had.

Both had long, silken, black hair I could envy if I had a moment to compare it to my shoulder-length, red-brown, frizz—except Jo—or "Jaybird," as I called her—had shaved the sides of her head to create a flowing blue-black Mohawk that hung down her back and crested over her face like a cocky Stellar's jay.

"What the hell are you doing here? You scared me half to death," I whispered.

Jaybird cocked one eyebrow at me. "I think the question is, what're *you* doin' here, girl?" She glanced at the island. "An' if it's what we're thinkin', do ya think we'd let ya do it alone?"

I looked from one sister to the other, and even in the darkness I could see the calm resolve that had made me let them into my life when I really didn't need anyone.

"You don't need any trouble. How'd you know I was here?"

The sisters exchanged too-knowing glances and I didn't like what that inferred: that I was becoming predictable. Predictable could get you killed.

"Great." I shook my head and held my resolve. "But you're not doing this, I am. I'm not letting this last bit of joy get sucked outta this world—sometimes joy's more important than meat."

"And who died and made you the savior of the environment?" Serena asked.

"I'm sitting here covered in mud. Where's the savior in that?"

"Joy is good…." Jaybird said, in mock thoughtfulness.

Serena rolled her eyes in disgust.

"Well, someone has to do it, don't they? Someone has to stand for the animals and forest," I said.

The two sisters looked at each other as if they shared a secret. Then Jaybird tossed her forelock of hair.

"Friggin' Robin Hood, that's what ya are. An' even he had his merry men to help him. Goin' in alone is really stupid. But I told Serena you would as soon as porpoise meat started showing up in markets. We've been tracking ya the last twenty-four hours."

And I hadn't noticed. Not good. That meant I wasn't paying attention enough—just like Granddad and Kirsten always complained.

"So you'll stay out here and watch my back while I do what needs to be done. You can hold my kayak."

"Not exactly what I had in mind." Serena studied the island. "That almost looks like fire, but it's too big. The Melanis would never waste the wood."

It did look like fire, when she said it. A flicker and jump across the twisted trees, which were all that still clung to the island after the flooding, the quakes, and the big blows.

"Who knows what they're doing? It just means you guys hang farther offshore."

Serena looked uncomfortable.

"What? What is it?"

She shrugged. "I don't know. Something about tonight. It feels like the dreamtime. Like the Elders are afoot tonight and things are changing. Maybe we should be careful. Maybe this isn't such a good idea."

"There she goes again." Jo rolled her eyes. "Always making out like you've got some connection to the before times. I tell ya, she does it just for attention. Pretending she's in touch with the Transformers and such."

"Transformers?"

"Those that made the world as it is," Serena said dreamily.

"Well, then they really fucked it up, didn't they?"

I struck out in a careful paddle along the curve of the island and S and J fell in behind, their paddle-fall as soft and careful as mine as we glided almost silently around Melani Island, except Jaybird took it upon herself to work her paddle so it sent a silent spray of water over me and her sister.

"Would you stop that?" I whispered.

"What?" she hissed back, innocently.

"Just cut the jokes, Jo," Serena reprimanded.

Jaybird rolled her eyes. "You are both sooo seriously boring."

I just kept paddling, but the spray stopped. Mostly.

Melani Island hadn't always been an island. Once, before the Big One of '35 dropped most of the coastline and the water flooded in, this had been a treed hilltop. After twenty years the tops of drowned trees still created a dangerous maze where they poked through the water.

The Melanis had shown their ugly resourcefulness by rigging nets across these standing dead, both above and below the surface. Then they'd used deep water explosions to drive schools of fish and porpoise pods into their bay of death. They fed Couver City and the camps that way—for a price. Meat wasn't cheap or plentiful these days, so the Melanis did pretty well. Last I'd heard they'd built a new house on their island with all the stuff they traded for. The trouble was, while they were doing well, the fish and wildlife around here weren't.

We came around the last curve of island. I ghosted past the outer ring of tree tops, careful of snags hidden just below the surface of the dark water that could take the bottom outta a boat hull if you weren't careful.

Everything was still over the bay. Water lapped peacefully on the shore. Too peacefully, except for a few places where the water rippled evilly against the steel netting.

There should be the churn of the porpoise surfacing, the mist of their breath, but the still night and the heavy cloud seemed to suck the breath right outta me, too.

"You sure they caught 'em?" Jaybird asked, studying the water as she came up beside me.

Dread made it hard to answer. I couldn't be too late, I couldn't. The Melanis wouldn't slaughter the porpoises all at once because there was more money in doling it out a bit at a time—taking them a few at a time while the remains of the pod waited trapped and terrified. Just the thought made my stomach turn sour. The beast inside me wrenched against his chains, but the chains held.

"I'm going in."

"Just don't get wet," Jaybird joked. "Killed, either."

Helpful always, that girl.

I ripped the spray-skirt loose from the cockpit and shimmied it over my head, then shrugged off my shirt so I was wearing only a threadbare singlet and my shorts. Good enough for what I was going to do. The old diver's knife at my hip that I'd long ago rescued from Granddad's attic was the only equipment I needed.

I hauled myself up onto the back of the cockpit, slid my legs over the sides, and glanced at my friends. "Thanks for coming."

Serena shook her head. "I still think this is a stupid idea."

"Well, coming for me was. You two stay far enough off shore." I grinned at her and the white crescent of her smile shone back as she shook her head.

Okay, so maybe Serena and Jaybird were better friends than I'd thought.

The water was bitch-cold as a *deepee* heart and shriveled my nipples to nothing. All the air left my chest in a whoosh as I sank up to my neck. Breath eluded me, but I released the side of the kayak and turned away.

"Be careful," Jaybird hissed, suddenly dead serious.

"Like I won't be?"

"I wish," Serena mumbled.

So I left them behind, breast-stroking silently through the dark water toward the glowing island. Stay away from the water, Melani. Let me be silent as revenge rising out of the deeps.

I hoped.

A few strokes and I reached the netting. The deadly pool lay silent before me, the shoreline uneven with boulders and rock ledges lapped by water that reflected the flickering, red glow from the island's interior. Where were the Melanis?

Smooth water in the cove when there should be arched backs. Too silent when there should be the gentle sigh and whoosh of porpoise breath. But there was only dark water all the way up to the shore, then boulders on the beach and then trees silhouetted by that strange light on them.

Was I wrong? Had the word in Couver been wrong?

But there was a metallic scent to the air and my skin went gooseflesh.

Noohnoohno. I tasted the water. Copper.

Blood.

The cold of the ocean cut through me and I hung there a moment, and strangled on tears. The pool was a killing field.

Damn them. Damn them all. Damn the whole fucking world for what we did. I wanted away from this place of death. Far away. But more than that I wanted to make the Melanis pay.

The beast growled deeply as I hauled out my knife.

If the porpoises were dead I'd at least make sure the Melanis didn't have a net anymore. It would take them months to rebuild it.

Damn them. I stabbed through the mesh and ripped down, sawing. The cold water numbed my hand, but it didn't matter. Anger kept me warm. The bastards. The fucking bastards had killed them.

I dove under water and felt my way deeper. Ripped net free of its moorings. Slashed it into small pieces, then let them drift away in the current and the rough part of me roared triumphant.

At least triumphant enough.

The cold froze my fist around the knife pommel as I beat the metal netting loose, as I slashed and hacked.

Above me the surface of the water glimmered and ran red with the light on shore, but something moved.

Inside the net two small, dark forms eased slowly past, flukes barely rippling the ruddy surface.

I drove up and splashed into air and two young porpoises turned tail and headed away back toward shore, one half supporting the other. Proof positive that the rumors had been true. These were the survivors.

"No," I cried, hoping the damned Melanis wouldn't hear. "This way."

I couldn't let them stay or the Melanis would catch them, and one of them was obviously hurt—something I might be able to do something about if I could catch them.

There was no help for it—I had to go into that place, that blood, that death. I glanced over my shoulder, thankful Jaybird and Serena weren't here. I didn't want to drag them into this anymore than they were. Then I gritted my teeth and followed the porpoise.

Young, barely three feet in length, which meant that they were probably still nursing.

No more, given there was no other movement in the netted area. I glanced to the shore.

Melani or one of his family could see me plain as day with my head up, breast stroking after the two little ones. I tried not to think about what I was swimming through.

Life blood. Spilled away.

Those poor little porpoises must be terrified. So I kept swimming after them, trying to find a way to herd them because if they just went free there was very little chance they'd survive on their own.

I ducked and dove and swore at their agility even though one was injured, but finally I managed to herd them toward the edge of the net by the shore. They didn't want to go there and started to cry—soft, sharp squeals of protest that would draw the attention of anyone listening.

It couldn't be helped. I drove them into the shallows, the two pathetic, sleek forms cowering against the netting as my feet found rock bottom, as I went to my knees, as I blocked them as the stronger one tried to dart past, but couldn't unless he left his injured partner. He wouldn't.

"It's okay. It's okay."

I glanced up at the island. No one had come. So far.

That was good.

I held out my hands and the two huddled back further, almost beaching themselves against one of the rock shelves along the shore.

I reached, intent on touching them, and they jerked back once more. The rock shelf shifted.

Not rock. Not rock at all.

A body.

Human.

To continue reading Terra Incognita look for it in your favorite bookstore

or

on line at your favorite e-tailer.

Fantasy, Romance and High Adventure
from Twisted Root Publishing

If you enjoyed this book, you might enjoy other
titles available from Karen L. Abrahamson in your
local bookstore or wherever e-books are sold.
www.karenlabrahamson.com

www.ingramcontent.com/pod-product-compliance
Lightning Source LLC
Chambersburg PA
CBHW031309210726
48287CB00005B/1477